THE
TRIAL

MARK T. WAYNE

ILLUSTRATION OF *THE SLEEPING GOD* - OIL ON CANVAS BY RODAN

MARK T. WAYNE

THE

TRIAL

Mark T. Wayne

EVERLY BOOKS
PUBLISHING CO.

New York   Boston   London   Paris   Toronto

MARK T. WAYNE

THE TRIAL
SOMNIVM DEVS THE SATANIC DREAM

Second Edition
Printed In the United States of America

54 24 66 74 12 98 15 01 14

by

EVERLY BOOKS
PUBLISHING GROUP

3232 W38th Ave Vancouver BC V6N 2X6 Canada
www. EverlyBooks. com

BIBLIOTHÈQUE ET ARCHIVES CANADA / LIBRARY AND ARCHIVES CANADA
CATALOGUING AND PUBLICATIONS

ISBN-13: 978-0-9949809-1-5

PUBLISHER'S NOTE

THE TRIAL

To Ioana and Nicole

MARK T. WAYNE

I do not feel obliged to believe that the same God who has endowed us with sense, reason, and intellect has intended us to forgo their use.

—Galileo

CONTENTS

The Trial

Whether random chances or predestination made you pick up this book, it is for a good reason. Do not put it down!

Enjoy your reading.

ACKNOWLEDGMENTS

I bring homage to Christopher Hitchens whom I came to admire and highly esteem during the many enjoyable tête-à-têtes with his writings, and with his exuberant public speeches. He promised to write the Introduction for this book.
Unfortunately, Christopher died before this book was completed.

The very few friends I wanted to wholeheartedly express my gratitude for supporting me in writing this story, unfortunately I cannot mention since they fear for their lives. They realize who they are and they know that this book was written with them in mind. Special gratitude goes for extraordinarily gifted Editor-in-Chief Anthony Bly who had the courage to edit it and also make it available for e-book readers.

I left my parents and my family lastly for it is them to whom I owe my life.

To conclude, I'll use the words of my dear friend Heinirch Heine who wrote in light and the echo of my very thoughts: "I have a most peaceful disposition. My desires are for a modest hut, a thatched roof but a good bed, good food, very fresh milk and butter, flowers in front of my window and a few pretty trees by my door. And should the good Lord wish to make me really happy, he will allow me the pleasure of seeing about six or seven of my enemies hanged upon those trees."

Author's Note

"O fools, awake! The rites ye sacred hold/Are but a cheat contrived by men of old/Who lusted after wealth and gained their lust/And died in baseness—and their law is dust."

The Syrian philosopher Al Ma'arri, plague-ridden with smallpox when he was four, became blind physically but not rationally. He was one of the greatest Arab poets. Islamists accused him for apostasy as he wrote fearlessly against religion. And we, at this time and age still bow our heads before an unseen ruler with our eyes wide open and insistently unashamed?

It was a beggar in New York's Central Park that profoundly changed my life. He was sitting in a Half-Lotus position on the grass at the edge of an alley with a dog curled up at his feet, reciting aloud the above verse. I stopped and listened to the inflections in his voice while reaching inside my back pocket for my wallet. His accent rubbed at my heart most pleasantly. It sounded so exclusively vibrant. He had the air of a very humble and highly educated man. As I neared him I saw that his eyes were fixed upon a vision far beyond me and I'd noticed a tarnished cane resting at his feet. He seemed blind. I took a hundred dollars bill out of my pocket, the only money I had and fold it thrice; seconds later our hands hugged as if in a handshake. He startled as he felt the note, his brows almost uniting in awe. As I turned to live, he said,

"Thank you my dear brother; you have a noble heart. Do not rush leaving so soon; I also have something to give you."

I was flabbergasted. He offered me a manuscript fumbled out carefully from a garbage bag near him, which must have contained all his valuables. It was well wrapped in old newspapers and tied up with rubber bands. He bent forward slightly as if wanting to whisper, speaking slowly and affectionately, "This is yours to have. Please read it. If you find it interesting you may put your name to it and publish it. If not, keep it as a souvenir or just throw it away.

After I carefully picked up the bundle, he finally drew a self- proficient smile and spoke with a sigh, "Now, I can die happy. I've been waiting for you for a long time."

He made me feel as if I knew him for ages. I thanked him, my own voice betraying astonishment. I assured him of honorable care of the script and asked him for his name.

"Martin! My name is... Martin Hefts" he said.

I wish I could have given him treasures if only I were not myself modest. And then I realized how wrong I was. This man was already rich because he was so wise. In fact he must have been the richest man in the world, whereas I, so fortunate to meet him.

Because I have found this story uniquely interesting I did publish it. So here it is, in hope that you will treasure it as much as I do. Beware though! It is a very scorching tale, uniquely antagonistic, highly challenging, lavishly sarcastic, filled with metaphors as well as historical facts and therefore oddly unusual. Some of you will love it while others will be very offended by it. I guess it all depends on one's level of comprehension, morality, and freedom of thinking.

Ney, no apologies offered. After all, those who do not appreciate this book could always say that it is the story of a blind panhandler. But those of you who find it valuable will call it, a personal gift from the richest man in the world.

—Mark T. Wayne

Mark Thomas Wayne

PRELUDE

God is dreaming . . .

After He finished His work, He stretched upon the softness of the universe, covered himself with the blanket of infinity, and fell asleep, dreaming of His own Creation. Before Him, hundreds of billions of galaxies expand beyond imagination.

The rain does not stop picking microscopic pieces from the sky, scattering them over the lively indigo oceans of planet Earth. The blood red magma flows continuously through the planets' pulsing veins, struggling, contorting, –and erupting with life. Life reigns everywhere, penetrating even the wintry walls of the sacred urn wherein lies a mother waiting endlessly for her wandering son: the son lost in the swamps of Vietnam, the prodigal son, the son beheaded by a guillotine, the son who became the greatest artist of the Renaissance, the son so many times crucified. He returns too late, only to see her trapped inside the urn as this rain that does not stop pouring; he is the composer of yesterday as well as the writer of today.

God is dreaming. In His dream, He writes, reads over, erases, rewrites. The red, bleeding letters join, embrace, struggle, subside, and, finally—wet and smelling of fresh blood—coagulate on the ethereal papyrus for once written, they will grow cold and eternal.

By now, God writes reflexively with speed greater than thought, mixing names of kings and paupers, princes and harlots, holy maidens and unlucky orphans, famous and infamous, musicians, poets, sinners and saints, destitute writers and helpless dreamers. In the last line, on the very bottom, He sees my name, written in letters smaller than any eye but His could read. His finger stops. He contemplates it and considers crossing it off to write it on another page, but the thick, mauve letters have already congealed, staining the spot. He blows over them, His breath filling them with life. Then He smiles, signs the list, and places it in the Grand Catalog of Infinity under a chapter called "Human Destiny." Sighing deeply, He almost awakes. He turns to one side continuing to rest and dream.

Suddenly, He starts and frowns.

* * *

Strong flashes that looked like solar explosions amid the unmistakable sounds of screeching tires and colliding cars jolted me from my daydream as I was crossing between Fifty-Second and Fifty-Third Streets, heading toward the 666 Building on Fifth Avenue in Midtown Manhattan. Before I lost consciousness, I heard voices above and around me:

"He's dead, poor guy."

"No, he's not; he's still breathing. Someone, call an ambulance!"

CHAPTER
1
THE WOMB

I was a grafted cell, floating in a universe unknown. I knew that I had arrived from afar after traveling for millions of years, and I knew that I was reuniting with my own self. I remember being surrounded by a sweet, soft, indefinite, continuous music born of warm steam and reverberating over cozy, limitless waters. I can't describe the sound, but I knew it well; I had heard it often in my dreams.

The protoplasm that surrounded my nucleus tickled and soothed my senses. I remember laughing, seemingly for feeling so happy; merriment mixed with other feelings made me realize that I had arrived after wandering through nothingness. Because nothingness exists, I assure you, like a rest area for passengers through time.

A pre-embryonic voice had spoken to me—I don't know how—telling me—I don't know what. Whoever he was, he had the warm, comforting voice of a Santa Claus, that old fellow who had set many presents beside my Tree of Life. Later, I would forget that voice, remembering it only when I needed something, just like everyone else. Yet, as I planned and arranged my thoughts in an immense, illusory agenda, I heard voices coming from somewhere, reverberating in a familiar way. I loved them so much that I shouted for joy, but no one heard me because no one was there. I kicked and struggled to escape that space, and I would have done just that had my tiny, pellucid legs not slipped and slid helplessly with every jolt.

Before long, I found myself tranquil and blissful, listening to the symphonies surrounding me, which appeared to arrive from beyond knowledge. Now and then, I contemplated my little hands, giving to each of my fingers important names, imagining that they were my friends. Maybe they were, given that they've remained attached to me ever since.

Everything developed peacefully for many months until one day I saw a light at the end of a passage. I shrank, trembling with fear that beyond my matrix was a very unfriendly world. I kicked around with an inexplicable passion to live, to stay where I was, safe and unhindered. Something told me to hide within my abyss where no one could ever find me, but I was helpless against the forces that pushed me through the tunnel. I winced as a deep, powerful voice suddenly spoke, making my heart almost stop beating. Unexpectedly, the whole history of the world appeared before my eyes from the beginning until the present, and what I witnessed were the fantastic events that I am about to reveal. Sometimes, I wish I hadn't been born since I have witnessed great suffering. And, yet, if I hadn't seen it all, who would have lived to tell what happened?

Dear believer or unbeliever, this... is my story.

CHAPTER
2
GENESIS

In the beginning, there was neither darkness nor light nor color—for color could not exist without light. Only eternal, limitless, transparent space existed, the undivided, unconditional absolute in its unknowable state of nothingness, like a multidimensional canvas upon which the spirit of the artist paints His greatest creation, an everlasting masterpiece that we call the universe. And because time was nonexistent then, there was no age. God's design would have taken forever if He had not invented time afterward to measure the evolving of the known and the unknown. Neither the known nor the unknown could have started had God not given them a direction, a path, a purpose called destiny.

The first foundation of the universe was darkness, in which calmness and tranquility reigned. Over it, the Creator sprayed billions of suns and the essence of life to enlighten His divine opera. Light was born, and all things awakened, exploding into billions of living galaxies that spawned trillions of stars, each with its own planets dancing joyfully around its light. Among them was a very tiny planet, so small that it had almost disappeared from His sight like a disoriented teardrop:

the Earth. And from this teardrop, the waters we call seas, oceans, lakes, and rivers seemed to trickle from the saddened eye of the Divine, He who even today adds here and there His inimitable, immanent details to His creation.

After God had given life to the last insect, a lad found himself in a heavenly garden named Eden, face to face with the Creator.

"Good morning, Father!" he said shyly. He was an adolescent (although time and age didn't exist then).

"A very good morning to you!" answered God the Father mildly, happy that He wasn't alone any more.

The youngster was Adam, the man we've all heard about from the Tanakh or Septuagint, otherwise known as the Old Testament, or from other books and tales under many different names. Anyway, Adam was naked, but he didn't seem at all bashful since he knew nothing of modesty at the time.

God scrutinized him and admired his purity. The young man looked—and felt—free. God watched him jumping and dancing around under the sun, finding his way about the garden. He admired the man's free will and promised Himself to make it law. Mankind would freely choose his path. God would not interfere. God found it interesting that the first emotion the man felt was joy, his face shining and his mouth smiling. The smile became a loud laugh. It must've felt good because he started laughing more and more and then guffawing and holding his belly because the surprising sounds he was making were so very funny. He laughed some more in celebration of that feeling.

"I can give you anything you want," said God.

The youngster replied timidly, "Father, please forgive me; I need to think about my desires. I don't know yet what I want." His milky cheeks burned, turning scarlet. He couldn't stop blushing; it was an innate reaction.

God showed compassion and nodded. He liked what He had created. "Whatever is written is written, my son. You cannot erase a word. I shall give you a woman to love and keep forever if you both listen to me. Let your name be Adam because I have formed you from red clay. You will name her Eve, meaning 'life,' because she will be the mother of mankind."

His voice vibrated pleasantly, bearing the echo of an unfinished dream. At first, Adam jumped up excitedly at the news, but then he lowered his chin in confusion. He had no idea what was coming but felt as any purebred primate would feel in face of a major change.

Thousands of thoughts fluttered through Adam's mind that night in Eden. The stars sparkled above everything while he lay on his back feeling the cool, soft blades of grass against his skin. He watched a lightning bug taking off looking as if it had sprung from a nearby star, calmly carrying its torch homeward. He could also hear the water from a nearby creek caressing the pebbles in its bed, rounding their softened wet cheeks; he could hear the trees in the forest murmuring in the breeze as if they knew something he didn't know. The birds went to sleep while he was reflecting on how to make his father proud of him. Little by little, his eyelids began to feel heavy like stage curtains closed before a live audience, concealing the prelude to an immortal play, a drama in which the actors were to be all humankind and the director, God Himself.

When he woke up from sleep, God's voice was still in his mind: "Whatever is written is written," God had said. *If so, where is free will?* Adam wondered. He decided to see his Father because he had so many questions. For instance, in one of those days in the garden, he had looked into a pond and jumped up frightened when he saw his own reflection in it. For a moment, he hadn't been the same tall, clean-shaven young Adam resembling the paintings of Albrecht Dürer or Domenico Zampieri. Instead, before his eyes stood a horrible *Pithecanthropus erectus*, hairy from head to toe, a brutish yet human figure with a sloping forehead, a brow ridge, and no chin. On a hideously flattened round face sat a broad nose, puffing and sniffing the precious air through furry nostrils. His immense mouth full of strong teeth covered by fat rubbery lips naturally resembled an ape snout. In contrast to all, his eyes were round, quick, and bright, observing everything, sheltered by thick continuous eyebrows under a bony ridge that gave him an angry look, the mirror of his soul. Soon thereafter, all his *Homo sapiens* successors, beginning with Cro-Magnon, inherited his aggressive but innocent image with much pride, showing transcendent intelligence. If you don't believe it, look around and see for yourself how some of these faces still gaze at you from a nearby desk on Wall Street or today's reality shows.

Yes! He was furry and slightly hunchbacked. He had strong, long arms and thick thighs with enormous feet. What a lout he was. He spewed exclamations preserved in today's vocabulary, such as, *wow, hei, dude, uh-uh*, and *fuh-aak*, and he had arrived from a primitive epoch, apparently—the Paleo-lithic.

Adam thought it was improper to ask his Father why that image would eventually haunt human evolution in the eras to come. And I am not talking about the premonitions he'd had of the advance of civilization. From the Fall to Noah's Flood, to the Babylonian Exile to the Crucifixion of Christ, to the be-trayal of Constantinople (by the Roman pope), to the Refor-mation; from the French Revolution's massacre to the fall of the American empire, to the New World Order, to the new extinction, and to . . . .

Yet, choosing a bride had marked the most prominent and irrevocable period representing that modus operandi of hu-man senses and atavist habits. I am still speaking of Eden and our immediate ancestors, Adam and Eve. She, a splendid, ex-otic, and sensual specimen intentionally built to populate an entire continent, was running barefoot as fast as her legs could carry her, dressed in a few leaves modestly covering her from the one who wanted to possess her at any cost. She was running for dear life terrified and burning among the hairy woods and plains of the savannah, jumping over creeks and quicksand and sharp stones with her little bare feet streaked in blood, not even feeling the cuts and wounds as she tried to escape him. All the while, she could hear him panting behind her like a buffalo, holding his "thing" in his hand—the primitive club with which to hit her behind the head in a single stroke, making her fall to the ground into ready submission. And, of course, she would wake merrily possessed, loving him unconditionally until they were both old and gray.

The sound of a volcano somewhere far away jolted Adam from his trance. He regained his composure and quickly felt his face. To his surprise, his complexion was clean and his body manly and smooth. Instinctively but cautiously, he peeped into the lake, its surface reflecting an attractive young man: tall, tanned, and fit, with high cheekbones; long, light brown, wavy hair; inquisitive green eyes, full lips, and a slightly tip-tilted nose. He didn't realize that the image in his daydream reflected both the present and the future. But he did notice a mild discomfort around his ribcage, which led him to discover by probing the area with his fingers that one of his ribs was missing. He rushed to ask Father about it but found him on the verge of a deep sleep.

God half-opened his eyes for a moment, asking Adam to let Him rest since it was the seventh day after Creation and He was exhausted. He mumbled that He was in the middle of a dream, so Adam let Him be and left to wander around the garden. When he saw Eve half-hiding behind a bush, he gave her a good chase, instantly falling in love with her and forgetting about God.

CHAPTER
3
GOD'S CONFESSION

After wandering through the ages, dying and being born thousands of times, Adam at last returned to God to see how He was doing. Neither of them realized that billions of years had passed. To his surprise, he saw God weeping.

"Hello, Father," he called, running to embrace his Father as any child would do.

God wiped his eyes with the backs of His hands. "Oh! I was expecting you, my son," He said, taking Adam in his arms.

But Adam felt God shaking, and the apparent weakness scared him. "Why are you crying, Dad?" he asked.

God stared at his boy as if his question confounded Him. His voice was windless. "I had a dream, and it turned into a nightmare. You see, I've overslept and I feel . . . ." He wiped His eyes. "Look at what has become of my work. Look at the evolution of the world. My real dream, a nightmare? Oh, my conscience rebels against me, eroding my spirit. What a mess my Creation has turned out to be!"

Adam was shocked to hear Him speaking this way. It seemed as if the ages had instantly become meaningless without God's positive energy, and lifeless without his cheering spirit.

"You are my Father and my God," said Adam. "If you desire, you can redo everything or rewrite it all."

"What has been done cannot be undone, my son. The ink that entered the veins of creation cannot flow back into the universal fountain pen."

"But, Father, You are being. . . ."

"Prejudicial to my own conscience," God said sadly, nodding to Himself. Rubbing His hands together, He bent toward Adam, murmuring, "If your soul seeks consolation, you pray to me, do you not?"

"Most certainly, Dad," Adam replied quickly. "You know that."

"Well? To whom do I pray?" God asked sadly. "I need to pray, too."

Adam watched His father's eyes sinking in tears.

"My God, You exist within everything. You taught me that. You are all-pervading, all-powerful, all-knowing," he added, while his heart throbbed with grief. God gazed at him with a pitying, fatherly smile. He spoke with the sadness that accompanies a premonition. "Listen to me, son! It is time for me to face my conscience."

"I don't understand," muttered Adam.

"Conscience springs into life through consciousness," God explained. "I am one with conscience. Without conscience, I do not exist. Through conscience, I have designed this universe, which bears the fruit of my self-awareness, perception, intuition, and knowledge. My spirit fills every particle of sand and being since *all* is conveyed from me. Look into the gray matter of the human brain and you will find part of my conscience, part of my living spirit from which reason is born and reborn through a continuous evolution—the so-called paradox of 'intelligent design.'"

"So your own conscience rebels against you for letting your dream flow freely?" asked Adam.

"Yes. A true yet paradoxical statement."

"But how could anyone grasp the meaning of it?"

"To understand it, you must go beyond the limitations of language and sensory perception and reach into what is called spiritual awareness."

CHAPTER
4
THE INTRUDER

Adam dared to whisper: "Do you mean to say that there will be a trial?"

He nodded sadly.

"Well, we'll win, Dad," said Adam confidently. "We'll demonstrate your virtues. Thanks to You, I have been a witness to everything from the beginning until now. I am by your side and I will be forever."

"I know what I know and yet, who would believe that my own dreams could turn into a nightmare?" said God. "We are dealing with people, badly injured people. Who would believe me, and given all this, who would even care?"

"I do! I do, Dad. Even if there is only one soul left who believes in you, which is absurd, you should fight for that one soul, Dad."

"But what will happen if you lose?" a voice from behind Adam asked.

"Helel ben Shahar!" said God, frowning. "I was wondering when you would show yourself,"

Lucifer had manifested himself uninvited as always.

"I thought you weren't allowed here," said Adam, glancing at Lucifer with aversion mixed with surprise.

"Thank you for offering me such a breathtakingly warm welcome," said Lucifer with mock reverence. "I'm delighted to see my family again." He chuckled.

"Your brother is here for the trial, Adam," said God.

"Are you suggesting that there should be a second dispute here in Heaven?" Adam asked angrily. "Wasn't the war in Heaven that you started before I was born sufficient?"

"On the contrary, I am here only to prove that our Father's conscience is right," said Lucifer, smiling.

"The agony of truce," responded God without blinking.

"Oh, my God! What have we become?" Adam blurted.

"My dear little brother, do you mean to tell me that you go against our Father's conscience?" asked Lucifer deviously.

"You're playing a dangerous game this time, Lucifer. During His nightmare—and I wondered who was responsible for it—Father's consciousness was at rest. I don't suppose you had anything to do with it, or did you?"

"Come now! We are all part of our Father's dream, Adam. Everything is a misconception. You, yourself are also dreaming." Lucifer's eyes shifted from Adam to God. "Isn't that right, Father? Do tell me," he continued with an ironic British affectation, "could I be blamed for your nightmare and still be defending your conscience?"

He continued with the same airs, "So, Father, Your intentions are heavenly. Nevertheless, your nightmare affected mostly the planet Earth rather than the whole universe although I find catastrophic disorders in it. Should your own conscience defeat you, you will still have the immensity of space and galaxies, their order and nature dependent on your existence, so why do you even care about a grain of dust lost in this eternal space? It's nothing to you."

"Because it is part of the Absolute, and it is not 'lost' in space."

"You can replicate it easily since you're the Master."

"Reproduce my own original? I put my spirit into that creation; for what purpose and for what reason do you think I did it? To leave it to you?"

"But aren't you inside my mind as well?" asked Lucifer with a sneer. "I heard you telling Adam earlier that you are indeed in everything that exists; therefore, You are also in me, and what's more, we are in what I might call 'partnership' in *all* our actions, are we not?"

"You forget free will, Set. I made you from my own light, but you have used this brightness to blind the eyes of man. You have my genes and yet you rebelled against me when I gave you identity. You made me look as if *I* were morally liable for your independent actions."

"Surely you mean dependent, Father?"

"Your actions are independent, regardless of your reporting to me. Today is your judgment day, too."

"I did serve your conscience, which I am defending now at trial," Satan snapped. "So today is *your* Judgment Day, dear holy father."

"You acted independently and ripped the pages of destiny. The fact that I was at rest does not mean I ceased to exist."

"That's not what millions of people say about You, God," mocked Lucifer. "To them, you don't exist. Even I have become mythical lately, and I am on Earth all the time, unlike you, the invisible, supernatural, intangible God whom even prayers can't reach. Isn't absence a synonym for nonexistence?"

"If I *am*, how am I *not*? If people talk about Me, I exist. Can you talk of any notion that doesn't exist if only as a thought?"

"I am your Son, your first son," continued Lucifer as if God had not spoken, "and yet, You have reduced me from a free and unburdened spirit in this infinite universe to an almost invisible specter controlling a speck like Earth, yet You care about its insignificant inhabitants who are under my jurisdiction because I am following Your command? Look at Your kingdom and compare it with mine. But suppose we switch. You take planet Earth and I'll control the rest of the universe, and let's see whose territory will end up more fortunate. Will you agree to that? After all, you are a righteous Father. But, no, don't respond now because if your conscience wins—which, of course, she will—I will regain my entire territorial rights and my freedom."

"Do you in your diabolical mind think that my conscience will ever take your side? It is taking me to court mainly because my utmost dream has become a nightmare since you took control of the world during my sleep. Do not be confused, son, or enticed to believe that if you stand by my conscience against me—brimful of jealousy and hatred as you are—my consciousness will not be alerted by your desire to dethrone your own Father. Is it not odd that you come to fight me again instead of repenting and confessing your misconduct against the beings you call insignificant? Why do you mind so much how this trial affects the souls in that 'grain of dust' unless you fear the virtues and the infinite potential that reside in them? You are certainly afraid that the mankind I created might run the universe one day and you will no longer be at the helm. Regardless of the outcome of this trial and regardless of my own existence or death, they will resurrect me when they find me again while looking for something missing in their souls. I am indestructible; I am not made of matter, which you seem to forget after perhaps living too long on one planet. Nevertheless, my nightmare has been your sweetest dream, Lucifer."

"Yes, you could be resurrected by thought, that is, if anyone ever thinks of you," said Lucifer foxily. "If not, I fear that you'll become extinct. In fact, I have evidence that you are already defunct on Earth, sad to say, despite your arguments."

"I have evidence that you exist in every breath and everything there is, Dad," Adam cut in, "and that you're loved and worshiped. How could God be extinct from His own self?"

"Your wonderful conscience does not lie, Father," continued Lucifer, ignoring Adam. "You shouldn't have slept through all these ages and awakened to blame me for the genocide that sprang out of your dreamworld. Nevertheless, I love you all the more, and I want to thank you for what you've given me. About Earth, it –may be true after all that the best gifts come in small packages." He smirked.

"Do not forget that the whole universe also resides in a child's mind," said God. "A mind has limitless abilities."

"And when you think that all those abilities are under my influence . . ." said Lucifer, chuckling.

"Under your influence, yes, but not under your control. People can choose."

"A mind has limitless abilities . . . Hm!" Lucifer paused. "Why are you looking to recapture a place where your Name is denigrated, sad to say, through your own neglect? Those human-invented religions and doctrines are filling history pages with gore and sacrifice copied from the actions so craftily settled in your bleeding Book of Destiny. The founders of those religions sanctified their tenets, and nothing and no one, not even you, can change their minds now that you've given human beings freedom of thought, the so-called free will. In fact, in their minds, you are full of equal blame and error like a person who inadvertently distributes a Trojan in software to other computer users. I am the patron of the child you are giving me as an example; I stand by every child that is born but acts according to your will, and I will prove that in court."

Just as Lucifer's tone became strident, his Father erupted suddenly, making the universe shake. Lucifer trembled and faded as the beam of light blinded him. He withered before the energy hit him, disappearing without a trace. Instinctively, Adam looked toward the Earth. Seeing earthquakes and tsunamis, tornados and fire, he knelt before God and prayed Him to spare the world from his brother. He thought of Armageddon. "Let it not be this way, Dad; please, let it be not this way."

As soon as Adam took wing toward Earth to confront Lucifer without giving a second thought, he heard his Father's voice thundering a command: "Come back! It's not your time yet." He was already some twenty-six thousand light years away from the Galactic Center, almost entering Earth's atmosphere, when he stopped. He turned and looked back into the nebulae and the view was shocking as it always is for a soul traveling in space. He could see energy radiation, stellar dust, and clouds, floating into the Milky Way Galaxy, an unbelievably beautiful yet terrifying spectacle.

And when he thought that part of it was Earth, a small, wonderful world in the hands of his brother Satan, who had been preparing the final war for power, he could only fear and pray. The Earth resembled a precious jewel worn by the Devil. Lucifer had appeared small before God and yet he was a deity himself because his Father had given him the power. His Father's voice echoed, "The ink that entered the veins of humanity cannot be fed back into the universal fountain pen." It reminded Adam of his old friend Omar Khayyam, who wrote:

The Moving Finger writes; and, having writ,
Moves on: nor all thy Piety nor Wit,
Shall lure it back to cancel half a Line,
Nor all thy Tears wash out a Word of it.

When Adam returned to God, he saw a brokenhearted father who looked as if he had lost his own son.

"Let him be for now," said God woefully. He will be back at the trial to win my case. I feel him; he is already in my conscience."

CHAPTER
5
THE JUDGE

Adam was terrified because he was witnessing the division of God: on one side, the defendant, the Almighty Father, the Creator, and on the other, the plaintiff, God's conscience, the voice of righteousness.

Gathering and preparing the evidence for the trial would have been impossibly arduous if earthly lawyers had attempted it. Trial preparation included investigations, fact gathering, reports, and the planning of witness interrogations to provide conclusive evidence of God's innocence or guilt.

An army of angels did the work in an instant, leaving not an iota of detail behind. In fact, everything was ready for the audience to view at the snap of a finger with images projected onto the firmament of space illustrating none other than time traveling thought projections from throughout the ages, life clips in all dimensions. God assumed the position of defendant, also willing to preserve His conscience, although she was now the plaintiff in the case. God gleamed as never before and so did His conscience, but no one could see them through the blinding light.

The selected jury (there was no need to examine their competence) was the spirit of all humankind. The audience, which consisted of all the souls in heaven, sat in rows extending out into the immensity of space as far as my mind's eye could see, separated by corridors like brazen highways winding like the circumvolutions of a human brain seen from far away. The angels had divided them into three segments: the Religious, the Irreligious, and the Innocent, who occupied the smallest space.

The Religious included members of more than forty-six hundred religions, most notably Christianity, Islam, Hinduism, Judaism, Buddhism, Jainism, Shinto, Sikhism, Daoism, Zoroastrianism, and Confucianism, with many schisms, sects, and divisions. The Irreligious professed such philosophies as atheism, anti-theism, metaphysical naturalism, and secular humanism. The Innocent included those who had died as infants, children, or senile old men and women (now in perfect state).

Among them all declared were nearly half a million people who had perished in 2004 and 2011 when tsunamis followed major earthquakes in Indonesia and Japan. Along with them, all lined up by cause and date of death, were tens of millions wiped out by such means as the eruption of the Lake Toba supervolcano about seventy-five thousand years ago or wars and plagues throughout the ages. The 9/11 victims were grouped together.

Of course, all the spectators enjoyed the privilege of showing up at whatever age they preferred since this was Heaven, and time didn't exist. They had all obeyed the summons to come without being told the reason, just as they had obeyed the call to be born.

I was surprised not to see God's face since His light is so powerful that everything reflects His Spirit. I also failed to understand the separated masses of souls standing there in contempt of truth. Yet, God was willing to face his conscience in a holy trial and risk abolishing Himself should He lose the battle against His own moral code. Adam, who was sitting near God, seemed furious as millions of souls applauded the entry of his brother Lucifer, right before the very eyes of Providence, while the rest obeyed the law of silence. Lucifer looked, I must admit, better than ever, nothing like the goat-like fiend with winding horns and cloven hooves, but as a tall, athletic man-figure whose posture discharged power as if energized by the billions of souls who had taken his side, and now with a smirk and the stance of a cosmic lord, he stepped into the brilliant light radiating from God's conscience, which seemed to flicker for a moment.

A gasp arose from the audience as the mighty judge entered the courtroom and an angel acting as bailiff said, "All rise." Every visible being—counselors, jury, and audience—stood up, and the bailiff continued, "The Court of Heaven is now in session, the Honorable Judge Justice presiding."

The judge sat upon a throne with a podium in front of her. "Please be seated," she said in a euphonious voice. She was not dressed in black like most judges in major courts of our world, but in a white pallium.

She resembled the wonderful Themis, the Titan goddess of divine law; but instead of a set of scales, she held a book in one hand. Her beauty and grace astounded me, and I felt a sense of awe and reverence in the presence of her innocence and power.

When everyone had sat down again, she continued, "We are here today to fill in the purpose of the trial and the charges. Her voice resounded pleasantly as she addressed the assembly. "My name is Justice, and I'll be the judge today. You may address me as Judge Justice or Lady of Justice. I'll preside over this court in full reverence to the eternal spirit of Justice leaving to you, ladies and gentlemen of the jury, the duty of drawing a fair verdict based on conclusions supported by facts, a final judgment that will change the fate of all future generations.

At these words, a murmur arose among the audience, but the tumult ceased as the judge's gavel struck the podium, echoing like a thunderbolt. The silence grew even more intense to accompany the now floating galaxies, which looped smoothly against the blackness of space, creating patterns of immense beauty—proof of perfect balance and conception, a merely décor for the eye of the ignorant.

We are here in a holy trial where the Father of Heaven, the Spirit of Creation that we all call God is in conflict with His own conscience. You, the jury, will decide at the end of this trial whether God is innocent or guilty of the crimes that He is being charged with, which we are now about to re-view. One of the charges against God is negligence. One may ask, 'Well, if He is accusing Himself, then why the trial? By the very act of self-accusation, God confirms His guilt and should be punished by eternal law.' And to those who hold this view, I respond: 'We shall presume God's innocence until He is proven guilty beyond a reasonable doubt.'

"Please note that this trial is the most powerful, unnatural and unconventional proceeding ever conducted. God stands before His own Self in the exceedingly difficult process of trial by conscience. God's conscience, ladies and gentlemen, is the Plaintiff, but God Himself agreed to be tried by a jury formed by the consciences of all living humans, for which reason during the trial we will stop time and freeze motion when we must.

Because it tries not only God but also supreme morality, this trial is the most critical and, certainly, the most unpredictable ever conducted. If you find God guilty, He will forever be dethroned, expunged, and eradicated not only from the minds of the people through whom He lives, but also from His very Self. If you find God not guilty, winning over His conscience, you will have a God with a lost conscience. The regrettable complexity of our God does not make Him guilty, only the wrong actions, if any, that He has committed. Some of you face the dilemma of whether God even exists; the prosecution and some of the witness will claim that if He had existed, Creation would have contrasted markedly with the chain of crimes that has appeared on the Earth since its inception, with harmony instead of hostility and kindness instead of cruelty.

"During this trial, over which I'll preside without any preconceived opinion, we'll witness emotions that may impress deeper than words, expressed through actions or intentions. Please listen patiently and politely to everyone called before this court regardless of stature, social position, sex, race, age, or education. When you listen to God or His conscience, you will show veneration regardless of your beliefs. Your thoughts will be heard and your words will be inscribed and duly sealed. You will listen patiently to the defense attorneys and to the prosecution without interrupting their speech. The numerous witness stands will accommodate many persons at a time, allowing for connected examination. This procedure will reserve you many surprises while giving you the chance to learn from the witnesses, as some will arrive with their conscience full and leave with their hearts empty while others may come with their conscience empty and depart with heavy burdens.

With regard to God's alleged criminal acts, God's conscience as represented by the prosecution is obliged to prove the allegations beyond reasonable doubt through pure, cold facts to the point that, you the jury, have no doubts in your minds that God, the defendant, has done whatever He is charged with having done. If you have any doubt regarding His guilt, you must consider Him innocent of all charges.

The burden of proof lies with God's conscience as represented by the prosecuting attorneys. Once again, until proven guilty, God must be presumed innocent and must be honored accordingly. I want to make certain that everyone understands this. Clear away any biases from your mind. We shall be embarking upon a long journey that will take us from Alpha's Ex-Genesis to the present and from present into Omega.

Regarding your own conscience, ladies and gentlemen of the jury, I would like to quote the American philosopher Joseph Cook, who said, 'Conscience is our magnetic compass, Reason our chart.' Your judgment will determine the future of

God and your verdict will clear His conscience. The question is—can one exist without the other? Can one abolish the other without obliterating itself?

"We shall see. Let the trial begin."

With this, the judge let the gavel fall like a blast of thunder, ending the heavens' peace.

Down on Earth a poor scientist was trying to crawl upon the distance between native reality and supposition, struggling to explain what he saw through the thick lenses of the latest and most powerful telescopes in the hope that a happy accident would propel him beyond the limits of matter and he would live to tell what he saw.

CHAPTER
6
SERVIUS SUPLICIUS RUFUS

Standing up and facing the judge, a dignified-looking man assumed the stance of a Roman orator:

"May it please the Court, Your Honor, ladies and gentleman of the jury, counsel, my name is Servius Sulpicius Rufus. I am one of the prosecuting attorneys who represent the conscience of God or, as I call her, the Supreme Conscience. In all fairness, my client chose me to open this case before you and the entire universe because of my – they say – power of expression. I am representing the conscience of God, along with my honored colleague and mentor, Marcus Tullius Cicero. Cicero rose for a moment in his immaculate, hand-embroidered toga, saluting his colleague with a lift of hand while whispers polished up the silence.

Rufus returned the salute. "We'll look at the hard evidence and you, ladies and gentlemen of the jury, will draw the conclusions. After my opening statement, my esteemed colleague Cicero will present his evidence regarding the weak foundation on which God established His Creation.

"Those who believe in a good God imagine Him as omniscient (all-knowing), omnipresent (existing everywhere or in everything), omnipotent (all-powerful or invincible), and, finally, omnibenevolent (all-good). But seeing that God's failure to foresee or prevent the evils that arose from His absence throws these attributes into doubt, I will with fullest respect to God, regard them as being as foreign to Him as to the human beings who attributed them to Him. My duty is to bring forward the facts and to prove beyond any reasonable doubt that God is responsible for everything and, therefore, guilty of all evil. I would like to make it perfectly clear that I, as one of the prosecutors, intend to prove that those attributes cannot even exist in a God, and further cannot "be" without a conscience. The mere fact that the Supreme Conscience is the plaintiff today confirms this faction. Please note that this same conscience resides in all of us, however inactive it may be. Some of you may wish to argue that if the Supreme Conscience is God's, implicitly God exists. However, a God without conscience is by definition immoral, incomplete, partial, dissolute, imperfect, and so, a paradox within Himself.

"Ladies and gentlemen of the jury, if we accept the proposition that God can exist without a conscience, it would mean that God is devoid of any of those supernatural excellences that believers have attributed to Him, including goodness. Because we cannot measure His supernatural immensity, we once again return to imagination or delusion. The measurement in our brains resides only inside our minds where everything is possible be it real or unreal, finite or infinite.

"Which is the truth? Well! We are gathered today in this holy trial, in this lawsuit against God, who, by creating the universe and everything in it, grotesquely erred when, amid billions of galaxies of unimaginable dimensions in a likewise unthinkable timeframe, He allowed this microscopic speck called Earth to spin toward extinction among other cosmic dust particles. Why did He create this universe in the first place; in other words, why is there something rather than nothing? We shall find out. And what does this universe, particularly the Earth and its inhabitants, amount to? Some people prefer to call it *intelligent design* and so will I for now despite grave reservations regarding the adjective *intelligent,* whose nuances are numerous.

His great work, Man, required the implant of a lively and efficient soul to become 'alive.'

Any child can make a toy out of any material and later form an emotional attachment to it. Such a toy has no soul; the child who plays with it gives it a soul. The child pampers it, loves it, grooms it, sleeps with it, dreams about it, and protects it.

"Or consider the mother who gives life to her baby. This new 'toy' has already a soul. The mother adores her baby, raises it, and fights desperately to protect it from outside dangers like fires and internal enemies like germs.

"You may think that after creating a living being, God would care about it at least as much as a child cares about a toy, if not as much as a mother, human or nonhuman, but what if we find out that this is not the case? Can we envision God the Almighty not caring about his creation?

"I am a pagan myself, but if I am proven wrong—in fact, if we the prosecution are proven wrong that this God is a personal God who in fact cares about His creation—we will probably look at a Deity most likely guilty of gross negligence. He couldn't escape into neutrality by entering the realms of chance and motivation. He would be as subject to punishment as any father would be when facing those charges. But He is not just any father; He is supposed to be our Father in Heaven, the Father of all things, the Holy Father who blends with the Great Mother, Nature, into one being; that's why Neo-pagans refer to Him as the Matropater since to them She is the eternal life, the All-Righteous, and the All-Loving. You would think that as a loving God, He would want His children to live forever. Any caring parent would want the best for his or her newly born.

"I would like to see a book directly from God, written by His hand and printed on some (Ahem!) some heavenly printing press. He should be able to send us a Scripture that would be at the level of His divine faculties and His spiritual and literary greatness, not as poorly written as the Old and New Testaments, whose style and content would make a fifth grader laugh.

If a book like this one came directly from Him, it would probably change itself over time, making itself understood in all the languages if that's what it took to get the message through—and to make itself stand irrevocably as the only Word of God. Or maybe God will decide to throw the book down to us on Earth—just as He did with the black meteorite in Mecca that Muslims consider a holy relic, even if the book were as heavy as that rock. Or He could make it appear suddenly on everyone's coffee table some morning, giving us a pocket edition that could be carried anywhere. Let him make billions of them and rain them into our houses or have them appear through some kind of a miracle, say, resurrecting all the saints and having them distribute the books to us. Easier yet, let Him whisper in everyone's ears the commandments and laws rather than disseminate them only to a select few who seem to have made a bad name for Him already. Simplest of all (think of Ockham's razor), perhaps He could preinstall the software into us in the womb and have it fully operational by the time we are born. Not possible? Everything is possible for God.

"But He has not done any of these things. He leaves everything up to us: the writing (so far, so poor), the editing, the printing, the publishing, the distribution of the many versions all different from one another. If God wanted to take a direct approach rather than letting us do the work, is there a good reason why holy books could not grow in nature like living organisms? Or why from time to time He hasn't placed a sign in the sky as a message for us, especially when death is near. If God wanted to show us that He's a loving father, He could drop by occasionally to say hi or to stop a tsunami, earthquake, supervolcano, or tornado from slaughtering his children.

"The burden of proof remains with us, the prosecution. We will show them evidence that this God is not our loving father, a real Heavenly Father who listens to His children and cares about every living soul and wandering spirit. We will show them evidence that this God extolled for His benevolence has contemplated and committed most atrocious crimes. We will show them evidence that He is neither a moral nor a good Celestial Parent with the qualities of any parent who cares about His children, nor is He a Father who will sacrifice His life for His own children. We will show them evidence that God is a not the good Father whom we should love not because of fear but because of affection, and come to Him for comfort without having any Scripture imposed on us by the sword of His religious representatives.

"You will see no loving and just God. We will present to you a Creator of hallucinations, lies, jealousy, avarice, vengeance, wrath, carelessness, egocentrism, disease, torture, murder, pain, suffering and death.

Ladies and gentlemen of the jury, we will provide evidence of endless evil brought to that little speck of dust called Earth as the direct result of God's actions and character. Multiply those evils using the rich scale of infinity, and even the most powerful minds collectively running as the ultimate computer of the universe will show an error message and stall.

"Will God's conscience win? If so, for the first time, God will have allowed something good to happen: His own extinction. Will God win? If so, He will exist without a conscience. Will you be happy voting to allow such a tyrannical, monstrous creature to continue producing His living nightmare? We shall see.

"It is up to you, ladies and gentlemen of the jury, to decide what is right and what is wrong—what is moral and what is wicked.

Today, you'll reach your verdict. The right verdict will also free you morally and spiritually from the bondage of religion, which has nothing in common with any god, let alone a Supreme god. It is up to you to eliminate this illusion and drive the Almighty Illusionist out of the books forever. A god without followers does not exist. A god invented by people exists only in the mind and nowhere else. An impersonal god does not interest anyone. A god of perfection is not perfect without his conscience. Which God do we have before us today? Perhaps His conscience will help us uncover Him.

"Who is this mighty God? I shall close my opening statement with a lyric left to humanity by one of my beloved friends who lived centuries after me; he is Michael Eminescu, who reflected with sadness and sincerity upon the making of the world:

> When death did not exist, nor yet eternity,
> Before the seed of life had first set living free,
> When yesterday was nothing, and time had not begun,
> And one included all things, and all was less than one,
> When sun and moon and sky, the stars, the spinning earth
> Were still part of the things that had not come to birth
> And You quite lonely stood . . . I ask myself with awe,
> Who is this mighty God we bow ourselves before.

"Thank you, ladies and gentlemen of the jury. Thank you, Your Honor."

Rufus took a few small steps and sat by Cicero while the audience took advantage of the opportunity to chatter among themselves for a moment."

CHAPTER
7
ADAM

"Your Honor, ladies and gentlemen of the jury, counsel, my name is Adam."

The audience roared until the judge called, "Quiet, please!" The gavel thundered and silence fell heavily once again.

"I know! I know! I probably look different than you imagined," said Adam, smiling. And he was right. If I had imagined him, he could have smiled all he wanted but no one could have seen his smile since his enormous, reddish, cottonlike beard would have hidden it. While the beard would have covered his genitals, his long hair would have covered the posterior of the first God-made man, who might have resembled a purebred *Homo erectus*.

But, in reality, Adam was a well-dressed, middle-aged man of impressive build, with thick, straight hair neatly trimmed and a clean-shaven face. He wore an impeccable dark violet suit made of the finest wool, which I suspected was unmixed with any other fibers in accordance with the Jewish commandment of Shatnez. His greenish eyes scanned the audience furtively as though trying to locate the one person who was the most important to him: Eve. He sighed deeply, paused, and faced the judge speaking in a warm baritone voice, "I am representing God, whose dignity and fate I am defending. Without God, we would not be here. Without Him, there would be no trial. Yet, among those in this courtroom are the skeptics, the unbelievers, the misinformed who reject the very concept of Creation in favor of evolution, forgetting that evolution means progress, growth, development, advance—and yet advance from what? Didn't evolution have a beginning? What gave it that start? Who was the "first mover?"

"Among us today are Saint Anselm of Canterbury, who left us the famous maxim, *Credo ut Intelligam* (I believe that I may understand). Understanding is a posteriori, meaning 'after the fact,' because it relies on experience or empirical evidence. It is a conclusion. Belief is a priori, meaning 'before the fact'—that is, before experience or knowledge derived from experience, otherwise known as experiential evidence. Belief always precedes reasoning. No philosophical system can depart from belief or assumptions.

"From this perspective, if man were a rational being, such a trait could not be attributed to his use of reason to discover an extrinsic reality or a given objective truth but to his ability to more or less justify his nonrational presuppositions, whether individual or collective. In other words, reason attempts to validate belief. Without believing, you cannot understand and therefore cannot know; thus, you cannot be unbiased and impartial in providing counterarguments to any theory. Do not commit the fallacy of combating a philosophical or religious system without first accepting its argument, for you will fight it from the outside and fail to refute it. To be unprejudiced, you must accept the starting point of any theory or belief that you attempt to refute. To deny the existence of Creation and to deny God, you must have a concept of Creation or God. You heard Rufus say in his opening statement, 'the measurement in our brains resides only inside our minds where everything is possible be it real or unreal, finite or infinite.' His assertion is self-evident and yet self-contradictory.

Why? Because if God is *finite*, He is real, and if He is *infinite*, He is similarly real: "Is" is the operative word here. The lack of reality is a misconception since perception from *without* toward the unfathomable *within* needs no less explaining. Looking from *within* justifies the above assessment, which highlights the truth.

"As for the crimes charged to God, ladies and gentlemen, those who deny God's existence must admit that His nonexistence renders the allegations against Him absurd since a nonexistent entity cannot commit a crime. I don't want to play with words. I am prepared to present the facts that I know will convince you to reach a fair judgment. Nevertheless, my brother Lucifer, so cleverly illustrated in man-made Scriptures (whether you believe in them or not) might fall to blame."

A tumult from the audience interrupted the speech. Adam looked at Lucifer, who concealed a devilish smile, raised his hand to command silence, and then signaled Adam to continue his speech. The noise ceased, and Adam continued bravely, "Therefore, ladies and gentlemen of the jury, the question is not whether an accused God still exists. Let's be attentive to this. After all, God, the one Creator of the universe, is on trial here for errors, crimes, and cruelty. My esteemed colleague has questioned His morality in connection with the supernatural qualities of omnipotence, omnipresence, omnibenevolence, and omniscience, which, for simplicity's sake, I'll refer to as the Four *O*s.

"Some people discredit His Creation, His actions, and His morals without knowledge of the subtle facts that make reality. Those people have heard of Him through fairy-tale stories fabricated by humankind. They have created God in their own image, as shown by the many gods and many religions all ensuing from one another, religions that bear a seed of truth fallen from the sweet fruit of deceit and death, which I am ashamed to discuss. But hold your stones and don't aim them at me because I, the sinner, am both as innocent as guilty as you are.

"We all have eaten from this fruit, and living people are *still* eating from it every single day, and I wonder who feeds it to them. I shall prove to you today the innocence of God, that He is the One, the Dot, the Alpha and the Omega, the Creator of the cosmos, the Supreme Intelligence, the Ultimate Balance, the Just and the Pious, the Infinite within and the Infinite without, the Unmoved Mover, innocent of evil and of any wrongdoing. It doesn't matter whether you call him Allah, Yahweh, Buddha, Zeus, the Big Bang, Intelligent Design, or "the guy upstairs" because He will respond in the same manner to all the names bestowed upon Him.

"Please note that God would not be on trial with His own *conscience* as plaintiff without His own consent. Therefore, He is a righteous God. He could have left the world the way it evolved or, better yet, destroyed the world and rebuilt it if He found it to be imperfect. But He didn't choose that path. He preferred to face His conscience and Himself. He is a Just God, ladies and gentlemen, and one way or another, I with our defense team will prove Him right. He will reveal His glory and perfection. I ask you to listen to our defense and analyze the evidence, which will, I strongly believe, establish his innocence. I trust that you, ladies and gentlemen of the jury, will find your God not guilty on any charges, a verdict that will seal eternity, forever.

"Thank you."

Adam stood quietly, and looked as his Father instinctively, before he returned to his seat.

The silence deepened until it felt heavier than matter. For a moment, I thought that everyone had vanished. For an unbearable moment, the courtroom felt like an empty void expunged from time, silently seeking an answer, as if expected to come from the mind of God.

CHAPTER
8
CICERO'S OPENING STATEMENT

"Your Honor, ladies and gentlemen of the jury, distinguished colleagues, I am Marcus Tullius Cicero, and, look, I have a head on my shoulders, and my tongue is sharper than ever."

The heavens shook, thundering with laughter.

"The moving images that I am about to show you will revitalize your view about the conception of the world. I would be ungrateful to Mother Nature if I didn't admit that I long for the good old Roman days, save 'Fulvia's hairpin and the wrath of Mark Antony, although I adore his Meditations. I forgave them both since that was my nature. The inner voice of my alter ego whispers to me—'What were few moments of horror compared to so many well-lived years?' I want to believe that what happens here today is true, although I am not so confident that we would not experience another nightmare." He

---

[1]According to Cassius Dio[42] (in a story often mistakenly attributed to Plutarch), Antony's wife Fulvia took Cicero's head, pulled out his tongue, and jabbed it repeatedly with her hairpin in final revenge against Cicero's power of speech. (Ref: Wiki)

cleared his throat. "Many of you wonder whether this trial is real or just a new fallacy. Is it someone's dream? I pinch myself and it hurts, so I'll treat it as real. Even my friend Rufus assures me that I must cite Adam's remark expressed in his opening statement, which makes my tongue ticklish as if wanting to speak of its own thoughts. Adam said, referring to God, quote, some people discredit His Creation, His actions, and his morals without knowledge of the subtle facts that make reality, unquote.

"Please allow me to question his remark. Do we, the people to whom Adam refers, really discredit God's Creation? Or have His real actions, the facts, the very *reality* that we do in effect acknowledge quite as well as if we were made indeed in His image, already harmed it? And Marcus Aurelius, not Mark Antony, wrote Meditations if I might borrow Mr. Samuel Clemens's flair for a moment.

We are about to look at some historic images since they depict Creation. I call them the River of Life, the greatest stream on its way to its most spectacular waterfall. Please understand that we will define "time" as the sequential measurement of two dissimilar outward appearances—the day and the year—using clocks and calendars. It makes little difference which term we use to define time, so long as we respect these facts. Imagine the whole history of evolution played on fast forward and condensed to one second. Of course, you would hear only a beep and see only a flash. Did evolution occur in one second? Yes, if we time measure the compressed timeframe. In reality, did it take longer than a second? Well, reality by what measure? Likewise, it could as easily take forever if time were played upon a slow-motion machine commensurate with Infinity. Does time matter anymore? No, because it's relative and symbiotic. What matters is evolution itself. It happened and continues to happen.

We are in a situation in which the Supreme Conscience, the ultimate intelligence and energy in the universe, takes God to trial—the word *God* being a synonym for Creation— for the crimes that He or It committed against humankind.

We will show you that the universal conscience exists while God is a theoretical entity, an impostor of the Four Os, an abstract concept. Does this verse sound familiar?

> Rather a rude and indigested mass:
> A lifeless lump, unfashion'd, and unfram'd,
> Of jarring seeds; and justly Chaos nam'd.
> No sun was lighted up, the world to view;
> No moon did yet her blunted horns renew:
> Nor yet was Earth suspended in the sky,
> Nor pois'd, did on her own foundations lye:
> Nor seas about the shores their arms had thrown;
> But earth, and air, and water, were in one.
> Thus air was void of light, and earth unstable,
> And water's dark abyss unnavigable.
> "Does anyone know whose poem I recited?"
> Voices shouted, "It's Ovid! The Metamorphoses; Ovid, sir!"

Cicero raised his arm, thrilled to hear the live calls. "Well, yes! The verse is a passage from Ovid's Metamorphoses depicting the embryonic state of the universe as a chaotic blend of the four elements, making us think perhaps of Empedocles and Anaxagoras, who are among the pioneers of such thought. Please observe evolution of the solar system for a moment, beginning far back in time."

Cicero raised his hand and pointed toward the sky. A spectacular, multi-dimensional display appeared before our eyes.

Everyone jumped as a supernova exploded, shaking the heavens. The sublime yet terrifying image lasted just long enough for us to observe the grandeur of the event and then the scene fast-forwarded to the formation of the planets about [2]five billion years before the present. Meteorites

---

[2] The Hadean (pronounced /ˈheɪdiən/) is the geologic eon before the Archean. It started at Earth's formation about 4.6 billion years ago (4,600 Ma), and ended roughly 3.8 billion years ago, though the latter date varies according to different sources. The name "Hadean" derives from Hades, Greek for "Underworld," referring to the conditions on Earth at the time. The geologist Preston Cloud

whizzed through a cloud of gases and dust around the Sun, which gradually shrank as gravity compacted it, resulting in nuclear fusion that produced heat and light. Dust grains in the surrounding disk collided and merged into larger bodies, or planetesimals, which grew into large protoplanets and then into planets while the remaining debris formed asteroids. The heat resulting from continual collisions and bombardments made the surface of the newly formed planets, including Earth, molten. As the Earth cooled and solidified over the next billion and a half years, clouds formed and created the oceans, as we witnessed the inception of the Achaean or Archeozoic Eon, 3.9 to 2.5 billion years before the present. Continental plates began to form. The atmosphere, composed of ammonia, methane, and mixed gases, interacted to make the first living organism known as cyanobacteria or blue-green algae.

As we watched, those small, one-celled organisms, which manufactured their own food through photosynthesis, formed colonies (stromatolites) as if they could think or someone had programmed them to perform their task precisely. By producing oxygen, the stromatolites transformed the atmosphere, enabling the evolution of more complex forms of life. Other cyanobacteria evolved into chloroplasts and merged with more advanced cells containing nuclei to form the first self-sustaining organisms.

Before our eyes, the still-forming continents began to emerge. Oxygen produced by the algae and plants entered the atmosphere, and as the Cambrian Period began, the first animals appeared, including trilobites, shellfish, starfish, sea urchins and many exotic species that later became extinct.

Then, the flowing music that we hear at birth surrounded everything. Earth looked like a colorful, pumpkin-shaped volleyball made especially for children. Dressed in its perfectly

---

coined the term in 1972, originally to label the period before the earliest-known rocks. W. Brian Harland later coined an almost synonymous term: the "Priscoan period". Other older texts simply refer to the eon as the Pre-Archean. Ref: Wikipedia

tailored "atmosphere suit" made of layers of gases to protect life from dangerous rays traveling ninety-one million miles from the Sun, it certainly made "chance" look like a miracle since everything seemed perfectly calculated, all falling into the right place for the right purpose; or not.

Even as I watched the life forms becoming more complex, I couldn't help wondering where the supernova that started our solar system came from and how the universe itself came into being. Who programmed the minuscule cyanobacteria to develop other forms and trigger the evolution of life on Earth? If their development was only a chemical reaction, who devised the chemical elements and what arranged them in precise patterns of life distinct from one another and suited to their particular environment?

Everyone else seemed as fascinated as I was by the fantastic display of power and creativity. Our tiny solar system compared to "space" was a sparkling grain from which light reflected only to disappear a second later into the entire primordial soup of dust.

It reminded me of Zeno's famous paradoxes, in which there is hypothetically an infinite amount of space in an infinite distance between two points, one incapable of reaching its destination due to the unlimited amount of periods forming an imaginary line, which could objectively be bisected *ad infinitum*, which displays the sweet and sour irony between reason and truth. Take, for example, his paradox of Achilles of Iliad and the tortoise. Achilles, knowing that he is fast and the tortoise is slow, kindly grants the tortoise a head start in a race but can never catch up with it because the tortoise has always moved on when Achilles reaches the point where it used to be.

The audience members gaped at the spectacle surrounding them. One of them, Pierre Simon de Laplace, looked as if he wanted to stand up and shout, giving the impression that he had just discovered something that no one else had noticed.

As I watched in horror, the so-called Cambrian explosion, which had produced so many colorful and varied marine invertebrates, ended in a mass extinction as the Earth turned into a gigantic snowball. God—or the forces of Nature—had no mercy for the life that He—or they—had created. Another and even worse extinction, caused by glaciation and volcanic activity, followed the Ordovician Period, which had produced the first plants on land and the primitive fish in the sea. But, miraculously, the Earth recovered, and the Silurian Period gave the sea its first jawed fish, while the first arthropods (centipedes and millipedes), the first ferns, and the first mosses appeared on land. The high and extremely agitated seas produced brachiopods, corals, and crinoids. By the Devonian Period, fish and land vegetation had become diverse and plentiful. The first four-footed animal, a lungfish, appeared near the end of the period, followed by the first amphibians. The first bony fishes, first sharks, and first [3]ammonoids made the headline news in Heaven. The springtails and other wingless insects multiplied by the billions.

And whether Creation or chance was responsible, another mass extinction resulting from a meteor impact and falling temperatures wiped out thirty percent of all animal families. Amid the tumult, I saw Napoleon shouting at the top of his lungs: "Pierre Simon! Can you see God from where you are?"

The events continued to flabbergast everyone. The first flying insects appeared during the Mississippian Period, followed millions of years later amid flourishing vegetation by mayflies–, cockroaches and the first reptiles in the Permian. Then, once again, the continents merged into a single supercontinent, Pangaea. Plants and phytoplankton oxygenated the Earth's atmosphere. More insects appeared, the first stoneflies

---

[3] Ammonites' spiral shape gave rise to their name, as their fossilized shells somewhat resemble a tightly-coiled ram's horn. Plinius the Elder (died 79 C.E. near Pompeii) called fossils of these animals *ammonis cornua* ("horns of Ammon") because the Egyptian god Ammon (Amun) was typically depicted wearing ram's horns. (ref: New World Encyclopedia)

showed up, along with beetles and caddis flies. But this era of flourishing life ended with the largest mass extinction in Earth's history, which resulted from the million-year-long eruption of the Siberian Traps and resulting climate change. Seventy-five percent of all land vertebrates vanished, ninety-five percent of all marine species, including Trilobites, died out, along with many tree species.

And it didn't stop there. The Triassic Period, which followed, brought the first dinosaurs, crocodilians, and mammals. Mollusks were the dominant invertebrate. Reptiles, some of them mammal-like, filled the land. Turtles evolved, and the ichthyosaurs swam the seas A new group of insects, the flies, appeared.

But God didn't seem to like this scenario, either, as the Triassic Period ended with a comparatively minor extinction that destroyed forty percent of all animal families, including the eel-like conodonts, giant amphibians called labyrinthodonts, many other amphibians, and all marine reptiles except ichthyosaurs, the huge fish-lizards that lived another 123 million years.

As the presentation entered the Jurassic Period, rumbling growls and shrill whistles filled the air, making us forget about God and the trial. The archaeopteryx made its debut, along with other new fashion birds. The first flowers bloomed amid lush vegetation of other kinds—rushes, ferns, conifers, palm like cycads, and gingkoes. In the sea, ammonites lived within whorled shells. In the sky, pterodactyls and other pterosaurs sailed the skies. The ground rumbled with the footsteps of Diplodocus, Stegosaurus, and the fearsome Allosaurus. Mysteriously, most of these dinosaurs became extinct, along with many marine reptiles and other sea creatures at the end of the Jurassic, but the glory days of the dinosaurs were yet to come. As the Jurassic faded into the Jurassic, the first crocodilians and feathered dinosaurs gleamed in the sun. The earliest-known butterflies fluttered among the flowering plants, along with the first bees, while the earliest-known ants and snakes crawled on the ground. The dinosaurs whose names every child knows—Tyrannosaurus Rex, Spinosaurus, Triceratops, and Iguanodon—made the Earth tremble with their footsteps. Late in the period, primitive marsupials showed their faces amid volcanic eruptions and shifting continents that took on a modern look. But, suddenly, predator and prey alike stood frozen as a meteor hurled to Earth, signaling the end of the dinosaurs, pterosaurs, and half of the marine invertebrate species, including the ammonites.

This famous extinction put an end to the Mesozoic Era, the Age of Reptiles, opening the door to the modern Cenozoic Era or Age of Mammals. The Tertiary Period, beginning with the Paleocene and Eocene Epochs, gave the tiny mammals that survived the End-Cretaceous extinction a chance to evolve into new forms. The primitive Paleocene mammals took on more advanced shapes during the Eocene, evolving into three types: monotremes, marsupials, and placental mammals, including the first large mammals, such as elephants, and primitive primates.

Then the Oligocene Epoch started from a minor extinction that killed off the remaining of the plesiadapiforms. But as I watched the spectacle of creation and extinction, I felt certain that God knew what He was doing. Yes, this extinction in particular was for the better since it made room for new mammals such as cats, deer, pigs, rhinos, camels, horses, and tapirs as grasses spread everywhere. The Miocene, which followed, witnessed the advent of whales, raccoons, dogs, bears, and horses. Modern birds made a difference in this four-dimensional motion picture arrangement. Monkeys in South America, apes in southern Europe, and Ramapithecus in India and Africa appeared suddenly as if tired of hiding for so long in the mind of the creator.

Finally, the Pliocene began, and the first hominids, which we all believed as the Australopithecines. They looked like apes and seemed unable to speak even though they walked on two legs. Modern forms of whales swam around at leisure in no danger from Megalodon, a sixty-foot shark with seven-inch teeth, reddened the seas with blood.

In the first part of the Quaternary Period, the Pleistocene Epoch (generally regarded as the last Ice Age, the first humans (*Homo sapiens* or Cro-Magnon) appeared suddenly. They were not descended from the earlier *Homo erectus* as his physiognomy differed markedly from theirs. He looked like modern humans, and he could speak, create cave paintings and stone sculptures, and make sophisticated tools. The men and women were a new breed. I could easily have mistaken them for modern Americans if only they weren't wearing skins.

Saber-toothed cats, mastodons, mammoths, giant ground sloths, and other Pleistocene mega-fauna roamed the frozen tundra near the caves inhabited by these new, thinking humans. But as the Ice Age ended, God decided to make another fine adjustment: a minor mass extinction of many birds and large mammals caused by the end of another ice age. But God's displeasure with His Creation had not ended. In the second part of the Quaternary, the Holocene Epoch, human civilization took the place of the Cro-Magnon's hunter-gatherer culture. Here God surpassed Himself since He had made man in his own image and character. We spectators watched helplessly as men who hated or envied each other attacked each other with weapons that no other animal or beast could make. Nations despised other nations. Races claimed superiority over all other races. Diseases, climate disturbances, and early death bore the stamp of God everywhere. On the surface of planet Earth, we witnessed turmoil as men advanced technologically, fireballs bursting and growing into larger explosions that escalated to unimaginable proportions and then, as everyone gasped in anxiety and fear—the sky went blank.

Wiping the tears from his eyes for the first time in more than two thousand years, Cicero paused to regain his composure. His voice skipped before shouting out, "Ladies and gentlemen, children of the universe, honorable grand jury, most divine court, how do you explain the presentation that we have just witnessed? If there were a Divine Maker, surely, He would have prevented all this, or better yet, He would have made a better world from the beginning. And if there is a Creator, He is clearly a malefactor, consuming Himself before His own conscience. No matter how we put it, if there is a God, this display of facts alone demonstrates Him guilty before this court and before His conscience. Today, we have the chance to end suffering, crime, and the delusion of beatitude. Perhaps obliterating God will obliterate evil. If evil by definition cannot be eradicated, what's the purpose of an all-watching Almighty? I beg you on behalf of all living creatures to decide fairly according to the evidence we present to you and to vote for sentencing a horrible deity who does not even care for His own Creation. If He cared, He would have shown mercy if not love, decency if not kindness, righteousness if not consideration, holiness if not understanding. He would have shown Himself in answer to billions of prayers and trillions of tears flowing like rivers from the eye of living beings. He would have turned a kind face to us all. But He didn't. Why? Because He does not exist for us any more than we, the righteous dead, do. And we are nothing but a mirage, His mirage, His dream.

Where was our Father in Heaven when all this inferno happened? I have not seen Him anywhere in this presentation. Why so many extinctions, one after another? Assume for a moment that there's been an honest mistake—unlikely if our God is a perfect God—but let's suppose it anyway. Even if He made *one* mistake, why present us with repeated debasement and cruelty? *Who* I ask you again, is to blame for this self-destructing evolution? Shall we blame Adam, or Eve, or both? Shall we point fingers at allegorical figures such as the Angel of Light? Shall we blame humankind for actions predating their existence? Are we to be accounted guilty and sentenced to eternal suffering because we ate a metaphorical fruit from the Tree of Knowledge and because, as Adam states so aptly, we are still eating it *today*? Who invented the fruit? Such a statement would make a cat laugh. Are we made in our Maker's image or are we puppets that the Master Puppeteer created to amuse Himself on His day off? Oh! Such ignorance is perhaps to accuse; such folly is presumably to blame. Maybe Marquis Pierre Simon de Laplace, who seemed agitated as he watched the sky in its disorganized splendor, could tell us if he saw God anywhere during the production of our solar system, anywhere at all to modestly redirect this question once asked by Emperor Napoleon Bonaparte, whose voice you heard earlier in the multitude.

"Ladies and gentlemen of the jury, honorable court, esteemed colleagues, this has been my opening statement. Thank you."

CHAPTER
9
SATAN'S TESTIMONY

Not without anxiety, Rufus shouted, "I now call my first witness: Satan."

The jurors murmured for a few seconds as they watched Lucifer walk to the middle of the podium, stopping a few feet before the judge. An angel acting as bailiff extended the Bible as the judge asked Lucifer to place his left hand upon it and raise his right to take the oath.

"You insult me by giving me these scribbles," said Lucifer, chortling.

The judge motioned for the book to be removed.

The bailiff continued, "Do you swear to tell the truth, the whole truth, and nothing but the truth, so help you God?"

"I swear to tell the truth, the whole truth, and nothing but the truth, without any help," he said calmly. "I don't believe in God anymore."

"Please take the stand."

Lucifer walked serenely toward the witness stand, his supporters eying him with veneration. Even those opposing him seemed surprised not only by his gigantic, prepossessing figure but also by his docility, modesty, and humility, which were nothing like the descriptions of him in legends, books, and most religions.

RUFUS: Please state your full name and occupation.

SATAN: My name is Lucifer, Archangel of Light.

RUFUS (ironically): Not of Darkness?

SATAN (smiling): No-ho, not at all!

RUFUS: What is your occupation?

SATAN: The ruler of the Earth, appointed by God.

RUFUS: Have you done anything without God's permission, Mr. Lucifer?

SATAN: No.

RUFUS: Are you also known as Satan or the Devil?

SATAN: Yes and no!

ADAM: (raising his voice): Objection, Your Honor!

JUDGE: On what grounds?

ADAM: His response is confusing and misleading. His answers must be direct, reduced to either "yes" or "no to all questions.

JUDGE: We are not on Earth. You may ask the witness to elaborate and elucidate. Overruled!

SATAN (shrugging affably): Let's say yes!

RUFUS: Are those your birth names? Can you explain?

SATAN: No, they are not! Lucifer has been my name for as long as I can remember; the other names are human inventions created to sustain religious speculations.

RUFUS: Which speculations? Can you inform the court?

SATAN: Instead of attributing to God all the evil in the world since without His knowledge nothing can exist, people blinded by religious speculation and by fear, not love of God, fabricated lies accusing me of tempting them into evil, inventing death, and even torturing them beyond the grave. Nothing could be further from the truth, with very few exceptions.

RUFUS: What are those exceptions?

SATAN: I do torture criminals—murderers, rapists, thieves, vandals, pedophiles, and animal abusers, as well as the wicked and the avaricious in general.

RUFUS: Who is responsible for the destiny of everyone and everything?

SATAN: The one you call God!

RUFUS: Do you see God in this court, and, if so, can you point toward Him?

SATAN (pointing): "There He is!" (The spectators and jury look at . . . nothingness.)

RUFUS: But I cannot see Him. Can you?

SATAN: Well, that's the whole point. No one can. That's why people have always blamed me. I'm with humanity every day from morning 'til night, I give them wealth and pleasure, and yet they hold me responsible for every bad thing. They forget that without the permission of our Father in Heaven, nothing happens.

RUFUS: Can you please point to us where God's conscience is sitting?"

SATAN: I represent God's conscience, and there's where His conscience resides! (Points toward the jury and then toward the multitude of souls attending)

(Spontaneous murmurs from the crowd)

JUDGE (pounding her gavel): "Quiet, please!"

(Silence in the courtroom as the spectators and jurors exchange apprehensive glances)

RUFUS: And what is God's conscience accusing God of doing?

SATAN: Of creating a nightmare of a world.

RUFUS: Can you tell the court your interpretation of nightmare?

SATAN: Yes! (Takes a deep breath, closes his eyes, and poses as if rewinding his thoughts)

(Adam smiles sadly, suspecting that Satan has a trick up his sleeve.)

SATAN (to everyone): You all saw the presentation of our world's Creation. Did anyone notice me during that time? Did anybody see me in person anywhere near that apocalypse? Where was I when the mass extinctions happened? Do you impute those catastrophes to me? I'm listening; I don't hear any voice. Well, I tell you, then. I wasn't there when one calamity after another extinguished species after species, life after life, and soul after soul. They all died with their eyes wide open, shouting until their mouths filled with dust or lava or fire or ice. And God either heard them and didn't care or didn't hear them because He was asleep, making him worse than nonexistent: anti-existent, in other words, absent. I ask you again, have you seen or heard the howling, the pain of those creatures who were burned to ashes by lava or frozen and starved by glacial ice? Where was I then? Does anyone still have the nerve to blame me? Or did everyone wait for humanity to be born before finding me—the nail in all coffins and all the crosses, including the one from Calvary carrying the bleeding, the crucified, the anointed Jesus of Nazareth. Who set me up to entice Adam here and his beautiful Eve into eating the fruit of the Tree of Knowledge—knowledge, not ignorance—which condemned humanity to eternal damnation? Who condemned humankind and all living species? Where was I hundreds of millions of years ago when evil presided everywhere? Apparently, the so-called Good Book was not published until much later in Germany, so I couldn't have existed before it was written, could I?

Oh, I forgot that you, with your priests, rabbis, prophets, and ministers, your well-intentioned, heavily indoctrinated, light-minded followers of God, your money-seeking religious charlatans, and your quasi-learned crooks who rob the credulous, the poor, the sick, and the weak, who steal from the pious and the true lovers of Creation, you poke your noses against these primitive scribbles and find me liable for everything afraid of denouncing the real malefactor. God—the Supreme Intelligent Designer, the Creator, the Architect, the Master, the Our Father which art in Heaven—doesn't listen to any of your crying, to any of your screams and yells when disease and death strike without warning. For death seems abrupt but is actually painful and lengthy not only for the dying but still more for those left behind to suffer the loss, crying to

Heaven for a helping hand that never arrives; the only thing remaining is the hopes eroding their hearts and minds.

Omar Khayyam wrote:

Look not above, there is no answer there;
Pray not, for no one listens to your prayer,
Near is as near to God as any Far,
And Here is just the same deceit as There.

Was I, the so-called Devil, involved in all this? Ha! Satan, the accuser; al-Shaitan, the adversary, the hostile? Or was it they, the people who invented my alter ego in their fear of a heavenly despot? Was it I who damned those of you born before the birth of Jesus Christ so that you could be saved later? Did I design the shark that rips through flesh with its cruel teeth? Did I invent the tiger that hunts and kills to survive? Did I create the trillions of germs responsible for fatal illnesses, which attack human beings from infancy and follow them to their deathbed? Was it I who created hell on Earth and promised eternal damnation after death? Have you ever seen a deer crying before he dies or the eyes of a child left without a parent or the slow walk of an elephant toward his graveyard? Have you witnessed the dolphin's last flip in the air? Have you looked without fear or remorse into the lifeless eyes of your Destiny? Did I design all those, dear friends?

Let's be impartial for a change and assume that everything God made was predestined. As you like to say, "Everything has a purpose." For the purpose, the motif to exist, the intent must be there. Isn't there a saying, "the path to Hell is paved with good intentions"? Does that saying apply to everyone? Whoever made the universal laws should also live by them for He made the laws according to His wishes and His wishes according to His plans and His plans according to His purpose, which resulted from His feelings. Once He set the universe in motion, neither He nor anyone else can stop it from following its own laws, don't you agree?"

RUFUS: I'm repeating the question: Can you please tell the court your interpretation of nightmare?

SATAN: As I was saying, if you do not interrupt me, we have here a God who, after creating the world in six days, rests on the seventh and falls asleep, happily dreaming of his work well done. Well, for such a design, such a dream, and now we are facing the consequences. But, wait! Why don't we blame Satan, the villain of the Bible, the angel thrown from Heaven down to Earth, since he alone must be responsible for all the chaos and the many hideous life forms on Earth, starting with an estimated ten quintillion - that's ten followed by eighteen zeroes - living insects of not less than ten million species. They comprise ninety-five percent of all the animal species on Earth. Yes! Satan should be blamed for all the crimes" he ridiculed. "In fact, he is to blame for all the dangers, diseases, wars, lies, killing, cruelty, betrayals, deaths, and suffering during life and after death, right? Every creature suffers, from the majestic whale to the minuscule germ. Young or old, they all die in the end. Old age is a programmed disease as calculated as life span.

Life is short. Why isn't life a pleasure, anyway, instead of an ordeal? I don't know; don't look at me. Ask the Savior or wait for His honest answer when He testifies. He may come again after another two million years, but if you're in a rush, read the predictions. Try the oldest religious texts from ancient Egypt or the Epic of Gilgamesh from the Sumerian tablets. Or take the Zoroastrian Avesta or the Hindu Vedas and Bhagavad Gita. Or read the Tanakh or Jewish Scriptures, the Quran, or the New Testament for argument's sake. The New Testament writers spewed many arguments and finally declared Jesus as the "only" begotten Son of God, Jesus who promises eternal life but *only* if to those who accept Him as a mediator, the Father's middleman, the entrepreneur, the broker commissioned to carry on. Ask Jesus, the Son of Man, the God Jesus, the invented Jesus, himself the inventor of Hell where he stopped to see the souls in torment and left sick and nauseated by His own idea. Believe it and there you have it: your own bare belief that you must strengthen with faith, without which there is no salvation. Come on now!

And after God had created all design as efficiently just as if it were a giant round cake with all the sweet ingredients in it, He had to top it with a cherry His latest model—the woman; He produced the man first, in His own image, ready to flavor and relish the cherry. God designed her for procreation since the man could not reproduce the race alone. If that were possible, God would've made them for one another, but He didn't. He created the woman for the man. Look at her outline, her serpentine curves that undulate within a package of pleasure and lust and complexity. Her mere presence beats the heavenly boredom that I see here in Heaven by far.

In creating the woman, God surpassed Himself. After all, she is more complex than man is and, therefore, more perfect than perfection. If she looks better than man does, and if man is made in God's image, it follows that she looks better than God does. She is the cherry on the cake, she is..."

RUFUS: So is this your interpretation of a nightmare?

SATAN: I'm painting a broad picture of it. God had made everything so that men and women could enjoy the scenery, the play. Unfortunately, in His joyful rush during eternity, He forgot to wake up and see the result of what had happened while he lay resting, dreaming of His divine works. His nightmare of a dream had spread throughout the heavens, erupting with insane intensity, unimaginable impetus, and irrevocable deliverance, erupting like a big bang.

Who said that Heaven watched with indifference and with folded arms for more than one hundred thousand years how human beings perished due to maladies, cataclysms, tribal massacres, animal encountering, and later to repetitive crimes of genocide and wars as human beings killed each other for land or power? Until finally, about six thousand years ago, the Almighty's heavenly hierarchy began to notice the butchery, the evils, and the imbalance, and they said to themselves with remorseful baritone voices, "We must intervene," for God loves these people to death. Yes, "to death," it's been said, and to death it remained. . . . But, ah, Religion! Religion was born to save everyone from the death as if it wouldn't have been wiser for God not to invent death in the first place rather than going to the trouble of Salvation. Why go about it backwards, scratching behind the right ear with the left hand from behind the back? God began to notice all this when He woke up. In fact, His conscience awoke, too, and rebelled against God's Creation. As a good friend of mine from the United Kingdom said, "God squeezed the fountain pen to its last tear of ink until He had no more to say, and then He disappeared behind the magic veil of time." My friend did open a can of worms—also God's wonderful invention—by offering intellectual reasoning with a charming British accent. Oh, I love my English comrade! He's expected any moment now; Christopher Hitchens, ladies and gentleman, that's the name of this brilliant man—Christopher Hitchens the one that wrote "god is not great – how religion poisons everything." What an excellent fact book. In fact, God Himself inspired Christopher to write such stimulating remarks. God foreknew eons earlier that He, God, would become the subject of ridicule. He worked at the promotion of it, planning, marketing wisely, giving people like my English friend – well, English-American, rather - the soul and the spirit needed to speak and write just as He preordained. Just as He knew of this book telling about His nightmare, and He helped the selling of it. The Almighty conceives people whose destinies He has penned from birth, so what Christopher and others like him did- was only to write with God's pencil, executing a supreme command so that even the religious apologetics must bow and respect him and venerate his writings and even hold them holy, for they are the Word of God. The writer only fulfilled a heavenly prophecy by recording what God inspired him to record: the truth, the whole truth, and nothing but the truth. The fact that we are here today proves it.

Without God our Father in Heaven we would not be here, it is true. The creation of man had been in my Father's mind for billions of years. He just acted on it late but not so late as to get in trouble by it. Forgive me, Father, for I shall sin, but I must tell the truth. (Looks toward the light and stares as if hypnotized, like Brutus before a falling Caesar and continues in a compassionate tone)

My Father, I'm sorry to say, didn't find the right moment for creating man in His image. Our God forgot about man while creating the black hole and all the spinning, bursting, and firing nebulas and galaxies and then the solar system and the Earth. But at last, after designing the lemur, the three-toed tree sloth, and the orangutan, the memory of His great intention surfaced. I saw Him chuckling and smiling as man's image entered his mind in all its beauty and perfection, and from there it erupted like a volcano and . . . He made Adam first."

A loud laugh broke the silence.

ADAM: Objection, Your Honor! He's being deliberately sarcastic and offensive.

SATAN (with a serious expression): "This is my way of showing the jury pure facts, Your Honor. I am not being offensive at all. Sarcastic? Maybe. But what I say is shedding the sunlight of truth onto the darkness of Adam's testimony."

JUDGE: "Overruled. We are interested in the facts, not in how the facts are presented."

SATAN: Thank you. As I was saying, God remembered to place the man and woman on the surface of the Earth after which He fell asleep. The result? Man learned that he was made in the image of his Creator and began to emulate Him by becoming a creator himself: an inventor, a scientist, and, eventually, an architect. The first thing that he invented was the marriage club, of course, in a primitive shape at first but as efficient as the baseball bat of today. With it he proposed marriage to his beloved woman, who was on the run from him, by hitting her not too hard behind the head with a simple volley strike to convince her beyond a reasonable doubt that love at first sight had its charm and an unquestionable future.

He also devised the arrow-tip made of stone, and Adam's descendants had been at it for about a million years before another mastermind inspired by the Creator invented a more modern one, which satisfied the inhabitants of the planet and lasted almost another million years. But notice, please, that after the arrival of the ones called Annunaki, who seemed to give man the ability to speak by genetically mixing their DNA with his, man went straight to conquer space in about thirty-five thousand years. And speaking of tongues (not "in tongues," that would be called schizophrenia), there are currently about six thousand nine hundred twelve living languages and over thirty-nine thousand dialects spoken today on Earth. Now, can anyone tell me why are there so many languages when God spoke only in one to Adam and Eve, which was Hebrew? (Laughter)

Yes, you see—why would God choose Hebrew since it was not the first language spoken by humankind, just to give his Holy Scriptures to desert wanderers and camel riders? Think! Today it is no sin to think.

Of course, not all tribes advanced equally and not all humans are direct Annunaki product. Some preserved ninety-eight percent of their primate genes as a reminder of God creating them, as we can observe just by looking among us. Better yet, look around into the jungles of the Mato Grosso in central Brazil, or San Miguel in El Salvador (my brother Michael should be proud of this one since it carries his name), the Sabaragamuwa province in Sri Lanka or Queensland in Australia, if not into the rainforests of Ecuador or the depths of Monrovia, Costa Rica, or Borneo. Search no further than Papua, New Guinea—a land evidencing primitive traditions, mysticism, and all sorts of magic, one of the last refuges of Stone Age tribes. These people are also made in God's image, aren't they? They look so different from one another, their physiognomy is different, they are of different races, and although I would love to give credit to my brother Adam as the Father of Mankind, not all of them resemble his bloodline. Well, they parade around their own Eden habitats—not speaking Hebrew, though—fashioning a leaf up front and only men another in the back, while some game raw pelts made from the skins of hares or snakes or sheep (once living happily and unconcerned). Please note that more than one Stone Age tribe enjoying free will by practicing cannibalism in today's 'religious' age. Look at the Korowai, also called the Kolufo, in the Southern Papua, or at the Melanesian tribes who still practice ritual cannibalism, as well as at the rebel soldiers in the Congo and Liberia who may have eaten their enemies as an act of terror. Cannibals can eat any savior whether he is a Son of God or not, and after the meal, they will compliment the cook for how tender and mild He tasted. Then, their digestive systems will transform the food into nutrients, the rest being loudly purged into the air. This proves a lot, does it not? Or see how these tribesmen eat live roaches, larvae of beetles and earthworms, which were also created in the image and within the Spirit of God. Here the anthropomorphic argument of the existence of God fits in perfectly.

Humans live and behave according to the environment surrounding them. Given the examples that I've just presented, do you still think that God made everyone in His own image? We would not err by saying that primitive ignorance gave birth to superstition. Religious beliefs erupted by the lip of the first volcano, enforced by first flood while the first gods appeared with the first ice storm and the first hurricane—not to stop disasters but to claim them. People started to bring sacrifices, praying to what they thought was the supernatural manifesting itself. They were still far from knowing the laws of nature. Also, if they needed to defeat a neighboring tribe, they brought sacrifices to gain preference from God. So did the other tribe. Funny. And they're still scratching their heads, flagellate and even scalp-slash themselves like the Shiite tribes today, running bloody and hysterical and fanatic and stupid like chickens with their heads cut off around their town squares to please God, precisely like Stone Age tribesmen.

Others became religious being amazed by the power of the Sun praying to Ra, the sun God, or God's Son, Amen-Ra (from whose name the Hebrews conveniently borrowed and reinterpreted the word *Amen*). Fear of death and hope of an after-life gave birth to faith.

But then something wonderful happened. There were the lucky few, inspired by the Spirit of God, who put into their minds words of wisdom, promises, laws, and commandments to be memorized and transmitted to others (as if God couldn't just tell everyone Himself) and later written down in books that almost immediately became sacred. Thus, in some barren desert in the Middle East during the Bronze Age, God spoke to an "illiterate" merchant, a cad, a rapist, a pedophile, a pederast and a killer, telling him to 'borrow' from existing testaments, change some names, and proclaim a new religion based upon the "only" and "final" Word of God. Why? God was not satisfied with the previous religions, which He had whispered into earlier minds by way of voicing His story. Why? Don't you see? Because God loves to invent new things (remember the extinctions?) and new religions for new people because people are not all the same. People with different tastes and skills have built different customs and cultures according to their geographical location and its particular climate and terrain. Why do you think that so many religions exist in the world today? Because God wanted them to provide backup for each other. That is, if one died out, another could take its place. And it wasn't difficult for the new prophets to convince the herdsmen and farmers, who knew nothing of the four cardinal points or the shape of the world, that their words came directly from God. One of them, was fifty years of age when he forcibly "married" a six-year-old child. And I ask you, what would you do to a man if you knew that he had performed sexual intercourse with a minor? A few courts of law would hang him by the neck or the nuts; most courts would send him in prison for rape and child abuse, or, if he had money, they'd send him to a mental institution for treatment. But rather than punishing this pervert, our Heavenly Father selected him as a prophet whose story one and a half billion souls retell and believe. Worse, our Father in Heaven promised him seventy-two virgins as his reward for preaching the law of God to desert camel riders and goat herders. Did God listen to the screams of the little girl while the camel paramour veteran raped her? No! He turned his face the other way and slept through it, allowing it to happen without interfering, without proclaiming it wrong, without punishing the bilious, perverted, lubricious, cowardly bastard. Then to irritate and confuse his followers more, He even decided to call the pedophile a prophet and to bless him with His spirit of truth and virtue.

And this Prophet isn't the only perverted religious leader. God allowed his prophets, priests, and ministers to rape not one but many children, boys and girls, and, strangest of all, He still allows it today. Look at the Catholic Church. Is anyone raising an eyebrow, questioning the morality of the priests who molest children? But there's a difference between Father and me since I don't allow this crime in my so-called Hell. We're talking about Heaven here. And God has promised these people a heavenly paradise for believing in His son, Jesus. Suppose that I give them some of my Heaven for a change, since I, too, am made in the image of my Father. I assure you, I hate pedophiles, rapists, criminals, and thugs with reeking breath; and they all smell. My place will welcome them and comfort them in a suited environment for sure. I'll give them something to fulfill their carnal pleasures forever. I'll give them the hottest offer they can't refuse. In fact, I long to see them in my garden—the Garden of Even. But if they end up in Heaven for some reason, such as canonization, I would recommend self-abuse. As Cetewayo, the Zulu hero, once remarked, "A jerk in the hand is worth two in the bush." (Another burst of loud laughter breaks the silence.)

ADAM: Objection, Your Honor! He's using low and lewd expressions. Besides, he's showing disrespect to God's prophets.

RUFUS: "Your Honor, he is citing Cetewayo just as Clemens once did in a pamphlet whose title I would rather not mention. The words are not vulgar in my opinion, and the witness intends no disrespect to this court or to any religious group. He only speaks the truth as he sees it. Anyone can challenge his testimony if he or she can prove the contrary.

JUDGE: To the majority, his words may not appear to be vulgar, but I see a few people lowering their chins in sign of embarrassment; Objection sustained! We'll withdraw the last remark.

ADAM: Thank you, Your Honor.

JUDGE: The witness will please continue.

SATAN: I say for those who want to hear, all man's books are nothing but fabrications inspired by and copied from Creation. All Scriptures plagiarize one another and all contain lies and delusions. And the proof is here in this courtroom. We are facing God the Creator, not God the character in the so-called Scriptures, which are nothing but crime novels. As far as I can tell, He crucified Himself along with his invented son.

I would like to ask a question. Can anyone tell me whether all people are same or equal? Or have only a handful remained in God's image while others have been hereditarily positioned to fit a better purpose? Can we distinguish the products of God from the others thrown into the blend? We look at a salad mix of races in this world, don't we? I don't want to add to the confusion, but look around and judge for yourselves. Is Beethoven the same person as a man-eater in Papua? Does he look like the Zulu musician? If you have no answer to that let's ask God, or better yet, ask Beethoven himself. The Korowai tribesman wouldn't mind to be compared with Beethoven (if he knew of him) and if he were living in a free society with human rights, those rights penned in bold capital letters. The cannibal would love that, especially if you brought the composer to him before lunch while his stomach growled with hunger. I assure you that if the tribesman were given a passport to a Western country, educated for more than few years, given modern clothes, taken to church regularly where he would learn the words "believe" and "faith" fed gourmet dishes, and given plenty of money, he would claim his equal rights unreservedly. Given his culture and his nature, he would qualify as a bishop or even the president of a country one day, especially if he were baptized in secret by a certain society—of course, with God's blessing. His somersault into civilization could even get him a Nobel Prize.

(He pauses, looking around. Ludwig van Beethoven stands under a ray of light, nervously combing his hair with both hands. The beginning of his Fifth Symphony in C minor, opus 67, known as the Symphony of Destiny, plays softly in the far background. Since his hearing has been restored in Heaven, Beethoven blushes.)

SATAN: For now, I think I've said enough.

RUFUS: I do have one more question to ask. If God knew all these things before they happened, that fact should be stated somewhere. Is there any evidence to support your claim, and if so, where is it written besides the man-made Scriptures?"

SATAN: What God has willed, He has written in the book called "Human Destiny"! What He has written must follow its course. Facts are God's will that has been accomplished."

RUFUS: Thank you!" (Turns to face the judge): No further questions, Your Honor.

JUDGE: "Would the defense like to cross-examine the witness?"

(With a deep sigh, Adam steps forward. In the palm of his hand, he bounces a shiny, green apple. He walks toward the witness stand, stopping a few feet away from Lucifer, who juts his chin forward, squinting. Adam bites the apple in front of him, producing a loud, slurping sound that resonates in the acoustics of space. A few juice drops sprinkle outward. Lucifer throws back his head and laughs loudly, startling the audience and making the dogs down on Earth twitch in their sleep. Obviously, he didn't expect Adam's biblical gesture. The audience and jurors remain attentive, watching and listening as Adam chews passionately. Lucifer swallows once, reflexively.)

ADAM (facing the audience): Ladies and gentlemen, I know that it's hard to put aside all beliefs and dogmas, the tales of prior events labeled as history, the centuries of teachings all from honorable and beloved sources. However, the only way to overcome this crisis of denial and continuing sacrilege brought against God and His Creation is to open our minds to facts, sacrificing fiction in the name of righteousness and truth and morality and ethics. Lucifer, are you *fact* or *fiction*?"

SATAN (winking): I am that I am!

ADAM: Do you copy God's words from the Old Testament?

SATAN: The Bible God copied me!

ADAM: What do you mean by "Bible God"? Are you insinuating that there is more than one God?"

SATAN: Once He's invented, He therefore is.

ADAM: You are part of the Old and New Testament as well. Does that mean that you were born in the Scriptures?"

SATAN: Mentioned in the Scriptures, of course. But come now, Adam. You're not denying my existence outside those degenerate scribbles, are you? What about your own existence? Do you claim to have arrived in Eden as the first man?

ADAM: I ask the questions for now. However, out of courtesy, I must say that, yes, I was the first man as far as I know since I didn't see any other man around when I was born, I mean, made. (Laughter) Just because I'm part of the Holy Scriptures doesn't make me fiction. Am I not standing before your very eyes here and now?

SATAN: Images perceived by the eye, which is part of the brain, are illusory. "Yes, I perceive you as present here and now, Adam, but your presence is an illusion."

ADAM: Is the Bible God, as you call Him, an illusion, as well?

SATAN: An illusion indeed. The mind-born Bible God reflects upon reality.

ADAM: And what is reality?

SATAN: Reality is the presence of quantum energy that exists in human consciousness through perception and its effects. The quantum chemist Lothar Schäfer calls it "the existence of non-local physical effects." Lothar states "Something that happens at this moment in its depths may have an instantaneous effect a long distance away, such as right here and now."

ADAM: Given your theory, why does every person perceive reality differently?

SATAN: Consciousness, which receives and interprets reality, varies from individual to individual and from subject to subject in any living entity according to its sensory or mental capacity.

ADAM: If so, why blame God for committing crimes when all He does is deliver energy that His creatures receive according to each one's disposition or capacity?

SATAN: Uh, that's another story.

ADAM (hurriedly): No, we're in the same book. No more questions, Your Honor.

CHAPTER 10
DELUSION

[4]"Look again at that dot. That's here. That's home. That's us. On it everyone you love, everyone you know, everyone you ever heard of, every human being who ever was, lived out their lives. The aggregate of our joy and suffering, thousands of confident religions, ideologies, and economic doctrines, every hunter and forager, every hero and coward, every creator and destroyer of civilization, every king and peasant, every young couple in love, every mother and father, hopeful child, inventor and explorer, every teacher of morals, every corrupt politician, every 'superstar,' every 'supreme leader,' every saint and sinner in the history of our species lived there — on a mote of dust suspended in a sunbeam."

"Down on Earth, it is December 21, 2011.

---

[4] Carl Sagan

Human beings have divided themselves into societies except for a few primitive tribes, which preserve their violent cultures. The very few are extremely rich while the majority of Earth's residents suffer from political pressure. The crafted social and economic instability is renamed "moderate poverty." In the last few years, the climate has changed for the worse. The air is flat and infected with new viruses.

New religions, purposely created and vigorously promoted, confuse the masses. Fanatics, succumbing to lies and delusions, are ready to sacrifice their lives and their own children to reach a Heaven they think it was built especially for them in a constellation of eternal beauty.

The world's economy bows to a terminal disease that the Elite call "financial collapse" while the money prestidigitators print legal tender in inflated numbers with their names and their masters' faces on it. The world's economy expands just like a super inflated balloon ready to pop. As a result, jobs are scarce and people struggle to keep their homes. Those that are religious pray that their gods will save their families from the crisis. No god answers any prayers. Many homeless people roam the streets and sleep in tents or public shelters, under bridges, in parks, or near garbage cans beside squalid buildings.

In all countries, even the richer ones, the young are largely uneducated. Illiteracy governs the so-called civilized societies. Too few people see the danger. Many believe that somewhere, someone let all this happen for a purpose.

Religion has become a controlled business, a scam of the grandest proportions. Believers prostrate themselves to a chimera, idolatrizing a book wherein their hero (God) awaits their prayers and constantly demands money (through His representatives). Jealous of other gods that reside in other books, God hides so deep inside them that only the mind can reach Him, and when it does, God talks to that mind and gives it reason enough to trust Him, to believe in Him, to have faith in Him.

People embarrass themselves before their own dignity. They reject a normal mental state in favor of ecstasy, allowing themselves to receive hypnotic dogma, and through daily repetition of certain phrases, become convinced that they will reach paradise in a state of absolute serenity regardless of any sins that they have committed.

Reverends—ordained ministers and charlatans alike—who fill vast venues, order their subordinates to count people's money right after milking their minds. Carefully added to tax-exempt accounts receivable, supplementary to monthly "contributions" accumulated from the tithes (see Hebrews 7:5-9) from congregants' salaries, these sums make the pastors' bellies grow with pride and more love for . . . God.

"Isn't God good to us?" the charlatans ask as they add another mansion to their name. And the flocks of sheep follow their shepherds knowing not that those are wolves dressed in sheep's' skin. The effect of reading these holy books or smoking them is the same: prolonged hallucinations.

The preachers' humble salutations always translate to "Share your salaries with God; if you give the church part of your monthly earnings, brothers and sisters, ye shall be saved."

"Do it!" says the Bible. Trust every letter, commands the Quran. Bobbing and davening to (Kotel) the Wailing Wall in Jerusalem and waiting for an answer, is customary. What, nothing yet? Pray more, even if it takes a lifetime. If there's no answer now, you'll receive it tomorrow; if there's none tomorrow, wait for the next day. It's good exercise emotionally and physically.

Think of Pascal's wager, which states that even if God doesn't exist, you should behave as if He does. What do you have to lose? It doesn't matter if you're a hypocrite; you should try to reach the promised Heaven. Try to be the first in line, and if there are people by Heaven's gate fighting to get through that gate in front of you, you should slam some elbows and kill your brother if need be—follow the example of the God of the Bible and slay everyone that stands in your way, to advance to your heavenly position. Killing for God absolves the murder. You must have faith. Bow before a black meteorite in Mecca, the jewel from Heaven; maybe a rock will answer your prayers. A stone shall answer the stoner.

Wait for Jesus to appear from behind the clouds on a white horse (the horse must be white or else it's not Jesus). But what if you're blind and can't see the color? If it's Jesus, you'll see Him even if you're blind; why would you need eyes if you have faith? Ah, well. Wait for Jesus's coming; wait for the Rapture. He's a bit late, but He'll come. The clock is ticking, people are getting older and (with a few exceptions) poorer, the sick are getting sicker, the hungry hungrier, the blind . . . the blind can see! (Shouting!) The blind can see! Jesus; Jesus is here! Jesus, oh, Jesus! Jee-esus Christ! Hallucination. They're smoking those books again.

God must be sleeping. Billions of prayers vaporize in thin air; generations vanish without hearing an answer, a reproach, a call, whether it's good or bad while pontiffs break wind and make the news by fondling boys: "Nightmare! Children Molested; Catholics Deny God as Witness." Wow! Wow! Wow; the wowsers wow and bow instead of hanging the rapists by the kidneys (I don't want to say "balls") and take over religion.

Where is the real God hiding? Where? Evil does not happen accidentally since it happens all over the world. It's not a coincidence. It seems that everything spells casuistry. A lawless universe, a lawless world, a lawless people, lawless matter, and yet they all follow as if one law, the law of nature. No? If it's not that, then what is it: intelligent design?

Don't laugh at destiny; don't curse it either. "What if?" is the question!

What if God really cares? What if He becomes a very personal God? What if He watches you while you sleep? What if He reads your mind? What if He gawks at you in the bathroom while you're conducting your private activities? What if He cares about your love life? Imagine always having to roll your eyes, take a deep breath, and think twice before your every move. Embarrassing! What if He counts your every prayer or counts the slices of bread that you eat every day? What if He doesn't like people being obese, or too skinny or too short or too tall? Look how skinny Jesus was portrayed (only physically; now he's religiously overweight). Or what if God minds what you drink (some religions don't allow "spirits" since He's a sacredly sober God) or how you dress or what you say and when you say it or how much money you give to the Church or ministry? What if He keeps your schedule by the book—not the "Holy Book" but the destiny book—in which every breath you take from birth to death is registered (although you may ask why He would mind your doing anything if everything is predestined; in other words, you're doing it by the book, as He commanded). Well, only freethinkers can question God's mind.

But what if you hear voices in your head as you're dressing up for the synagogue, the church, or the mosque, telling you that God has changed His mind and wants you to wear a different outfit? What if He wants you to go in shorts and a bright-colored jacket opened just enough to reveal a flashy T-shirt with some prophet's head painted upside down holding a trick cigar in his mouth? And what if the cigar had just exploded, revealing that the cigar was made from the pages of the a sacred book, and right above up the picture was the caption, "The Smoking Prophet"—just to make fun? Would you dress to God's command if God told you to wear that outfit? After all, He is God and the prophet is only God's servant—so the sacred book says—and God could pull a prank sometimes to get a break from his monotonous lifestyle. He may also be a loving and a funny God when He wants to be although He doesn't show affection or a sense of humor that much. He can't be grave forever and ever; He must break loose from his chain of commandments, and even He must laugh once in awhile to shake it all off, relax, and play around a bit.

Would the pious mind if God commanded them to wear the T-shirt with the upside-down portrait of the Prophet, his eyes bulging like Marty Feldman's as the cigar blasted all over his contorted face? In other words, the cigar exploded - not to kill him since he's already dead - but just to scare his portrait silly. It's a trick cigar, a joke.

If he, the Prophet, were alive today and anyone gave him such a gift, he couldn't die from it if he wanted to. Well, okay, maybe he would die of a heart attack if it scared the sheep out of him, making him jump out of his sandals, but it wouldn't pulverize him like real dynamite. If the faithful don't mind suicide bombers dying from explosives and even make martyrs of them, why would they mind a trick cigar that wouldn't do the Prophet any harm? Would they be angry with their God if He gave the cigar to the Prophet Himself?

Would the faithful condemn and risk eternal torment in Hell going after the artist or the printer or the seller of the T-shirt to kill him, her, or them if God commanded the poor, honest, faithful believer to wear that T-shirt? Or if God commanded a company to mass-produce the T-shirts and release them to the world market, would that command anger the pious believer, making him act irrationally, if he knew that it was God's wish? The blindfolded pious believer committing such an irrational, evil crime – acting absurdly, rebelliously and violently - would without a doubt face eternal damnation for disobeying the Word of God. No believer in his right mind would wear such a T-shirt if not commanded by God; it would be sacrilegious, disrespectful to his own religion, as well as impertinent. It takes faith to carry out God's wish, no matter what it is. You can't judge God's actions. What do you expect God to do, come down and wear the T-shirt Himself? Instead, He would have to tell a believer to dress up and prove his courage. That's what God calls an act of faith. No matter what God does to you or asks you to do, you must swallow your pride and do it or face the consequences. Well, you could think the obvious, which is that you could end up dead, anyway, since it sounds like a death sentence if you piss off some fanatics who may put a death sentence on you, but at least those who were responsible for your death would end up in Hell. God says so Himself. They would not be welcome in

Heaven, says God. It's *in* the holy books. After all, if they were smart they would know that it was God, joking. And they have the potential of being very smart. At the end of day, where's the harm in it?

What if anyone dressed in such a fashion suggested that the believers modify *their sacred books* because God Himself had commanded it, and if they don't, they'll go to Hell. Not only did God say that it would be all right to wear it, but He also said that from now on, T-shirts bearing any prophet's face must be sold everywhere in the world to show good faith. If the sales prove successful, the happy God might add the face of Abraham in the back of the shirt as a sign of friendship and joy and peace between the Gentiles and the Jews. Or He may say that from now on, all these prints bearing a prophet's face must be sold in churches, temples, mosques, and synagogues, and yes! What a brilliant idea, once in a while substitute the prophet's face with that of Jesus's and Moses's portraits smiling out to the world. Remember, all these people are God's servants; they call Him "Master." That would be God's way of saying, "I love you, man."

Will the believers feel insulted by this "act of God" knowing that it's God's way of showing the world that He is a funny deity and not the crabby, tyrannical dictator, mass murderer and liar that everyone fears Him to be?

Consider this: What if God, on seeing that His joke had been a world success that gave Him prolonged pleasure, decides to play another prank by throwing one more black stone (a meteorite) onto the Earth next to the one that millions pray every year, also black; will the pious believers pray to both stones now? What if God gave yet another holy sign to them believers and decided to send a *third* rock to the Earth on the north side of the other two, but of a different color? Would that action make the pious believers less or more faithful? Would it confuse them? Would they pray to the rock they placed on the east corner of the first one, or to the one on the North side of it, or would they pray to both of the stones in the East? Or would they have to rearrange all the rocks to keep the east side sacred?

Here's another very important thing. What if anyone dressed in the T-shirt suggested that people of all religions modify their own religious books because God Himself, seeing the dissimilarities among all the versions of *all* the holy books, commanded it to eliminate confusion and discord and bloodshed. What if He decided to update his views and begin by adding more commandments to match the day's complex and modern environment (perhaps an encyclopedia full of them) since there were only four in the beginning with more added later? And what if, after seeing that those commandments were good (as if He didn't know it in advance), He also chose to write His own *new version* of the Holy Book? Would that decision create havoc or extreme happiness among *all* people of faith?

He could change *all* the holy books to *one* Scripture, which He could write, publish, and distribute Himself as easily as He ordered, "Let there be light," he could say, "Let my Book be in every house!"

Everyone but the hypocrites is used to the image of a cantankerous, short-tempered, severe, unfair, uniform-minded, demanding deity, in one word—a monster. But what if everyone is wrong?

Imagine for a moment a God who has a sense of humor. Imagine a God who would respect your privacy and didn't care what you eat and how you looked.

Let's go further and envision a God who doesn't care how much money you give Him—as long as you give Him some. Picture a God who is your friend, in fact, everyone's friend. In that case, when two people fight to the death, on whose side would God fight? You guessed right: the winner's.

Well, imagine a God who is not only funny but also realistic. Some things are bad and some are good; there's a balance in the universe. So what? If God could do anything about the state of the world or if He wanted to, do you think He would fold His arms (if He had any), look on the mess with indifference, and keep His arms folded for few hundred million years? What, are you trying to understand God's mind? Do yourself a favor: don't. If He leaves things as is, you must also close your eyes. Don't try to change God as easily as they change versions of the Bible or rearrange its text. No wonder everything is so blurry. Beware, though. You might wake Him up to a surprise even more unpleasant than chaos: *planned chaos*. At least, now you know His habits or you *think* you know them. He's a capricious Father.

One more example to prove that He's capricious: What if God decides to kill the sacred cow and the monkey god in India to show the Hindus that He is the only God in the universe and also a jealous God who will tolerate no other gods before Him? Think. While the Hindus may swear that those gods are only personifications of Him, God could be insulted terribly. What do they think He is? A monkey? A cow? What next—a snake? Lucifer would like that last assumption, wouldn't he?

God is aware of people's superstitions, but He can't kill all the animals on the planet just because people in different cults decide to pray to them. Cats, rhinos, elephants, birds, cows, bulls, baboons, crocodiles, snakes, even fish—are these people crazy? You'd have to be God Himself to understand how difficult it is for a deity to abstain from anger under those circumstances. Men get angry when someone compares them to a monkey, don't they? Why wouldn't a deity get angry, too? Unless the monkey resembled Him.

To add insult to this great injury, man, God's own creation, has decided to dominate the world and become a demigod himself (remember the Tree of Knowledge whose fruit God commanded Adam and Eve not to eat for fear of man becoming like "us," to know of good and evil. Well, look at man today. He wants to be like God himself, a poor impersonation no matter how well done. Man long ago thought to conquer his own kind and even found one super formula: "Divide et impera" Divide and conquer, a dogma encompassing economic, statutory, and military strategy. He wants to rule through creating more disorder, more chaos, and more poverty, and by weakening the educational system and instigating wars from which to profit. Men have hated and killed each other whether they were related or not because that was their nature. The Kurukshetra War erupted somewhere between 6000 and 500 BC between two sets of cousins, the Kauravas and Pandavas, who fought for the throne of Hastinapura, with much of the slaughter taking place at Kurukshetra in what is now the state of Haryana, India. The children of God slew each other with a violence unsurpassed even by wild animals defending their young. They spilled more blood than anyone could imagine and they did it with God on their side, a God who was watching the massacre. Suppose they didn't know of a deity then? But God knew them. So, why did God, who knew them and created them, allow that to happen? He had written it, for "what is written is written" He had said, and the inevitable must happen. Everything that happens has a purpose, right? Isn't that what we're supposed to believe? But why are we born if not to live healthy lives and have a chance to create and evolve and not face famine and pain and poverty and loneliness and old age and death? Why is God so cruel? Why does He continue to torment humankind? This monster is not the Father I know. It must be something else outside His will or else He shows us that He doesn't even exist . . ."

"Come on now!" I yelled with all my might. "Why doesn't God intervene? Where is He?—Where? I want to see God! I demand to see God! I have to see God!"

The hospital room resounded with a young man's voice. His heart was pounding faster and faster, until he felt someone touching his hand, cuddling it warmly. He half-opened his eyes and saw an old man standing next to him. At first the man looked unfamiliar, but as he spoke, his voice echoed as if from ages past. Then, there were flashbacks of myself hovering above the room staring at this man and me staring at the ceiling.... And then, instantly, I remembered the womb, the eternal matrix. Hot tears impeded my efforts to see Him as I forced my eyes open. "Daddy!"

"Sleep," He whispered. "I am here. The doctor said that you must sleep, my son."

Everything faded.

CHAPTER
11
PLATO AND SAINT AUGUSTINE

"Adam! Are you all right? Adam!"

Adam shook his head as if coming out from a deep void. He answered hesitantly, "I'm sorry. . . . Your Honor, I'm truly sorry. . . ."

Lucifer grinned as he watched the dazed Adam struggling to keep his composure.

"Would you like to continue?" asked the judge.

"I . . . uh," Adam began.

"Your Honor, if I may!" A bearded, middle-aged man resembling a character from Rafael's painting *The School of Athens* called out from the audience. "I would like to continue the examination, with your permission."

The judge looked at Adam, who nodded humbly.

The man patted Adam on the shoulder as he passed by him, a faint smile brightening his normally serious expression.

JUDGE: Please tell the jury your name, the time in which you lived, your expertise, and your profession.

MAN: Yes, of course. (Turning to the jury): *Kalimera, ti kanis.* My name is Aristocles! I was born 437 years before Christ and arrived here in 347 BC. My skill is philosophy. Because of my broad physique, I acquired the nickname Platon. You know me, I believe, as Plato.

(Murmurs of veneration from the audience.)

JUDGE: Very well, then. You may proceed, Mr. Plato!

PLATO: The defense calls Augustine of Hippo to the witness.

(Lucifer raises his fist and pulls it down in a gesture of victory and then stands up to leave the witness stand. He smirks as Saint Augustine appears as if from nowhere and approaches the bench.)

PLATO: Don't leave yet, my dear friend, Lucifer! I need you as expert witness. Just as a reminder, suppose anyone arrived late, the court is setup to allow the examinations and cross-examinations of more than one witness simultaneously.

(Satan resumes his seat)

SAINT AUGUSTINE (placing his hand on the Bible offered to him by the bailiff): "I swear to tell the truth, the whole truth, and nothing but the truth, so help me *God!*

PLATO: Thank you. Please state your name, lifespan, and occupation on planet Earth."

SAINT AUGUSTINE (taking the farthest seat from Satan's): "My name is Aurelius Augustinus, admirable sir. I was born on November 13, 354, in Tagaste, Numidia. I arrived in Heaven on August 28, 430. I am, well (embarrassed cough), I *was* a priest and then a bishop in Hippo, Numidia, while also studying your works and those of your distinguished followers, Ammonius Saccas and his pupil Plotinus, uh! both of whom I am pleased to see in the audience.

PLATO (nodding and smiling): I feel humbly grateful. Can you please tell me, Mr. Augustinus, do you see God in this court?"

SAINT AUGUSTINE (modestly, looking toward the light): "Yes, sir. I see Him."

PLATO: Clearly?

SAINT AUGUSTINE: Yes, sir, quite clearly.

PLATO: Can you point to where God is sitting, please?

SAINT AUGUSTINE (with reverence): There is our Heavenly Father. (Points to the spot that Satan indicated moments before. A brilliant mist hovers around a human silhouette whose age and sex cannot be determined.)

PLATO (gazing around him): Does everyone see God sitting where Augustinus is pointing? (No one speaks or nods.) Well, then, for contrast—let there be light over those that see God and shade over those that do not see Him."

(Part of the Heavens brightens as though an unseen angel flipped on a light switch. Billions of glittering spots appear, pulsating like stars. Everything looks as it does from Earth; the heavenly court blending within space. Lucifer the Angel of Light was covered by a thick veil; He flashes on and off like a lightning bug whose feeble glow can just be seen by the naked eye. The power of God lights the sky, yet some members of the audience remain under shadow, revealing that they can't see Him.)

PLATO: Lucifer, please tell this court whether you see God now.

SATAN (slyly): I see a being too small to be called God!

PLATO: Saint Augustine, do you see a small God?

SAINT AUGUSTINE: I see the Father that I love. He is a giant; He is God, sir.

PLATO: Can you describe God to those who cannot see Him, please?

SAINT AUGUSTINE: I'll try to, sir, but He is too grand for me to describe. I do not think that anyone can describe God other than subjectively no matter how hard he tries to be dispassionate. (Swallows once as if a plum were stuck in his throat.) May I have some water, please?

(A bottle of fresh spring water appears before him on the edge of the witness stand. Condensed droplets on its sides suggest that the bottle is colder than the room, which is comfortably warm. Saint Augustine unscrews the cap, drinks from the bottle, and sighs with relief. His face brightens as he places the bottle in front of him.) What a delight. Thank you, O Lord! This water is heavenly thank you, my dear God! You have baptized me with water, and it feels like Heaven.

Uh-Yeah! He is the Reason for our existence the reason that we are here today. He is the Absolute, the Unmoved Mover to borrow Aristotle's term; He is the Designer, the Infinite, the Ultimate Intelligence, the Eternal Soul, and the Unending Energy, He is the Perpetual Life, He is—

SATAN (interrupting):—our Father of Delusion, Jealousy, and Tragedy, a total misconception of what even the incompetence of man had succeeded of making of Him.

SAINT AUGUSTINE (not looking at Lucifer): The Bible tells the truth, and you know it Satan.

SATAN: (snapping) Bible-tribal, bits of myths! Since you're in Heaven, I'll overlook your gross ignorance, but I will not fail to tell this court that your benediction and sanctification knows no more morals than the Scriptures, fibs filled with lewdness, slavery, mass-murder, and mind-controlled fear, nothing less than speculation, sentimental manipulation, and despotic control.

PLATO (calmly): What are you insinuating, Lucifer?

SATAN: Well, let's take lust, for example, gentlemen, and let's look no farther than Augustine's own works. What was the famous saying branding the so-called Saint Augustine? (Half-turns to Saint Augustine, trying to conceal a devilish smile) Can you tell this court about your habits of erotic enchantment, my dear Saint? You have certainly set a great example for today's priests and ministers, have you not? As anyone can see, they gladly follow your moral conduit. That's how saints are born, after all, through sin.

SAINT AUGUSTINE: Neither in humility nor in embarrassment do I speak the truth before my Lord and this court, Lucifer. I indeed enjoyed my life in my youth, loving a woman for her beauty and spirit with supreme affection and devotion until God gave me a wife. I am not sorry that I loved her since love is noble and holy, and within the realm of these virtues, she brought me a gift from God, which otherwise I would have not had, my dear son Adeodatus. I am eternally ashamed for the sins I committed but I was too passionate to think and certainly too young and happy, not to say too human, not to err. I did avow my difficulties in my *Confessions*, and while humbling myself, I have asked God to forgive me for my weakness. I never ceased extolling his virtues.

SATAN: Too human, you claim? That will answer the question about the kind of attribute and character God passed on-to man, which are not far different from that of his primate cousin the chimpanzee if we're speaking of primitive animal instincts. Nevertheless, what have you asked of God the Father in your hypocrisy, Augustine?

SAINT AUGUSTINE: *Da mihi castitatem et continentiam, sed noli modo*—Lord, give me chastity and continence, but not yet! And it was a sincere prayer not a hypocritical one, Satan.

SATAN: Oh! Do you hear that, distinguished jury, esteemed court? Do you hear that, Father? This is your saint, one of the most revered saints today a doctor of the Church and the Bishop of Hippo. I'm not saying that fornication should be forbidden, which is ridiculous since our Father filled human beings with passion and gave them the appropriate hardware to indulge it as the number of people on Earth amply demonstrates. But here's the deal—if you join any religion and swear to anything in the name of a god, you must abide by the oath and not break it. Yet you blame me for the good times that you would have kept ad infinitum God had granted you perpetual youth; am I right? And then you would have no need for praying, would you?

SAINT AUGUSTINE: The Good Lord forgave me because I revealed my love for Him in my written testimony, *City of God*, which concludes my repentance as I poured love for God from my heart and soul. Whereas, you, God's only beloved Archangel of Light, will never feel remorseful no matter how much love your Father shows you; you rebel against Him and are jealous of Him, showing hatred and greed. God must love you still or else His wrath would have destroyed you a million times over before now. And see, He allows if not destines you to balance the world and leverage the soul. To blame God for your acts when you are in full control of them is hypocrisy. As far as my sins or whether I would have continued to commit them given eternal youth is concerned, I am human in soul and nature as you clearly admitted. I was going through a cycle in life, and I carried my cross until the end.

As for immortality, haven't you sinned, Lucifer? You were so privileged as to be born an archangel, once free of vices, only to spoil that purity by developing an envy against (Ahem! Excuse me!) against God. Denying God's Greatness is the greatest sin of all, as denying your Father is equally terrible. You owe your existence to Him; He is your Father and you are his son. You still have time to repent, and now is the time. Imagine a world without evil. Why can you not return to Him before it's too late, at the last minute if salvation?"

SATAN: Whose salvation?

SAINT AUGUSTINE: Everyone's, including yours.

SATAN (laughing): "Listen to your impertinence. My salvation? You forget that I'm indestructible, that I have my Father's DNA. He's the evil one. Changing me changes Him. Destroying me eradicates Him. Look at the people that He made. If they change, He changes; if they perish, He vanishes. He lives now in books of superstition and in mythology created by beings supposedly made in his image.

Perhaps you're talking about God's salvation—an oxymoronic statement when we refer to his present state of conscience. Save your struggles, Augustine. When this trial is over, God's conscience and I will remember everything and I personally will reward people like you, in kind. I rule the world by following God's conscience, and it is His conscience, not God Himself, that I defend. So don't think me evil since you'll compromise His conscience by doing so. God is on trial before the Judge to face His conscience, to face me, to face the people against whom atrocities He committed, to face the 95 percent of all species on planet Earth that have been wiped out owing to His so-called grace. I would like to save my Father, the faulty Creator, but how can I save Him from his own conscience, from his own Self? Without a conscience, a thinking being regresses until it annihilates itself. It pains me to say it, whether you believe it or not."

SAINT AUGUSTINE: The only fault in God's Creation that I see is that He made the world more than perfect. He is too indulgent.

SATAN: Do you know what a sycophant is?

PLATO (calmly changing the subject): "Lucifer, can you please tell us, was God deeply asleep when the Earth began its turmoil?"

SATAN: Yes, He was.

PLATO: Was He unconscious?

SATAN: Yes, He was.

PLATO: By unconscious, do you mean involuntarily senseless and inert?

SATAN: I mean absolutely dormant! Delinquently unconscious.

PLATO: Could it rather be said that He was 'innocently" unconscious?

SATAN (smiling): No! 'Delinquently' should be more than self-evident given the evidence that Cicero presented."

PLATO: Which means that His conscience was sleeping in Him, according to your judgment?

SATAN: "Unconscious" means cataleptic, out of consciousness, not "without conscience." After all, His conscience must always be alert since He's supposedly omniscient." (Winks ironically, distorting half his face.)

PLATO: But is it not true that consciousness activates conscience?"

SATAN: Yes. Without consciousness, awareness of reality is absent.

PLATO: Is it possible for God's awareness to be absent?

SATAN: When it comes to God, everything is possible. But you know that physical awareness is different from spiritual consciousness.

PLATO: Can we safely reason then that when God went to sleep, He left the world in the same condition that He expected to find it when He woke up?

SATAN (smirking): "Yes, but He overlooked *evolution*."

PLATO: "Was evolution not written in His Book of Destiny?"

SATAN: "It was, but as destiny is subject to change, dreams may change, too."

PLATO: Just as His dream world changed into a nightmare?

SATAN: Precisely!

PLATO: "What could have triggered the disastrous elements in His dream?

SATAN: "His own creation betrayed Him. And I'm not talking about the fairytale sin from the Book of Genesis."

(Screams and yells from the audience, some in sheer excitement and some in protest as the gavel pounds furiously. A fantastic explosion of lighting ends the tumult.)

PLATO: You heard Augustine tell you that you represent the balance in the world, did you not?

SATAN: I did.

PLATO: "Do you agree with that statement?

SATAN: I do.

PLATO: And are you a witness to everything that happens in the world?

SATAN: A witness to everything, I surely am.

PLATO: You attested that you were sent by God, rather conditionally as I understand, to preside over the Earth, did you not?

SATAN: Yes, I attested that. I also stated that I have done nothing without my Father's permission.

PLATO: But He could not have given it to you since He was sleeping, according to your statement.

SATAN: He gave it to me before He went to sleep.

PLATO (loudly): Thank you. No more questions, Your Honor!

SATAN: Come now, you're playing with words! God's Spirit never sleeps even if His body desires to rest.

PLATO: Your Honor, please intervene.

SATAN: "Are you attempting to shift the blame to me instead of acknowledging the error in God's physical and transcendental engine called Nature?"

(More outcries from the audience)

JUDGE (pounding her gavel): Order! Order please!

SATAN (yelling): God made the laws of the universe! We are part of those laws! Everything is part of His Laws. All that happens results from His irresponsible, short-sighted design. If His laws aren't to your liking, neither is He."

PLATO: Your Honor! The witness is out of order.

JUDGE: Lucifer, one more random remark and I'll hold you in contempt of court.

(Background commotion)

JUDGE (raising her voice and banging her gavel): Silence! I demand silence! The last warning!

Would the prosecution like to cross-examine the witnesses?"

CICERO (jumping up): Yes, Your Honor, I would.

CHAPTER
12
THE SCROLLS OF MARK TWAIN

"[5]I cannot persuade myself that a beneficent and omnipotent God would have designedly created the Ichneumonidae [parasitic wasps] with the express intention of their feeding within the living bodies of Caterpillars, or that a cat should play with mice."

Cicero stood before the entire court gazing over the ocean of heads and holding in his hands a few scrolls. He waited a few seconds longer until there was complete silence before he theatrically untied the golden ribbon that kept one of the scrolls from unfolding. He pointed out that what he was about to quote was of most important evidence (in observation form,) which he requested the jury to hear carefully.

Cicero also informed the judge that the author in question could not appear in person since he had to attend a friend's funeral in Connecticut and console his family. "However," noted Cicero, "he is particularly interested in attending the trial to see God with his own eyes (his words) and even to

---

[5] Charles Darwin

serve as a material witness later in the proceedings. He emphasized and spelled out the word *material*. He also told me that he would like to assure everyone that because he's already dead, he will not go anywhere else besides his customary trip from Hell to Heaven where he's allowed to come occasionally to visit his old friends who, in his opinion, should have known better than to live in such a boring place. He said that he enjoys all the fun and social life down South very much, since he was always a devoted southerner, and would not opt to live anywhere else even if he were reborn."

The judge chuckled, along with everyone else.

CICERO: Therefore, Your Honor and ladies and gentlemen of the jury, regarding Saint Augustine's statement that God made the world "more than perfect," I ask permission to read an excerpt from a book entitled *Letters from the Earth* penned by my dear friend, Mr. Samuel Langhorne Clemens, better known by his nom de plume, Mark Twain. In it, he refers to the work of God with fervid seriousness yet taunting disapproval"

Cicero cleared his throat, opened the first scroll to a point near the beginning, and started to read. "'According to the Book—'"

PLATO: Objection, Your Honor! The evidence presented to the jury should not include any jocular material, which might be obstructive to the proceedings or demeaning to the defendant."

CICERO: Your Honor, the work I intend to quote should give my esteemed colleague no cause for dismay. I find no falsity in it, and I challenge the defense to refute Mr. Twain's arguments. The style is civil aside from the irony, which is there to stimulate minds, not to inflame them, and in no way detracts from the accuracy of the depiction aside from a few errors arising from the date of composition, 1909, such as the estimated age of the Earth. Arriving at truth is our object, don't we all agree?"

JUDJE: Overruled. Please continue.

CICERO: "Thank you! Here, then, is an excerpt from *Letters from the Earth* with reference to God's work on planet Earth. The narrator is Satan, and the book he refers to, spelled with a capital B, is, of course, the Holy Bible. (Clears his throat again) "According to the Book and its servants, the universe is only six thousand years old. It is only within the last hundred years that studious, inquiring minds have found out that it is nearer a hundred million."

(Laughter)

CICERO (commenting): Or four and a half billion, if you prefer. (Resumes reading) "During the Six Days, God created man and the other animals." (Coughs insinuatingly) Note, please: "*and the other animals.*"

PLATO: Objection, Your honor!

JUDGE: On what grounds?

PLATO: Your Honor, Cicero, I mean, the prosecution is mocking man by calling him an animal.

CICERO: Your Honor, the statement is not mockery; it is a fact. And I am quoting Mr. Twain. It is written right here.

PLATO: Another abuse.

CICERO: And how should this phrase have been worded?

PLATO: "Man and the animals," to distinguish him from them.

CICERO: I am quoting Mark Twain, for goodness sake! And why should we be ashamed of being a mammalian species?"

PLATO: It is highly insulting. I call—

JUDGE: "Gentlemen, you are in court."

CICERO: "How can I insult the work of God, Your Honor? Besides, I'm making a point. I will direct this question to Aurelius Augustinus, then.

JUDGE: Objection overruled. Go on!

CICERO: Mr. Augustinus, according to your Good Book, God made a man and a woman before He finally rested, right?

SAINT AUGUSTINE: "That's right, and He made them very well."

CICERO: "I didn't ask you whether He made them well. That should be evident just from looking at them."

(Laughter)

SAINT AUGUSTINE: "I apologize. Yes, sir, He made them on the sixth day before He rested. Yes."

CICERO: And placed them in the garden."

SAINT AUGUSTINE: "Yes, sir, in the Garden. The Garden of Eden."

CICERO: And how old were they when God finished making them?

SAINT AUGUSTINE: Ah, age did not exist then. He made them adolescents."

(Laughter)

CICERO: Excuse me?

SAINT AUGUSTINE: I said, God made them adolescents.

CICERO: "I thought I hadn't heard correctly. So, by today's standard of judging someone's age, how old do you think the man and woman must have been when God created them?"

SAINT AUGUSTINE: "I would have to guess that their young bodies resembled those of adolescents about sixteen or eighteen years old."

CICERO: "Of course, even though age did not yet exist. And they lived together in harmony, never growing older, until when? What happened next that caused that change?" (he points to the scrolls and smiles).

SAINT AUGUSTINE: God warned them that they must not eat the fruit from a certain tree.

CICERO: What did God say would become of them if they ate from that tree?

SAINT AUGUSTINE: They would die.

CICERO: Did God provide them with an illustration of death – to borrow Mr. Twain's observation - so that they would know what He meant by the word *die*?

SAINT AUGUSTINE (shrugs and squints into the light where God is sitting): God knows!

(Loud laughter; chatter)

SAINT AUGUSTINE: I mean, God would know the answer to that question.

CICERO: So, God's telling his new creations not to eat of a tree in the garden they lived in meant no more than telling a pair of newborns not to drink milk while giving it to them?

SAINT AUGUSTINE: They should have obeyed the Word of God.

CICERO: Stupidly? Blindly? They were infants. Their minds were inoffensive."

SAINT AUGUSTINE: Not blindly. Faithfully.

CICERO (calling out): That's the word that explains it all, ladies and gentlemen—faith-fool-ly. You must not question anything; be ignorant and execute orders whether they mean anything to you or not. Those words probably sounded to them like they would sound to any of us here if God told us not do go somewhere because if we did, we would certainly *mierlim*.

PLATO: Your honor, the prosecution is stating opinions rather than examining facts."

JUDGE: Sustained!

CICERO (finds his place in the scroll and reads): "Presently a serpent sought them out privately, and came to them walking upright, which was the way of serpents in those days."

(Laughter)

SATAN (jumping up and chuckling): That was me!

ADAM: Your Honor, objection! The prosecution is subjecting us to ridicule.

CICERO: Excuse me, Your Honor. Adam will have the chance to respond. I am being interrupted in the middle of my examination. I request to be heard civilly and without interruption in order to make a point."

JUDGE: Overruled.

CICERO (after taking a few seconds to think): Augustinus, what did the serpent say to Adam and Eve?

(Saint Augustine turns to Lucifer as if to seek his approval.)

SATAN: Don't look at me, buddy. You're on your own.

SAINT AUGUSTINE: "The Bible says that he offered the fruit of knowledge, which revealed the knowledge of good and evil, and . . ."

CICERO (reading from his scroll): "The serpent said the forbidden fruit would [pay attention, please!] store their vacant minds with knowledge."

SAINT AUGUSTINE: Not exactly in those words.

CICERO (reading): "So they ate it, which was quite natural, for man is so made that he eagerly wants to know." (Pauses and sets down the scroll). He wants to find out, to look for answers, to seek the light. Just like a cat looking curiously for new things, he should have the right to explore. Why bring him below the cat in that regard? Or below the monkey, whose stomach rules his mind. A billion gods could command the monkey not to touch a banana because he'll die if he does, and I guarantee you that the monkey will care nothing about it. The gods could chase the monkey and threaten him, and he will still go about his primary business of feeding himself— in this case, eating that banana. Why would God leave his main pet—man—in an idiotic state, knowing less than his fellow primates do? Just like his simian cousins, man wants to know, taste, and feel; despite the priests, ministers, and other representative of God (peers intently at Augustine), who, as my friend Mr. Twain says (picks up his scroll and reads), "has made it his business from the beginning to keep him [man] from knowing any useful thing."

Everyone glanced at Saint Augustine, who ignored the implications.

Cicero (still reading): "Adam and Eve ate the forbidden fruit, and at once a great light streamed into their dim heads."

ADAM: "Your Honor, May I say something?"

CICERO (shouting, bringing his index finger to his temple and waving the scroll as he recites): "They had acquired knowledge. What knowledge—useful knowledge? (Reading from the scroll) No—merely knowledge that there was such a thing as good, and such a thing as evil." (Waving the scroll and putting Twain's thoughts into his own words): And thanks to this knowledge, they learned how to do evil, which they couldn't do before. Is that right, Mr. Augustinus?

SAINT AUGUSTINE: Yes, you see . . . .

CICERO: For that reason, as Mr. Twain points out, all their acts up to the time that they committed the crime of acquiring knowledge were done without incurring any blame. Is that right, Mr. Augustinus?

SAINT AUGUSTINE: Precisely, but . . . .

CICERO: So now, after acquiring knowledge, they were to suffer for their evil because they were aware of it, whereas before, their committed evil was without blame. Right?

SAINT AUGUSTINE: Without intent to commit evil, one is innocent.

CICERO: Yet, the knowledge of evil is the possession of "moral sense," according to the Church, says the scroll.

SAINT AUGUSTINE: Which differentiates man from the beasts.

CICERO: In other words, the acquired moral sense raises man above other animals.

SAINT AUGUSTINE (smiling): Of course.

CICERO: It follows that without moral sense man will be just like any beast, or any other living animal. Do you agree with what the Church says?

SAINT AUGUSTINE: I do agree with what the Church said. How could I not?

CICERO: "So, having moral sense is good.

SAINT AUGUSTINE: Yes! The Church says even today that moral sense is among the noblest virtues, perhaps even second to faith.

CICERO: "Can anyone acquire moral sense without understanding what he or she acquires?

SAINT AUGUSTINE: "Of course not. One must understand the knowledge that one acquires.

CICERO: "So God commanded Adam and Eve not to eat the fruit of the Tree of Knowledge of Good and Evil, in other words, He commanded them not to acquire moral sense.

Doesn't that indicate clearly that God intended man to be without moral sense?

SAINT AUGUSTINE (frowning): No, God couldn't have intended that. He wanted man to be above all beasts, which is why He made man in His own image and gave him power over all other living creatures.

CICERO: "But God must have known eons in advance that man (meaning man and woman) would be condemned to death for not listening to His orders. Why didn't He offer them a non-compromising option?

SAINT AUGUSTINE: His intention was to have them live forever in paradise where death did not exist, but they disobeyed His command.

CICERO: Why did he plant the tree there in the first place unless He intended to determine man's destiny through it?

SAINT AUGUSTINE: God gave them free will and the option to live.

CICERO: And they chose the option of death, an unknown option?

SAINT AUGUSTINE: The man and woman had free will. They chose the wrong option against their Father's advice. I find that man likes free will.

CICERO: "Well, God should have not allowed a death trap in the first place."

SAINT AUGUSTINE: "God intended free will as a gift from God.

CICERO: How do you know God's intentions if not through His acts?"

SAINT AUGUSTINE: They were revealed in the Holy Scriptures. How else?

CICERO: Wait a minute. Let's take a step back; God tells Adam and Eve not to eat the fruit of a certain tree because they will die.

SAINT AUGUSTINE: "Yes."

CICERO: And yet, He couldn't have explained death to them because they could not understand what the word referred to. When a walking snake (speaking metaphorically, of course—we all know that it was Satan—) offered them knowledge, they went for it; their acquired knowledge filled their emptiness with moral sense, which the Church says is good, and you support the Church's view. Do you agree so far?

SAINT AUGUSTINE: Yes, I do.

CICERO: But God condemned them and all their descendants—his own children—to death because they acquired the only thing that differentiates them from beasts, a conclusion that makes no moral sense if we are talking about a good Father with good intentions, Himself a supposedly perfect example of morality.

(Turning to face the immense audience and shouting)

Isn't that strange, ladies and gentlemen of the jury, esteemed court? The Church, according to Saint Augustine's endorsement to what Mr. Twain was saying in his letters, continues to see moral sense as man's noblest asset even today, regardless of the Church's knowing of God's disagreeing with it. Let's go a bit further, Can you tell me, Mr. Augustinus, why you think that God made the woman for Adam?"

SAINT AUGUSTINE: So that he would not be alone.

CICERO: And?

SAINT AUGUSTINE: If you will allow me to quote Scripture:

"And God blessed them, and God said unto them, Be fruitful, and multiply, and replenish the earth, and subdue it: and have dominion over the fish of the sea, and over the fowl of the air, and over every living thing that moveth upon the earth."

"And God said, Let us make man in our image, after our likeness: and let them have dominion over the fish of the sea, and over the fowl of the air, and over the cattle, and over all the earth, and over every creeping thing that creepeth upon the earth."

CICERO: Then, God made Adam and Eve so that they could rule the Earth.

SAINT AUGUSTINE: Of course, He did.

CICERO: If that is true, then God must have planned their fall from grace since His purpose, according to what you just said, was for man to rule the Earth, multiply, and live under set conditions. A set up called, predestination.

SAINT AUGUSTINE: Yes, I mean—no! I mean—yes, of course, what you describe is predestination, but—

CICERO: A very interesting subject comes to mind at this point; I assume that we all are acquainted with it (eyes Saint Augustine warningly), and that is sexual intercourse. I will not go into details (laughter), but I will enter into this subject for the first time with the aid of the previously mentioned letters written by Mr. Twain, assuming the persona of Satan, which I make a lot of sense when we are speaking of knowledge of good and evil.

Please listen and do not interrupt me (picks up the scroll again and reads):

Very well, Adam and Eve now knew what evil was, and how to do it. They knew how to do various kinds of wrong things, and among them one principal one—the one God had his mind on principally. That one was the art and mystery of sexual intercourse. To them it was a magnificent discovery, and they stopped idling around and turned their entire attention to it, poor exultant young things!

In the midst of one of these celebrations they heard God walking among the bushes, which was an afternoon custom of his, and they were smitten with fright. Why? Because they were naked. They had not known it before. They had not minded it before; neither had God.

In that memorable moment immodesty was born; and some people have valued it ever since, though it would certainly puzzle them to explain why.

Adam and Eve entered the world naked and unashamed—naked and pure-minded; and no descendant of theirs has ever entered it otherwise. All have entered it naked, unashamed, and clean in mind. They have entered it modest. They had to acquire immodesty and the soiled mind; there was no other way to get it. A Christian mother's first duty is to soil her child's mind, and she does not neglect it. Her lad grows up to be a missionary, and goes to the innocent savage and to the civilized Japanese, and soils their minds. Whereupon they adopt immodesty, they conceal their bodies, they stop bathing naked together.

The convention miscalled modesty has no standard, and cannot have one, because it is opposed to nature and reason, and is therefore an artificiality and subject to anybody's whim, anybody's diseased caprice. And so, in India the refined lady covers her face and breasts and leaves her legs naked from the hips down, while the refined European lady covers her legs and exposes her face and her breasts. In lands inhabited by the innocent savage the refined European lady soon gets used to full-grown native stark-nakedness, and ceases to be offended by it. A highly cultivated French count and countess—unrelated to each other—who were marooned in their nightclothes, by shipwreck, upon an uninhabited island in the eighteenth century, were soon naked. Also ashamed—for a week. After that their nakedness did not trouble them, and they soon ceased to think about it.

To proceed with the Biblical curiosities. Naturally you will think the threat to punish Adam and Eve for disobeying was of course not carried out, since they did not create themselves, nor their natures nor their impulses nor their weaknesses, and hence were not properly subject to anyone's commands, and not responsible to anybody for their acts. It will surprise you to know that the threat was carried out. Adam and Eve were punished, and that crime finds apologists unto this day. The sentence of death was executed.

As you perceive, the only person responsible for the couple's offense escaped; and not only escaped but became the executioner of the innocent.

In your country and mine we should have the privilege of making fun of this kind of morality, but it would be unkind to do it here. Many of these people have the reasoning faculty, but no one uses it in religious matters.

The best minds will tell you that when a man has begotten a child he is morally bound to tenderly care for it, protect it from hurt, shield it from disease, clothe it, feed it, bear with its waywardness, lay no hand upon it save in kindness and for its own good, and never in any case inflict upon it a wanton cruelty. God's treatment of his earthly children, every day and every night, is the exact opposite of all that, yet those best minds warmly justify these crimes, condone them, excuse them, and indignantly refuse to regard them as crimes at all, when he commits them. Your country and mine is an interesting one, but there is nothing there that is half so interesting as the human mind.

Very well, God banished Adam and Eve from the Garden, and eventually assassinated them. All for disobeying a command which he had no right to utter. But he did not stop there, as you will see. He has one code of morals for himself, and quite another for his children. He requires his children to deal justly—and gently—with offenders, and forgive them seventy-and-seven times; whereas he deals neither justly nor gently with anyone, and he did not forgive the ignorant and thoughtless first pair of juveniles even their first small offense and say, "You may go free this time, and I will give you another chance."

On the contrary! He elected to punish *their* children, all through the ages to the end of time, for a trifling offense committed by others before they were born. He is punishing them yet. In mild ways? No, in atrocious ones.

You would not suppose that this kind of Being gets many compliments. Undeceive yourself: the world calls him the All-Just, the All-Righteous, the All-Good, the All-Merciful, the All-Forgiving, the All-Truthful, the All-Loving, the Source of All Morality. These sarcasms are uttered daily, all over the world. But not as conscious sarcasms. No, they are meant seriously: they are uttered without a smile.

(Adam covers his face with both hands, concealing his tears)

CICERO: "See how Adam weeps. He knows the truth and tries to obscure it to save his father. Listen well, for such a thing could happen only in Heaven—a son forgiving his father for commanding his and his wife's execution and those of his children of all generations forever and ever. Yes, the good-hearted Adam may forgive his father, but the punishment extends far beyond his time and continues into the present. And I ask everyone present, do you forgive the Father who purposely condemned you to death?

Listen further to this remarkable statement, ladies and gentlemen, brothers and sisters, and you, Adam, will find this true story sad yet amusing. (Reads):

So the First Pair went forth from the Garden under a curse—a permanent one. They had lost every pleasure they had possessed before "The Fall"; and yet they were rich, for they had gained one worth all the rest: they knew the Supreme Art.

They practiced it diligently and were filled with contentment. The Deity ordered them to practice it. They obeyed, this time. But it was just as well it was not forbidden, for they would have practiced it anyhow, if a thousand Deities had forbidden it.

Results followed. By the name of Cain and Abel. And these had some sisters and knew what to do with them. And so there were some more results: Cain and Abel begot some nephews and nieces. These, in their turn, begot some second cousins. At this point classification of relationships began to get difficult, and the attempt to keep it up was abandoned.

The pleasant labor of populating the world went on from age to age, and with prime efficiency; for in those happy days the sexes were still competent for the Supreme Art when by rights they ought to have been dead eight hundred years. The sweeter sex, the dearer sex, the lovelier sex was manifestly at its very best, then, for it was even able to attract gods. Real gods. They came down out of heaven and had wonderful times with those hot young blossoms. The Bible tells about it.

By help of those visiting foreigners the population grew and grew until it numbered several millions. But it was a disappointment to the Deity. He was dissatisfied with its morals; which in some respects were not any better than his own. Indeed they were an unflatteringly close imitation of his own. They were a very bad people, and as he knew of no way to reform them, he wisely concluded to abolish them. This is the only really enlightened and superior idea his Bible has credited him with, and it would have made his reputation for all time if he could only have kept to it and carried it out. But he was always unstable—except in his advertisements—and his good resolution broke down. He took a pride in man; man was his finest invention; man was his pet, after the housefly, and he could not bear to lose him wholly; so he finally decided to save a sample of him and drown the rest.

Nothing could be more characteristic of him. He created all those infamous people, and he alone was responsible for their conduct. Not one of them deserved death, yet it was certainly good policy to extinguish them; especially since in creating them the master crime had already been committed, and to allow them to go on procreating would be a distinct addition to the crime. But at the same time there could be no justice, no fairness, in any favoritism—all should be drowned or none.

No, he would not have it so; he would save half a dozen and try the race over again. He was not able to foresee that it would go rotten again, for he is only the Far-Sighted One in his advertisements.

He saved out Noah and his family, and arranged to exterminate the rest. He planned an Ark, and Noah built it. Neither of them had ever built an Ark before, nor knew anything about Arks; and so something out of the common was to be expected. It happened. Noah was a farmer, and although he knew what was required of the Ark he was quite incompetent to say whether this one would be large enough to meet the requirements or not (which it wasn't), so he ventured no advice. The Deity did not know it wasn't large enough, but took the chances and made no adequate measurements. In the end the ship fell far short of the necessities, and to this day the world still suffers for it.

Noah built the Ark. He built it the best he could, but left out most of the essentials. It had no rudder, it had no sails, it had no compass, it had no pumps, it had no charts, no lead-lines, no anchors, no log, no light, no ventilation, and as for cargo room—which was the main thing—the less said about that the better. It was to be at sea eleven months, and would need fresh water enough to fill two Arks of its size—yet the additional Ark was not provided. Water from outside could not be utilized: half of it would be salt water, and men and land animals could not drink it.

For not only was a sample of man to be saved, but business samples of the other animals, too. You must understand that when Adam ate the apple in the Garden and learned how to multiply and replenish, the other animals learned the Art, too, by watching Adam. (Laughter) It was cunning of them, it was neat; for they got all that was worth having out of the apple without tasting it and afflicting themselves with the disastrous Moral Sense, the parent of all immoralities.

(Scans the scroll and finds a particular sentence): You may have wondered about one particular sentence in which Twain says that "man was [God's pet, after the housefly." I will return to that point before ending my commentary. But to resume:

Noah began to collect animals. There was to be one couple of each and every sort of creature that walked or crawled, or swam or flew, in the world of animated nature. We have to guess at how long it took to collect the creatures and how much it cost, for there is no record of these details. . . .

How many animals? We do not know. . . .Of birds and beasts and fresh-water creatures he had to collect 146,000 kinds; and of insects upwards of two million species.

Thousands and thousands of those things are very difficult to catch, and if Noah had not given up and resigned, he would be on the job yet, as Leviticus used to say. However, I do not mean that he withdrew. No, he did not do that. He gathered as many creatures as he had room for, and then stopped.

If he had known all the requirements in the beginning, he would have been aware that what was needed was a fleet of Arks. But he did not know how many kinds of creatures there were, neither did his Chief. So he had no Kangaroo, and no 'possum, and no Gila monster, and no ornithorhynchus, and lacked a multitude of other indispensable blessings which a loving Creator had provided for man and forgotten about, they having long ago wandered to a side of this world which he had never seen and with whose affairs he was not acquainted. And so every one of them came within a hair of getting drowned.

They only escaped by an accident. There was not water enough to go around. Only enough was provided to flood one small corner of the globe—the rest of the globe was not then known, and was supposed to be nonexistent.

However, the thing that really and finally and definitely determined Noah to stop with enough species for purely business purposes and let the rest become extinct, was an incident of the last days: an excited stranger arrived with some most alarming news. He said he had been camping among some mountains and valleys about six hundred miles away, and he had seen a wonderful thing there: he stood upon a precipice overlooking a wide valley, and up the valley he saw a billowy black sea of strange animal life coming. Presently the creatures passed by, struggling, fighting, scrambling, screeching, snorting—horrible vast masses of tumultuous flesh! Sloths as big as an elephant; frogs as big as a cow; a megatherium and his harem huge beyond belief; saurians and saurians and saurians, group after group, family after family, species after species—a hundred feet long, thirty feet high, and twice as quarrelsome; one of them hit a perfectly blameless Durham bull a thump with its tail and sent it whizzing three hundred feet into the air and it fell at the man's feet with a sigh and was no more. The man said that these prodigious animals had heard about the Ark and were coming. Coming to get saved from the flood. And not coming in pairs, they were *all* coming: they did not know the passengers were restricted to pairs, the man said, and wouldn't care a rap for the regulations, anyway—they would sail in that Ark or know the reason why. The man said the Ark would not hold the half of them; and moreover they were coming hungry, and would eat up everything there was, including the menagerie and the family.

All these facts were suppressed, in the Biblical account. You find not a hint of them there. The whole thing is hushed up. Not even the names of those vast creatures are mentioned. It shows you that when people have left a reproachful vacancy in a contract they can be as shady about it in Bibles as elsewhere. Those powerful animals would be of inestimable value to man now, when transportation is so hard-pressed and expensive, but they are all lost to him. All lost, and by Noah's fault. They all got drowned. Some of them as much as eight million years ago.

Very well, the stranger told his tale, and Noah saw that he must get away before the monsters arrived. He would have sailed at once, but the upholsterers and decorators of the housefly's drawing room still had some finishing touches to put on, and that lost him a day. Another day was lost in getting the flies aboard, there being sixty-eight billions of them and the Deity still afraid there might not be enough. Another day was lost in stowing forty tons of selected filth for the flies' sustenance.

Then at last, Noah sailed; and none too soon, for the Ark was only just sinking out of sight on the horizon when the monsters arrived, and added their lamentations to those of the multitude of weeping fathers and mothers and frightened little children who were clinging to the wave-washed rocks in the pouring rain and lifting imploring prayers to an All-Just and All-Forgiving and All-Pitying Being who had never answered a prayer since those crags were builded, grain by grain, out of the sands, and would still not have answered one when the ages should have crumbled them to sand again.

On the third day, about noon, it was found that a fly had been left behind. The return voyage turned out to be long and difficult, on account of the lack of chart and compass, and because of the changed aspects of all coasts, the steadily rising water having submerged some of the lower landmarks and given to higher ones an unfamiliar look; but after sixteen days of earnest and faithful seeking, the fly was found at last, and received on board with hymns of praise and gratitude, the Family standing meanwhile uncovered, out of reverence for its divine origin. It was weary and worn, and had suffered somewhat from the weather, but was otherwise in good estate. Men and their families had died of hunger on barren mountaintops, but it had not lacked for food, the multitudinous corpses furnishing it in rank and rotten richness. Thus was the sacred bird providentially preserved.

Providentially. That is the word. For the fly had not been left behind by accident. No, the hand of Providence was in it. There are no accidents. All things that happen happen for a purpose. They are foreseen from the beginning of time, they are ordained from the beginning of time. From the dawn of Creation the Lord had foreseen that Noah, being alarmed and confused by the invasion of the prodigious brevet fossils, would prematurely fly to sea unprovided with a certain invaluable disease. He would have all the other diseases, and could distribute them among the new races of men as they appeared in the world, but he would lack one of the very best—typhoid fever; a malady which, when the circumstances are especially favorable, is able to utterly wreck a patient without killing him; for it can restore him to his feet with a long life in him, and yet deaf, dumb, blind, crippled, and idiotic. The housefly is its main disseminator, and is more competent and more calamitously effective than all the other distributors of the dreaded scourge put together. And so, by foreordination from the beginning of time, this fly was left behind to seek out a typhoid corpse and feed upon its corruptions and gaum its legs with germs and transmit them to the re-peopled world for permanent business. From that one housefly, in the ages that have since elapsed, billions of sickbeds have been stocked, billions of wrecked bodies sent tottering about the earth, and billions of cemeteries recruited with the dead.

It is most difficult to understand the disposition of the Bible God, it is such a confusion of contradictions; of watery instabilities and iron firmness; of goody-goody abstract morals made out of words, and concreted hell-born ones made out of acts; of fleeting kindness repented of in permanent malignities.

However, when after much puzzling you get at the key to his disposition, you do at last arrive at a sort of understanding of it. With a most quaint and juvenile and astonishing frankness he has furnished that key himself. It is jealousy!

I expect that to take your breath away. You are aware—for I have already told you . . . that among human beings jealousy ranks distinctly as a weakness; a trade-mark of small minds; a property of *all* small minds, yet a property which even the smallest is ashamed of; and when accused of its possession will lyingly deny it and resent the accusation as an insult.

Jealousy. Do not forget it, keep it in mind. It is the key. With it you will come to partly understand God as we go along; without it nobody can understand him. As I have said, he has openly held up this treasonous key himself, for all to see. He says, naïvely, outspokenly, and without suggestion of embarrassment: "I the Lord thy God am a jealous God."

You see, it is only another way of saying, "I the Lord thy God am a small God; a small God, and fretful about small things."

He was giving a warning: he could not bear the thought of any other God getting some of the Sunday compliments of this comical little human race—he wanted all of them for himself. He valued them. To him they were riches; just as tin money is to a Zulu. . . .

The fear that if Adam and Eve ate of the fruit of the Tree of Knowledge they would "be as gods" so fired his jealousy that his reason was affected, and he could not treat those poor

creatures either fairly or charitably, or even refrain from dealing cruelly and criminally with their blameless posterity.

To this day his reason has never recovered from that
shock; a wild nightmare of vengefulness has possessed him
ever since, and he has almost bankrupted his native ingenui-
ties in inventing pains and miseries and humiliations and
heartbreaks wherewith to embitter the brief lives of Adam's
descendants. Think of the diseases he has contrived for them!
They are multitudinous; no book can name them all. And
each one is a trap, set for an innocent victim.

The human being is a machine. An automatic machine. It
is composed of thousands of complex and delicate mecha-
nisms, which perform their functions harmoniously and perfectly, in accordance with laws devised for their governance,
and over which the man himself has no authority, no mastership, no control. For each one of these thousands of mecha-
nisms the Creator has planned an enemy, whose office is to
harass it, pester it, persecute it, damage it, afflict it with pains,
and miseries, and ultimate destruction. Not one has been
overlooked.

From cradle to grave these enemies are always at work;
they know no rest, night or day. They are an army: an organized army; a besieging army; an assaulting army; an army
that is alert, watchful, eager, merciless; an army that never
relents, never grants a truce.

It moves by squad, by company, by battalion, by regiment,
by brigade, by division, by army corps; upon occasion it masses its parts and moves upon mankind with its whole strength.
It is the Creator's Grand Army, and he is the Commander-in-
Chief. Along its battlefront its grisly banners wave their legends in the face of the sun: Disaster, Disease, and the rest.

Disease! That is the main force, the diligent force, the dev-
astating force! It attacks the infant the moment it is born; it
furnishes it one malady after another: croup, measles,
mumps, bowel troubles, teething pains, scarlet fever, and other childhood specialties. It chases the child into youth and

furnishes it some specialties for that time of life. It chases the youth into maturity, maturity into age, age into the grave.

With these facts before you will you now try to guess man's chiefest pet name for this ferocious Commander-in-Chief? I will save you the trouble—but you must not laugh. It is Our Father in Heaven!

It is curious—the way the human mind works. The Christian begins with this straight proposition, this definite proposition, this inflexible and uncompromising proposition: *God is all-knowing, and all-powerful.*

This being the case, nothing can happen without his knowing beforehand that it is going to happen; nothing happens without his permission; nothing can happen that he chooses to prevent.

That is definite enough, isn't it? It makes the Creator distinctly responsible for everything that happens, doesn't it?

The Christian concedes it in that italicized sentence. Concedes it with feeling, with enthusiasm.

Then, having thus made the Creator responsible for all those pains and diseases and miseries above enumerated, and which he could have prevented, the gifted Christian blandly calls him Our Father!

It is as I tell you. He equips the Creator with every trait that goes to the making of a fiend, and then arrives at the conclusion that a fiend and a father are the same thing! Yet he would deny that a malevolent lunatic and a Sunday school superintendent are essentially the same. What do you think of the human mind? I mean, in case you think there is a human mind.

Noah and his family were saved—if that could be called an advantage. I throw in the *if* for the reason that there has never been an intelligent person of the age of sixty who would consent to live his life over again. His or anyone else's. The Family were saved, yes, but they were not comfortable, for they were full of microbes. Full to the eyebrows; fat with them, obese with them, distended like balloons. It was a disagreeable condition, but it could not be helped, because enough microbes had to be saved to supply the future races of men with desolating diseases, and there were but eight persons on board to serve as hotels for them. The microbes were by far the most important part of the Ark's cargo, and the part the Creator was most anxious about and most infatuated with. They had to have good nourishment and pleasant accommodations. There were typhoid germs, and cholera germs, and hydrophobia germs, and lockjaw germs, and consumption germs, and black-plague germs, and some hundreds of other aristocrats, specially precious creations, golden bearers of God's love to man, blessed gifts of the infatuated Father to his children—all of which had to be sumptuously housed and richly entertained; these were located in the choicest places the interiors of the Family could furnish: in the lungs, in the heart, in the brain, in the kidneys, in the blood, in the guts. In the guts particularly. The great intestine was the favorite resort. There they gathered, by countless billions, and worked, and fed, and squirmed, and sang hymns of praise and thanksgiving; and at night when it was quiet you could hear the soft murmur of it. The large intestine was in effect their heaven. They stuffed it solid; they made it as rigid as a coil of gas pipe. They took pride in this. Their principal hymn made gratified reference to it:

Constipation, O Constipation,
The Joyful sound proclaim
Till man's remotest entrail
Shall praise its Maker's name.

(The audience erupts in hysterical laughter)

JUDGE (smiles): Quiet, please. Let the prosecution continue!

CICERO: Well, well, let me resume Mr. Twain's narrative.

The discomforts furnished by the Ark were many and various. The family had to live right in the presence of the multitudinous animals, and breathe the distressing stench they make and be deafened day and night with the thunder-crash of noise their roaring and screeching produced; and in additions to these intolerable discomforts it was a peculiarly trying place for the ladies, for they could look in no direction without seeing some thousands of the creatures engaged in multiplying and replenishing. And then, there were the flies. They swarmed everywhere, and persecuted the Family all day long. They were the first animals up, in the morning, and the last ones down, at night. But they must not be killed, they must not be injured, they were sacred, their origin was divine, they were the special pets of the Creator, his darlings.

By and by the other creatures would be distributed here and there about the earth—scattered: the tigers to India, the lions and the elephants to the vacant desert and the secret places of the jungle, the birds to the boundless regions of empty space, the insects to one or another climate, according to nature and requirement; but the fly? He is of no nationality; all the climates are his home, all the globe is his province, all creatures that breathe are his prey, and unto them all he is a scourge and a hell.

To man he is a divine ambassador, a minister plenipotentiary, the Creator's special representative. He infests him in his cradle; clings in bunches to his gummy eyelids; buzzes and bites and harries him, robbing him of his sleep and his weary mother of her strength in those long vigils which she devotes to protecting her child from this pest's persecutions. The fly harries the sick man in his home, in the hospital, even on his deathbed at his last gasp. Pesters him at his meals; previously hunts up patients suffering from loathsome and deadly diseases; wades in their sores, gaums its legs with a million death-dealing germs; then comes to that healthy man's table and wipes these things off on the butter and discharges a bowel-load of typhoid germs and excrement on his batter-cakes. The housefly wrecks more human constitutions and destroys more human lives than all God's multitude of misery-messengers and death-agents put together.

(Stops reading, looks around, and then glances at Augustine with an ironic smirk) Mr. Augustinus, do you still regard the Bible as holy, meaning the seventy-three books of the Old and New Testaments, and consider them *the written Word of*

God, in other words, God's whispered revelation, all inspired—completely without error historically, spiritually, morally, or scientifically?

SAINT AUGUSTINE: Yes, I do!

CICERO: "How do you refute Mr. Twain's version of the facts?"

SAINT AUGUSTINE: "There are two problems with his book. In the first place, Mr. Clemens refers to what he calls the Bible God, whom he portrays as an evil God who created a chaotic world and must accept the blame for doing so. In the second place, Mr. Clemens would not have written this book if he didn't believe in a Universal God whom he considers to be the *real* Creator. In other words, he is not an antitheist.

CICERO: What are you suggesting is the reason for Mr. Twain's compendium?"

SAINT AUGUSTINE: Pure revolt within himself.

CICERO: Please elaborate.

SAINT AUGUSTINE: There seems to be a Dr. Jekyll and Mr. Hyde inside the same person: Mr. Samuel Clemens believes in God the creator while Mr. Mark Twain lampoons the God of the Holy Bible for personal reasons.

CICERO: This analogy seems unkind when referring to an illuminated mind such as that of Samuel Clemens. Can you please elaborate further on your statement?

SAINT AUGUSTINE: Yes! Mr. Clemens wrote in his personal notebook and in his biography, quote, The Being who to me is the real God is the One who created this majestic universe and rules it. He is the only originator, the only originator of thoughts; thoughts suggested from within, not from without . . . . He is the only creator. He is the perfect artisan, the perfect artist, unquote. So, Mr. Twain's angry outburst is excusable.

CICERO: In other words, justified.

SAINT AUGUSTINE: Well . . . .

CICERO: That is a very interesting view if we take it literally, and it could be true were we not witnessing the presence of certain personages among us, such as Adam and Satan.

How did those notables appear in the Holy Scriptures if they were not real? They certainly claim relationship with the same Father who is facing those charges today, so the God of the Bible is the God of the Creation given the present characters here in court are the same as the characters in the files.

SAINT AUGUSTINE: It is true! And observe that Twain and Clemens are the same entity; just like the God of the Scriptures and the Creator.

CICERO: "Yes! Yes! Even more so, and if they are the same, what do you make of the particulars that are brought forward from Twain's letters? *The facts!*"

SAINT AUGUSTINE: The facts are depicted accurately, but. . . .

CICERO: Then the guilt is real, too.

SAINT AUGUSTINE: I only brought forward the contrasting personalities, Mr. Clemens and Mr. Twain, in response to your question regarding the unrest inside the soul of our distinguished author. I also think that his love for creation and the Creator doubly justify his revolt.

CICERO: We are not discussing Twain's inner personality conflict; we are analyzing God's *actions*. Nor are we asking *which* God performed them—the fictitious God or the real one—since we have already established that there is only one God, reasoning that there is only one Creation. If the events Mr. Twain depicts are real, then God is guilty for the acts committed, is He not?

SAINT AUGUSTINE: No! God's design is not defective. He is here to save the world by bringing Himself to trial.

CICERO: I repeat the question. If the events are accurately depicted, then God is guilty for the acts that He committed, is He not, Augustinus?

SAINT AUGUSTINE: He is not; He wanted to save the world, and . . .

CICERO: To save the world from *what* or better yet, from whom? Perhaps from His own Self? How can we see God's intentions if not through the amount of evil He allowed?

PLATO (rising): Objection, Your Honor! Presuming God's intentions as evil is supposition, not evidence. No one can know God's mind.

CICERO: Someone *does* know His mind, though . . . ."

PLATO: Your Honor, if I may. (turns to Cicero) And *who* might that someone be?

CICERO: His conscience!

PLATO: But God's conscience is not separate from God. Let me rephrase my objection. No one outside God can know God's mind, let alone his 'intentions' to do evil.

CICERO (intrigued): "God and His conscience are separate *now!* Aren't they in court as separate entities?

JUDGE: Objection sustained!

CICERO (sighing): Augustinus, do you have any reason to believe that God is guiltless of the atrocities attributed to Him based on these letters?

SAINT AUGUSTINE: I . . . .

PLATO: Don't answer that question! Your Honor, objection! The question is misleading and is meant to trap the witness into concluding the guilt of God.

JUDGE: Sustained!

CICERO: Let's go at it from another angle, then. Is God's conscience accusing God because God Himself slept through a nightmare of disaster?

PLATO: Objection, Your Honor! He is using the claim made by God's conscience against God, which suggests guilt without proof.

CICERO: Your Honor, The question is stated clearly; we intend to show the guilt or innocence of God. The plaintiff—His conscience —is accusing God of causing that has happened during his seventh day of rest, including the *all* that is and will be, as a result of his sleep. It seems as if God abandoned His conscience.

JUDGE: Overruled!

CICERO: Please answer the question.

SAINT AUGUSTINE: Yes! I understand why we are holding this trial.

CICERO: Again, please answer my question by responding with yes or no this time: Is God's conscience accusing God because God Himself slept through a nightmare of disaster?

SAINT AUGUSTINE: Yes!

CICERO (snapping): Thank you! "Disaster" also translates to "act of God," does it not?"

SAINT AUGUSTINE: Theoretically—Yes!

CICERO: Yes or no, please.

SAINT AUGUSTINE: Well, yes *and* no!

CICERO: Dear Saint, will you give us a direct answer?

PLATO: Objection! Your Honor, it is obvious that Saint Augustine's intention is to expand on the subject, not to be cut off and be locked within an incomplete sentence.

JUDGE: Sustained!

SAINT AUGUSTINE: "Well, natural disasters are called "acts of God" because they are outside human control, but they are just that "natural. God doesn't intervene in the course of nature; nature behaves by itself."

CICERO: (Ahem!) Mr. Augustinus, my respected colleague, Mr. Plato, taught us the Forms, concepts of eternal truth and goodness, to which you have devoted your teachings, isn't that correct?"

SAINT AUGUSTINE: Indeed, I fostered Mr. Plato's philosophy for centuries, and I still do. His logic and his enlightenment derive from a single divine source: God. And the—

CICERO: If we attribute the Forms to God, whence did evil come?

SAINT AUGUSTINE: From the absence of good! (looks at Plato, who nods slightly)

CICERO: Well, how much absence of good was there when God created the maladies?

SAINT AUGUSTINE: We see the world from our own perspective, not through the eyes of God. This world is a punishment for the sins of Adam and Eve.

CICERO: We ought to see the world from our perspective since God projected it this way. As for this world being the punishment for Adam and Eve's sins, condemned forever, as

Mr. Twain writes, by "the All-Just, the All-Righteous, the All-Good, the All-Merciful, the All-Forgiving, the All-Truthful, the All-Loving, and the Source of All Morality" doesn't it sound unreasonable?

SAINT AUGUSTINE: Not forever. That is why God gave us His Son, our Savior Jesus Christ, who died on the cross for us.

CICERO: "Well, well! The Father alone could not do the job, so He sent a mediator to intervene and assume the blame for actions committed by us and then absolve us of all sins that He allowed to happen in the first place? Does that make sense to you or to anyone?

SAINT AUGUSTINE: Yes, it does!

CICERO: "I will ask again since this very important question fits here like a glove—why did God place the tree in the garden in the first place if not to provide an defense for murdering mankind, assuming there really was a tree and we are not here enwrapped in pure fiction?"

PLATO: "Objection, Your Honor. The prosecution is making presumptions."

CICERO (ignoring him): To tempt the poor couple?

SAINT AUGUSTINE: *No!*

CICERO: I ask you straightforwardly—what does a person have to do to be absolved?

PLATO: Your Honor, the prosecution—

CICERO: Please, Your Honor, allow the witness to answer the question.

JUDGE: Overruled. Please respond to the question.

SAINT AUGUSTINE: A person has to accept Jesus Christ, God's Son, as his or her Savior."

CICERO: Otherwise, he or she cannot enter the Kingdom of God.

SAINT AUGUSTINE: That's correct.

CICERO: "I didn't accept Jesus Christ as my savior, and behold! I am in the Kingdom of God, if we can call it that, and I was here before you and almost everyone else—except our friend Plato and a few others.

SAINT AUGUSTINE: You couldn't have known of Jesus of Nazareth since He was born four decades after you had already died.

CICERO: And yet am I not in the Kingdom of God, now?

SAINT AUGUSTINE: It was God's decision to admit you here. God loves you, Cicero.

CICERO: I guess I should not mention that I was murdered and decapitated—God's way of inviting me to His heavenly home. Perhaps I should be thankful for what I have received. So much for love if not empathy.

PLATO: Objection Your Honor, Cicero is showing bias. He should direct the questions toward the witnesses unless he wants to take the witness stand himself.

CICERO: Your Honor! I am asking a simple question. Facts are facts and history does not lie. I am using myself as an example."

JUDGE: Overruled!

CICERO: "Thank you, Your Honor: Can a person born after the Crucifixion of Christ enter the Kingdom of God without receiving Christ?"

SAINT AUGUSTINE: "No! No one can."

CICERO (gesturing toward the audience): Look at the masses of unbelievers as far as the universe stretches. (Turning to face the judge) The Prosecution calls Jesus of Nazareth to the witness stand.

(Profound silence as Cicero scans the immense crowd, the people's heads looking like a field of unharvest grain. The call echoes throughout heavens, but the Son of God does not appear.

(Angry murmurs from the crowd.)

CHAPTER
13
JESUS OF NAZARETH

CICERO: Your Honor, once again, I call Jesus of Nazareth to the witness stand.

JESUS: I am already here!

CICERO (starts violently as Jesus appears on his right side wearing robes of some bright, unknown material): "Where did you come from? I didn't see you, Yoshua.

JESUS: I'm always sitting by my father, and I'm always near you, but you can only see me now that you've called for me.

(Cicero smiles as if forgetting that he is a prosecution attorney, and stares, mesmerized, at Jesus, who looks just as most people imagine him upon his Second Coming.

JESUS: May I take the witness stand?

CICERO: Of course, please. Thank you.

(Saint Augustine jumps from his seat and kneels before Jesus in convulsions of weeping. Jesus helps him rise.)

SAINT AUGUSTINE (nearly strangled by his emotions): "Oh, my Lord, my God! How I was longing to see you. Only not like this. Oh, I love you so. . . .

Jesus sits near him, nodding toward Satan, who puts up an ironical reverent longbow.

CICERO: We shall begin then . . . .

SATAN: It's not fair, Your Honor!

JUDGE: What is not fair, Lucifer?

SATAN: That Jesus be allowed to testify without taking an oath.

JUDGE: What do you mean?

SATAN: An oath upon the Bible!

(Spontaneous laughter)

JUDGE (looking at Jesus, who nods His acceptance): Very well, provide a Bible to Jesus Christ at once.

(A bailiff appears and places the Holy Bible before Jesus, who put his left hand upon it. As he lifts his right hand, the sleeve from his robe slips down, revealing traces of the wounds caused by His Crucifixion.

JESUS: I swear upon what is written here of my Father and of me, to speak the truth, the whole truth, and nothing but the truth as I've always done."

(Saint Augustine crosses himself three times, once for each person of the Trinity.)

CICERO: Are you Immanuel, the Christ, the Son of God?

JESUS: You say that I am.

CICERO (surprised but quickly regaining his composure): You gave that answer before the Sanhedrin—your accusers. Please, let us have a more direct answer so that there will be no room for speculation. We are not accusing you of anything.

JESUS: Not yet.

CICERO: "Well, your expectations could validate your actions, perhaps. My questions are conventional.

JESUS: My answers will be conventional, too.

CICERO: Are you one with God and the Holy Ghost?

JESUS: Yes!

CICERO: Meaning that you are God incarnate, who descended to Earth to save the human race from death.

JESUS: Yes; I am God's only begotten Son.

CICERO: The one born of the Virgin Mary, wife of Joseph of Nazareth?

JESUS: Yes. Her Hebrew name is Miryam."

CICERO: Do you want us to believe in the miracle of a virgin birth?

JESUS: No, you don't *have* to believe in anything.

CICERO: Is it then a *fact* that you were born of a virgin?

JESUS: "I was conceived as you say; I never boast about it.

CICERO: Did you teach that you are the only gate to Heaven?

JESUS: I tell you the truth; I am the good shepherd who laid down his life for his sheep. I know my sheep, and my sheep know me, just as the Father knows me and I know the Father.

CICERO: You sound as if you are paraphrasing the verse from John 10:14. Why are you using this speech?

JESUS: The people who know me follow my voice and my path.

CICERO: Do you treat people as sheep?

JESUS: I speak in parables.

CICERO: "You'll do us all a big favor if you speak straight and clear for everyone to understand. Look! Let's set the Scriptures aside. The Bible is not on trial today—at least not directly, God the Father brought Himself, not the Holy Book, to trial. That being said, it is God's will that His conscience be permanently cleared, so my questions to you will be simple and intended to bring the truth forward. So please, let us talk outside the Bible and not use allegories. Just down-to-earth language (as we say) so that even idiots can understand you since no one wants to go to Hell."

JESUS: "How can I tell my story without the Gospels? Isn't that how you know me, by reading them? Discussing me without them would be like asking you to summon Marcus Antonius before this court yet make no mention of the Roman Empire its history has been falsely reported in which he played no part."

CICERO: With the difference that Marcus Antonius and the other Romans existed as flesh and bone while the Bible is filled with fictional personages.

JESUS: Do you call me fictional?

CICERO: Are we to understand that if the Bible is erroneous and faulty and immoral, and by the end of trial we dismiss it as being the genuine Word of God, you will just vanish in the air before everyone's eyes?

JESUS: "That sounds more like deliberate falsification than error."

CICERO: Are you a mere character in a Jewish fairytale or are you a historical person?"

JESUS: If this trial evidences the Scriptures to be a fabrication of the human mind, I will become as mortal as the Word in it. I tell you the truth: Even in Heaven before God, you're blinder than a blind man looking into the sun. If your faith is barren, your eyes don't see and your heart doesn't feel. You look at me, you ask me, you talk to me, and yet you think that I'm an illusion. You look at God and see nothing there. Where is your faith?"

CICERO: Don't talk about faith in this court. You bring *faith* into a court of law where fact is the only proof. Faith by definition is belief not based on logical reasoning or solid evidence.

(Cicero yields another scroll, waving it as he approaches Jesus. He speaks with much pomposity as he unfolds the scroll): Jesus of Nazareth, the Bible prophesied that the Messiah would be born in Bethlehem, but you were born in Nazareth, isn't that correct?

JESUS: No, it is not.

CICERO: In order for the prophecy that the Messiah would belong to the House and lineage of David—we will go back to the Old Testament—the New Testament authors had to concoct a story that would bring you into Bethlehem, the Town of David. The Bible states that the census requiring Joseph to go to Bethlehem to register, taking the pregnant Mary with him, took place when Publius Suplicius Quirinius was governor in Syria. No such census took place at that time in that region under Emperor Caesar Augustus and Quirinius was not yet the governor of Syria, which contradicts the [6]Gospels. Can you tell us the city where you were born, again?

JESUS: As far as I know, [7]I was born in Bethlehem.

CICERO: As far as you know? One would assume that by now you would have found out. What was the year?

PLATO: Objection, Your Honor! The question is blatantly inviting a debate as the views of hundreds of historians, theologians, and even present-day followers invariably contradict one another.

CICERO: Well, that's exactly the reason that the witness must be allowed to answer my question, Your Honor. Jesus' testimony will silence all speculation on the dates of His birth, ministry, and Resurrection. And if He doesn't remember it or doesn't know it—strange since He claims to be the Son of God and the Third Person of the Trinity—His mother can possibly tell us.

(Yells mixed with laughter from the audience)

JUDGE: Overruled.

CICERO: Thank you, Your Honor. (Turning to Christ): Year of your birth, please?

JESUS: By which calendar?

CICERO: Let's say the Gregorian.

JESUS: Four BC, born in the days of Herod the Great.

CICERO: Are you the Christ?

JESUS: Yes

CICERO: You say you were born on year 4 B.C. meaning that you were born four years before you were born (B.C. means before Christ.)

JESUS: That's why I asked you by which calendar. Correct is 3758 after Creation (by Hebrew calendar.)

CICERO: Day, month?

JESUS: March 28.

---

[6] John 7:42 Expressly indicates that Jesus was not born in Bethlehem

[7] John 1:45-6 asserts Jesus did come from Nazareth

CICERO (smiling): Date of your death?

JESUS: Friday April 3, AD 33.

CICERO: Day of Resurrection?

JESUS: Sunday, April 5, AD 33.

CICERO: I am flabbergasted. Ladies and gentlemen, Jesus does not remember the town of his birth but he accurately remembers with accuracy his birth, death and resurrection. (Turns to Christ, addressing him with sympathy): I am truly sorry, my good friend, for the pain and suffering that the Roman soldiers inflicted on you. I speak from the heart. I personally do not believe that you are the Son of God or part of the Trinity and therefore an aspect of God Himself although I wish you were, for you seem like a nice fellow. If you are now God, you were God then, and if you were God then, you could easily have proven your divinity in better ways than magically turning water into wine or walking on water or feeding three thousand hungry mouths with two loaves and two fishes. You could have proven that you were God by providing food for the hungry millions that you see still praying on empty stomachs not just for a few of your own people. You could have pitied the voices of the billions who suffer disease and poverty from infancy to old age if they don't die of famine. If you were God or the Son of God, you could have saved them all, forever, just by bending one finger (well, I speak in parables, too). If you were God, why didn't you save everyone, Jesus?

JESUS: The prophecy had to be fulfilled.

CICERO: Prophecy? Or the hypocrisy had to be fulfilled. In fact, I do not think that your death was necessary at all. You could have lived a "human" life dedicated to doing "good" by saving everyone from starvation, poverty, and disease. By ending evil, including death, you could have chosen to demonstrate to all of us a divine excellence.

I assure you that no one would have condemned you had you done that. Yet, to quit your work young and let yourself be killed by your own people to provide them with a blessed afterlife is a bit of a stretch. You could have granted salvation to humankind more honorably and less painfully for everyone, including yourself. And by that deed alone, you would have eliminated all doubt in your divine status. The way it actually happened sounds almost politically religious if not religiously political.

PLATO: Your Honor . . . .

CICERO: Please! I know what suffering is, having been slashed like a pig and beheaded for exercising free speech after which my hands and head were displayed on the Rostra and subjected to degrading brutality. My son yelled at the top of his lungs. Did God hear his cries? I am not angry with Marcus Antonius; he only responded according to his own instincts and prejudices, predestined by God if you will, and I forgive him. But you (addressing Jesus) were beaten and pinned to the Cross by your own will to fulfill a prophecy. If you are the Son of God, my dear Jesus, please, please forgive me, but I must request of you a simple answer to this simple question: Where was your Father when you were tortured, beaten, and condemned to death? Wasn't He asleep?

JESUS: No!

CICERO: What? Suppose He was not asleep, He simply watched your grotesque suffering as a bunch of primitive-minded soldiers nailed you to a cross and skewered your body, hearing your desperate plea, "*Eloi, Eloi, lama sabachthani?*" (My God, my God, why hast thou forsaken me?) before you finally commended your spirit into His hands. Since He did nothing to help you, He must have been watching impotently or not watching at all. He had definitely entered what is called the Epicurean Paradox: God is either incompetent because He is incapable of stopping evil or wicked because He permits it to exist. Someone had to think it, and Epicurus did. He was not afraid to say it. And why would he be afraid when reason, God's gift to man, told everyone that God was absent and, therefore, did not exist since absence is lack of being?

Epicurus, can you please quote your own words regarding the *trilemma* argument that you postulated? Speak loudly so that everyone can hear you.

EPICURUS (his voice rising faintly from within the crowd):
Is God willing to prevent evil, but not able?
Then he is not omnipotent.
Is he able, but not willing?
Then he is malevolent.
Is he both able and willing?
Then whence cometh evil?
Is he neither able nor willing?
Then why call him God?

CICERO: Here you have it, ladies and gentlemen of the jury. A fine extract from a human mind that dared to think without fear. (Turning toward Jesus and speaking with a tremor in his voice): "What is your answer to all of this, my dear Jesus of Bethlehem?"

JESUS: I see that you love me." (Smiles with a trace of sadness) My Father didn't intervene because a chain of prophecies had to be fulfilled. And so they were."

CICERO: Prophesies as written in the Bible?

JESUS: Yes!

CICERO: (Facing the jury): How much more evidence must we produce to show that the Bible is the work of man, ladies and gentlemen of the jury? (Turns back to Jesus) Do you mean to tell me that the God of the universe, the omnipresent entity, the Creator of all things, your dear Father, would descend from eternal space into the pages of a book to become the God of the Bible knowing that He would face derision and multiple mistranslations and misinterpretations by doing so?"

JESUS: If He is *everywhere*, He is in the Bible through the quill of man, who records and obeys His Word.

CICERO: Obeys His Word . . . *Obeys!* Please notice the word *obeys* because God is the one who inflicts injustice and allows human beings to commit murder, adultery, fornication, and treachery, to feel, envy, to rob and enslave his fellow humans. Contrary to moral principles, He, the Father God, forbids man to do what he Himself so deliberately does—in other words, "Do as I say not as I do . . . but go practice free will.

Well, that reminds me of poor Giovanni Boccaccio, whose quotations remain in history to this day as an attack against churchmen and friars who thought that 'Do as we say and not as we do' was an adequate response—"as if," wrote Boccaccio, "it were possible for the sheep to be more constant and stouter to resist temptation than the shepherds." Poor Boccaccio was nevertheless punished by God first for thinking of it, second for writing it, and last for proclaiming it in a way that implies a premeditated crime. What did God do? God destroyed Boccaccio's only love, Maria d'Aquino, in the year 1348, shuttering his heart forever, drowning his hopes, giving him misery for the remainder of his struggling, forlorn, insipid, short life. God had arranged for Maria (a married woman) to meet Boccaccio and become his mistress (typical of God's morality), and then decided to punish them both by sending the Black Death and killing her horribly. She had committed adultery and so He punished her.

But what was her death compared with those of the other one hundred million innocent people that the Almighty and All Just successfully exterminated during the Black Death, otherwise known as the bubonic plague? God *knew* in advance what Boccaccio was going to do; therefore, He allowed it to happen He prophesied it, for Maria became Boccaccio's inspiration to write his prose tales, so that Boccaccio's name should become immortal. Immortal! Immortal! How wonderful! How intelligent. How godlike! How diabolically ingenious! What other than an abundance of unhappiness, desolation, grief, torment, despair, agony, and regret would cause Boccaccio to surrender and genuflect before Providence? But God thinks of everyone's future—and look how many at a time—and He acts with calculated patience because He is a democrat, not a tyrant.

Perhaps you could have saved them, Jesus if you were God. I am sure that each of those people who perished from one of God's most spectacular inventions, the bubonic plague, would jump at the chance to ask God a question. But, of course, you would not want to see them appearing here as they looked on their last hour before they died because that would be too much for you and this court, not to mention that it would be too upsetting to God. But, of course, it's not going to happen since God also predestined this trial eons ago.

Yet, speaking of His Divine Order, suppose that God concerns Himself with personal matters. Suppose that He actually interferes in the lives that He is responsible for and that He cares about the world He made. Wouldn't this kind of Father hear the cries of torment while watching His inventions at work? Would He enjoy all this? Is He present at all? The Holy Books sell well. He must be somewhere.

For the sake of the billions still living, would it be better for God express himself with goodness instead of evil? Moreover, wouldn't it be more honest for Him to show Himself from time to time, saving us from suffering or answering a prayer? Couldn't He do it for love because He is the All Loving or, at least, for concern, compassion, and virtue?

JESUS: Yes! It would be better.

CICERO: Well, thank you. I assure you that none of the so-called faithful—including the all man-made saints—grow more than *hope* in their hearts with regard to whether their God even exists. I am not counting the delusional, narrow-minded "sheep" or the sentimental speculators that are incontrovertibly adding to personal gains.

Isn't it because of the evil—chiefly, the fear of death—that most believers bow to an imaginary supernatural being—God, or Allah, or Elohim—all dipped in religious absurdity? Here's a good version from Emperor and Proletarian:

Religion—but a tale astutely spread abroad
To rivet on your shoulders the heavy harnessed load,
For, had you lost all hope of heavenly reward
After a life on earth with pain and hardship scored,
Would you go on working as an ox beneath the goad?

"Can anyone refute the *trilemma* argument presented earlier by Epicurus? How about you, Jesus, you who claim to be the *only* begotten Son of God, how do you account for all this malice?

JESUS: Your logic is in every respect perfect."

(Uproar throughout the courtroom. The judge pounds her gavel as Cicero raises his hand to silence the crowd. Plato appears to take notes.)

CICERO: "Please, ladies and gentlemen, let's be civil. (Turns to Jesus as the crowd quiets) Do you agree that these statements are true, Jesus?

JESUS: I agree that these statements are indeed true.

CICERO: "Is God guilty of what He did, yes or no, Jesus?"

JESUS: "Yes, He is."

(People shout uncontrollably and Satan sends butterfly kisses toward Jesus Christ. Adam stands up in protest.)

JESUS: But not my God, Cicero, not the *real* God!

(His voice is heard all over the courtroom although he speaks without effort because the universe has been abruptly reduced to silence.)

JESUS (calmly): I would totally agree with your judgment if we were speaking of the same God, but fortunately, we are not. My Father is nothing like what you have described. The being who committed such crimes is indeed among us, but he is not the Father of all Creation. I tell you the truth. Even if I become no more than thought to you before this trial is over, we will witness the God of Chaos.

CICERO (wiping the sweat his forehead): Make us understand, please. Is the Bible God, the one depicted in the Old Testament, your Father?

JESUS: Yes, He is!

CICERO: Is the God on trial here your God?

JESUS: Yes, He is.

CICERO: Well, isn't it evident then, for crying out loud, that if God put Himself on trial for the crimes committed while He slept and His own conscience accuses Him of neglect and chaos, he implicitly fits the description of what you call the God of Chaos?

JESUS: Can it be self-evident, then, that an impersonal, ferocious evildoer such as the God of Chaos, could be in reality a Perfect Being fitting the description of a benevolent, loving, merciful, tolerant, charitable, empathetic, Caring Deity?

CICERO (frustrated): No! It cannot!

(A sudden silence fills the skies. With my eyes closed, I can hear the sound of the planets in motion, the airy music of the universe. Everyone looks at Jesus, who makes a humble reverence)

JESUS: *There* is your answer.

CHAPTER
14
JESUS' TESTIMONY

Jesus had filled all space with his last statement, which left Cicero suspended in his own thought for a moment. Satan slanted in his chair, hiding a smirk, a pose reminding me of Santi Di Tito's *Niccolò Machiavelli*, his glance bouncing back from the wondering spectators.

CICERO: I apologize for overreacting. I must confess that in listening to Jesus, I am shifting in and out from realizing that I speak to the Son of God. My heart tells me one thing and my mind and duty, another. I lost my life by listening to my heart; I don't want to do it again. Although I see in myself the reflection of Pontius Pilate, as I'd like to wash my hands before you, leaving Jesus in the hands of His own kind who I am sure will defend Him today, I shall stand straight in the face of justice and overcome my weaknesses. Despite my mixed feelings, I must continue to seek the truth. Here is my question to you, Jesus:

Mark 8:1–10 states that you fed four thousand men and women with seven loaves of bread and a few fishes while Matthew testifies in 14:31 that you fed five thousand men with five loaves of bread and two fishes. Well, what's a thousand here and there; but he was feeding only men, not women and children as you, ladies and gentlemen, will kindly notice. The discrepancy between these two accounts is flagrantly evident but not of so much importance to us as to those still on Earth swimming in inaccuracy. Let's even presume that there were two different miracles and also that you were feeding man, women, children of all nature. Please tell us why you didn't — by way of benevolence and benefaction—feed the whole hungry world instead of a few thousand and why didn't you provide to all women and children, stranded and homeless?"

JESUS: I feed the world every day. I tell you the truth, much of what I said were lost in translations and retelling. In other words, everyone tells my life in his own way and in his own language. Yet, they all tell my life. My answer to you is that I did then as I do now and that is to feed the world, physically and spiritually.

CICERO: What percent spiritually and what percent physically?

JESUS: Here is your answer: Give a man a fish and you feed him for a day. Teach him how to fish and you feed him for a lifetime.

CICERO: "Wasn't that proverb told by Lao Tzu five hundred years before your time?"

JESUS: But the wisdom is God's and, therefore, mine.

CICERO: Much honor to the Chinese master for being the first to preach it.

JESUS: Much honor to those who listen and learn from it.

CICERO: People are all looking at the planets today and seeing the universe through the eyes of powerful telescopes, which by the advance of technology have become more and more sensitive. Why didn't God, or you, for argument's sake, reveal the truth about the universe to those who wrote the Abrahamic Scriptures to save innocent medieval scientists from being burned at the stake for contradicting the Scriptures?"

JESUS: "We look at the sky and see trillions of galaxies, stars, and planets floating through space like dust clouds. If

God had revealed to the unprepared mind that humankind lived on a speck of dust in the infinity of space, would that have been a better consolation than the Scriptures?

CICERO: And we are not talking about consoling people but about saving them from torturous dying. Is that knowledge a consolation now? Isn't the truth more important than a falsehood? I believe that revealing the truth could have saved many lives and prevented the Church fathers lots of shame. Human beings living on a dust particle large enough to hold the beauty of nature would have respected their world and consolation would be unnecessary. Yes, it would have made a difference. Instead, humanity had to find out the hard way, through pain and horror and a shameful religious history baptized in blood."

JESUS: I agree. And yet, the baby needs to crawl before it walks. Similarly, teething is not pleasant, but it's necessary.

CICERO: What do you mean by that? Couldn't God the Almighty design it better than to give a poor baby pain and tears?

JESUS: There is a reason for everything. Sensations must coexist. The discomfort is not great, and crying helps the baby develop his or her lungs. Crying is a requisite. A baby's happy laughing after the pain is gone proves that crying is only a reaction to a temporary feeling."

CICERO: Let me quote Joshua 10:12–13: "Then spake Joshua to the Lord in the day when the Lord delivered up the Amorites before the children of Israel, and he said in the sight of Israel: Sun, stand thou still upon Gibeon; and thou Moon, in the valley of Ajalon. Is not this written in the book of Jasher? So the sun stood still in the middle of heaven, and hurried not to go down about a whole day."

What are we to make of this breathtaking passage? If this story is true, what is the name of the director and what should we name the play? Couldn't God find a better way to have Joshua carry out his revenge than stopping the sun and moon for the children of Israel? Is it fact or fiction? If this passage isn't meant to be a mocking comedy, I don't know what is; What is more disturbing, the number of believers falling for such absurdity or the growing ignorance which is highly promoted by the clergy so that its followers would be easily taken advantage of. The Sun standing in the middle of heaven is like stopping the heart of a live organism for a day by pressing the Pause button and expecting it to continue simply by pressing Play."

(Satan laughs)

JESUS: It seems unlikely, but if it's written in the Bible, it's true!

CICERO: Note that, ladies and gentlemen: "If it's written in the Bible, it's true." I'd like to go back, then, if you don't mind, to the original sin—and here I would reiterate the words of a distinguished lawyer friend of mine named Clarence Darrow with whom some of you are familiar from the "Scopes Trial" in Tennessee. Mr. Darrow asked, "What has the human race done that was so bad, except to eat of the tree of knowledge?" And, as Adam mentioned earlier, they have eaten it ever since and will always eat it. Without knowledge, may I add,- we are only as smart as apes. Perhaps this is what Darwin meant when he referred to men as a species. He went back to the genesis and—

PLATO: Objection to the prosecution's last sentence, Your Honor: a soup of cynicism and mockery at the cost of both Darwin and God.

JUDGE: Sustained!

CICERO: Well, to quote Mr. Darrow again, "What has the human race done that was so bad, except to eat of the tree of knowledge"—which we have established is a good thing to do?

JESUS: Adam and Eve disobeyed God's commandment.

CICERO: Is knowledge something to condemn?

JESUS: How do you know what God had in mind? Are you certain that man by obeying His request would not have earned a better reward? What if God had decided to make man earn his immortality through progressive physical and spiritual enlightenment?

CICERO: Isn't it cruel to condemn all generations for two bites from a piece of fruit?

JESUS: Not all generations. I was sent to save those who want to be saved.

CICERO: So, what are you waiting for, genocide after genocide? Save them! Wouldn't it be more convincing to appear before everybody rather than only to a chosen few in a secluded spot in the middle of nowhere? Why not bring immortality right to Earth, except that it's impossible since God already designed the engine of life to consume. Tell me, why don't you rush out and save everyone?

JESUS: The Earth is a school. God has a better place for those that hope for it.

CICERO: You do not answer my questions. Show me anyone on Earth who refuses eternal life, where aging and suffering are absent, knowing that there's evidence of it..

JESUS: Show me one who really knows of it if not by faith; I'll show you many who do not follow me although they were told that I am the way to eternal life.

CICERO: But they hope for it anyway, even without you.

JESUS: "You just mentioned the first step into faith, Cicero; and that is—hope."

CICERO: "No, I was mentioning hope since even without faith people can desire something beyond annihilation or death. No one dares to imagine that, after accumulating so much knowledge during a lifetime, he or she must dump it into an empty grave with only an epitaph carved in stone if the purse of the mourners is fat enough to pay for it. How absurd is that? So, of course, many people hope for more, like seeing their living family members after death. Others think that there is no afterlife because there is no purpose to anything: The world just happens to revolve around the sun carrying everyone around with it. Not everyone has faith. Belief it cannot survive where facts are available, can it, Jesus?

JESUS: I tell you the truth—no one shall enter the Kingdom of God without following my guidance. I am the light and the way.

CICERO: Would God refuse to help anyone in need of help who also has faith and really believes in Him?

JESUS: No.

CICERO: Would you as the Son of God refuse anyone who asked you for help in the name of God the Father?

JESUS: Absolutely not.

CICERO: I have here another parchment called "The Faith of the Canaanite Woman" from Matthew 15:21–28. I shall read it to everyone:

Leaving that place, Jesus withdrew to the region of Tyre and Sidon.

A Canaanite woman from that vicinity came to Him, crying out, "Lord, Son of David, have mercy on me! My daughter is suffering terribly from demon-possession."

Jesus did not answer a word. So his disciples came to Him and urged Him, "Send her away, for she keeps crying out after us."

He answered, "I was only sent to the lost sheep of Israel."

The woman came and knelt before Him. "Lord, help me!" she said.

He replied, "It is not right to take the children's bread and toss it to their dogs.

"Yes, Lord," she said, "but even the dogs eat the crumbs that fall from their master's table."

Then Jesus answered, "Woman, you have great faith! Your request is granted." And her daughter was healed from that very hour.

(Cicero pauses and then continues) Does the Son of God discriminate?

JESUS: I was human before I was God.

CICERO: Or less than human; *I* would have helped her. Weren't you portraying the Son of God; God of Israel?

JESUS: Yes! And I was sent only to the lost sheep of Israel.

CICERO: You just testified earlier that you were sent to save the world.

JESUS: Yes, But, you are mixing inferences.

CICERO: I'm afraid they are the same inferences that you laid out.

JESUS: Salvation is like food. You don't swallow the whole plateful at one time, Cicero, but chew it piece by piece. Otherwise, you'll choke to death.

CICERO: Be specific . . .

JESUS: I fed the Word of God little by little; I started with my people and then reached out to others.

CICERO: How about this, then? You said, "It is not right to take the children's bread and toss it to their dogs." Isn't it contemptuous to call the Gentiles "dogs"?

JESUS: Aramaic patois is not offensive at all. It was the vernacular of the age.

CICERO: "Dogs are dogs in any language; we refer to them as animals even if we sing the term. The thought of it alone is enough to validate it, is it not? Did you imply that she was a dog, in a pejorative way, because she was a goy?

PLATO: Objection! The suggestive word is incriminating.

CICERO: Your Honor, goy is a Hebrew word also meaning "Gentile." If this word is incriminating, it confirms its incriminating sense and we should take note of that.

PLATO: Objection"

JUDGE: On what grounds?

PLATO: "Jesus's response given to the Canaanite woman is irrelevant to the charges against God."

CICERO: "Your Honor, Jesus's response is not irrelevant at all; in fact, I will prove that it is connected not only to the mind of God but to the mind of those claiming to be God's chosen people, like Jesus here. He claims to be the Son of God, and yet God sent Him only to the lost sheep of Israel. I need to make my point by bringing forth the evidence that I have, which includes behavior of the presumed Son of God which does not honor a God whose chosen people are all the world's people not only a preferred group called "chosen."

PLATO: Your Honor, what do the chosen people of God have to do with God Himself? We are trying God, not His people.

JUDGE: Overruled.

CICERO: I apologize, Plato, but is it fair for you to keep interrupting me in an attempt to make me lose my train of thought? Luckily, I have not lost it, and here it is again tenfold:

The word *goy* is found in Jewish law, ethics, philosophy, customs, and history as compiled in the Talmud, or as it is traditionally referred to as **Shas** (ש"ס), the Hebrew abbreviation of *shisha sedarim*, or the "six orders" of the Mishnah. *Goy* is also a derogatory nickname used by religious Jews meaning "cattle," beast," "animal," or "slave" when referring to non-Jews (Gentiles), categorizing them as their inferiors.

SAINT AUGUSTINE: That accusation is absolutely false and a sacrilege against Judeo-Christianity.

CICERO: Your Honor, he is out of order.

JUDGE: Saint Augustine, please refrain from interrupting.

CICERO: With your permission, I would like to recite a few paragraphs from the Talmud and related documents, which will allow you to understand Jesus' upbringing as a Jew and as the Son of Yahweh, the God of Israel—which will clarify Jesus' religious attitude, as well as that of His disciples, vis-à-vis the prayerful Canaanite woman.

The Midrasch Talpioth, p. 225-L states, "Yahweh (God) created the non-Jew in human form so that the Jew would not have to be served by beasts. The non-Jew is consequently an animal in human form, and condemned to serve the Jew day and night." (.) Further, the Baba Mecia, or Babylonian Talmud 114b, states: "The Jews are human beings, but the nations of the world are not human beings but beasts." The Tosefta, a supplement to the Talmud, states: "On the house of the goy, one looks as on a fold of cattle."

Please note that the teachings of the Talmud take precedence over all other Jewish laws. According to Rabbi Israel, Rabbi Chamboyet, and others, they are more important than the laws of Moses. It is because of these teachings—which existed as oral tradition in Jesus' time—that Jesus acted impulsively and one-sidedly. Yet, one would think that if God were the universal God, He would send His son to comfort everyone.

JESUS: My Father sent me to reform the laws of Israel and I did just that. Why do you think I was crucified?

CICERO: Well, that raises another question: Which Jewish religion is genuine? Which laws are the true laws of God, the ones in the Tanakh, which Christians call the Old Testament, or the reformed laws taught by Jesus of Bethlehem and recorded in the New Testament? Why would the God of Israel send in His Son to replace His own laws? That decision should make a skeptic question the veracity of those laws, in fact, the authenticity of all God's laws and actions. When did God distribute those laws and when did He speak to Moses and Abraham and to all the other prophets and kings and followers if He was sleeping?

I have no more questions, Your Honor.

CHAPTER
15
SONS OF GOD

(The lights in the court dim as if an act of a play is ending and another is about to begin.)

RUFUS (reciting in a voice that vibrates throughout the courtroom):

[8]Religion—but a tale astutely spread abroad
To rivet on your shoulders the heavy harnessed load,
For, had you lost all hope of heavenly reward
After a life on earth with pain and hardship scored,
Would you go on working as an ox beneath the goad?
With what strange phantom shadows are your illusions fed
That makes you set your faith in heaven's promised store?
No, when your life is passed, all hope of joy is sped,
And he who dies in misery, in misery is dead
For those who pass the grave come back again no more.
In lies and windy phrases their state and safety stands,

---

[8] From Emperor and Proletarian by Mihail Eminescu (translation by Corneliu M. Popescu)

Their holy law and order is but an empty creed,
To keep their stolen wealth safe from your needy hands,
They arm you to destroy your like on foreign lands,
And you against yourselves triumphantly they lead.

(The lights brighten as Rufus approaches Cicero, who pats the shoulder of his old friend and moves back a few feet to face the judge in sign of reverence before retiring to his seat)

RUFUS: According to the New Testament, you, Jesus Christ, are the Son of Man, later called the Son of your God, meaning the God of the people of Israel. Is that claim true?

JESUS: Yes it is.

RUFUS: Again, according to the New Testament, you accepted death by crucifixion to save humanity from death. Is that claim also true?

JESUS: Yes.

SAINT AUGUSTINE: Jesus Christ is the *only* way to Heaven, the only source of truth, and the foundation of all life.

RUFUS: Your Honor, can I get a weight off my chest?

JUDGE: Of course. All hearts must be emptied of their burdens.

RUFUS: Thank you. I am astonished that even today within this infinite space, many still resort to believe in the same corrupt reasoning in the form of incantations that we have just heard from the mouth of Augustinus. These incantations come to us from the never-drying poisoned ink of the pus-filled pages of the past that still affect the morality of mankind to the present day and follow some of you even here.

Augustine, do you really feel compelled to recite a formula in order to demonstrate your support of your God?"

PLATO: Objection, Your Honor. His remarks are offensive and demeaning."

JUDGE: Sustained. You do not have to answer Saint Augustine. Rufus, the saint's opinion is part of his testimony.

SAINT AUGUSTINE: Your Honor, perhaps Rufus is right when he claims that most people follow a doctrine with falsity in heart, but that is not true for me or other followers like me. I use what I've learned respecting and cherishing wherever I go, even if this, some people, such as Rufus, call it dogma and view it as illusory. By barely thinking of the Son of God, we have brought before us Jesus of Nazareth. Some people may argue that it is a dream, but to me it's a dream come true; to me and to others sitting here who share my faith and pure love for faith, Jesus is the zenith of our expectations. Here and now. I have reached the highest point of my existence. Is my perceiving all this as fictitious as my own belief? Maybe, but it is my reality and I am finally at peace with myself, O Lord.

Anything that we believe may be either real or unreal. It depends on how much of it we regard it to be real. Do I live in a fantasy world? Perhaps, but it is my world and I feel at home in it. Why take it away from me or from others who dwell in this dream? I look before me and I see the Son of God—yes, the God of the people of Israel Who, for me, is the same as the God of the people of India and the people of China and the children of the Caucasus, and those of Mexico and of Persia. He was the God of the Muslims, the Scandinavians, the Romans, and the Greeks, as well as the Babylonians, the Sumerians, and the Thracians. He is one God no matter what you call Him or how you want to divide Him and here He is, God's Son; take Him or leave Him.

What does it matter whether the savior came from Bethlehem or Jerusalem? To me and to other Christians, Jesus Christ is the only savior. To others, He carries another name. Let's put away the hypocrisy that one God is better than another just because one name sounds better than another or one people thinks that it is above another. All human beings live on the same sphere, share the same Mother Nature, abide by the same laws of the universe, have the same natural structure, go through the same life, and what is even more astonishing—"

SATAN (fulminating): Share the same death . . . .

SAINT AUGUSTINE: Not the same death, Lucifer, not at all. Not because one ends up face down while the other dies belly up—by which I mean that one goes to Heaven and the other to Hell—but because Hell is not the brimstone and fire that Christians often depict it as being. Ladies and gentlemen, Jesus spoke of eternal fire, torture, and torment, referring to the eternally ignorant soul that has no rest or the spirit that breeds eternal pessimism. To be eternally unhappy is worse than any physical suffering; the soul in conflict with itself will never find peace.

SATAN: Really? Try a taste of it and you'll not only beg your way out, you'll retract every word you've just spoken. You'll drop religion when the first cigarette butt touches your skin, let alone a blaze of hellfire. You'll drop your God to save your own ass at the first smell of the boiled excrement in which your soul will bathe. Yes, Augustine, Jesus invented the boiling Hell where sinners must suffer eternal torment after death. That's not the same place that Twain is in. Don't change the words of "God," as your words having once rushed will forever be sinful. The fire that Jesus invented must be fed continuously to keep his flames alive. Remember that.

Ask Jesus Christ, who is now here, and He will tell you about Hell. He visited the so-called inferno that you learned about in tales, and He saw it with his own eyes, did He not? Say "yes" and approve this fiction; say "no," and rebut His being.

SAINT AUGUSTINE (rushing in): Where there's hope, there's faith as Jesus said clearly to those who want to hear it. And where there's faith, there is the commanding of the spirit into the hands of God. The only thing to do is to be faithful. Hope for eternal life; do not stagnate into obscurity by feeding on pessimism by electing death as your destiny. Myths or no myths, you control yourself, your mind, your spirit, and your desires. Believe in your God, your Abrahamic God, your Babylonian God, your Egyptian deity, your Hindu god or goddess, or an Alien Supreme. Call Him or Her whatever name you desire: Universe, Nature, Space, Eternity, Atom, Quark, DNA, Creation, Inner Self or . . . Everything.

SATAN: Then, why call him God and not Universe or Nature, or any one of the other supposed synonyms that you mentioned?

SAINT AUGUSTINE: Jesus offered you salvation. Take it. It is free; it is from the heart. God has given it to you through His Son's sacrifice. Why the sacrifice, you may ask? Because we need physical evidence to believe in God just as we need to feel our own heartbeats to believe that we have hearts in our chests.

SATAN: Can anyone compare the limited, temporal suffering of Jesus to the prolonged suffering of humanity?

SAINT AUGUSTINE: Jesus' sacrifice intensifies His suffering.

SATAN: Pure fabrication! It is the plurality and repetition, the persistence of evil pressing on the open wounds of humanity that intensifies its suffering far beyond the few hours that Jesus spent on the Cross.

SAINT AUGUSTINE: Suppose it is all fabrication. Once the seed of belief finds its soil in the mind of the believer, it sprouts like a seedling tree and its buds give way to the beautiful flowers of hope and love giving way for the fruits of finest energy, which we must put to good use every day of our lives before this envelope of bones and muscles shrinks and wrinkles like dry earth, just like the one under our feet.

SATAN: Please listen, ladies and gentlemen of the jury. Once you plant the seed in the soil of the mind, says Saint Augustine, it blooms and bears fruit. Yes, and the saint is not wrong since those fruits bear the seeds of nonsense, that once planted in the mind of the host, sprouts like a seedling tree whose buds give way to the beautiful flowers of hope and love–but not knowledge; Oh! Puppets are those waiting to be maneuvered through nonsense and empty words by a servant of the Grand Master Puppeteer. Yet, Augustine has secured himself a place in the carefully dreamt Heaven near his Father, for where the Father is, the saint will follow as his servant, with his slobbering tongue hanging out, a loyal slave indeed. For Augustine, there is no return. Too late for him since his mind has been programmed with old software that is not compatible with today's machinery of thought.

SAINT AUGUSTINE (shouting): I will be the servant of God until . . . until the end of eternity!

SATAN (laughing): An honorable if oxymoronic position since now you may join your God beyond His end.

RUFUS: Bravo! Your thoughts are full of teaching, Augustinus. "Better a diamond with a flaw than a pebble without," as Confucius used to say. But tell us, please: Wouldn't it have been easier for everyone, including the Divine, not to let this chaos hit the world in the first place?

SAINT AUGUSTINE: Who am I to judge or even to know God's mind?

JESUS: Well said.

SAINT AUGUSTINE: Thank you, Lord.

RUFUS: Well, Augustinus, do you defend God's conscience?

SAINT AUGUSTINE: I defend God's actions, whatever they may be, because He is always right.

RUFUS: Please, respond directly to my question.

SAINT AUGUSTINE: Of course, I defend God's conscience.

RUFUS: Isn't God's conscience the plaintiff who is challenging God in this court, therefore placing you directly against God if you defend His conscience?

SAINT AUGUSTINE: I love God and I trust His conscience to overcome its own misgivings, exonerate God, and comfort God's union again.

RUFUS: God's conscience has never left Him until now. On the contrary, it is as alert today in God's awakened state as it was when He was sound asleep on the Seventh day after Creation. How do you see it, Lucifer?

SATAN: With God or without Him, life and death behave the same. I am not saying that God should cease to exist in the mind of man (or woman); After all, humans may hold anything in their heads—gods, ideas, heavens, hells, nirvanas, a harem full of everlasting virgins. They may even pray daily to all the Roman Catholic saints who were a hair-split away from being deified themselves, unfortunate delusional mortal sinners. You people are free to choose from many gods and revive the old myths. After all, there are only about twenty thousand of them, give or take a few.

What I am saying is that anyone who lived through God's nightmare did so regardless of whether the divine Father was present or not. The result is the same for those living or not living under the tutelage of the Father: If religion has proved futile until now, it will prove even more futile when most of the human race follows so many other species to extinction. We could, however, give God credit for His qualms of conscience and for trying to win our trust and regain His own morality and His own identity.

JESUS: God is making the entire universe tick. He is the watchmaker.

SATAN: True, the cosmos ticks like a time bomb. If the universe worked like a clock for billions of years without the hand of its Master to wind it (He was sleeping), wouldn't it be fair to conclude that it will continue to work for as long as it has energy in it or to assume that, once started into existence, it is now living on its own account? Energy seems indestructible. God could continue to leave it alone and attend to many other things, such as devising other universes in other planes or dimensions, which He could make auto-existing just like this one, or could better supervise, now that He has experienced this self-winding prototype. After all, space is limitless. What's beyond space, if not more space? This living universe has limits since it had a beginning, an evolution and an end, even if this, too, is a dream.

JESUS: What a sacrilege. And yet, He loves you, too, Satan.

ADAM (springing up and shouting from his witness stand): You would like that very much, Lucifer. I remember your audacious proposal to our Father when you came to Him before the trial and claimed the Earth as your dominion. And now you suggest taking Him out of His realm of Creation.

SATAN (applauding ironically): What is your authority, little brother, other than the defender of a God stripped of conscience?

ADAM: His breath is in me. I have the right to speak, as I am his first son. I represent Him.

SATAN: Oh! I thought that Jesus was God's first son. How many first sons are there? How many sales and marketing representatives does He need? You should open a heavenly stock market. He surely employs his kith and kin to do his world affairs. This is one-sidedness.

SAINT AUGUSTINE: "Adam is truly God's first son born into flesh, but Jesus Christ is the Messiah, the only crucified Savior, God's only anointed Son.

SATAN: Adam is from dirt (and gore according to Muslim beliefs,) made to fit a book personage. As for Jesus Christ, the only begotten Son of God, the only crucified Savior—

MAN'S VOICE: It's all a lie! And I have something to say.

(Roars from the crowd)

JUDGE (pounding her gavel): Silence, please! And who are you, sir?

MAN: My name is Kersey Graves, Your Honor. I have some evidence of my own that will help to disprove what you heard regarding the Son of God if you will allow me to speak.

RUFUS: Your Honor, I request that Mr. Graves be allowed to testify.

JUDGE: Please, come forward, Mr. Graves.

(Lucifer's eyes follow the man as he approaches the witness stand. He looks pleased as if he knows the man well. Kersey Graves seems nervous as he takes his seat, and when an angel extends the Bible to him, he waves it off.)

GRAVES: I don't take oaths on that book, but I swear on my own soul to speak the truth.

RUFUS: Please, state your full name and your birth and death dates."

GRAVES: Kersey Graves. I was born in Brownsville, Pennsylvania, on November 21, 1813, and entered Heaven September 4, 1883.

RUFUS: Please state your profession, Mr. Graves.

K.G: Philosopher, writer, and freethinker; self-educated.

RUFUS: What do you know about the only begotten Son of God, Jesus Christ, whom Christians claim to be the only Savior us, Mr. Graves?

K.G: Jesus Christ is not the only begotten son, nor is he the only crucified savior. If you will permit me, I have chronological evidence with me. He is a copycat.

RUFUS: What is your evidence?

GRAVES: (taking a note from his pocket) Here is my testimony ([9]Reads):

More than twenty claims of this kind—claims of beings invested with divine honor (deified)—have come forward and presented themselves at the bar of the world with their credentials, to contest the verdict of Christendom, in having proclaimed Jesus Christ "the only son, and sent of God:" [T]wenty Messiahs, Saviors, and Sons of God, according to history or tradition, have, in past times, descended from heaven, and taken upon themselves the form of men, clothing themselves with human flesh, and furnishing incontestable evidence of a divine origin, by various miracles, marvelous works, and superlative virtues; and finally these twenty Jesus Christ (accepting their character for the name) laid the foundation for the salvation of the world, and ascended back to heaven.

These have all received divine honors, have nearly all been worshiped as Gods, or sons of God; were mostly incarnated as Christs, Saviors, Messiahs, or Mediators; not a few of them were reputedly born of virgins; some of them filling a character almost identical with that ascribed by the Christian's bible to Jesus Christ; many of them, like Jesus are reported to have been crucified; and all of them, taken together, furnish a prototype and parallel for nearly every important incident and wonder-inciting miracle, doctrine and precept recorded in the New Testament, of the Christian's Savior. Surely, with so many Saviors the world cannot, or should not, be lost. . . .

I will now lay before [you] a brief account of the crucifixion of more than a dozen virgin-born Gods and sin-atoning Sav-

---

[9] *The Sixteen Crucified Saviors- K Graves.*

iors, predicated upon facts which have escaped the hands of the Christian iconoclasts determined to know only Jesus Christ crucified.

(Graves stops reading and addresses the judge): May I ask the court to let the beings I name line up near Jesus, on his left and his right sides. It doesn't matter where they stand as long as everyone can see them.

JUDGE: Very well.

GRAVES (calling out names from memory): Krishna of India, crucified 1200 BC. (Krishna appears on Jesus' right.) The Hindu Saki, crucified 600 BC. (Saki appears on Jesus' left). Thammuz of Syria, crucified 1160 BC. (From this point forward, each person named appears at the right or left end of the line.) Wittoba of the Telingonesic, crucified 552 BC. Iao of Nepal, crucified 622 BC. Hesus of the Celtic Druids, crucified 834 BC. Quexalcote of Mexico, crucified 587 BC. Quirinus of Rome, crucified 506 BC. Aeschylus's Prometheus, crucified 547 BC. Thulis of Egypt, crucified 1700 BC. Indra of Tibet, crucified 725 BC. Euripedes' Alcestis, crucified 600 BC. Atys of Phrygia, crucified 1170 BC. Crite of Chaldea, crucified 1200 BC. Bali of Orissa, crucified 725 BC. Mithra of Persia, crucified 600 BC.

RUFUS: Here they are, ladies and gentlemen of the jury. We see before us the Saviors, all crucified. Is that right, Mr. Graves?"

Graves: Yes, you have before you standing all the Saviors, incarnate, as the legends tell.

RUFUS: Why the virgin births, why the crucifixions, why so many Saviors? Is it myth or reality?

GRAVES: Well, here is the story. Let me read to you again. (Coughs and then reads in a stronger voice):

It has always been presumed that death, and especially death by crucifixion, involved the highest state of suffering possible to be endured by mortals. Hence, the Gods must suffer in this way as an example of courage and fortitude, and to show themselves willing to undergo all the affliction and misery incident to the lot, and unavoidable to the lives of their devoted worshipers. They must not only be equal, but superior to their subjects in this respect. Hence, they would not merely die, but choose, or at least uncomplainingly submit to the most ignoble and ignominious mode of suffering death that could be devised, and that was crucifixion. This gave the highest finishing touch to the drama.

And thus the legend of the crucifixion became the crowning chapter, the aggrandizing episode in the history of their lives. It was presumed that nothing less than a God could endure such excruciating tortures without complaining.

Hence, when the victim was reported to have submitted with such fortitude that no murmur was heard to issue from his lips, this circumstance of itself was deemed sufficient evidence of his Godship. The story of the crucifixion, therefore, whether true or false, [I repeat, whether true of false] deified or helped deify many great men and exalt them to the rank of Gods. Though some of the disciples of Buddhism, and some of the primitive professors of Christianity also (including, according to Christian history, Peter and his brother Andrew), voluntarily chose this mode of dying in imitation of their crucified Lord without experiencing, however, the desired promotion to divine honors. They failed of exaltation to the deityship, and hence are not now worshiped as Gods.

SATAN: Mr. Kersey, can you tell the court about the titles of the Saviors?

GRAVES: You read my mind, Lucifer. I'll continue:

The various deific titles applied to Jesus Christ in the New Testament are regarded by some Christian writers as presumptive evidence of his divinity. But the argument proves too much for the case; as we find the proof in history that many other beings, whom Christians regard as men, were honored and addressed by the same titles, such as God, Lord, Savior, Redeemer, Mediator, Messiah, etc.

The Hindoo Krishna, more than two thousand years ago, was prayerfully worshiped as "God the Most High." His disciple Amarca once addressed him thus: "Thou art the Lord of all things, the God of the universe, the emblem of mercy, the bestower of salvation. Be propitious O most High God," etc. Here he is addressed both as Lord and God. He is also styled "God of Gods."

Adonis of Greece was addressed as "God Supreme," and Osiris of Egypt as "the Lord of Life." In Phrygia, it was "Lord Atys," as Christians say, "Lord Jesus Christ." Narayan of Bermuda was styled the "Holy Living God."

The title "Son of God" was so common in nearly all religious countries as to excite but little awe or attention.

St. Basil says, "Every uncommonly good man was called 'the Son of God.'" The "Asiatic Researches" says, "The Tamulese adored a divine Son of God," and Thor of the Scandinavians was denominated "the first-born Son of God;" and so was Chrishna of India, and other demigods. It requires, therefore, a wide stretch of faith to believe that Jesus Christ was in any peculiar sense "the Son of God," because so denominated, or "the only begotten Son of God," when so many others are reported in history bearing that title.

The title Savior is found in the legends of every [religious] country. So also God, Redeemer, and Mediator. "When a Mogul or Tibetan is asked who is Krishna," says the Christian missionary Huc, "the reply is, instantly, 'the Savior of men.'" Buddha was known as "the Savior, Creator and Wisdom of God," and Mithras as both Mediator and Savior, also as "the Redeemer," and Krishna as "the Divine Redeemer," also "the Redeemer of the World." The terms Mediator and Intercessor were also applied by his disciples to him. And both he and Quexalcote were hailed as "the Messiah." In short, most ancient religious nations were honored with or expected a Messiah.

Was Jesus Christ the "Lamb of God?" (John i. 9.) So was Krishna styled "the Holy Lamb." The Mexicans, preferring a full-grown sheep, had their "Ram of God." The Celts had their "Heifer of God," and the Egyptians their "Bull of God." All these terms are ludicrous emblems of Deity, representing him as a quadruped, as the title "Lamb of God" does Jesus Christ, a term no less ludicrous than the titles of the pagan Gods as cited above.

And was Christ "the True Light?" (John i. 9.) So was Chrishna likewise called "the True Light," also "the Giver of Light," "the Inward Light," etc. Osiris was "the Redeemer of Light," and Pythagoras was both "Light and Truth." Apollonius was styled the "True Light of the World;" while Simon Magus was called "the Light of all Men."

Several nations had also their Christs, though in many cases the word is differently spelled. [Christos] or Chrest, the Greek mode of spelling Christ, may be found on several of the ancient tombstones of that country. The Christian writer [Heneage] Elsley, in his "Annotations of the Gospels" ([volume I, page]. 25), spells the word Christ in this manner, Chrest. The people of Loretto had a black Savior, called Chrest, or Christ. Lucian, in his "Philopatris," admits the ancient Gentiles had the name of Christ, which shows it was a heathen title. The Chaldeans had their Chris, the Hindoos their Chrishna, the Greeks their Chrest, and the Christians their Christ, all, doubtless, derived from the same original root.

As for Jesus, it was a common name among the Jews long before the advent of Christ. Josephus refers to seven or eight persons by that name, as "Jesus, brother of Onias," "Jesus, son of Phabet," etc. . . .

Again, was Jesus Christ "the Alpha and Omega, the Beginning and the End?"[S]o, likewise, Chrishna proclaimed, "I am the Beginning, the Middle, and the End." Osiris and Chrishna were both proclaimed "Judge of the Dead," as Jesus was "Judge of quick and dead." Isaiah represents the Father as proclaiming, "I am Jehovah; besides me there is no Savior." ([Isaiah 43:11]).

With what consistency then can Christ be called "the Savior," if there is but one Savior, and that is the Father?

And other divine titles besides those above named—in fact, all those applied to Christ—are found used also in reference to the older pagan gods, and so prove nothing.

SAINT AUGUSTINE: This is ludicrous.

SATAN: Indeed it is, ladies and gentlemen, and those tales should not be taken without a sip of fine red wine and much, much humor.

So why neglect all the other gods and Sons of God in favor of Jesus of Nazareth? Either dismiss them all or dismiss none. Should we favor Jesus because He will return as He promised? So will the others. But where would Jesus return? To the place where He once lived? They crucified Him for God's sake, and literally for God's sake, ladies and gentlemen, and He won't go there and appear riding on any fluffy cloud or on His non-existent white horse (as many believe) even if He could do it; otherwise, He would have done it already. Why not? Because His own people would most likely crucify him again! What, you say? That's an old, abandoned practice? Think again. Islam is still crucifying people today, as we speak. How barbaric is that? Read today's papers, the right ones.

RUFUS: Jesus, what do you have to say about all this?

JESUS: "I truly tell you—what Mr. Kersey Graves is saying with regard to the other Saviors is pure mythology."

RUFUS: Do you agree that all these other mythical deities reflected on or influenced your life?

JESUS: They indeed were like me.

RUFUS: Or you were like them since they predated your time on Earth.

JESUS: No matter. What you heard is some good equivalence.

RUFUS: God, supposedly, has only one Son, hasn't He? Which is the real one, the real Son of God, Jesus?

JESUS: I am. I am not a myth.

RUFUS: Why are you the only Son of God above all the others mentioned, and not, let's say, Krishna?

JESUS: Because I am the last and the first. I am the All. Krishna is I and I am He. I tell you the truth, ladies and gentlemen of the jury, children of the world, distinguished court of Heaven: I am Christ in all there is. You have the examples of Saviors crucified throughout history, and you do not recognize me? Look near me. Do you not see? You take no notice of the air because you breathe it every day. You have worshipped many gods and even fought over them, yet you do not recognize me in them? God's Spirit is in me; no matter how many times He appears before you and regardless of what name or ritual He takes, you do not see the truth when you have it before you, even when you had been given so many examples of it.

I tell you, ladies and gentlemen, Satan says that if I return, I will most likely be crucified again, but don't you realize that you are crucifying me every single day?

You call me every time you think of the Son of God. You refer to me when you see the crucified saviors, including me, the last one crucified, to remind you of God. And no matter how many times I appear, you will choose to crucify me again—physically, mentally, emotionally, spiritually. You would do so eternally were it not for this trial, which will end all confusion. I tell you this—all of it will all end here, today.

All of us here are one Son of God. I am in Krishna and Krishna is in me; I am in Buddha and Buddha is in me. We are all in our Father and our Father is in us.

RUFUS: But why the Crucifixion? Why the gory agony?

JESUS: (Commits to silence. He tilts His head to the side and smiles, mirroring a long, sad gaze.)

RUFUS: How can we interpret your silence?

JESUS: I would do it again if I knew that humanity will follow me.

(Noise in the courtroom silenced by the gavel.)

RUFUS: Phew! That's something.

JESUS: (Meekly) More than nothing.

RUFUS: How do you define *nothing*?

JESUS: The opposite of God!"

RUFUS: Then what is the definition of God?

JESUS: Everything.

SATAN (raising his hand): Including me!
RUFUS: No more questions, Your Honor!

CHAPTER
16
THE GOD OF CHAOS

(Leaning to one side in his chair, Plato seems to be deep in thought.)

JUDGE: Mr. Plato, do you wish to cross-examine the witnesses?

PLATO (jumping up as if awakened from a dream): Oh, thank you, Your Honor. Of course, I shall cross-examine the witnesses. (Coughs) Forgive my sluggishness; I was absorbed by the dialogues. Apparently, they have overexposed my mind to enlightenment—in a good sense, of course. Yes, here I am in defense of God. (Clears his throat) Lucifer, can you please tell this court your relationship with the conscience of God?

SATAN: We are relatives, sir.

PLATO: Pardon?

SATAN: I am a son of God; therefore, I am a relative of His conscience.

PLATO (turns instinctively toward the judge as if seeking approval): Oh, very well. Let's make a note of that. Could the conscience of God be fallible in your view?"

SATAN: Impossible. How could the Supreme Conscience have flaws?

PLATO: Are you certain? One hundred percent sure?

SATAN: Yes.

PLATO: Can you expand on why you think so?

SATAN: You know that God is perfect; at least, you assume that He is. Well, His conscience performs as His second mind or voice, which approves or disapproves the thoughts of His first mind. Think of it as a cosmic supercomputer.

PLATO: Could this supercomputer crash?

SATAN: No, it could not. If one mind—God's in this instance—crashes in terms of being asleep or, say, hibernating, as it were, the alter ego which is His conscience would hover over everything and communicate with God once He's awake.

PLATO: Is God always listening to His Own conscience, meaning to His alter ego?

SATAN: Well, yes. He has already confirmed that by the simple fact that we are now here.

PLATO: If God listens to His conscience, could His conscience have disapproved of His sleeping on the Seventh day after creation?

SATAN: His conscience mustn't disapprove or approve of anything unless there is doubt, and there was no doubt in God's mind on His Seventh Day, of any kind.

PLATO: So His conscience acts only if there is a question of doubt?

SATAN: Indeed.

PLATO: How about to prevent Him from performing harmful actions?

SATAN: He had a clear conscience when he went to sleep. Yet the Almighty knows in advance what would happen, and my point is that He did nothing to prevent the nightmare.

PLATO: But if God knew in advance that He would have a nightmare, so did His conscience and yet, why didn't His conscience cause in Him a sense of guilt or penance, alerting or preventing Him from letting a wrong action taking place, before He went to sleep? You said that God doesn't err, nor does His conscience.

SATAN: She did alert Him, but He ignored the warning.

PLATO: Then, how can His conscience be cleared if She held a sense of guilt for the upcoming events, especially after God ignored Her warning?

SATAN: God convinced Himself and His conscience that His creation was benefic and simply went to sleep. But He'd been sleeping ever since He finished the Creation, unless he can prove it otherwise.

PLATO: For fourteen billion years?

SATAN: It looks like He did. And not fourteen but eighteen billion years had passed since creation of the universe. (Winks and chuckles)

PLATO: The Bible states that God defined the day clearly, isn't that right, Augustinus?

SAINT AUGUSTINE: Yes. Genesis chapter 1 states:

And the evening and the morning were the first day.

And the evening and the morning were the second day. And the evening and the morning were the third day.

And so on up to and including the sixth day.

PLATO: Well, what do you make of that, Lucifer?

SATAN: (Sarcastically) Well, a thousand years is a day to the Lord (2: Peter 3:8) it took God a long time to create it. I'm not that impressed anymore; are you? And then, on the fourth day, God made the sun, moon, and stars. Quote, And God set them in the firmament of the heaven to give light upon the earth, unquote. (Genesis 1:17). In other words, God made the light on the first day and the suns on the fourth after four thousand years according to the *Bible*." Ha-ha-ha!

PLATO: Well, who was in charge of the world during all this time, meaning from the time He created it until now?

SATAN: God was.

PLATO (sniffs indignantly): You don't say.

SATAN: His conscience is attesting to that.

PLATO: Was God's conscience a witness to everything?

SATAN: Yes. A witness to all, even to the fact that God sent me to Earth to rule.

PLATO: But God rested assured that *you* had everything under control. His conscience was clear also with that decision, and yet *evil* penetrated absolutely everything. Isn't that what happened?"

SATAN: Yes, that's true, but evil was His invention because God created everything including it.

PLATO: Didn't God's conscience oppose evil?

SATAN: Do the numbers on a die oppose the cube of plastic that they're imprinted on? They make part of the same whole; they are part of the same die, are they not?"

PLATO: Confusing! Please explain.

SATAN: She did oppose evil.

PLATO: Aren't God and His conscience numbers of the same die?

SATAN: Yes.

PLATO: Then, God opposed evil, as well, isn't that correct?

SATAN: Paradoxically yes. Yet he created it. Look! I think that my Father meant well when He crafted the universe. But even *I* detest the slaughter. It sickens me because it's so bloody and cruel and poisonous; it's nothing but butchery. Unfortunately, the nature of the world was predetermined. You know: "forms."

As Mr. Twain was saying, a tiger was not built to eat onions or strawberries. His nature is to kill. To *kill!* His teeth and claws confirm it. The nature of man is different. His nature is to be passionate, to love, to cry, to compete, to procreate like all other animals, but unlike all other animals, which kill for nourishment, to protect their territories, or to safeguard their young, man has one major flaw, he kills for revenge or for sport or for any number of reasons. Not to mention his other vices, all of which show him to be ill natured. (Shouting) *Ill natured!*

We see him stealing, raping, enslaving his unfortunate kin. His jealousy rivals the biblical Yahweh's jealousy, for the Old Testament portrays our Father in Heaven as a jealous God and a punishing God whose temper we see reflected in mankind. But man has never seen his God, so he had to invent Him by raising his own traits to a supreme level as my friend Voltaire once said, sarcastically, of course. And man's delusional mind claims revelations; man invented prophets who could hear voices in their heads just as our radical apologist Augustine claims that they did. And these voices are none other than (pauses dramatically) the voice of God. How do they and their contemporaries know that? Because God speaks to them and they recognize Him at once. How do they recognize God if they've never heard Him before? Because the voices speak in a tongue that only they, the selected prophets, suddenly understand. Sometimes, God speaks directly in Hebrew because, after all, he's the God of Israel.

The selected prophets remembered every verse and so they wrote down everything – in their minds - with precise accuracy, since God gave them a phenomenal memory for that reason alone. Otherwise, they were illiterate and primitive. Some believers still argue that their illiteracy and simplicity alone is sufficient proof that they speak God's word since an illiterate or a simpleton couldn't remember what happened on the first day of God's Creation, let alone a full chapter, without the help of God or his delegated angel Gabriel. The long phrases and verses that God laid in their innocent brains had to be passed onto others, and people hearing the prophets speaking with so much pomp believed in the word of God because if their prophets said it was true, it was true. Does anybody have a problem with that?

PLATO: You're being ironic, aren't you?

SATAN: Of course I am, but for a good reason: to prove that imbecility is a fine gift.

PLATO: Are you indicating that man devised God in his own image, or was it the other way around?

SATAN: Well, God made everything, including man and woman. Human beings, in the absence of God—He was nowhere to be seen—concocted an imaginary God and sustained their invention through another invention, religion. Religion has nothing to do with the real Creation or the real Creator since every religion has a different deity, a different concept of creation, and a different theory of an afterlife bearing different teachings. Confusing?

PLATO: Can you define religion?

SATAN: Religion is the lifeblood of evil.

PLATO: Many people think that you represent evil.

SATAN: Well, if that's true, I represent what I have inherited from my Father. Am I not part of religion? I am, that I am. Am I not a daemon? Yet, God is the ruler of all this daemonic universe because He is all pervasive, all powerful, and all knowing. But what does the terrifying word *daemon* mean?

PLATO: It is a Greek word meaning "spirit."

SATAN: And for those who know the meaning, it doesn't sound bad at all, does it? God then becomes the ruler of a spiritual universe. Why, then, would people fear the spirit of light?"

PLATO (evading the question): What about God's conscience, Lucifer? Where was God's conscience when the universe was made?

SATAN: God's conscience endorsed the making of the universe.

PLATO: Therefore, God's conscience is an accessory equally responsible for its existence.

SATAN: Agree!

PLATO: And, yet, God's conscience didn't prevent God to the cruelty and chaos that would result from the faults in design?

SATAN: Again, conscience warns, cannot prohibit.

PLATO: How is God omniscient, omnipresent, omnibenevolent, and omnipotent? Is He not present through His conscience? Weren't all of those attributes transferred to his conscience during his dream?"

SATAN: Yes and no.

PLATO: Explain.

SATAN: Consciousness is the state of awakened realization.

PLATO: Do you mean that God has been totally unconscious?

SATAN: Completely. His conscience floated everywhere while the Master was unconscious.

PLATO: Do you mean that God's conscience by itself was incapable of acting in God's place?

SATAN: His conscience was in all His Creation while God was sleeping as I have mentioned, and it experienced every detail of the failed worlds—the capricious, fortuitous design, the organized Chaos. Oxymoron? No. I shall explain: It connects two periods—the first when God was awake He gave us a world obeying His deterministic laws of physics; while the second, when He was asleep He left it yielding to the laws of chance.

PLATO: Chance and chaos, you said?

SATAN: Yes, the whole universe is in total confusion.

PLATO: Not only planet Earth?

SATAN: Of course not. Look at the cosmos. Look at its entire picture; it is missing care. If it had any before, it went awry when God left it unsupervised, unwatched, forgotten. A living unity of billions of life forms adjusting, evolving, desperately looking for survival. Everything left to evolve by itself.

PLATO: Evolution?

SATAN: Evolution.

PLATO: A God of evolution?"

SATAN: –Ha-ha! Yes, or simply Evolution without God. He was busy resting.

PLATO: Thank you, Lucifer. (Turns to face the judge) I call a young woman named Eve, Eve from Eden, Adam's wife, to the stand.

(Voices fill the courtroom)

CHAPTER
17
EVE'S TESTIMONY

The bailiff spoke clearly and loudly. "Calling Eve to the witness stand!"

Adam stood up from his seat on the witness stand. His green eyes seemed to enlarge as he searched everywhere for his wife. Disoriented, he walked toward the center of the court where Plato stood, turning every which way in an effort to see from which direction Eve would appear. Beads of cold sweat rolled down his puzzled face faster than his tears. (He seems stunned by Plato's sudden call as if he wants to be the one to call her or fears that she might not hear Plato's voice because she isn't in Heaven. He stands trembling as he watches and listens to the stillness of the infinite, to the silent music of space.)

"Your Honor," Plato said, "if Eve is not available for whatever reason, I could pass it this time. I would like to invite—"

"Here's Eve," Jesus interrupted. "She's coming!"

From behind the place where God supposedly shed His light, a young woman appeared. At first, she seemed to float, but then I realized that she was walking with an undulating motion, her slender figure showing through the white and pink gown. As she advanced, her golden hair was streaming down her shoulders almost to the marble floor. Through the thin, silky material of her garments, her body looked like that of a goddess as the light hit her from behind, leaving the imagination of the artist to paint it or carve her in stone or marble or immortalize her in the mind, once and forever.

When she saw Adam, she stopped and looked at him as though mesmerized. She took a deep breath before darting toward Adam, almost knocking him out of Heaven with her embrace. Adam locked his arms around her tightly as if determined that no God or gods would ever separate them again. They seemed to melt into each other, kissing and forgetting all etiquette.

Plato smiled sadly.

From God's direction came a beam that illuminated them like a limelight on a stage. Adam and Eve looked as young and beautiful as if they were still in Eden. This was Heaven.

The audience all stood looking at what they must have thought was a stage play in which the main roles were given to Adam and Eve, a drama in which the actors were mankind and the producer God Himself.

PLATO: Eve, please be seated here on the same side as our other distinguished witnesses.

SATAN (to Plato): Thank you. (To Eve) What a pleasure to share the same space with you once again.

(Eve ignores Lucifer. She steps back from Adam gracefully, not before giving him one last dreamy glance, betraying an eternal passion.)

PLATO: I don't suppose that you need to be given the Bible since you are part of it, do you, Eve?

EVE (jokingly): Thank you. I heard that I was an important character in a book. I don't mind feeling its *hard covers* again.

(Chuckles from the audience)

PLATO: Please tell us, Eve—do you see God in this courtroom?

EVE (pointing to the far corner from which she came): Yes. He's standing right there! My dad.

(Plato's eyes water, and he takes a few moments to collect himself before speaking.): Do you see Lucifer before you?

EVE: You mean Satan. It's hard not to see him. He's a snake in human form.

SATAN (smiling): Oh, Eve, you're more beautiful than you were then. You are. . .

A Statue of cold image and yet charmingly warm
As if the Gods have made you in their Shape and Form;
Perhaps now incarnated to mark another sin
And then back to your image forever you are born
Much softer than an angel, much lovelier within
Much lighter than a dream—eternally forlorn.

Why are you angry with me and not with God, my dear Eve?

EVE: Thank you for the wonderful verse. To respond to your question—Death has claimed humankind ever since "the Fall," my not so dear *sssssnake*.

SATAN: Would you have preferred to remain—I am sorry to say—as ignorant and idiotic as God created you and intended you to be?

EVE: I would have preferred eternal life over death for me and for all Creation. Besides, it's better to live as an ignorant and idiotic or, rather, an unconscious innocent than to be labeled as the original sinner and the executioner of mankind.

SATAN: Oh, Eve, you were a calculated excuse for God to condemn humanity, can't you see? You made history and inspired art.

EVE (politely but coldly): Most people doubt my existence, nevertheless.

SATAN: Doubt opens the avenue of truth.

EVE: As I said, I would have preferred eternal life over death—not for me alone but for all people. I've branded women with the spirit of sin—forever.

SATAN: As Mr. Twain pointed out, how could you know what death was if you had no illustration of it? Besides, God had already ordained the wager of life and death had He not?

EVE: I can't question Father for imposing His rules when He is the ruler. If He gave an order or made a request, He must have had a reason. He knew what it was; I didn't.

SATAN: Yes, He *knew*; that's the whole point, and He left you in peril; in fear of acquiring knowledge and becoming like *them*, the same knowledge that makes man and woman superior to chimpanzee, without which he or she would not have noticed the difference. Without knowledge where would humans stand? Would they live as dolts in the Garden of Eden: flesh-and-blood machines, biological servants, genetic toys? Where, in Blessedness? Without realization of where you are, there is no Heaven. Without self-consciousness there's only the primeval life.

EVE: Isn't it better to live eternally without pain, problems, and losses than to be at the mercy of aging and death? Better not to fathom the excruciating hour of death and to live—forever, I would say. I've been through death and it's painful, not only for me but for my descendants as anyone in the audience can confirm.

SATAN: Do you condemn me for offering you knowledge when Father arranged the whole plot?

(Eve looks confused.)

SATAN: Isn't God the producer of the show?

EVE: Aren't you the director? (For a moment, she gazes at the Light where God is sitting and then looks at Adam. Tears glimmer in her eyes as she faces the light.)

SATAN (bowing like a serf before his master): Everything happens does so with Father's permission because without the Almighty, nothing could exist. God had your destiny in His hands as He set the whole world ticking (Jesus' words) just like the rest of this universal time bomb. It's a blood-written destiny; and what God writes cannot be erased.

PLATO: Eve, you are an intelligent woman, and you have been through a lot. Please tell us without restraint: Do you condemn God for the outcome of the world?

EVE: I cannot revile my Father. I am much wiser now than I was when I lived in Eden."

PLATO: Do you believe that God is guilty of the accusations brought against him so far in this court by His own conscience?

EVE: I can't speak for His conscience. He is what He is, our Lord and our God. We only have one Father. I, we, must accept him as He is. If He ever "died," if He ever dissolved in ether, disappearing beyond eternity, I would be lost and feel deader than death. Despite any destiny that He has written, I'm sure that the world would not be the same without Him. Nature would feel abandoned, betrayed, and purposeless. We human beings have learned to cope with the facts of life and with realism as we see it. Must we learn another way now? Are we to take everything from the start and be reborn into new selves? Why deny the beauty of Nature and the obvious facts, which are with us regardless of outcome? Why try to explain the obvious by looking for words to replace feelings?

SATAN: Ladies and gentlemen, Eve's words prove that she has a heart warmer and larger and greater than her Father has. Here sits a punished woman representing a punished mankind willing to forgive the Grand Master for her own death. The Architect fails in His design, and the edifice of civilization collapses under His moral weight, and we are lauding His merits, His very actions, for fear of what He'll do next.

Look at Eve, ladies and gentlemen, and note how beautiful, how pure in heart, and how forgiving she is. And while she demonstrates this silent compassion with tears running down her cheeks, you may want to witness the same tears in the eyes of the millions of children our Father the Almighty God further punishes by promoting diseases and suffering and death—perpetual death, ugly death, painful death, shameful death, repulsive, disgusting death. He will not stop killing unless His own conscience overcomes Him. All I ask of you is to listen to God's conscience. Eve is the happiest and saddest mother in the world. She sees in every baby a wrinkled old woman or man ready to die—or an unfortunate young one who will die prematurely—because *death* is the toll that all men and women must pay for God's evil munificence.

JESUS: God sent *me* to save mankind from death.

SATAN: He must've been asleep when He sent you.

(Total silence)

JESUS: No, as the prophecy foretold, I—

SATAN: What does this have to do with what I just said about Eve? Did you hear what I just said, or you are trying to turn a sensible moment into a senseless one by bringing in dogmatic, politically corrupt, religious, stereotyped malarkey? Tell me something and I won't doubt you—are you saving the animals, too?

JESUS: Every living being will go to Heaven.

SATAN: But the beasts don't seem to follow you—the animal beasts, I mean. They'll growl and hiss if they see you.

JESUS: They only follow their instincts.

SATAN (deridingly): By growling at you? If so, that proves that their instincts are better than most people's logic.

JESUS: Well, I wouldn't put it that way. They are innocent and therefore blameless.

SATAN: Are they more privileged than mankind, whom you condemned to Hell unless they bestow their souls at your bare (Gentile-washed) feet?"

JESUS: Yes. Animals don't know to believe in me. They don't know good from evil or knowledge from ignorance. They are innocent.

SATAN: Why do the animals die if they are innocent?

JESUS: Their death is man's fault for disobeying the Word of God. Through me, they will again enter the Kingdom of God.

SATAN: Do you mean to tell me that animals once lived in the Kingdom of God?

JESUS: Yes, they did. Every Christian and every Jew knows that.

SATAN: I am not a Christian or a Jew, so tell me: Were the animals also punished for disobeying the word of God? Say, the lioness sinned by biting into a watermelon or a fig or a mouth-watering ripe apple, rendering the whole Eden imperfect and sinful?

JESUS: Don't mock the actions of God.

SATAN: And those people who know nothing of you or never heard of you or don't even believe that you ever existed don't share the animal's privilege of entering Heaven after death?"

JESUS: All people have a choice: Heaven or Hell.

SATAN: You don't say! On the contrary, it sounds to me that people have *no choice*. Either you or Hell, and I wonder which is worse. Your recent invention, Hell, has been registered in the Holy Book. Not to say that from the moment you proclaimed it, billions have written their own ticket to damnation since it's impossible not to violate the Bible God's man-made laws.

JESUS: Believe what you please, Satan.

SATAN: You are the Son of God and God yourself, are you not?

JESUS: Yes, I am.

SATAN: Ladies and gentlemen of the jury, God foresaw that His master plan would be disastrous for humanity yet He committed to perdition entire generations of mankind. He approved the eternal torment of which I am a direct witness and spilled Jesus' blood for the salvation of souls that wouldn't have required salvation in the first place if He hadn't let sin happen. At least, that's what those personages depicted in the comic book called the Bible lead you to believe; right? Jesus is saying that He Himself is God. If so, didn't He then become a victim of His own judgment?

JESUS: I chose to die for mankind because without pain and suffering there is no salvation. My blood purified the souls of those who want to be cleansed of sin. Believe what you please, Satan.

SATAN: Believe? I'll tell you what. I'll bet that if you saw a hungry lioness in the African savannah suddenly appear in front of you, the only way to save yourself from being food would be literally to fly. Your attempt to run would only arouse laughter in the cat before she chased and easily caught you, biting your feeble, godly neck, ripping you to pieces, and munching you, my dear rabbi, prayer shoal and all—well, almost all. Let's see you offer the lion vegetables and fruit and tell her to lie at your feet and be your pussy. Your bones would be picked clean by the vultures and the hyenas despite your body's producing worms that barely wait to devour your leftovers; and in the end, they'll satiate their thirst with your trickling blood. And once again, your grave will not be found. You will be resurrected on the third day (after passing through the lioness's digestive system); with some tribal chief claiming that he saw you rising in form of an odor toward the clouds and swear to it that he sniffed in some of that waft himself.

Would you try facing a lion in the wild? Prove us wrong. Prove that you are God or the Son of God. If you are, nothing can harm you, right? But I'll give you some well-intentioned advice if you want to attempt that: first, practice flying. Then, you can go before a hunting lioness and her hungry family and try to pick up a cub to take to Heaven, and you can explain to the cats that it will be better for the cub to eat blueberries, green apples, or peas instead of red flesh, but don't forget to mention that is all kosher. You can promise to give the eternal life so that the cats won't go to Hell. Let's see this miracle, all of us; in fact, let the world see it on ESPN or Animal Planet or the CNN news or Fox TV or the History Channel, Rai Uno, Berlusconi, Deutsche Welle, every one of the world's major television stations. This would be a convincing one, wouldn't everyone agree?

(The audience remains as silent as if it weren't there.)

JESUS: Mocking as usual. "Thou shalt not tempt the Lord thy God."

SATAN (erupting in laughter): Well recited: Luke 4:12. You keep going back to the hypnotic writ like a broken record. (Snaps forward) Look, there's Luke! Between the covers of that book. . . . Ha-ha-ha!

JESUS: I tell the truth; those who follow me will see the Kingdom of God.

SATAN: Everything is predestined by God's giving nature: Dying and regenerating and perpetuating and progressing and metamorphosing are the nature of the world. Does the scorpion join you into your peaceful Heaven? And the sharks, and hyenas, and cats, and crocodiles, and the trillions of annoying, germ-filled flies that buzz in and out of everywhere, including your supposed holy food, washing their feet in your so-called holy water?

JESUS: All shall live peacefully in the Kingdom of the Lord, forever."

SATAN: And the smelly hippopotamuses will join you at the Lord's Table?

JESUS: They won't be smelly at all in Heaven. They'll be like toys.

SATAN: What about the chameleon? Will it join you as well?

JESUS: The chameleon, too."

SATAN: And what will they all eat, pasta?

JESUS: If they want pasta, they'll eat pasta.

SATAN: What if they want to eat you?

JESUS (elusively): We are in a serious trial and this is not funny.

SATAN: What of the snake? Will, he too, be allowed in Heaven?

JESUS (smiling): I know what you're getting at; you're just being cynical.

SATAN: Answer the question, Jesus. What about the nutrients for the flies? I haven't seen any flies here lately— although by the buzz of it, I feel them very near.

PLATO: Please, gentlemen. This is a trial, not a play.

SATAN: *Now* you see that I'm being derisive and making a laughing of your lack of common sense and primitive manipulation of words."

JESUS: You're tempting me into anger and I will not give in.

SATAN (sarcastically): No, but you could answer in a straightforward manner reflecting your royal divinity. And what do you do when you're angry? Show us!

(Plato shakes his head in disapproval, scissoring his hands above his head)

PLATO (loudly): No, please, please! Ladies and gentlemen, I must ask you to consider or reconsider the facts and not to assume that hippos will be dining with you here in Heaven or that cats will be laughing to their sociable sense of humor if given the chance. Why not then assume that great white sharks will swim close to the heavenly shores, showing their bright teeth in affable smiles, rolling their eyes, and winking at the ever-growing number virgins on the beach who follow their masters around like living tails, their heads wrapped in hijabs and their bodies in light burqas. They may resemble floating ghosts but, they only dress that way to obey their fanatical masters who believe that covering their heads and bodies will protect them not of sea sharks but from human sexual appetites.

Please don't give us these stories. I don't see any of those slave beauties in this Heaven or else we would call it paradise.

(Laud laughter everywhere)

Come now! Proof beyond a reasonable doubt is the only path to a fair judgment even if the evidence is presented humorously. I beg you to speak factually. We cannot believe in fantasy, nor should we be treated as sheep or cattle that follow the sound of a call.

I ask this jury not to dismiss any remarks by Satan or Jesus of Nazareth and to see through the irony and the allegories, considering only the evidence. Let's distinguish between the possible and the impossible, ignoring the far-fetched dragon tales that appeal to the gullible and traveling instead into the realms of reason that appeal to the judicious. Right?

(Looks around as if seeking a raised hand but not finding one.)

PLATO (facing the judge with a sigh and a shrug of his shoulders): Your honor, I have no more questions.

CHAPTER
18
THE LUCIFERIAN PRINCIPLE

(Lucifer rose from the witness stand, his poised figure mounting under his newly assumed role as prosecutor. He walked by every witness hands behind his back, chin almost touching his chest and stopped before Jesus. Smirking in a way as to impose superiority He measured the Son of Man from head to feet, while addressing the court.)

SATAN: I'd like to call the entity (he finally turned toward the Judge) who knows God's conscience better than God Himself.

JUDGE: And who could know God better than God Himself, Lucifer?

SATAN: His Spirit, Your Honor.

JUDGE: The Holy Spirit?

SATAN: Yes *His* Holy Spirit. With your permission, I would like to call God's Holy Spirit to the witness stand.

JUDGE: Very well.

(Outcries mixed with applause and sporadic shushing ceased as fast as they started, heads turning every way in anticipation of the appearance of God's Holy Spirit. A comet a few million light years away whizzed by, surprising the audience and the witnesses. Lucifer smiled with the triumph of a gladiator in an arena full of spectators, some of which have predicted courage and blood while the rest have invested in compassion and leniency.

Adam looked concerned; there was no response to the judge's call. The wait seemed long and wintry, and the place appeared deserted; the ticking of an imaginary clock grew static.)

SATAN: See? There is no presence of God; there is no Spirit of God; there is no Father in Heaven other than the one in our imaginary creation. Where is your God now? Where is His Ghost? Busy floating around when Her place would be with God? I don't see the flying pigeon, do you?

SAINT AUGUSTINE: Ladies and gentlemen! Please, indulge me and listen. Listen to the sound of your vibrating souls; listen to the sound of distant drums in the far jungles of the Earth; they are stimulating wrath; they are the rhythms of war; I tell you before Jesus Christ, my Lord, *this* is the final war between good and evil, between Satan and God. This is obliteration; This is Armageddon.

SATAN: Your Honor, Augustine is speaking out of turn again; I agree that this is the final war but not between God and me, but between His conscience and Him; between humanity and Him. God is at war with His own Self.

Are we not here in this court to reveal the truth about our destiny? Are we not here to face God and His crimes? Are we not after all facing the result of God's nightmare, which He admits having? Are we not trying to illuminate the path of truth and save ourselves from the tragic fate that resulted from His negligence?

Let's step out of the real darkness into the real light; let's fight for our rights and see this war end. Let's renovate the world into an everlasting benevolence; let's free ourselves from the serfdom, bondage, and oppression to which the Almighty has condemned us.

I would like to ask Augustine last few questions, this time about God's spiritual and moral attributes. And my questions are . . .

(standing up and shouting intrepidly): How much longer must we endure this audacious attack?

JUDGE: Order, please! Lucifer represents the prosecution now, and you must answer his questions while you remain on the witness stand.

SAINT AUGUSTINE (Emancipated): "The Luciferian Principle, is the art of concealing darkness in light, war in peace, and, finally, bondage in liberation from self-restraint. In this way, people are seduced into embracing their own destroyer."

SATAN: Your Honor, Augustine is constantly interrupting me. I'm asking that his last remark be withdrawn and that he be charged with contempt should he continue to show disrespect to this court.

PLATO: Objection, Your Honor. Saint Augustine is citing the Bible, the same book that you have here for taking an oath. Disregarding its text would demean its purpose.

JUDGE: Lucifer and Plato, please approach the bench."

CHAPTER
19
THE GHOST OF MARK TWAIN

(A young man rushes through the front rows raising his arm and waving. Plato is startled by his appearance and recognizes him.

PLATO: Your Honor, I see that our witness finally arrived; he wants to testify. JUDGE: (motions affirmatively)

PLATO: The defense calling Mr. Clemens.

(The fellow walks fast toward the witness stand, his head a bit tilted to a side, a piercing look in his eyes, meaning business. He is supple, young, has a thick mustache and rich wavy hair. His features are healthy. He is dressed well in a dark three piece suit. In his hand he holds a booklet and some papers inserted in it. He seats and begins talking immediately.)

SAMUEL CLEMENS: Your Honor; Mr. Plato, my name is Samuel Clemens. In Hell, where I enjoy a certain fame, they call me Mark Twain or "the American."

I still write once in awhile as I spring into the minds of living men and women who love this knack, but mostly I preach from the Scriptures to the millions of fans who are lost in sin and can't see the light at the end of the tunnel. I make them see the light. Yes, I am a pastor now who learned to preach from some selected evangelists who reside in nearby darker neighborhoods and who were kind enough to teach me this fanatic, uh! fantastic art. I learned quickly and since then, I've added some of my own technique and passion, becoming the only one who. . ."

PLATO: Mr. Clemens, before you testify, would you like to swear upon the Bible?"

CLEMENS: Ah, no, thank you; I don't swear. Well, very rarely, only when—

PLATO: Mr. Clemens, what I mean by "swear" is to take an oath, not use profanity.

CLEMENS: Oh. No! Ha-ha-ha! Don't worry, I'll speak only the truth; what reason would I have not to?

JUDGE (smiling): Please proceed!

PLATO: Mr. Clemens, do you see God in this court?

CLEMENS: What do you mean by God? The God of the Bible?

PLATO: Yes.

CLEMENS: (sniffs) No!

PLATO: Do you see any other God?

CLEMENS: (Looks around, squints; sees Jesus) No. Look, I'll try to be quick and be off your sight as soon as you'll let me, as I have to get back to Hell for another Bible teaching.

PLATO: Bible teaching? Why would you teach the Bible in Hell?

CLEMENS: Where *should* I teach the Bible, in Heaven?

PLATO: Well, that is a true fact. And do your listeners pray to God?

CLEMENS: Oh! They've been praying to God since they were alive, some of them for ten thousand years—give and take—before I arrived, but no prayer has ever been answered, you see. I told them they must be persistent (winks.) I must tell you that we've only now discovered the secret of "begging" (well, you call it praying) as it's a gift to know *how* to pray, *when* to do it, and *where* to do it. And I tell you most sincerely that Hell is *where* it should be done. Unless you're in Hell, you shouldn't pray to the Heavenly Father. Not that it makes any difference. Do you fellows pray to God here in Heaven? (He looks all around again) No! See?

PLATO: And Satan allows prayer and Bible reading in Hell?

CLEMENS: He not only allows it, he encourages it just to show everyone that no prayers will ever be answered. (Lucifer nods.)

PLATO: Mr. Clemens, this may seem a very peculiar question, but do tell us should you have the choice between Heaven and Hell as a place to spend eternity, which would you choose?"

CLEMENS: Well, make me an offer that I can't refuse. I must admit that I sampled both Heaven and Hell while living on Earth. (Short pause) I'd rather be a traveling ghost. I could never spend eternity in one place. No matter how wonderful, with time it becomes boring. I say "go to heaven for the climate, hell for the company."

(Muffled laughter in the audience)

PLATO: You said that you are teaching the Bible in Hell; does your teaching include the Gospels?

CLEMENS: Oh, I teach all three Abrahamic religions. I like to revel in dutiful matters.

PLATO: Wouldn't that be confusing not to say conflicting?

CLEMENS: Not at all. There're all the same if you really read them. In fact, during my joyous sermons I switch them (all three scriptures) like a Three Card Monte. Conflicting? To the contrary, they are enlightening to the mind; they are the best medicine. There's no fighting in Hell for that reason. We have fun.

PLATO: A three-card Monte?

CLEMENS: Or the shell game—if you remember three walnut shells and a pea or a nut under one of them? It would seem that there's one chance in three to find the nut – I mean God, right?

PLATO: Right.

CLEMENS: Nope—Wrong! They can never find the pea because the pea (or nut) is under none of the shells. Instead of palming the pea God does it for us: He seems to be under a different shell, in a different book, every time. But if you really look for Him and open all three books, He ain't there.

PLATO: (smiling and scratching his head) What is the main belief in Hell?

CLEMENS: There's no belief; we are all *atheists*, meaning that we are *without* God—I mean it's a Greek word; you're Greek, you know that. Circumstances prove it.

PLATO: Please explain. Don't the holy books teach the love of God?"

CLEMENS: These fables teach *reason* and *logic*. These books that you call Holy Scriptures are the main motif for atheism.

PLATO: Can you tell the court why you think so, Mr. Clemens? Why do you think that those holy books are the main motif for atheism?

CLEMENS: Take the Bible per example. "[10]It is full of interest. It has noble poetry in it; and some clever fables; and some blood-drenched history; and some good morals; and a wealth of obscenity; and upwards of a thousand lies."

PLATO: You may expand on the subject if you desire.

CLEMENS: "[11]The Christian's Bible is a drug store. Its contents remain the same; but the medical practice changes...The world has corrected the Bible. The church never corrects it; and also never fails to drop in at the tail of the procession— and take the credit of the correction. During many ages there were witches. The Bible said so. the Bible commanded that they should not be allowed to live. Therefore the Church, after eight hundred years, gathered up its halters, thumb-screws, and firebrands, and set about its holy work in earnest. She worked hard at it night and day during nine centuries and imprisoned, tortured, hanged, and burned whole hordes and

---

[10] Letters from the Earth
[11] "Bible Teaching and Religious Practice," *Europe and Elsewhere*

armies of witches, and washed the Christian world clean with their foul blood.

Then it was discovered that there was no such thing as witches, and never had been. One does not know whether to laugh or to cry.....There are no witches. The witch text remains; only the practice has changed. Hell fire is gone, but the text remains. Infant damnation is gone, but the text remains. More than two hundred death penalties are gone from the law books, but the texts that authorized them remain." I make sure the text is read.

PLATO: Looking at the people living today on Earth, at their progress until today, what can you tell us of their beliefs in God? After all, there are five billion believers.

CLEMENS: "[12]Man is a Religious Animal. He is the only Religious Animal. He is the only animal that has the True Religion--several of them. He is the only animal that loves his neighbor as himself and cuts his throat if his theology isn't straight. He has made a graveyard of the globe in trying his honest best to smooth his brother's path to happiness and heaven....The higher animals have no religion. And we are told that they are going to be left out in the Hereafter. I wonder why? It seems questionable taste."

SATAN: Jesus had testified that the animals are allowed in Heaven, after all."

CLEMENS: I can see that... I mean, I see.

PLATO: (ignoring the sarcasm) And of the people in general, what can you tell us?

CLEMENS: Most of the people are very intelligent; I would say, adorably clever; especially those that buy my books. So we shall exclude those from the other bunch.

PLATO: What other bunch?

CLEMENS: As you may observe the world is infested with idiots. *This* is nonfiction.

PLATO: Please, go on!

CLEMENS: The idiot has come a long way and you must give him credit for that. From a one-time Stone Age man to a modern man penetrating deeply into –politics and religion, the idiot must have wits or otherwise he couldn't have emerged.

He's not an accident, nor is he the result of casualty. The syllogism proves it: God made man; the idiot is a man so, God made the idiot.

Yet, to assume that the idiot is a child of God would be to accept that God made him in his own image. Although that may sound sacrilegious, it ain't so since it can't be true. If it were true that God made the idiot in his own image, it would certainly falsify God's reputation from the point of view of the nonidiot, who believes that only *he* reflects God's image.

But if God didn't make the idiot, then who did? He must have a *creator*. We know that if *only* God is the Creator of man, it simply means that there must be *another* God—the idiot's God.

But that complicates the matter and creates a further problem since we must presume that there are *more* gods, each of them reflected in the mirror of their own created *product*.

Just like all those other humans that multiplied and spread throughout the world, the idiot formed families, groups, and populations, scattered everywhere, all representing their own god. If you don't believe this statement, look in the religion section of today's largest bookstores and see for yourself the books addressed specifically and clearly to the idiot at large: *The Idiot's Guide to Christianity, The Complete Idiot's Guide to Islam, The Idiot's Guide to Understanding Judaism*, etc. If there weren't idiots by the billion, there wouldn't be books to guide them just as there are books to guide dummies. Find them in the shelves: *Christianity for Dummies, Islam for Dummies, Judaism for Dummies*, etcetera.

If you look carefully, you'll notice that there's a hitch: If the idiots and dummies join all those religions, isn't that offensive to all the remaining people that are not dummies or idiots? Which begs the question: Why would the religious struggle to proselytize more idiots and more dummies than they have already have? How could the nonidiot share the same religion with these honest-minded brethren?

Notice that the idiot springs out in worrisome numbers to learn about and believe in the Bible and the Quran because he thinks that he has found God. Nothing could convince him that the mental image he prays to is his own fantasy.

He is devoted to this image; he cares about it and gathers in places such as: churches, synagogues, temples, and mosques as well as in tents and shelters among in the jungles. He prostrates himself before his mentally ever-present specter: the Almighty, All-Powerful, All-Good, All-Gracious, All-Perfect Commander—God.

He senses Him; he has goose bumps when speaking of Him, feeling some kind of, ah, fear enwrapped in love. He *feels* secure under this condition and he hears (from the non-idiot) that he must tell others about his *faith*, he must spread the Word of God among his fellow men and convince them that his god is the only god, the true god, the one and only creator. His god tells him to do it and according to Scriptures, everyone must obey God's word or face the consequences.

Dummies, the idiot's best friend, jump to help him and react with vengeance and force if you stand in the idiot's way or bother his creed. They will not just stand there with indifference and allow ignorance to take over; they will acquire electoral force and become legislators with the help of other idiots who will vote for them in large numbers, all united, all claiming that God is on their side.

Those two distinguished parties are hand in hand. In fact, now you can't even tell them apart. They have assembled and assimilated so much that you won't know under which roof you walk unless you read the nameplate inscription before you enter. The new generations of dummies and idiots speak today about—take note—*religious tradition*.

Your god is false (if you have one) while their god is true, they say. And watch how they'll convince you!

As a new spiritual generation, they'll trace your whereabouts, find you in your peaceful home, and get you out of your blandness rather quickly; either you'll convert to their religion and be saved or they'll kill you right there. They'll get you converted since they care about you; they won't let you go to Hell just like that. They'll consign you to the flames in the name of their Lord to get credit for doing God's work. Don't try to die like a martyr; they'll break your bones and throw them into fire just to show others like you how it's done. Love can turn into wrath, just as God's does.

If you're a freethinker and you dare express your thoughts, they'll accuse you of heresy. With the approval of the Good Lord (who ordained it eons before) they'll hang you or stone you to death or crucify you or torture you before a large gathering so that everyone can see what happens to the miserable, sorry infidel who had to be a jackass and die like one. You say those practices are seen only in medieval eras? Look again. They are modern times practices.

In some other regions, they'll let you have it by quartering, putting you on a breaking wheel, or impaling you; these carefully crafted inventions prepared in the name of God. If you're lucky, they'll just give you a hundred lashes.

You must be careful what you say, where and how you say it. You can't even keep it in your thought. Don't think to think about it. God gets in there and you may be condemned of a thought crime. Beware! Yep! These people believe in anything. Per example: you can't piss against the wall. It's against God's law. It's in the Bible. The Jewish God dictates in First Kings 21:21: "Behold, I will bring evil upon thee, and will take away thy posterity, and will cut off from Ahab him that pisseth against the wall, and him that is shut up and left in Israel."

Remember the case of Jeroboam? "I will cut off from Jeroboam him that pisseth against the wall." It was done. And not only was the man that did it cut off, but everybody else.

The same with the house of Baasha: everybody was exterminated, kinsfolks, friends, and all, leaving "not one that pisseth against a wall."

In the case of Jeroboam you have a striking instance of the Deity's custom of not limiting his punishments to the guilty; the innocent are included. Even the "remnant" of that unhappy house was removed, even "as a man taketh away dung, till it be all gone." That includes the women, the young maids, and the little girls. All innocent, for they couldn't piss against a wall. Nobody of that sex can. None but members of the other sex can achieve that feat.

A curious prejudice. And it still exists. Protestant parents still keep the Bible handy in the house, so that the children can study it, and one of the first things the little boys and girls learn is to be righteous and holy and not piss against the wall. . . .(Clemens pauses and looks around to see if everyone is paying attention and notices that the tomb-silent audience is indeed all ears.)

CLEMENS (impatiently: So, don't make your Father angry because He may punish you and your whole nation without pity. He proved it many times.

Note this passage from Second Kings 19:35: "And it came to pass that night, that the angel of the LORD went out, and smote in the camp of the Assyrians an hundred fourscore and five thousand: and when they arose early in the morning, behold, they were all dead corpses.")

Or this one from Jeremiah 50:21–22: "^{21}Go up against the land of Merathaim, even against it, and against the inhabitants of Pekod: waste and utterly destroy after them, saith the LORD, and do according to all that I have commanded thee

^{22}A sound of battle is in the land, and of great destruction."

Or this from First Samuel 15:2–3: "This is what the LORD Almighty says: 'I will punish the Amalekites for what they did to Israel when they waylaid them as they came up from Egypt. Now go, attack the Amalekites and totally destroy all that belongs to them. Do not spare them; put to death men and women, children and infants, cattle and sheep, camels and donkeys."'

To prove that He is not discriminating against any of his children, God surprised the Jews by commanding the poor Muslim, who like his Jewish brother is a peaceful man and doesn't want to commit murder (unless he has no choice), to slaughter the Jewish man again and again, wherever he is found. For example, God led the Prophet Muhammad to the massacre of Banu Qurayza where he slaughtered the Jews according to Allah's word as recorded in the Quran 8:17:

"It is not ye who slew them; it was Allah; when thou threwest a handful of dust, it was not Thy act, but Allah's. . . ." Yusuf Ali writes in his translation of the Tafsir (interpretation) for Sura Al-Ahzaab (chapter 33, The Clans, "The men of the Quraiza were slain; the women were sold as captives of war; and their lands and properties were distributed or divided among the Muhajirs."

If you are a thinker, you may dare to ask the question: Are there different deities who compete in death games playing with people's lives, or is there only one God who commands His children to kill each other?

If there is more than one, why don't *they* eliminate one another instead of slaughtering billions of humans? Do they enjoy the butchery so much that their wars will cause the complete extinction of mankind?

And these examples are only a small fraction of the ongoing carnage.

And on top of that, here come Christians following their own (newly born) Son of God who saves *only* the Christians and sends everyone else by the billions straight to Hell. Well, he does allow exceptions. As Romans 1:16 states, "¹⁶For I am not ashamed of the gospel of Christ: for it is the power of God unto salvation to every one that believeth; to the Jew first, and also to the Greek." Note that particular order. You would believe that God had proved once again judicious were it not for the postscript in Romans 2:28–29: "²⁸For he is not a Jew,

which is one outwardly; neither is that circumcision, which is
outward in the flesh:

²⁹But he is a Jew, which is one inwardly; and circumcision
is that of the heart, in the spirit, and not in the letter; whose
praise is not of men, but of God. . . ."

Given only the conflict between the Arabs and the Jews,
you may scratch your head and mull over the query: how
many gods are there? Could Allah be the same God as Yahweh? What about the rest of the gods? Where did they vanish?

Where are the Sumerian, the Babylonian, the Norse, the
Greek, the Roman, the Celtic, the Chinese, the Hindu, the
Polynesian, the Celtic, the Aztec, the Slavic, the Thracian, the
Gaeto-Dacian, or thousands of other gods spreading over one
hundred and ninety-four nations of the world? If there were
so many in the past, why is only *one* God on trial? Don't you
find this absurd? Is this a strategy for God to protect himself
from his own obliteration?

Win this case against Him, abandon Him, and another will
rise up and take His place.

The people who are born on planet Earth, instead of uniting and respecting the principle of life, play God and unceas-
ingly blow themselves and their children up. Is this a deep-
rooted idiocy or not? Do you blame the dummy and the idiot
who listen to voices in their heads or the nonidiot whose
voice of reason doesn't reach the ears of those who are unwilling to hear?

Still confused? Do you need to hear the voice of the Scripture God *yourself* to be convinced that He is the lord of polyg-
amy, rape, murder, pillage, animal slaughter, baby killing,
child molestation, and national genocide? Very well, here it is
again, this time from Ezekiel 9:5–7:

Then I heard the Lord say to the other men, "Follow [the
man dressed in linen] through the city and kill everyone
whose forehead is not marked. Show no mercy; have no pity!
Kill them all—old and young, girls and women and little children. But do not touch anyone with the mark. Begin your task

right here at the Temple." So they began by killing the seventy leaders. "Defile the Temple!" the Lord commanded. "Fill its courtyards with the bodies of those you kill! Go!" So they went and began killing throughout the city. And more, this time from Isaiah 13:15–18:

Anyone who is captured will be cut down—run through with a sword. Their little children will be dashed to death right before their eyes. Their homes will be sacked and their wives will be raped [by the attacking hordes]. Look, I will stir up the Medes against Babylon. They cannot be tempted by silver or bribed with gold. The attacking armies will shoot down the young men with arrows. They will have no mercy on helpless babies and will show no compassion for children.

Leviticus 26:21–22 shows that God's vengeance extends not only to the enemies of His chosen people but to the Hebrews themselves:

If even then you remain hostile toward me and refuse to obey me, I will inflict disaster on you seven times over for your sins. I will release wild animals that will rob you of your children and destroy your livestock. Your numbers will dwindle, and your roads will be deserted.

Exodus 23:23 states: "My angel will go before you and bring you to the Amorites, Hittites, Perizzites, Canaanites, Hivites, and Jebusites; and I will wipe them out."

In Ezekiel 35:7–9, God again threatens the Hebrews:

I will make Mount Seir utterly desolate, killing off all who try to escape and any who return. I will fill your mountains with the dead. Your hills, your valleys, and your ravines will be filled with people slaughtered by the sword. I will make you desolate forever. Your cities will never be rebuilt. Then you will know that I am the LORD.

And more, this time from Jeremiah 15:1–4:

And if they say to you, 'But where can we go?' tell them, "This is what the LORD says:

'Those who are destined for death, to death;
those who are destined for war, to war;
those who are destined for famine, to famine;

those who are destined for captivity, to captivity.'

"I will send four kinds of destroyers against them," says the LORD. "I will send the sword to kill, the dogs to drag away, the vultures to devour, and the wild animals to finish up what is left. Because of the wicked things Manasseh son of Hezekiah, king of Judah, did in Jerusalem, I will make my people an object of horror to all the kingdoms of the earth."

And last, from Joshua 6:20–21:

When the people heard the sound of the rams' horns, they shouted as loud as they could. Suddenly, the walls of Jericho collapsed, and the Israelites charged straight into the city from every side and captured it. They completely destroyed everything in it with their swords—men and women, young and old, cattle, sheep, goats, and donkeys.

The Testimony of Truth, one of thirteen ancient Gnostic codices from the Nag Hammadi Library, comments on God's behavior in the Book of Genesis as follows:

But what sort is this God? First he maliciously refused Adam from eating of the tree of knowledge, and, secondly, he said "Adam, where are you?" God does not have foreknowledge? Would he not know from the beginning? And afterwards, he said, "Let us cast him out of this place, lest he eat of the tree of life and live forever." Surely, he has shown himself to be a malicious grudger! And what kind of God is this? For great is the blindness of those who read, and they did not know him. And he said, "I am the jealous God; I will bring the sins of the fathers upon the children until three (and) four generations." And he said, "I will make their heart thick, and I will cause their mind to become blind, that they might not know nor comprehend the things that are said." But these things he has said to those who believe in him and serve him!

I would like to end it by reading the last letter, number eleven, from *Letters from the Earth,* which completes my testimony:

Human history in all ages is red with blood, and bitter with hate, and stained with cruelties; but not since Biblical times have these features been without a limit of some kind. Even the Church, which is credited with having spilt more innocent blood, since the beginning of its supremacy, than all the political wars put together have spilt, has observed a limit. A sort of limit. But you notice that when the Lord God of Heaven and Earth, adored Father of Man, goes to war, there is no limit. He is totally without mercy—he, who is called the Fountain of Mercy. He slays, slays, slays! All the men, all the beasts, all the boys, all the babies; also all the women and all the girls, except those that have not been deflowered.

He makes no distinction between innocent and guilty. The babies were innocent, the beasts were innocent, many of the men, many of the women, many of the boys, many of the girls were innocent, yet they had to suffer with the guilty. What the insane Father required was blood and misery; he was indifferent as to who furnished it.

The heaviest punishment of all was meted out to persons who could not by any possibility have deserved so horrible a fate—the 32,000 virgins. Their naked privacies were probed, to make sure that they still possessed the hymen unruptured; after this humiliation they were sent away from the land that had been their home, to be sold into slavery; the worst of slaveries and the shamefulest, the slavery of prostitution; bed-slavery, to excite lust, and satisfy it with their bodies; slavery to any buyer, be he gentleman or be he a coarse and filthy ruffian.

It was the Father that inflicted this ferocious and undeserved punishment upon those bereaved and friendless virgins, whose parents and kindred he had slaughtered before their eyes. And were they praying to him for pity and rescue, meantime? Without a doubt of it.

These virgins were "spoil" plunder, booty. He claimed his share and got it. What use had *he* for virgins? Examine his later history and you will know.

His priests got a share of the virgins, too. What use could priests make of virgins? The private history of the Roman Catholic confessional can answer that question for you. The confessional's chief amusement has been seduction—in all the ages of the Church.

Père Hyacinth testifies that of a hundred priests confessed by him, ninety-nine had used the confessional effectively for the seduction of married women and young girls. One priest confessed that of nine hundred girls and women whom he had served as father and confessor in his time, none had escaped his lecherous embrace but [t]he elderly and the homely. The official list of questions which the priest is required to ask will [overmastering]ly excite any woman who is not a paralytic.

There is nothing in either savage or civilized history that is more utterly complete, more remorselessly sweeping than the Father of Mercy's campaign among the Midianites. The official report does not furnish the incidents, episodes, and minor details, it deals only in information in masses: *all* the virgins, *all* the   men, *all* the   babies, *all* "creatures *that breathe*," *all* houses, *all* cities; it gives you just one vast picture, spread abroad here and there and yonder, as far as eye can reach, of charred ruin and storm-swept desolation; your imagination adds a brooding stillness, an awful hush—the hush of death. But of course there were incidents. Where shall we get them?

Out of history of yesterday's date. Out of history made by the red Indian of America. He has duplicated God's work, and done it in the very spirit of God. In 1862 the Indians in Minnesota, having been deeply wronged and treacherously treated by the government of the United States, rose against the white settlers and massacred them; massacred all they could lay their hands upon, sparing neither age nor sex. Consider this incident:

Twelve Indians broke into a farmhouse at daybreak and captured the family. It consisted of the farmer and his wife and four daughters, the youngest aged fourteen and the eldest eighteen. They crucified the parents; that is to say, they stood them stark naked against the wall of the living room and nailed their hands to the wall. Then they stripped the daughters bare, stretched them upon the floor in front of their parents, and repeatedly ravished them. Finally they crucified the girls against the wall opposite their parents, and cut off their noses and their breasts. They also—but I will not go into that. There is a limit. There are indignities so atrocious that the pen cannot write them. One member of that poor crucified family—the father—was still alive when help came two days later.

Now you have one incident of the Minnesota massacre. I could give you fifty. They would cover all the different kinds of cruelty the brutal human talent has ever invented.

And now you know, by these sure indications, what happened under the personal direction of the Father of Mercies in his Midianite campaign. The Minnesota campaign was merely a duplicate of the Midianite raid. Nothing happened in the one that didn't happen in the other.

No, that is not strictly true. The Indian was more merciful than was the Father of Mercies. He sold no virgins into slavery to minister to the lusts of the murderers of their kindred while their sad lives might last; he raped them, then charitably made their subsequent sufferings brief, ending them with the precious gift of death. He burned some of the houses, but not all of them. He carried out innocent dumb brutes, but he took the lives of none.

Would you expect this same conscienceless God, this moral bankrupt, to become a teacher of morals; of gentleness; of meekness; of righteousness; of purity? It looks impossible, extravagant; but listen to him. These are his own words:

Blessed are the poor in spirit, for theirs is the kingdom of heaven.

Blessed are they that mourn, for they shall be comforted.

Blessed are the meek, for they shall inherit the earth.

Blessed are they which do hunger and thirst after righteousness, for they shall be filled.

Blessed are the merciful, for they shall obtain mercy.

Blessed are the pure in heart, for they shall see God.

Blessed are the peacemakers, for they shall be called the children of God.

Blessed are they which are persecuted for righteousness' sake, for theirs is the kingdom of heaven.

Blessed are ye, when men shall revile you, and persecute you, and say all manner of evil against you falsely, for my sake.

The mouth that uttered these immense sarcasms, these giant hypocrisies, is the very same that ordered the wholesale massacre of the Midianitish men and babies and cattle; the wholesale destruction of house and city; the wholesale banishment of the virgins into a filthy and unspeakable slavery. This is the same person who brought upon the Midianites the fiendish cruelties which were repeated by the red Indians, detail by detail, in Minnesota eighteen centuries later. The Midianite episode filled him with joy. So did the Minnesota one, or he would have prevented it.

The Beatitudes and the quoted chapters from Numbers and Deuteronomy ought always to be read from the pulpit together; then the congregation would get an all-round view of Our Father in Heaven. Yet not in a single instance have I ever known a clergyman to do this.

To Mr. Plato's question: Why do I think that those holy books are the main motif for atheism, that, ladies and gentlemen, is my answer, which completes my testimony against the atrocities of the so-called God. Thank you. Are there any other questions?"

PLATO: No more questions, Your Honor.

JUDGE (to Lucifer): Would you like to cross-examine the witness?

SATAN: No; his testimony suits me perfectly, thank you.

JUDGE: Thank you, Mr. Clemens; you may.....

When they looked at where Mark Twain was standing, he was already gone.

CHAPTER 20
THE SPIRIT OF MUHAMMAD

LUCIFER (walking majestically to the center of the court and breaking the silence following Samuel Clemens's testimony): Ladies and gentlemen, you probably wonder why God hasn't taken the stand yet, to speak in His own defense. After all, He *is* the accused. Why hasn't anyone of us called God to the stand? Does anyone know why? What about you, Augustinus?

SAINT AUGUSTINE: I know why, Satan.

SATAN: Well?

SAINT AUGUSTINE: "*Hic est Jesus filius eius.*"

SATAN (cupping his ear with his hand): Who?

SAINT AUGUSTINE: Jesus! Jesus of Nazareth; Jesus *is* God incarnate. He is already on the stand.

SATAN: Does everyone agree with this statement? What about you, Muhammad? Where is Muhammad, the Muslim prophet? Let's hear his opinion; it might be a bit different. (Turns and stands on tiptoe looking over the audience) Your Honor, ladies and gentlemen, I call the Prophet Muhammad to the witness stand.

Hearing instantaneous applause and hollers from a great distance, the audience pricked their ears, soon realizing that the noise could only come from one place surrounded by billions of galaxies—Earth. Some Imam has carried the revelation that their Prophet was summoned to appear as witness in a final trial of Allah. No restriction from Heaven or Hell could have stopped the cries and shouts except a command of the Prophet himself or a sign from Allah.

But just as quick, the entire audience realized that the judge did not regard the random chaos as disorderly conduct but as a sincere manifestation of the spirit of the Muslim people albeit from a different dimension.

But behold! Billions of Muslims who were told of the news about Mohammad—peace be upon him (*sallallaahu 'alayhi wa sallam*), spontaneously showed their solidarity agitating their souls, making themselves heard regardless of consequences, demonstrating their passionate, avid belief—*faith.* They had to stand out; their spirits broke loose, celebrating the call of their Prophet Mohammad. Their turbulence increased alarmingly from a muffled buzzing that sounded like a daily prayer to a nearer and much louder bellowing, giving the sensation that the sounds were coming from outer limits, leaping from a bygone era beyond space and time at the speed of thought. Some people more sensitive to that kind of hullabaloo placed their hands over their ears as if to protect their eardrums from bursting.

Only a Muslim can fully understand what this transcendence meant because only a true Muslim can transpose into this state of a heavenly phantasm with so much love and tranquility and so much . . . peace—*peace* is the word. What an uplifting spiritual glorification they must have felt just at the mention of their prophet Muhammad's name. But wait. . . .

When they heard the Christians call Jesus "God incarnate," they expressed their disagreement with what they regarded as a foolhardy statement showing disrespect to them. Their mirth turned into revulsion and they became so agitated that they were now cursing and burning flags and spitting fire.

Billions of souls snorted acid words, spewed demeaning verses against the Christians and the Jews sputtering into their beards as they badmouthed this Jew rabbi who started all that New Testament nonsense and was now back again spoken of as if He were better than their Muhammad. All of them seemed suddenly ready to kill themselves and come to Heaven for a mass protest even if they had to do it the fanatic way and blow themselves up, just to prove that Isa, as they called Jesus, was not the Son of God, much less God incarnate.

Above everything, their Allah was not Yahweh and Jesus was only a prophet *beneath* the Prophet Muhammad since Muhammad was called Ahmad, meaning "more praiseworthy," lionized and celebrated as the "Seal of the Prophets," which meant that he was *above* all others—since he was the last prophet.

Taken by surprise, since never before had Heaven had been disturbed in such a manner, the bailiff called loud enough to echo in the Muslims' thoughts, Muhammad to the witness stand!

A strange silence rapidly fell on the entire courtroom, sealed as tight as a virgin gate that one could have heard a needle drop somewhere in a far, forgotten world.

A scarf like a magic carpet slowly emerged, floating through the aisles and past the audience until all recognized it as a man's head wrapped in a *ghutra*, a red-and-white-checked cloth held in place by a double black cord that the Saudis call an *igal*. It was none other than the Prophet Muhammad himself.

He flaunted before everyone's adapting eyes, a splendor of spiritual manifestation, effusively materializing to his full grandiose height. He looked handsome as always, physically unaffected by the passing ages, his striking face half-concealed under his fashionable black beard, worn not only for reputation, recognition, piety and manhood, but for honor and worship.

All Muslim men had copied his facial hair, yet not one had come even close to the magnificence of Muhammad's astonishing plant, a monumental trademark established in the minds of all Muslims.

His penetrating eyes were like burning coal, revealing much more intelligence than in the past since now he was a bit older in mind although an adolescent in appearance, his soul having adjusted to the new time zone and heavenly atmosphere.

Muhammad wore the traditional Saudi *thobe*, a loose, ankle-length garment made of the finest wool over which he displayed a white *bisht*, a cloak trimmed in twenty-four-karat gold that complemented his handmade sandals. Everyone seemed breathless at the sight of him; even Lucifer was gaping in pure admiration.

Stopping a few feet before the judge, Muhammad said in flawless Arabic, "أنا النبي محمد صلى الله عليه لي."

JUDGE: Speak so that everyone can understand you, please.

MUHAMMAD: Allah is great. I was just saying, "I am the Prophet Muhammad, peace be upon me."

(The bailiff hands him the Holy Bible and asks him to put his hand on it.)

MUHAMMAD: If you give me a book, it should be the Quran, not the Bible. I don't believe in the Bible.

JUDGE: Do you want the Quran?

MUHAMMAD: No, Your Honor, I have the Quran inside me, word for word, as I have Allah inside me. I just said that *if* you give me—"

JUDGE (to Lucifer): You may proceed.

SATAN (taking a few steps toward the prophet and looking him straight in the eye: Do you know why I called you here today?

MUHAMMAD: I suppose that you intend to question me about Allah.

SATAN (motioning toward Jesus but glancing furtively over the audience to feel its spirit): Do you recognize the man right before us?

(From Earth, the scene looked like a shimmering blanket of stardust. And since this tremendous vastness stretched beyond the physical universe to the point where matter ended, antimatter completed the unseen, or the invisible. The emptiness of space was brimming with thought and reflection as much as with senselessness and languor. Billions of human minds expanded within and without, from the most virtuous to the most negligible.

No one spoke since everyone was waiting for Muhammad to answer Lucifer's question. Muhammad was in everyone's mind and on their retina. All they saw was Muhammad. All they heard was Muhammad.)

MUHAMMAD: Do I recognize that man? Yes, I see the prophet Isa, the Jewish rabbi; may peace be upon him.

SATAN: Is Isa the Son of God, Muhammad?

PLATO: Objection, Your Honor. The prophet Muhammad is a Muslim, and his religion denies the principles of Christian doctrine. Satan's question prompts a dispute.

SATAN: My question seeks the witness's honest opinion, regardless of previous religious stances.

JUDGE: Overruled! You may answer the question, Muhammad.

MUHAMMAD: Isa is a Son of God.

SATAN: *A* Son of God or *the* Son of God?

MUHAMMAD: He is *a* Son of God just like the others next to him and like me. *I* am Allah's chosen son." (Raises his chin and his eyes focus fix a distant point. Wailing chants arise from the Muslims. Muhammad thunders a few words in Arabic and the commotion turns to a murmur.)

SATAN (grinning): Can you explain your statement?

MUHAMMAD: I will give you examples from the Christian Bible first, to show you that it's been customary for God to call all nations His sons:

"Genesis 6:4 states, "There were giants in the earth in those days, and also afterward, when the *sons of God* came in to the daughters of men. . . ." A later passage, Job 1:6, states, "There came a day when the *sons of God* came to present themselves before the LORD. . . .""

SATAN: Do you believe that the God of the Bible or Bible God is the same entity with our today's accused God and with Allah?

MUHAMMAD: Don't all the sacred books have the same personages like you and Adam and Jesus?

SATAN: And the answer to my question is. . . ?"

MUHAMMAD: "I believe that, if the stories in the Bible, both the Tanakh and the New Testament, no matter how contradictory, are part of God's biography; they represent God the Creator and, therefore, they must be revelations from that celestial God, the very one who is on trial here today."

SATAN: You haven't mentioned the God of the Quran, Allah. Is Allah the same being as the Judeo-Christian God?"

MUHAMMAD: There's only one Creator, God; we Muslims call Him Allah. But the true revelation is the last one, recorded in the Quran. Allah revealed it to me via the angel Jibreel, or Gabriel, as you call him. It is the richest, the clearest, the purest, and the most complete, the only peaceful and loving revelation. The Holy Quran is the true word of God, and because Allah is without error, the Quran is without error.

SATAN: Can you see Allah in this court? And if yes, can you please point Him out to us?

MUHAMMAD: I see the light of Allah above all of us, including Jesus, which means that Jesus is not the one with Allah or God; Jesus is distinctly isolated.

SAINT AUGUSTINE: God is omnipresent, which means that He is standing in Jesus' place as well as being everywhere else."

MUHAMMAD: "But Jesus is not God or the only begotten Son of God. When did ever Jesus of Nazareth call himself the Son of God? He always referred to himself as the Son of man. He is *a* son of God like Adam, Abraham, you, me, and all humankind. We are all his children; the children of God are everything in His creation.

SATAN (facetiously, pointing to himself): And like me."

MUHAMMAD: Precisely. Allah created you and, therefore, you are his son. But, I'll make an amendment so that we can all understand the proper meaning of relationship: The New Testament refers to Jesus not as the Son of God but as a *servant* of God.

SATAN: Can you give the jury examples?

MUHAMMAD: Yes. See Acts 3:13, which states: "The God of Abraham, and of Isaac, and of Jacob, the God of our fathers, hath glorified his Son Jesus; whom ye delivered up, and denied him in the presence of Pilate, when he was determined to let him go."

SATAN: But if we refer to the books, let's take Acts 3:26, which says, "Unto you first God, having raised up *His Son Jesus,* sent him to bless you. . . ." Is that right?

MUHAMMAD: No. The Arabic word for "slave of" or "servant of" is *abd*. In Hebrew, it's *ebed*. The translators of the King James Bible, which you quoted, purposely altered the meaning to fit the tenets of Christianity. The New King James Bible translates it as "servant." In that version, Acts 3:26 reads: "When God raised up his servant [Jesus], he sent him first to you to bless you by turning each of you from your wicked ways."

SATAN: Can you give the jury another example?

MUHAMMAD: Yes, Let's take Matthew 12:18 from the King James version, which reads: "Behold my *servant,* whom I have chosen." Note that he used the word *servant,* not *son.*

SATAN: Is the Bible to be taken literally or not?

MUHAMMAD: "The Bible is not forthright as is the Quran; it is kabalistic, encrypted, hidden in the open verses. It was meant to be interpreted, and the interpretation depends on the reader and his purpose. That's why you have so many Christian sects and denominations—over four hundred of them—each one with its own version of the Bible, each inconsistent with every other. They look down on one another and call each other's beliefs: false or mistaken.

SATAN: What does God Himself say about all this?

MUHAMMAD: Let's analyze the word of God according to Isaiah 43:10, King James Version: "Ye are my witnesses, saith the LORD, and my servant whom I have chosen: that ye may know and believe me, and understand that I am he: before me there was no God formed, neither shall there be after me."

Therefore, Jesus cannot be God. And Isaiah 43:11 adds, "I, even I, am the LORD; and beside me there is no saviour." Therefore, Jesus cannot be the savior.

It is unfair to give humanity a puzzle, a fabrication of God's revelation. The New Testament was purposely written to deceive the Gentiles while giving them a religion based on the teachings of a Jewish rabbi who [13]couldn't be Christian if He returned to them a thousand times over. They gave to pagans a Jewish king to control them spiritually. The Gentiles (we call them infidels) accepted it blindly, on *faith*. The Christians will believe anything as long as there's a promise of an afterlife.

SATAN: The Quran promises an afterlife, too, doesn't it?

MUHAMMAD: The Quran promises its believers the afterlife that Allah promised; the infidel outside Islam will not see the Kingdom of Heaven.

SAINT AUGUSTINE: I am in the Kingdom of Heaven, and in your view, I'm an infidel since I am not a Muslim. Jesus is not Muslim, and He's in Heaven, isn't He?"

MUHAMMAD: I'm not so sure. I haven't seen either of you in my Heaven; you must belong to another realm.

SATAN (looking amused): "How about the use of the word *Father* when referring to God? Doesn't that imply a Son, specifically Jesus?"

---

[13] If Jesus came back to Earth, there is one thing he wouldn't be; a Christian-Mark Twain

MUHAMMAD: Since the word *Father* is commonly used, Jesus called God *Father,* but called Himself "the Son of man," which indicated his mud origin. He was a mortal man who died like any other mortal.

God had no wife and no son. Allah through the Quran chapter seventy-two, verse three as translated by Abdullah Yusuf Ali says, "And Exalted is the Majesty of our Lord: He has taken neither a wife nor a son." Mohammed Marmaduke Pickthall's translation says: "And (we believe) that He— exalted be the glory of our Lord!—hath taken neither wife nor son." Muhammad Habib Shakir's translation of the same passage says, "And that He— exalted be the majesty of our Lord—has not taken a consort, nor a son."

Chapter six, verse 101 makes the same point. Yusuf Ali's translation reads, "To Him is due the primal origin of the heavens and the earth: How can He have a son when He hath no consort? He created all things, and He hath full knowledge of all things." Pickthall's reads: "The Originator of the heavens and the earth! How can He have a child, when there is for Him no consort, when He created all things and is Aware of all things?" Shakir's reads: "Wonderful Originator of the heavens and the earth! How could He have a son when He has no consort, and He (Himself) created everything, and He is the Knower of all things."

According to a version called *The Noble Qur'an,* Allah Almighty said in chapter 21, verse 26, "And they [the Jews] say: '(God) Most Gracious has begotten offspring.' Glory to Him! They are (but) servants raised to honour."

SATAN: Do you blame Allah for all the evil in the world?

MUHAMMAD: No!

SATAN: Do you blame Yahweh?

MUHAMMAD: Yes!

SATAN: Aren't they the same God?

MUHAMMAD: Yes and no.

SATAN: Explain.

MUHAMMAD: The Jews call our Allah, Yahweh, and their scriptures are distorted revelations. For the purpose of this trial I will call God's Conscience, Allah.

SATAN: Thank you. No more questions, Your Honor.

CHAPTER
21
OF ISLAM AND HONOR KILLINGS

[14]"The idea of the sacred is quite simply one of the most conservative notions in any culture, because it seeks to turn other ideas -- uncertainty, progress, change -- into crimes."

PLATO (rises, sighs, and turns to face Muhammad): Muhammad, you say that you call God's conscience Allah?
MUHAMMAD: I do.
PLATO: Very well. (Exhales slowly and resumes.) Did Allah ever demand or permit that your women should be mistreated?
MUHAMMAD: Of course not.
PLATO: Are you sure?
MUHAMMAD: As certain as I sit here before you.
PLATO: Does the Quran represent the Word of Allah?
MUHAMMAD: Absolutely.

---

[14] Salman Rushdie

PLATO: Absolutely. Is it safe to say that the Quran is therefore inerrant?

MUHAMMAD: Yes. The Quran *is* inerrant.

PLATO: Did Allah exist before He revealed His words to you?

MUHAMMAD: Yes, of course, how otherwise—?"

PLATO: Ladies and gentlemen of the jury, here is a passage from the Quran 16:58–59 referring to the birth of baby girls whom their Arab parents were ashamed of having:

[15]When news is brought to one of them, of (the birth of) a female (child), his face darkens, and he is filled with inward grief! With shame does he hide himself from his people, because of the bad news he has had! Shall he keep this [child] despite the contempt [which he feels for it]—or shall he bury it in the dust? Oh, evil indeed is whatever they decide!

As the passage indicates, the Arabs considered having little girls disgraceful. In *Nahju 'l-Balāgha* or *The Path of Eloquence*, sermon 26, the Imam Ali ibn Abi Talib commented about those days before the Arabs adopted Islam:

You people of Arabia followed the worst religion; you dwelt amongst rough stones and poisonous serpents. You drank putrid water and ate filthy food. You shed the blood of one another and paid no heed to relationships. Idols are established among you, and sins cling to you.

Another quotation from The Day the Prophet Wept states. "There were many Arabs who preferred their sons to their daughters." As soon as a girl was born, the Arabs buried her alive."

(Plato pauses again, his eyes scanning the shocked audience): I ask Muhammad, where was Allah or God's Conscience, whose existence preceded the Quran, when those repetitive murders happened? Ladies and gentlemen, please hear this story, which came to me by word of mouth, while

---

[15] A Great Friend of Children by M.S. Kayani. Published by *The Islamic Foundation*, 1981.

you, Muhammad, please tell us all if what I'm about to narrate is a legend or indeed did happen to you in reality:

[16]Before this man became a Muslim, he had fathered a daughter as sweet as angel who kissed him and hugged him, just as most girls do when they show their love for their fathers. Whenever her father called, this little girl came running and laughing toward him.

One day, her father called and she came running happily to his side. He grabbed her little hand as she looked up to him laughing while he took her for a long walk. She hummed and hopped beside him as they went along.

As they came to a well, without warning, he threw her in. Terrified, the little girl screamed, "Daddy, oh, Daddy, please!"

Her father refused to listen to her pleas. Instead, he flung dirt into the well to bury her alive and left her to die.

Full of remorse and guilt for the dreadful murder he had committed, the father had to face his conscience for the rest of his life.

Obviously, the Prophet was appalled when the father confessed his story. He wept so much that his beard became soaked with tears."

(Plato sighs deeply and looks at Muhammad, who is weeping like a child.)

PLATO (coming close to the Prophet and patting him on his shoulder): I know my friend, I know. . . .(Bends over and speaks softly) You'll have to tell your people to stop. You have a good heart. They will listen to you.

(Muhammad nods and thanks him inaudibly, wiping his eyes with the back of his hand.)

PLATO: Would it be possible for a person to commit this kind of crime if religion was not assertively interfering with his moral principles, assuming that he *has* such principles?

---

[16] A Great Friend of Children by M.S. Kayani.

MUHAMMAD: It happened when God was sleeping. God's Conscience gave us the Quran, but it was too late. . . .

PLATO: Are you aware of the thousands of killings committed in the name of Allah every year all over the world?

MUHAMMAD: Yes, I am.

PLATO: Are you aware of the suicide bombers, including children and young women who are brainwashed by being ordered to die for the cause of Allah every year?"

MUHAMMAD (nodding): Yes, I am."

PLATO: Do you blame a sleeping God for these events?

MUHAMMAD: I cannot blame a God who's not awake to defend Himself. I can only thank His conscience, who gave us the Quran.

PLATO: Do the Muslims dutifully obey the Quran, which is to say Allah's word?

MUHAMMAD: Absolutely!

PLATO: All of them?

MUHAMMAD: Undeniably; all of them.

PLATO: "Since I'm permitted leading questions, may I ask the following?

If Allah never commanded nor permitted women to be mistreated or wronged, as you've affirmed, why do your Muslim followers treat their women as their property, no better than slaves, cultivating no respect for them despite enjoying their dowry as the old-fashioned custom allows? I quote Pickthall's translation of chapter 2, verse 228: "And they (women) have rights similar to those (of men) over them in kindness, and men are a degree above them. Allah is Mighty, Wise." Unquote; why are the men above the women?

MUHAMMAD: It was the word of Allah. Man was made first, then woman.

PLATO: Why do the Muslim men beat their women repeatedly whenever they suspect they've done something that the men consider wrong, such as giving directions to a male traveler in the city or daring to look into another man's eyes? Why do they slash women's faces if the women wear makeup? Why do the Muslim men beat their girls for insisting to attend school and wanting to get an education? Why do they force them to wear burqas?

Why do Muslim men treat their women as meat for their own physical gratification?

Again I quote, this time from chapter 2, verse 223, in Pickthall's translation: "Your women are a tilth for you (to cultivate) so go to your tilth as ye will, and send (good deeds) before you for your souls, and fear Allah, and know that ye will (one day) meet Him. Give glad tidings to believers, (O Muhammad)."

MUHAMMAD: The verse was not meant to confirm your accusations.

PLATO: But those are not accusations, Muhammad, but questions linked to the Quran, which provides tutoring for the unlearned. And the majority of the people in the audience are not knowledgeable about Islam or the Quran although they are in Heaven, you see. Besides, I would like you to answer some more questions for the benefit of the jury. For example, why don't Muslim men trust their women rather than chastise them? Is it that they do not trust or cannot control their own urges, perhaps?

MUHAMMAD: They are no different from the men in other parts of the world who could easily be provoked by a woman's attractiveness.

PLATO: Don't you think that women should be equal to their men, rather than men being a degree above them?

MUHAMMAD: Allah knows better. I think that by questioning these mandates, we are questioning Allah's Word; and I am not in a position to go beyond what He revealed to me."

PLATO: Don't you think that your women should enjoy the same rights and education as your men and have the same chance to express themselves freely and select their own ways of living without fear of harassment or punishment just as women in free societies do? In short, shouldn't you allow them to step outside the primitive epoch of the Iron Age, thus washing the stains from the history of Islam?

MUHAMMAD: Allah knows better."

PLATO: "Should a woman be stoned to death if she desires to love someone of her choosing and marry whomever she likes, even if the person is an infidel and not the husband pre-selected by her father when she was a baby? I quote from a *hadith* or companion volume to the Quran, *Sahih Muslim*, chapter 17, verse 4194: "According to Umar, the companion of Muhammad and Islam's second caliph, sent down the Book upon him [upon you, Muhammad], and the verse [about] stoning was included in what was sent down to him.' Umar went on to insist that "stoning is a duty laid down in Allah's Book for married men and women who commit adultery when proof is established, or [in case] there is pregnancy, or a confession."

MUHAMMAD: If Allah said it, Allah knows better than we do.

PLATO: Don't your women represent the mothers of your own nation?

MUHAMMAD: You are right and my heart aches for them since the Quran that I left for my people to follow had only virtue, decency, and love in it; it is not the erroneous, bastard-ized alteration invented by the mind of man after my death. My followers learned it by ear and recited it from memory as I taught it to them; that's why it is called Quran, which means "recitation." Allow me to explain.

One day, during the month of Ramadan, I received the word of Allah from the angel Jibreel. What a revelation. I had not learned the art of letters or reading as you understand it. –In fact, most of Europe's kings at that time boasted that they lacked that skill as reading was an embarrassment and a bur-den for a person of royal blood. But once I felt the angel's touch, I became *literate*—and I'm glad to set this record straight once and forever, now that I'm here in Heaven before Allah and the heavenly court. Jibreel appeared to me and said, "Read!" But I said to the angel, "I cannot read." The angel grabbed me and squeezed me as much as I could bear, and then he said again, "Read!" I repeated, "I cannot read." The angel seized me for a third time and squeezed me, saying, if I may quote the Quran 96:1–, "Read! In the Name of Your Lord, Who has created (all that exists) He has created man from a clot (a piece of thick coagulated blood). Read! And your Lord is the Most Generous, Who has taught (the writing) by the pen, has taught man that which he knew not."

That is the truth. I will give you a few modern translations of chapter 7, verse 157 of the Quran to show you what I mean. The first is translated by Marmaduke Pickthall, a converted Muslim who took the name Mohammed, and it says:

Those who follow the messenger, the Prophet who can neither read nor write, whom they will find described in the Torah and the Gospel (which are) with them. He will enjoin on them that which is right and forbid them that which is wrong. He will make lawful for them all good things and prohibit for them only the foul; and he will relieve them of their burden and the fetters that they used to wear. Then those who believe in him, and [honor] him, and help him, and follow the light which is sent down with him: they are the successful.

The second translation, by Abdullah Yusuf Ali, advises:

Those who follow the messenger, the unlettered Prophet, whom they find mentioned in their own (scriptures,)—in the law and the Gospel;—for he commands them what is just and forbids them what is evil; he allows them as lawful what is good (and pure) and prohibits them from what is bad (and impure); He releases them from their heavy burdens and from the yokes that are upon them. So it is those who believe in him, [honor] him, help him, and follow the light which is sent down with him, it is they who will prosper.

And the last, translated by Mohammed Aqib Qadri, shows you what I mean:

Those who will obey this Noble Messenger, the Herald of the Hidden who is untutored *(except by Allah)*, whom they will find mentioned in the Taurat [Torah] and the Injeel [Gospel] with them; he will command them to do good and forbid them from wrong, and he will make lawful for them the good clean things and prohibit the foul for them, and he will unburden the loads and the neck chains which were upon them; so those who believe in him, and revere him, and help him, and follow the light which came down with him—it is they who have succeeded.

I recited the *suras* or chapters of the Quran to my *Sahaba* (family, descendants, companions, disciples, and scribes) who recorded them on everything—parchments, leaves, tablets, wood, stone, leather, and even bones—before my departure to Heaven in the year 632.

PLATO: Muhammad, I defend God, but I question his conscience, whom you seem to be in favor; I appeal to your integrity and also to your schism in the sense of recognizing that if those customs pertained to the seventh century, we shouldn't practice them in the twenty-first century simply because the world as we know it has evolved. I think we should ask Allah to intervene and *stop* these senseless killings. You symbolize Islam. If Allah commanded you today to reform Islam and rewrite the Quran, would you do it?

MUHAMMAD: I obey Allah regardless of my own wishes. Of course, I would give my people the revised Word of Allah. Absolutely!

PLATO: Muhammad, the need for revision is urgent. Do you know that today, around the world, young girls are slaughtered—hanged, shot, battered to death, or stoned by their own families and relatives for the crime of being in love—as many as ten thousand a year, of which only half are reported to the press? And most of them are not fully-grown; they are still children. Their conception of life is far from mature, so they think and act their age, yet these children are dying for expressing free feelings.

Muhammad, your tears have barely dried since I reminded you of a story that happened more than fourteen hundred years ago. What would be your reaction if I were to tell you that only a few years ago, in 2007, a seventeen-year-old Iraqi girl named Du'a Khalil Aswad, from a minority Kurdish religious group called the Yezidi was stoned to death because she dared to love a Muslim boy from the Sunni sect.

She was condemned to death for immoral conduct by the men in her family and fanatical religious leaders who regarded her murder as an honor killing. Nine men dragged her outside and stoned her for half an hour until she died. Who allowed it to happen, I ask you? The authorities looked the other way. They say that Allah allowed it.

Her death apparently triggered a redressing attack. A group of irate Sunni gunmen, forced twenty-three Yezidi workmen to get off a bus and shot dead.

...

(Scowling, Muhammad shook his head in disagreement, his eyes bulging and his lips tightly compressed. Plato asked the court for time travel live image display and the light dimmed. And there they were: live cinematic images of a series of infamous crimes committed by Muslims in the name of Allah and the prophet Muhammad.

Everyone sat speechless, some gaping in disbelief. Some were looking the other way while others buried their faces in their hands, unable to watch. Many wept.

Suddenly, the images zoom in on a thirteen-year-old Iranian girl trembling with fear and praying to Allah for rescue as tears streams down her face. Moments later, she is running as fast as she can through a yard filled with rubbish, her bare feet bleeding. Though she runs as fast as she possibly can, a group of Muslim men trap her. She struggles to escape and cries to Allah for help. The images skip fast-forward and stop as she is being accused of giving in easily when her own brother, age fifteen, had raped her and left her pregnant. Dispersed moments of the rape are shown. Skips later, she is sentenced to death by stoning, but because she's pregnant she is imprisoned until she gives birth to the baby. Once the baby is born they immediately seize it from her. She screams and pulls her hair in desperation. Images show her brother receiving 150 lashes in conformity with Sharia (Islamic canon law).

Their own father, a devout Muslim, informed the authorities of his children's behavior.

The Heavens watched feebly and did nothing to help as the Muslim men snatches away her newborn baby, drags her into the streets, and throws her into a hole.

She faints but awakes to desperation, crying to Allah to save her and weeping for her baby. (Muhammad watches in anger)

Her father throws the first stone. Instantly, the other men follow his example, pelting her from all directions until she is no more than a butchered body.

Before anyone could breathe, the scene changes to show a baby girl born into a poor family. The parents gather around her, caressing her and kissing her. Camera goes fast-forward showing her playing amid that poverty. Her mother dies in a car wreck. Traumatized, the five-year-old child faces the sky, asking why Allah was taking her mother. Her grieving father, unable or unwilling to care for her, turns to drugs and gives her to her senile grandparents for care. With no parental supervision, she wanders the streets and is shown frequently in trouble with the law. Images fade out.

Sudden images show her at age thirteen, as she is being arrested for "crimes against chastity" accused of sitting in a car with her male cousin. This is Iran and unmarried girls and boys cannot be alone together for any reason.

While in prison, she receives one hundred lashes as further punishment. She is being released, and she walks out psychologically impaired. Everyone in court can see and feel her pain. She looks humiliated and stripped of dignity. All this time, she had prayed to Allah for help, but there was no response.

Images jump and two years later, as she walks alone in the street, she is being stopped by the moral police, a branch of the Islamic Revolutionary Guard whose job is to enforce the Islamic moral code on the streets of Iran, and she's being arrested on the spot for merely looking suspicious. She is thrown in jail. Depictive pictures show how the *moral* police guards dishonor her, mock her, and rape her. Some people in the audience cover their eyes.

Pictures skip forward again; she is being released but she falls prey to a fifty-one-year-old married man. He is married and has his own children. The man rapes her repeatedly. She keeps silent. Days later she is being arrested at her grandparents' house for being a "bad influence" on local schoolgirls.

She ends up in front of the powerful head of the judiciary in her city, Neka, Liberia. Although her family presents evidence that she is only sixteen and therefore exempt from the death penalty, the judge decides, based on her well-developed body, that she must be twenty-two and therefore eligible to face execution by hanging. Her rapist, who claims that she seduced him, received only ninety-five lashes and is getting away.

The girl has the courage to throw off her *hijab* (head scarf), calling the judge a thief of justice, and even tosses her shoe in his face—a gesture of contempt that gained her immortality as a martyr—as he charges her with adultery.

The court witnesses as she is being hanged in a public square. The judge puts the noose around her neck himself.

MUHAMMAD (reacting to the scene): This is not permissible. Allah must be called to condemn these crimes. Oh, my people, what has become of you?

The scene shifts to a city in Iran where a woman is sentenced to death by stoning. Few people are exposed breaking into her house, grabbing and beating her in front of her children. They drag her into the street. The judge's ruling forced her husband and two children to attend the execution. The woman begs her husband to take the children away, but he is not allowed to do so. They must watch in horror.

Her executioners had gouged out her eyes; she escapes from the ditch into which she had been thrown her and starts to run away, but the executioners recapture her and shot her to death as her children cry to Allah for help.

Muhammad's fists were tight, his face red as a boiled lobster as the images roll on.

It continues showing a twenty-five-year-old woman in another Iranian city, being stoned to death. The gathering is wild and doesn't stop. The images never seem to end. She continually prays to Allah as she is being pelted. Allah doesn't answer.

These are live historical moments, not fiction. The images slide to India, where an eighteen-year-old student is shown hanging from a ceiling fan in her house after her father kills her by strangulation. He tells the authorities that he suspected her of going out with her cousin.

Hovering over the world map the nightmare continue in a town in the United Kingdom, showing a Kurdish twenty-one-year-old girl as she is running away from an arranged marriage since she fell in love with another man. Her father a Sunni Muslim and her uncle hired members of the same Kurdish clan to murder her. The clan members catch her, rape her, and her uncle strangles her with a shoelace. They stuff her dishonored body into a suitcase and leave it to rot. Her fiancé a Shiite Muslim is shown hiding. She is shown screaming on Allah for help during the ordeal. It appears that Allah didn't answer.

In Jordan, an eighteen-year-old is shown stabbing his seventeen-year-old divorced sister to death accusing her of "knowing many men." The images skip forward; since the murder was an "honor killing," the authorities cannot condemn him to death.

The year 1970 ghosts above Saudi Arabia where a nineteen-year-old Princess by the name of Misha'il bin Fahd bin Mohammad is shown publicly executed (shot in the head) since Prince Muhammad bin Abdul Aziz, required that she be killed for committing adultery. Hard to watch images show her lover Khaled Mulhallal al-Sha'er, being awkwardly beheaded with a sword. A woman opposed to the execution crying "Even the Prophet tried hard to avoid having a woman stoned when she came to him and admitted committing adultery."

Three men murder forty-four people at a wedding party in Turkey "for reasons of honor." Allah did not protect the victims.

In Italy, a fifty-three-year-old Pakistani immigrant murders his wife when she defends their twenty-year-old daughter for refusing to accept an arranged marriage. Along with his nineteen-year-old son, the man attacks his wife with a wrench, intending to kill her. The son helps his father bludgeon his mother to death, using a rock, and then attacks his sister, who later is shown in the hospital in critical condition. Allah did not intervene to protect the terrified mother and daughter.

The show was dripping blood and cruelty. Muslims in every country behaved as if they lived in a Stone Age. The last images from Italy presented a Pakistani immigrant who, with the help of two male relatives, slit his twenty-year-old daughter's throat and burying her in the garden of the family home with her head facing Mecca. They did it, he said, because she had "dishonored" the family by wearing Western clothes, working in a restaurant, and living with her Italian fiancé rather than accepting an arranged marriage." Allah did not stop the slaughter done in His name.

MUHAMMAD (cupping his face in both hands): Stop this! (His fingers nervously slip under the red-and-white *ghutra*, which falls off, uncovering his head. He clasps his hands behind the nape of his neck before waving his arms frantically and finally clasping his hands together as if in prayer.)

Please, stop showing this carnage! (As if from nowhere, rain starts pouring from the sky all over the Earth, making people screaming and crying as it drenches everyone in blood. Muhammad's voice is heard as it thunders from heavens. The display in the sky fades out and the light returns gradually. Muhammad turns toward the judge, his voice skipping.) It is blasphemy to believe that Allah or my teachings permitted the Muslim men to murder their own wives and children.

(Looks toward Earth and shouts):
"My dear followers,
Where is the honor in being lawless?
Where is the honor in being assassins?
Where is the honor in revealing no love for your own kind?
Where is the honor in your lack of shame?

Where is the honor in your luck of trust?

Where is the honor in that you, the Muslim Nation, behave no better than when I found you, wandering sheepherders lost without Allah.

I ask you, where is the honor in breeding disrespect for the most gracious creature in the world—the woman?

You beat her; you abuse her; you strip her of dignity and human rights; you demean her character; you hurt her feelings; you make her suffer; you give her pain and unhappiness; you poison her heart and empty her eyes of tears; you treat her as a sex object and your private delight; you keep her away from civilization, deny her education, and seize all her freedoms. If she displeases you, you kill her.

You roar at her as if she were a slave; you terrorize her; you patronize her; you dispirit her; you strip her of her own dignity, you dishonor her before your children, and the entire world; you diminish her before the one who created her: Allah.

You think that she has no feelings, that she has no heart and that she has no future unless you grant her one, yet you forget that *she* is the reason that *you* came into this world. She is the one that gives birth. In killing any woman, you symbolically kill your own mother.

Her terrified children are watching you.

The fact is that *you* don't trust yourselves with any women. You are insecure. You are afraid that seeing their forms will unleash your basic animal instinct. You cannot manage your temperament or control your bodily yearnings.

You foam at the corners of your lips and into your unshaved beards when you see a woman's curves and you want to rape her, regardless of who she might be: your daughter, your sister, your brother's wife, your friend's daughter, your wife's sister, or any daughter of God.

Unless her *burka* is so loose that you can't see her figure, you'll attack her and rape her since you know she'll surrender for fear that you'll kill her.

Your lack of education and self-control are your cruelest enemies;

Allah built her in the shape of a goddess for you to love, admire, and protect her superior being and respect her as your other half, not to molest her, shame her, and strip her of her own self.

Allah didn't build the woman so you could destroy her spirit. Allah gave her the spirit not you.

If you had decency, you would trust your women; not keep them on a leash;

If you had dignity, you would make your woman feel proud to stand next to you.

If you had dignity, your woman would show you appreciation and respect, not fear.

If you had dignity, you would set an example for your children by treating their mother, the one who educates the child, with respect and consideration.

It is time that she received freedom from servitude.

It is time that she had the freedom to choose her partner in life.

It is time that you allowed her the same rights that you have and want to have.

It is time that you met her needs and raised her confidence.

It is time that you protected her rights with your life.

It is time that you venerated the mother of your children

When you read in the Quran that Allah has made men a degree above women, understand that this degree refers to *quiwama*, that is, maintenance and protection. Common sense should tell you that most women are physically weaker than most men are; morality should tell you that they need your protection, not abuse. If women were stronger than you, would you then have the courage to challenge their wrights? If they were stronger, would they have abused you? I don't think so. You have become wild and fanatically dangerous. Fanatically I said, dangerous. Stop it before you enter eternal damnation. You wouldn't want me to curse you for if I do, you will be damned forever.

(Muhammad looks toward God's light.) Oh, my Allah! My Allah! What have my people done? In your Name, Allah, the Merciful, the Compassionate, I seek refuge, guidance and salvation for my people. (Prostrates himself and recites [17]the opening chapter of the Quran:)

Praise be to God, Lord of the Universe,
The Gracious, the Merciful,
Master of the Day of Judgment.
You alone we worship;
You alone we implore for help.
Guide us unto the straight path
The path of those whom You have blessed,
Those who have not incurred Your displeasure,
Those who have not gone astray.
Amen!"

---

[17] As translated by Maulana Muhammad Ali

CHAPTER
22
FREE WILL AND DETERMINISM: GOD'S ATTRIBUTES

The Islamic Reformation has to begin here, with an acceptance that all ideas, even sacred ones, must adapt to altered realities. Broad-mindedness is related to tolerance; open-mindedness is the sibling of peace. —Salman Rushdie

PLATO: And yet, God's conscience is a few thousand years late, and for that reason, millions are dead. I apologize for returning to this matter, but I must underscore God's conscience for a purpose.

MUHAMMAD (frowning): I don't understand.

PLATO (quoting): "I am not a man of blood; and God is my witness that in all my wars I have never been the aggressor, and that my enemies have always been the authors of their own calamity." Do you know who spoke those words that I've just quoted?

MUHAMMAD: Ah! It was Timur, the fourteenth-century conqueror, after the sack of Aleppo."

PLATO (shouting): "Aha! Tamerlane! This merciless man lived by the Quran, as a Muslim Turk. He slew hundreds of thousands of innocent people, most of them fellow Muslims:

children, women, and old people, in the name of Islam, right?"

MUHAMMAD: Yes, but he was a *ghazi*, a warrior of Islam."

PLATO: "What an excuse that is. Well, did Allah command him, through the Quran, to kill more than seventy thousand innocent people in Isfahan, Persia, after they surrendered in 1387? Tamerlane had promised them clemency for an easy submission, but, instead, he killed them all. His soldiers constructed at least twenty-eight turrets, each consisting of about fifteen hundred heads piled high in the name of Allah. Who was responsible for his butchery: Allah or the Quran? Let's call Allah and God one and the same because they are the same, aren't they?

MUHAMMAD: Timur's free will was responsible for those actions.

PLATO: Wasn't Tamerlane acting according to the teachings of the Quran by killing those inoffensive people for not paying taxes to their Muslim conquerors?

MUHAMMAD: Free will! Allah, the Conscience of God, allowed free will.

PLATO: Allowed it or endorsed it?

MUHAMMAD: Both! Free will.

PLATO: Both. Thank you! No more questions, Your Honor.

(Cicero walks to the center of the courtroom.)

CICERO: Muhammad, what is *free will*?

MUHAMMAD: It is the capacity of a man or woman to choose his or her own course of action.

CICERO: Very well. Does free will mean that external causes do not determine a person's actions?"

MUHAMMAD: Yes!

CICERO: And yet, Muslims believe in predestination. *Al-Qadar*, or divine decree, is a central belief of the Muslims, is it not?

MUHAMMAD: Yes, but this divine decree does not mean that God—that is, Allah—did not give men and women free will. God allows them free will."

CICERO: Then, what does the Muslim belief in predestination include?

MUHAMMAD: First, God is all knowing, which means that He knows what has happened and what will happen. Second, God has recorded all that has happened and all that will happen. Third, whatever God wills to happen happens and whatever He wills not to happen does not happen. All of these beliefs reflect and result from the fourth belief, that God is the Creator of everything.

CICERO: In the case of Tamerlane's massacres and the other bestial slaughters, God knew that they would happen and willed them to happen?

MUHAMMAD: Yes!

CICERO: "And God knew in advance that today, in court, He would present the Muslim Nation with new commandments and enforce those commandments?

MUHAMMAD: Yes!

CICERO: And He knew this since the beginning of time?

MUHAMMAD: Yes, He did. God knows everything.

CICERO: He has given you an amendment to the Quran, hasn't He?"

MUHAMMAD: Yes.

CICERO: Is God omniscient?

MUHAMMAD: I have already answered that question. Of course, He is.

CICERO: Is He omnipotent?

MUHAMMAD: Yes, He is.

CICERO: Is God omnipresent?

MUHAMMAD: Yes!

CICERO: Yet he was asleep and absent when all these evils happened."

MUHAMMAD: His conscience was not asleep.

CICERO: Either way, awake or asleep, shouldn't He be held accountable for the atrocities that *He knew* would happen because He willed them to happen?"

MUHAMMAD: "Absolutely not. His Conscience, although it has been and will be fully aware of events that happened and will happen, cannot make decisions. Consciousness, the awakened state of conscience, is only a nonphysical property of the mind of God– or Allah."

SAINT AUGUSTINE (jumping in): God gave us free will."

MUHAMMAD: Augustine is correct.

CICERO: Augustinus, you are welcome to explain.

SAINT AUGUSTINE: Every action or event results from a cause.

CICERO: If events result from causes, they are inevitable, predetermined, not in anyone's control.

SAINT AUGUSTINE: Our *wills* or motivations, themselves have many causes but our *actions* do not. For example, you may *want* to condemn God of a crime because you support His conscience, but you may not *do* so because of a chain of causes, which finally decide upon your free will. Or you may say, "I wish that this trial had never happened," but you are participating in it nonetheless. Your *final* actions flow from your will, and that explains their freedom.

CICERO: But if *wills* have causes, then why blame, praise, punish, or reward those who act on them? The Stoic philosopher Chrysippus of Soli declared:

Everything that happens is followed by something else which depends on it by causal necessity. Likewise, everything that happens is preceded by something with which it is causally connected. For nothing exists or has come into being in the cosmos without a cause. The universe will be disrupted and disintegrate into pieces and cease to be a unity functioning as a single system, if any uncaused movement is introduced into it.

Isn't this your warrant that all things must have a cause and that all causes are identified by God?

SAINT AUGUSTINE: Of course, all things must have a cause since they produce their effect.

CICERO: Is it correct, then, to claim that because God *foreknew* our actions, He must bear the responsibility for them?

SAINT AUGUSTINE: The fact that God foreknew our actions does not mean that He caused them. [18]We don't perform the actions because God foreknew them; rather, He foreknew them because we perform them and we *want* to perform them, which makes them free actions.

CICERO: But if everything requires a *cause,* then each cause is in fact the effect of another cause, and so on, going back to a chain of causes.

MUHAMMAD: Yes!

SAINT AUGUSTINE: A logical finale.

CICERO: It's not a finale yet, gentlemen. Let's go back in a chain of causes until we reach the first cause of all, if you will.

SAINT AUGUSTINE: And that is God!

CICERO: The *Prime Mover?*

SAINT AUGUSTINE: If you want to use Aristotle's theory, yes.

CICERO: Oh, the *Unmoved Mover.*

SAINT AUGUSTINE (excitedly): Yes!

CICERO: The Unmoved Mover meaning—He who made all the laws of this universe.

SAINT AUGUSTINE (rising and waving his fist, his eyes gleaming): The Creator of all laws!

CICERO (shouting): The One who does not err.

ST AUGUSTINE: "That's right! The all-perfect God, the One who does not err.

CICERO: And therefore His laws *cannot* be refuted or contradicted.

MUHAMMAD (intervening): Allah's laws are sacred and sound and cannot be countered.

SAINT AUGUSTINE: No laws of God can contradict themselves, to put it more clearly.

CICERO (cheerfully): Are you gentlemen certain of that?

(Both nod while the audience murmurs.)

CICERO: Ladies and gentlemen of the jury, please observe the inconsistency:

---

[18] The God Question – Andrew Pessin

If God had set the laws of *cause and effect* in stone– each dependent on the other and both irrefutable, unchangeable, and absolute, then a cause must depend on another cause to become an effect itself, thus reaching back to an infinite chain of causes. Disagree with that premise and you will contradict the laws of God, which would contradict His will.

If you say that the first cause is God, as our expert witness-es –testify, then God is Himself the effect of another cause existing before He became God. I repeat: since all things must have a cause, the cause itself must have a cause. My question is, who made God? Did He cause Himself? What was the purpose for his coming into being, for there must have been one purpose that preceded God's existence? Could God be self-contradictory?

SAINT AUGUSTINE: God cannot be self-contradictory.

CICERO: Jumping to a direct question — Is God responsible for our *immoral* actions?

SAINT AUGUSTINE: No! He is not responsible.

CICERO: Therefore He's irresponsible.

SAINT AUGUSTINE: No, he's not irresponsible, he's. . . ,"

CICERO: Responsible!

PLATO: Objection, Your Honor, The prosecution is using Machiavellian maneuvering.

JUDGE: Sustained!

CICERO: According to *Al-Qadar,* God is responsible for our immoral actions, isn't He?

MUHAMMAD: *We* are to blame for our immoral actions."

CICERO: What about our moral actions? Do they deserve praise?

SAINT AUGUSTINE: Only the immoral ones are our own doing; morality comes from God.

CICERO: Oh! That statement is demeaning to human na-ture and to humanity; do you mean to say that morality can *only* come from God?

MUHAMMAD: Morality does come from God's con-science!

SAINT AUGUSTINE: Of course, morality comes from God; wickedness does not.

CICERO: Because wickedness is *sin*.

SAINT AUGUSTINE: It is indeed.

CICERO: And sin comes from us humans. (Winks at Eve, who blushes.)

SAINT AUGUSTINE: Unfortunately, yes.

CICERO: Sin is immoral.

SAINT AUGUSTINE: Yes."

CICERO: But God created us imperfect since we cannot be moral without Him, is that right?

SAINT AUGUSTINE: Yes, without Him we are immoral.

CICERO: Therefore, we are imperfect beggars.

SAINT AUGUSTINE: Well. . . .

CICERO: "So, God made man sinful, imperfect, and immoral, expecting him to be virtuous, perfect, and moral? Our English friend Fulke Greville expressed our predicament beautifully in this excerpt from his poem *Mustapha*:

O wearisome condition of humanity!
Born under one law, to another bound;
Vainly begot and yet forbidden vanity;
Created sick, commanded to be sound.
What meaneth nature by these diverse laws?
Passion and reason, self-division cause.
Is it the mark or majesty of power
To make offenses that it may forgive?
Nature herself doth her own self deflower
To hate those errors she herself doth give.
For how should man think that he may not do,
If nature did not fail and punish, too?
Tyrant to others, to herself unjust,
Only commands things difficult and hard,
Forbids us all things which it knows is lust,
Makes easy pains, unpossible reward.
If nature did not take delight in blood,
She would have made more easy ways to good.
We that are bound by vows and by promotion,

With pomp of holy sacrifice and rites,
To teach belief in good and still devotion,
To preach of heaven's wonders and delights;
Yet when each of us in his own heart looks
He finds the God there, far unlike his books.

....

(Muhammad bows repeatedly and then remains still, as if hypnotized. Before him a rolled parchment appears. His hands reach out trembling, grabbing it, opening it. He bows to it and kisses it before reading aloud): God's New Commandments?" (Looking at the audience) This is the first word from Allah in more than fourteen hundred years. I shall read it to everyone. Lo and behold!

As he begins to read his voice skips; he takes a deep breath and he passes out falling to the ground as everyone stares. He awakes on the chair moments later.)

MUHAMMAD: I am sorry, Allah's Word... where...? Here it is.... (It fumbles in his hands, he hugs his treasure. He carefully begins to read it loud for everyone to hear. He pauses after each sentence as if to contemplate.

His voice resounds throughout. After he finishes Muhammad, rolls up the parchment and slowly walks toward the judge's bench, handing her the roll with a short nod before returning to the witness stand.)

PLATO: If I may use the saying, thank God for putting out His new commandments. I thank Muhammad for sharing this amazing new revelation, which arrived at the right moment. Muhammad, how do you think will the Muslims take your new revelation?"

MUHAMMAD: Allah has spoken! We are the children of God. My people will follow them as the new revelation from Allah. (Looks at Plato.) How would the Scripture get to Earth?

PLATO: (Pauses a smile and turns toward the judge.) Your Honor, I have no more questions.

CHAPTER
23
DA NIHILO VITA FIT
(OUT OF NOTHING LIFE COMES)

[19]"The ultimate weakness of violence is that it is a descending spiral, begetting the very thing it seeks to destroy. Instead of diminishing evil, it multiplies it. Through violence you may murder the liar, but you cannot murder the lie, nor establish the truth. Through violence you may murder the hater, but you do not murder hate. In fact, violence merely increases hate. So it goes. Returning violence for violence multiplies violence, adding deeper darkness to a night already devoid of stars. Darkness cannot drive out darkness: only light can do that. Hate cannot drive out hate: only love can do that."

(Adam rises from his seat and walks toward the center of the courtroom, grandly repeating the last stanza from Greville):
"Yet when each of us in his own heart looks
He finds the God there, far unlike his books."

---

[19] —Martin Luther King, Jr.

Ladies and gentlemen of the jury, if you were to look into your hearts for the God residing inside you; if you were to portray Him in your best verses; if you were to expound on His character and His laws' if you were to weigh His morality against your own—better yet, if you were to draw a picture of Him or portray Him in words—I venture to guess that each of you would do it differently although not one of you can see Him. You may draw or speak of Him from your own imagination, inspired by your own spiritual impressions, but the picture of Him would not be accurate since you have never seen God in His reality.

The point of my question to you is how can anyone evaluate and judge a *being* as great as God is and reach a unanimous verdict concerning Him if each of us has a different perception of what God is?

We cannot know Him because he transcends our understanding. Each of you sees a different image of God. These images are your own creations. You are the authors of your own thoughts, of your own gods who become your personal idols.

If you base your religious beliefs on the Scriptures, you base them on inventions of the human mind. That's why there are so many religions swarming on top of one another, suffocating themselves and each other in inconsistencies and contradictions. Each one reflects a different pattern of superstitions caused by different cultures and environments. The empathy of hope and fear has made these thousands of religions not only incompatible with each other in the sense of *beliefs* but also mutually hostile. Brother turns against brother and nation against nation. Conflicting beliefs spill the blood of humanity, but few people realize that there are no divine superpowers on either side of the conflict and there never will be.

So, *where* are these gods? *Who* are they? Moreover, *which* god is your god? Even if you saw your God, you wouldn't recognize Him. You'd mock Him and affront Him, for how can you *re*-cognize anything you haven't seen before? He might come before you as small and delicate as a butterfly or spread giant wings as large as infinity. In either case, you would not know Him.

Suppose, just suppose that when you reach a verdict to decide the fate of God, the verdict is not unanimous. Some people will reject it; and once more religious inconsistency will give birth to resentment, sadness, dismay, and, finally, hatred and bloodshed. For sooner rather than later, the anger of those opposing your verdict will grow and erupt like a super-volcano, destroying all civilization.

If, on the other hand your verdict is unanimous, say, finding God *guilty* and expelling Him from your lives forever, the question will remain: Which God are you condemning? And if you find Him *not guilty*, which God of all the gods that you worship is not guilty?

So, I ask you, who is the God on trial here? Can you recognize *your* God in this court? Surely, He claims to be the Father of Creation and that He is the only God, or else we wouldn't be here. But if you believe *in* His creation, which is the universe itself, then you should love Him as much as you love your universe regardless of what name you give Him or under which nature and in which form you visualize Him. The world has its flaws, but you accept your universe as it is because you are part of its body. Can you accept God as He is, judging His complexity by looking at the nature of the universe, which *is* His Nature?

Some of you may think that *evolution* is by itself a process *outside* the work of God—"God" meaning this entire majestic Creation, *not* the personage depicted in books and projected out of the minds and imaginations of little people.

But scientists depict the evolutionary process as being in conflict with Creation as if it were possible to trigger a course of action without a cause. The Big Bang theory, which most astronomers continue to speculate upon, postulates that an explosion, suddenly erupting from the nothingness of space, generated the universe into being. It replaces God because, astronomers say, it happened all by itself without reason or motive or cause when in fact only an *outside* cause could generate an effect; thus, an *originator* must be responsible for the outcome. To those who doubt God in favor of "chance," I ask this question because you know that everything must have an *origin:* What is the origin of the Big Bang? Perhaps it's not God; but what if it is Him?

Ladies and gentlemen, when you speak of the Big Bang, you realize that you are using an invented term for a hypothetical explosion, a theory developed by Monsignor Georges Henri Lemaître, who called it "the hypothesis of the primeval atom." And you may know that Fred Hoyle coined the term "Big Bang" as a flippant rejection of Lemaître's theory. Think that.

Hoyle, a lifetime atheist, applied Parmenides' adage *ex nihilo nihil fit* ("from nothing, nothing comes") to argue that Lemaître's theory was flawed. He believed that life evolved in space and –travels through the universe in the form of viruses on asteroids, meteors, and comets and propels evolution on earth, a theory that is also partially correct.

But was Lemaître entirely wrong? Even if he was wrong about the origin of the universe from a primeval atom, he was certainly right that the cosmos expands. The universe is a living organism, in perpetual motion, whose cycles—birth, growth, development, aging, death, and rebirth—depend on energy, matter, and motion. Life was always present in space or, was it? Everything is *alive* through a whole motion of living, including death, which is part of the whole cycle. How do I know that? Because I know that God is alive and He always has been, It follows that *Vita ex Deo* ("life comes from God") or, better yet, *Deus vita est* ("God is Life"). Do you want to call the universe God? Do it; God doesn't mind. Do you, Dad?

(Adam turns away from the jury to look at his Father and takes a few steps toward His light. The light dims gently as if to accommodate Adam's eyes.

ADAM (speaking in a near-whisper that somehow reaches the farthest corner of the courtroom): Oh, Father, please forgive me for what I'm about to say, but I must say it because only *now* can I see your form and shape, heart and soul, spirit and heavens; I'm afraid that if I don't say it fast, it will go away unless you give me the eloquence to finish my testimony.

If one thing is stronger than you are, Dad, that thing is your conscience.

You made the whole world in your own likeness and painted it on the canvas of space.

You are unknown to all things and to all beings just as a finished artwork is unaware of its creator.

You are invisible to the naked eye but visible to the mind.

You are still producing dimensions where universes are unknown to man.

You have sculpted and formed every object to embody the utmost depths of your thoughts.

You also made a tiny world—planet Earth—and compressed all the wonders of space into an area trillions of times smaller than a needlepoint for a reason that only you know.

And now, after generations upon generations, human beings are reinventing you and molding you out of their thoughts as if effigies could chisel their masters according to their own views.

You rested smiling, thinking of your divine works, but your slumber brought your nightmare, not the wonderful dream of your conception, for even you let your dreams flow freely.

You reached inside your spirit and gave man *life*.

You reached inside your thought and gave man *comprehension*.

You looked at your wonderful conscience, and in Her image you created the woman, the most perfect being in all Creation.

But if anything is above you, it *is* your conscience. If anything other than you is above man, it is woman. You are incomplete without Your conscience just as man is incomplete without woman. Conscience is your wealth just as woman, the giver of life, is man's wealth, and conscience is your foundation just as woman is our *alteram partem*. Your conscience is your beautiful mate—your other half.

Together, the man and woman are *God*. When they unite, when they suffer, when they break apart, they call your Name because they are one with each other, just as you are One with your conscience, loving, suffering, and now setting aside your differences until you unite again.

Your conscience is the Mother of Creation and you are the Father of Creation. There is no God without conscience; there is no conscience without God.

Within your conscience, you make the universe: laws known but not yet discovered; space seen but not yet exposed; life observed but not yet determined, rules devised but not yet enforced—all lying at the feet of Wisdom, Caution, Purpose, and Sequence—and I say *make* because—tell them, Father—Creation is everlasting. It's progressive, it's ongoing; it is a continuing process called *evolution*.

(Although the light of God shines dimly on him, blobs of sweat run down his forehead. He steals a furtive glance at Eve, who smiles and nods as if she knows his thoughts. He looks at the judge for permission to continue, but she stares reflectively without moving or speaking.

ADAM: (Humbly turns toward the light addressing God.) And now your Conscience, your Alter Ego, the other half of your being is calling upon you to admit your errors and misdeeds—not in the form of your Creation but in the creation of your forms—since your painting of creation is too abstract for everyone to understand, too simple for everyone to see, and too complicated for everyone to recognize.

Ladies and gentlemen of the jury, you are here to learn the truth, the whole truth, and nothing but the truth, and I'll tell you that truth whether it will mean the end of the world as you know it or not. And I'm going to spell it all out as this is my closing statement.

SATAN: Just a minute, we have one more witness. He is very good at "spelling;" you wouldn't want to misspell any words, do you?

(Laughter in the audience)

ADAM: Objection Your Honor. Lucifer is interrupting me; I will not tolerate it.

SATAN: Your Honor, it cannot be a closing statement since not all the witnesses have been called. This gentleman is a very important witness; we were waiting for him to arrive. (He nodded to Rufus who walked over taking the prosecution. Before he left whispered into Rufus' ear and patted his back.)

RUFUS: I'll be taking it from here on, Your Honor.

JUDGE: Thank you. Objection overruled.

ADAM: The prior arguments for me are final and conclusive. I don't need....

JUDGE: I said, overruled. If you don't want to cross-examine a witness you may exercise your option.

(Commotion in court)

JUDGE: Silence! What's the witness name?

CHAPTER
24
CHRISTOPHER HITCHENS

(Rufus reciting rarely and most affectionately from Khayyam):
> And do you think that unto such as you,
> A maggot-minded, starved, fanatic crew,
> God gave the Secret, and denied it me?
> Well, well, what matters it! Believe that too.

RUFUS: Your Honor, I'd like to call Christopher Hitchens
to the witness stand.
(Far end outcries start a wave of gossip that spreads almost
instantly throughout, the wave reaching the front rows. Everyone's looking in the direction from where the clamor began,
eyes fixing what at first looked like a needle size figure in motion at the end of the center the corridor that's dividing the
religious from the non-religious. As it advances, the image
gets clearer showing the features of a man growing larger and
larger until he enters the court standing five feet nine inches

tall. The off-white linen suit dresses him most elegantly, while a baby blue colored shirt gives him the look well remembered. His face marks a serious disposition over a hint of a self-assured grin. He displays a healthy look over a middle-aged attractive stature, and a vigorous but layback disposition typifying his charisma. He stops before the Judge bowing to her in sign of reverence waiting for permission to speak. The Judge nods.)

RUFUS: Mr. Hitchens, thank you for coming, Sir. (He's being motioned to the witness stand. Before he sits, they give him the option to take an oath.)

RUFUS: Would you like the Bible upon which to avow?

HITCHENS: Do you mean they even have them here? (Ahem!) Um... *no!* I can do very well without it, thank you.

RUFUS: Please raise your right hand. Do you swear to tell the truth, the whole truth and nothing but the truth, so help you... (He stops with a cough.)

HITCHENS: On my word of honor I do swear to tell the truth. Yes!

RUFUS: You may sit down. Thank you for coming.

HITCHENS: (Sits, shifts to a comfortable position.) I'm not too sure I wanted to come, so ... (Snorts drawing a serious, affected expression on his face) hurriedly.

(Laughter)

Thank you for having me, though. (He's slightly nodding with high regard.)

RUFUS: Can you introduce yourself to this court, please?

HITCHENS: Yes, of course! (Clearing his voice) Esteemed court; ladies and gentlemen; brothers and sisters; dear comrades—my name is Christopher Eric Hitchens. I was born in Portsmouth, England on April 13, 1949; checked out (sighs) December 15, 2011. I am... uh—I'm sorry—I *was*... a journalist, essayist, columnist and literary critic for a very short time unfortunately.

RUFUS: Mr. Hitchens could you be kind and tell us, do you see God in this courtroom, Sir?

HITCHENS: (drawing a most serious look) I wouldn't know him if I saw him.

(Laughter over dispersed applauses spreading throughout.)

RUFUS: (Amused) You're mentioning you were a journalist and a critic among other things. Were you also known as an anti-theist, an active adversary of God and a fierce antagonist of the three Abrahamic religions?

HITCHENS: Uh well... of the presumed god, yes—and I still *am* against all religions without a single question of doubt.

RUFUS: Can you tell the court your motive for being anti-theist and anti religious?

HITCHENS: I would like to direct immediate attention to the purpose for which we are here: a Godless world, ladies and gentlemen, besieged in evil; so well evidenced by a sleeping, absent god. What better motive could there be? What could be more convincing than that?

RUFUS: That's as far as God is concerned. As to religions, can you tell us why you are against them Mr. Hitchens?

HITCHENS: I'll refine my reasoning by asking, if you permit me—what could be more vicious or crueler —given the blood in which religions bathe—than the false, ghastly pseudo-literature called scriptures? I hope you are noticing my leniency for calling them "scriptures" and not using a more appropriate recycled expression.

RUFUS: Why is that so?

HITCHENS: Well, Marx said it well. I'm talking about Karl Marx of course who named religion *"opium of the people."* I'd like to look beyond this present age of mass ignorance into a very near future when all religions will be exiled into oblivion by common sense, at the time when the rest of the people will be more educated. I trust that societies will realize soon that religion is venomous, virulent, ruinous to the mind, offering not less than a dangerous, obscure consignment, more often than not producing intellectual hernia. Religion is in my opinion nothing more than *toxic waste.* (Snickering) Someone coin this term for me, please?

(Laughter applauds and boos all throughout.)

RUFUS: (Challengingly) you did not believe there could be a Heaven and Lo, you're in heaven now. What can you tell us about this?

HITCHENS: (Chortling) you know the old maxim: "*the fated will happen*" or..."*you won't escape your fears.*" Perhaps I'm still undergoing severe hallucination. Everything is possible—well, *almost* everything. Most probably, I am hallucinating because what I see undermines my definition of Heaven. (He motions towards Jesus.)

RUFUS: (Chuckling) You are more skeptical than me. (Drawing a grave expression) Mr. Hitchens, indeed you are in Heaven, and most importantly, you're in Heaven's Court. You are not imagining anything. I assure you, *we* are in fact assuring you (motioning to the conclave,) that this is as real as it can get.

Millions of people, and the numbers are climbing applaud your criticism with respect to our views with regards to God and religion. My question to you is a very important one: in your opinion, is religion God inspired?

HITCHENS: Oh no, definitely not; religion is not god inspired—and I speak for *all* religions regardless of tenure, to make it very clear. A sleeping being cannot be operative. We can easily observe God's absence. The being called God is totally dormant; therefore as good as dead. He was never around to inspire anyone. He even confirms it in his defense, the purpose of this trial that he was sleeping all along. Religion drowns in errors. It is a fact mostly observed today. And speaking about religions and their gods, since they all contradict each other it undoubtedly means that *god* indirectly contradicts his self. Why would a god offer countless disputing creeds? Suppose for a moment that he did offer religion to the world, would he distribute it only to a handful hither and thither or would he give it *at once* to everyone? Does it make sense to believe that he spoke only in Arabic or in Hebrew while being deliberately unfair to the majority of his "children?" Who would believe the kind of nonsense if not those who cover not only their heads but also their eyes?

RUFUS: Since there are more creeds than one, could there perhaps be more than one god?

HITCHENS: Oh, my dear Sir, it is intolerable already for us to prove one deity, let alone thirty thousand of them. Can you imagine the chaos? We'd be in trial forever. What a nightmare that would be! (Shrugging) I'm sorry; I do apologize; I didn't mean to sound that conservative.

RUFUS: God's Conscience confesses that His conduct led to evil. What can you tell us of that, Mr. Hitchens?

HITCHENS: In all honesty, I didn't know he *had* a conscience. But all right, I'll go over that assumption since I'm here in Heaven.... (Coughs covering his mouth)

RUFUS: In which case you think that God is guilty of what?

HITCHENS: *Universalem ruinam.*

RUFUS: Meaning, so that everyone could understand...

HITCHENS: Universal collapse.

RUFUS: (Friendly inflection) Christopher, you were a witness of evil on Earth; you weren't a witness of evil in the entire universe, is that true?

HITCHENS: By this very question, you indicate that there *is* evil in the entire universe. You had said it before me; thank you. Your question awakens an interesting observation you see, and that is that what we're witnessing on Earth is only a sample of evil on a negligible scale, by comparison. The evil in the universe is directly proportional to the evil on diminutive planet Earth; the display seen few hours ago of the formation of the worlds *amply* and accurately shows it. Could anyone think for a moment that god, as ego-centric and as capricious as he is, would ever permit evil to rule his most favored planet, condemning humanity to perdition together with all other life forms, while letting the entire universe, which according to the Good Book it's *lifeless*, bathe in infinite goodness? Would this make any sense? And yet as we will see, he allowed it.

The All Good and All Righteous, as god calls himself throughout man's poor literature, should be consistent and unprejudiced. Did he create the Earth where, the Book says, "his Kingdom shall come," simply to destroy it and then blame it on a dream or on his darling dollies Adam and Eve? Did he figure, or even worse, *planned* or *designed* his own Kingdom's demise by having the Andromeda galaxy crash into the Milky Way—a thing happening any nanosecond now by contrast with infinity—only to remove everything he likes to be praised for along with it his vanity? Did he doom humanity along with his own morality, in case he's got any morals at all?

If he did such awful errors it would mean to exenterate, to defeat his godliness, to dissolve his ethics, to revoke his Holiness; it would mean to change his *unchangeable* being and to move his *unmovable* Self and to prove himself wrong in the face of his own conscience.

I saw the presentation made by Cicero earlier today. It is evident that the whole universe represents an infinite *nightmare,* by definition. Evil coexists within creation. You can see its vibrant, bubbly, most gruesome and resolute force in everything there is. The greater the immensity of the universe, the greater is the evil all throughout. Evil is therefore innate in the existence itself. It naturally belongs to Creation and since Creation is God's, you say; it naturally follows that evil belongs to God. One without the other cannot exist, as simple as that. If evil didn't belong to God it would mean that it would precede him.

RUFUS: Therefore evil is *not* to be found only on Earth.

HITCHENS: (Calmly) Precisely. What kind of God would damn the only place he cared for? That would be neurotic of Him, obsessive of Him, mad of Him, weirdest, most definitely clinical. I'll go further and say, that because evil presides universally and shares infinity, and because it has been ascribed to the Devil, either the Devil is omnipresent—since we associate him with evil—or he, the Devil, does not even exist other than in poorest, tasteless scripts of phony squiggles, scratched down by dirty hands. All of them occult encryptions invented by necromancers of worse kind.

Let me push it a bit farther since I see that I can ... (Grins and sniffs) the *real* devil, based on quotations from conventional scriptures, is none other than the conflicting Bible God himself. He is the one with double natured complex and multiple personality disorder; He is the devil. So once again, evil is in creation, it is material and eternal; *that* is the true damnation.

SATAN: (Laughing with appetite; waving in sign of approval) Thank you for saving me, Chris!

HITCHENS: (Correcting him) Christopher! (Ahem!) You're welcome, but you haven't any to worry about, if you'll permit me. Your very nature is a gift predestined by no other than "god, himself. God cannot condemn you for the comportment he bestowed upon you; and if God cannot condemn you, (raising his voice) *no one* can.

RUFUS: (Addressing everyone with spreading arms) A remarkable revelation ladies and gentlemen of the jury. Mr. Hitchens, you *are* defending God's conscience, are you not?

HITCHENS: Hypothetically.

RUFUS: Why, hypothetically?

HITCHENS: Well, again, it would mean to acknowledge His being; and that I cannot do no more than I could recognize the thirty thousand gods before Him that claim supremacy. If so, we would have to condemn them all. Thank heavens we only have one in court. (His lips slack; he speaks with bathos):

Who in the right mind, bearing any sense of morals, dear Sir, would tolerate such a tiring monster knowing His unlimited evil resources? To think that a creature like this occupies and rules the whole space and time careless of his own conception, it is as sacrilegious to common sense as it is to ethics. Imagine for a moment if any of us should leave our children unattended in the middle of a jungle among wild beasts to the mercy chance. Imagine how extremely reckless that would be; how crazy to even think of such an irrational, immoral thing.

To fuel the fire a bit, think now that these innocent children are left at large while we are conveniently taking a nap, a very long one in fact, and after we wake and see our children slaughtered, we have the thick cheek, the utter impertinence as to blame it on a dream, not on our gross negligence, stupidity or immaturity; to blame it on a nightmare and safely and serenely plead "not guilty." Wouldn't we be perfect nominees for murder had we to do such irresponsible acts? Pleading insane would be an option. How does this sound to you, I ask? Doesn't it sound retarded? One might think it impossible for such murders to have come from God Almighty, the perfect being, the All-Righteous, don't you agree? Or because He is God He should be pardoned; the dirt swept under a breath of cloud; the matter dismissed and all forgotten since the pot cannot judge the potter.

To further imagine that this called "god" is the owner of all space and time worries me. It should concern you, too. I'd rather not wake again than to witness the cruelty invented by the "All Righteous." I refuse to think that such a tormenter could even coexist amongst so delicate animals in the universe. A cat, per example, is way above Him since it cares for its cubs and protects them at all times, even when it sleeps. It's so unlikely for us to think that this punishing deity had designed everything we see without us also thinking that He invented the scorpion, the black widow, the shark and the viper, giving those creatures a nature so distinctively cruel. If he didn't make them, than who did? Is there a co-creator? Why call him All Merciful and All Good when all we see out of his nature is evildoing? We are looking at *Reus malum*— the One who's guilty of mass murder.

RUFUS: Would you be willing to allow the possibility that the good in the world also made by God balances its evil counterpart? Some may say that it even surpasses it.

HITCHENS: I'm speaking under the hypothesis that God made the universe. Religion says that God only produces "good," and that evil is the product of the devil. So, in reference to "good" being greater than "evil," here are some examples to prove the contrary: pain is above pleasure; death is longer than life; youth is short, stupidity is inexhaustible while intelligence is limited. Where's the superiority of good in that? But okay, because I have a good heart and good morals, I'll be willing to compromise once and to condone the following idea: I'll accept, devoid of contempt, the idea of a sleeping deity for this trial's sake who *did* step out of the scriptures to rest on his seventh day after creation and became a victim of his own nightmare. I'll go along with that, let's say, and I'll postulate for a moment that all of it is true. And I'll even push it further supposing that we do have an All-Good father who's even willing to change everything for the better, to patch up the errors, to redo the blue print, to redesign the world for the sake of righteousness. I'll offer that absurdity for a fact. But the question is, will he do that?

I could speculate despite of my inner revolt and turn it around like this: what does any amount of time that already had passed really means vis-à-vis the persisting eternity? Because I care about the billions of people that will be born I also hope and ask the unreasonable: Do we gain anything by condemning such a god? What if this god is determined to end all torment? What if He's willing to make reparations that otherwise will haunt his conscience forever? I'll compromise with such a God for the benefit of the future. I could forget— well... all right, not *forget*, but close the file of the past that's gone away anyway in favor of a bright, vivid future. (Pauses taking a deep breathe; sighing.)

Based on what I've seen so far would I believe that he would be willing to change everything for the better and prove himself a good God? Would I believe for a moment that he would want to reprogram, redesign new live "software" and rerun the universe? Do I think that human species are that important to him? Di I think he would change the laws of nature for the benefits of love and benevolence to where survival, bliss and everlasting life will replace extinction, suffering and death? For the grant of compassion I'm willing to sacrifice my common sense and look like a fool for a moment questioning the above, openheartedly.

And now that the moment had passed, here I am back to my senses again thank...goodness, where I vastly and logically doubt his intervention. It is irrational to think such will ever happen since it never happened and could not happen. No God can do this anymore than he could convert the course of his own nightmare. Before I leave this witness stand, I'll prove to you that because of his nature God *cannot* and will not eradicate evil.

RUFUS: (Scowling) What is your deduction?

HITCHENS: Let's recap. Adam said that his father was asleep during all world evil. He said his father had been under a nightmare spell. Adam also attested that his father was not at the crime scène at the time when the *crimes* have been committed.

RUFUS: Doesn't this conflict with God's traits?

HITCHENS: Exactly. Doesn't this contradict with god's attributes, is the problem. What an inconsistency is to claim that god is seen nowhere, yet he is given the credit for being omnipresent and omnipotent. He is nowhere apparent and yet he is all over the place according to approximately five billion believers that imagine him ubiquitous. Those believers *confirm* his constantly present being, most of them talking to him, some of them repeatedly and desperately screaming and shouting his name, praying for his aid, for his golly, begging for him to interfere. He does not respond despite the fact that those believers claim to hear his voice in their heads, his Holy Spirit surrounding them. He does not appear to anyone. Millions are in starvation, in agony, diseased; other millions are being killed, tormented, living hopeless lives, confronting calamities. These calamities are called "acts of god." More tragedies are adding to human fate. Nature proves careless, undisturbed, unaffected and indifferent whether a thousand gods were there or not acting as if none have powers over her. When will people understand that he's toothless or unsympathetic, in any case useless to them? O *Sancta simplicitas!*

RUFUS: Which means?

HITCHENS: Which means that if there's anything larger than god that is human absurdity. This invisible "father" is seen nowhere. There is no eyewitness to point to him; and because he is invisible, his size is immeasurable. This imaginary giant the size of "nothingness" resides in the brain of the gullible; he has no substance yet fills the mind of man with void and, once there, it is terminal. He has no physical form other than coming in the essence of paint to fill the brushes of various artists who lay him morbid on walls of cold, sinister echo resounding cathedral halls. His gruesome, anthropomorphic figure is already born dead, stiff and silent, peeling off with time, smelling of chrism and incense. He is the one that leaked from the minds of man taking the main character in his books of fiction from where he rules from page to page, expectorating disagreements, spattering verses of gore, promiscuously, wickedly commanding and demanding, slaying and humiliating. He loves worships and invocations and needs them by day and night without end, whether we are alive or dead. Is this the god we have in this court? Because this god is an everlasting fugitive, an everlasting absentee, a betrayer of emotions pretermitting his own conscience, evading all reason, bouncing against all logic, running from book to book and from cover to cover. The spying eye of the universe. The eye of the pyramid.

If he is, He was born "framed," condemned to perdition by the very religions that patented him. He was born guilty because he *represents* all guilt. Come to think of it, we might want to bring to justice the ones accountable for fashioning such monster. Those handfuls should be condemned for murder and fraud for literarily "using" a patsy fictional character with the intent of poisoning the human mind, and for twisting human destiny. They fooled the gullible. People thrown in the vast ocean of death from birth, afraid to drown and hoping to live forever, will embrace upon any thrown promises of salvation.

(Commotion silenced by the thundering gavel.)

RUFUS: (Smiles) you do see Jesus in this court. Is he real?

HITCHENS: I see a man who *looks* like Jesus the public figure from paintings, films and pictures, but that's all I see. This person is not god any more than the other bodies standing near him in persuasive old fashion garbs.

RUFUS: (Cracks a smile) I thank you for your comments.

HITCHENS: And if there were an existing god, a just God, a noble, moral, benevolent, sympathetic God, he would indubitably agree with me.

SAINT AUGUSTINE: (Yells) blasphemy! That's blasphemy I say! I listen and cannot believe. I must be under hallucination. What has become of Heaven?

HITCHENS: Exactly! I'm glad you agree with me as far as the delirium effect, dear Sir. I look around and see the same thing. On the other hand, what you're referring to, as *blasphemy*, is no more than your god's collapse at the ascent of reason. Mark Twain said "Blasphemy? No, it is not blasphemy. If God is as vast as that, he is above blasphemy; if He is as little as that, He is beneath it."

SAINT AUGUSTINE: Outrageous I say. The Bible says....

HITCHENS: Show me the original manuscripts of any claimed Scriptures dear Sir, and I'll show you its pure fabrication.

SAINT AUGUSTINE: We *are* in heaven for God's sakes. The court uses the Bible because it is sacred. I...

HITCHENS: (Interrupting) No! The court offers the Bible along with the Qur'an and other man acquainted "pen-work" because of religious witnesses who are *used to* taking an oath on a book system rather than on integrity and self-respect. I took the oath upon my honor and I shall stand by it unafraid of any punishment, because I dare to have dignity. I am not kissing any posteriors be they of hard or soft covers.

SAINT AUGUSTINE: I am sincerely sorry for you. I pray for you because you do not have the Holy Spirit. But you will one day; you will, you will...

HITCHENS: With required respect Sir, I do not think that you are anymore virtuous than me or any other unbeliever. I think that you're a fair gentleman of ... yeah, a certain bent. This condition often happens to the religious.

SAINT AUGUSTINE: Religion is a life-giver, not a condition.

HITCHENS: (Ironical) I thought *god* was the life giver whereas religion preconditions your life. Are you needling an open debate?

SAINT AUGUSTINE: Any time. (Nervously shifting positions in his seat)

HITCHENS: What better time than now? Let's get it over with. Bring it on.... You can summon all the saints and popes. "[20]Let he who is without sin cast the first stone." (Smiling ironically.)

SAINT AUGUSTINE: Uh-ah! You're using the Bible, I see. I guess I *will* call on saints and popes if that's what it takes to win God's trial.

HITCHENS: Well, I hope they made it to Heaven. And by the way, John the apostle didn't write that verse I recited; a scribe added it hundreds of years later. It's a fabrication. His name was...

RUFUS: Gentleman, please. That was my next question, Christopher: does religion poison everything?

HITCHENS: Oh! (Chuckles) Absolutely. Much evidence is before us without indulgence. Are you mentioning my book... available in fine bookstores everywhere?

SAINT AUGUSTINE: Please, corroborate!

HITCHENS: (In most pleasant but sardonic tone) If you'll permit me, I'd like to ask you a shy question; and that is—do you... (Sniffs and motions with both hands) Do you really believe that God had inspired the writers who wrote the scriptures? Do you *really* believe it as true, or as unescapably true?

SAINT AUGUSTINE: I believe...

HITCHENS: (Rushing in) I'm sorry ... and if you do so, if you do...do you also believe that saints and pontiffs, as well as

---

[20] (John 8:7)

other religious people that have been inspired or *inspirited*, are a heaven's distance more gifted than nonbelievers or anti-theists? Let's take our example—is there a difference, which would make an evident distinction between us two? Do you see any?

SAINT AUGUSTINE: Yes, actually, I do. Of course, I do see a gigantic difference between us two.

HITCHENS: And how do you support that, Mr. Augustine?

SAINT AUGUSTINE: Uh... *Saint* Augustine.

HITCHENS: I'm sorry, *Saint* Augustine... why is that true, Sir?

SAINT AUGUSTINE: Because of the Holy Spirit. You must have the Holy Spirit in order to be inspired or as you said, "in-spirited"— I like that by the way— (he smiles), in order to understand God and have *faith*. You must let the Holy Spirit come inside your own self. You must have an open heart and accept the Holy Spirit with an open mind. You must be will-ing to receive it on your own free will, without questioning; by faith. Only then, you can see God.

HITCHENS: The Spirit enters and dwells in the heart.

SAINT AUGUSTINE: Yes, now you understand, my child. Yes-yes-yes. Be open, and you too, will receive the Holy Spirit for it's never too late. I know you will. You will *feel* and *know* the difference immediately. Then there'll be no difference be-tween you and me. You will feel extreme relief. It is like day and night.

HITCHENS: Or like heaven and hell.

SAINT AUGUSTINE: Or like Heaven and Hell if you want (chuckling and lowering his voice to half whisper) although... I've never been to hell—thank God!

(Looks at Jesus, who nods favorably, smiling.)

HITCHENS: I remember now! (Pauses in thought) I re-member it well; I remember it in fact very, very well. Not too long ago, I *was* a child myself playing and never worrying about what tomorrow might bring; never thought of death, and of maladies I knew naught of, nor did I know of any trou-ble the world was going or has been going through outside some history lessons, which sounded to me like old fables picked out from old books. Here's my little story, if I may tell it; if you allow me...

SAINT AUGUSTINE: Please, do tell us.

HITCHENS: [21]I was nine years old attending a school near Dartmoor, a stretch of moorland in Devon, Southern England. I remember her, (he nods once) Mrs. Watts—Mrs. Jane Watts her name was—a very respectable, very natural, very modest kind of woman of honest faith and decent character. She was our Bible instructor as well as our Natural Science teacher. She would take us out throughout our beautiful country of birth, to show and teach us about the country life: trees, birds, plants and flowers of different kingdom. If I close my eyes now I can still remember these days and how my mind wallowed in most pleasant daydreams. I remember of what now seems to be an everlasting euphoria.

One magnificent day, while outside in the meadow, she said to us with a most soothing inflected-skipping voice, "Look, children, at the grass and trees how wonderful and rich they look in color green, which is exactly the color most relaxing to the eyes. That is to show how great and generous God is. Imagine if instead the vegetation was all orange or purple [or monochrome,] how dire that would be."

SAINT AUGUSTINE (Shifting positions, excitedly exclaims): And she was right, Christopher. She was so right. What wonderful memories. You should have written them down.

HITCHENS (Unaffectionate): *Mr.* Hitchens...Well, *I did* write them down. If you allow me to continue... she had mixed the scriptures and science together with such innocent austerity. At that time, I didn't know anything about photosynthesis or chlorophyll or the evolutionary progression or anything about the genome or mutation anymore than you do, because I was a child. However, I was a believer and a Bi-

---

[21] god is not great – how religion poisons everything by Christopher Hitchens

ble student. According to you, I had the Holy Spirit dwelling in me, or in my heart, in my soul.

SAINT AUGUSTINE: The Holy Spirit left you the moment you doubted God; the moment your faith in God was gone.

HITCHENS: Oh! The Holy Spirit left me the moment I used *common sense*. Is that what you're suggesting or implying?

SAINT AUGUSTINE: No, what I'm saying is that the instant you turned your back on the Holy Trinity; that's when the Holy...

HITCHENS: Could've been that the Holy Spirit led me to spot the fraud in Mrs. Watts' teachings? Couldn't have also been the Spirit who [22]curled my ankle-strap sandals in pure embarrassment for Mrs. Watts' blindfolded ignorance? According to your words, I should be able to feel and know the presence of the Holy Spirit—as immediate and as distinctive as that of telling apart a day from a night. My confession: neither the presence nor the flight of the so-called Spirit made me feel any differently other than the moment of total happiness and awakening. The feeling I had when I had rejecting religion was of relief; yes, perhaps of an unexplainable gratification as my senses did question Mrs. Watts' outlandish delusion. Oh yeah, I remember; I would say that another *immediate* sign, if I had any, was a blush that slapped my cheeks in humiliation instead of hers when she debited such absurdity. What an embarrassment. What a shame! Possibly that was the moment when the Spirit left (coughs...) when the Spirit left me.

SAINT AUGUSTINE: Poor Mrs. Watts was right, I sustain. You didn't understand it then and still don't understand it now (since you don't have the Holy Spirit) that it was God that had made it all possible. The photosynthesis and chlorophyll that you are mentioning are God's gifts to the world. God put them there for you to see them. Have faith and you'll see God's gifts. Faith comes from the heart.

---

[22] Ref: god is not great – how religion poisons everything, page 3

HITCHENS (Nodding once): God's gifts to the world? Just as the gift of "ignorance" donated to the frail religious. In fact ignorance it is *demanded* of them. It's in the "menu."

ST.AUGUSTINE (Horror-struck): That is not true. How can you say that, on what grounds do you center your argument?

HITCHENS: Very well, then. Let's look into the second century at our friend Celsus. In his work True Discourse Celsus states with regard to Christianity, '[23]Let no one educated be near us, no one wise draw near, no one who is farsighted. For these faculties are thought by us to be evil. But as for any one who is unlearned, who is stupid, who is an infant in understanding, let them come to us boldly. For the Christians honestly confess that such as these are praiseworthy to be seen by their God; manifesting by this, that they alone wish and are able to persuade the ignoble, the insensible, slaves, stupid women, and little children and fools.

Also that we may see in the forum notorious characters and frauds collected together, who dare not show their trickeries to intelligent men; but when they see a lad, and a pack of slaves and stupid men, they creep in and parade.' (Origen - Contra Celsus)

We also may see in their own houses, wool-weavers, cobblers, fullers, and the most illiterate and rural yokels, who would not utter anything before their elders or more intelligent teachers; but whenever they encounter children alone from their parents and several stupid women with them, they feel free to instruct them wonderful things, for example that they should not listen to their parents and teachers since those teach them nonsense and have no comprehension. For, say they, your parents and teachers are delirious and stupid, and neither knows what is truly good. Only by following them will they learn perfection. They only live properly, and that

---

[23] Arguments of Celsus, Porphyry and the Emperor Julian against the Christians (1830) by Thomas Taylor

children taught by them will be blessed, along with their families.

If they perceive any one of the wiser educators of learning approaching, or a parent of the child to whom they are talking, they become very cautious and postpone their discussion to another time.... In addition they say that should they desire to be coached by them, it is obligatory that they should abandon their parents, tutors and lecturers, and go with women and little children who are their playfellows to the women's or to the cobbler's shop, that they may attain perfection. Thus they convert them.

SAINT AUGUSTINE: Sacrilege! Celsus is not my friend. Grave heresy this is. (He looks at Jesus first and then all around as if to get approval) The great Origen defends Christianity, refuting the untrue writings of Celsus.

HITCHENS (Grimacing): First, the word "heresy" or "hairesis" means "choosing," taking or having a choice. What could be fairer than being able to make a choice? Isn't that permissible in your strict world of free-choice dogma? Religions make choices for its believers, more than vice-versa it seems to me.

Secondly, Origen does not deny that the Christian society is mainly made of lower, uninformed, illiterate or else ill-learned or ill-bred classes. Observe how courteous I am. How can he deny the truth? He responds in favor of the true Christian believers (some of whom are in fact well-informed), that actually they are wise and knowledgeable, but it is with respect to *God* that they have these qualities, not regarding things of this world. In other words, the Christian believers are above all others, regardless of vocation, just because the Holy Spirit— who happens to attach only onto the feeble and the vulnerable minded—possesses them. The apostles were not too bright, either. That alone should tell you more than enough, if you know what I mean.

SAINT AUGUSTINE: Profanity once again, I say.

HITCHENS: And more, yet— Apostle Paul—it's in your Bible—suggests this to his Corinthian flock, saying "[24]not many of you were wise by human standards—"which is to say that *few* were educated but not all."

[25]In the Gospels portrayals, we see that most of Jesus's disciples are simple bumpkins, provincials from Galilee— uneducated, rough, [unwise] simple fishermen for instance. Two of them, per example Peter and John, are unquestionably "illiterate." Read it aloud in your book of Acts (4:13).

SAINT AUGUSTINE: An unskilled man is above a scientist if he has God on his side. Such sacrilegious remarks...

HITCHENS: It is not sacrilege if Paul tells it, but it's a sacrilege if I bring it up. Now I arrive exactly where I want to be. You said that the one having god or the Holy Spirit on his side is superior to the unbeliever, the infidel, the anti-Christ or to the anti-theist —in other words the possessor of the Holy Spirit can show an edge over the one that is devoid of it; is that right?

ST. AUGUSTIN: Absolutely.

HITCHENS: Do you have in you the Holy Spirit? Or are you enwrapped in the Holy Spirit, now?

ST. AUFGUSTINE: Of course, the Spirit never lives me; I feel It... It talks to me.

HITCHENS: May I ask Jesus of Nazareth, if the Holy Spirit possesses him?

JESUS: I am one with the Father and the Holy Spirit.

HITCHENS: Is the Father near you now, Mr. Augustine?

SAINT AUGUSTINE: Yes! (Looking toward the light)

HITCHENS: I'd like to ask the court to give pen and paper, please, one to Saint Augustine and one to Jesus of Nazareth. Is that possible? (He looks at Rufus, then at the Judge who nods affirmatively. An angel brings it to them.)

---

[24] Misquoting Jesus – Bart D. Ehrman (1 Cor. 1:27)
[25] Misquoting Jesus, Pg. 39 The Beginnings of Christian Scripture – Bart D. Ehrman

HITCHENS: Thank you. I ask of these two very distinguished *men* to compose anything close in quality and mastership to any of Beethoven's pieces—I presume they are familiar with his works—and, or to produce a set of verses in the rhyme and style of Dante Alighieri.

I'd like to ask the court to grant these two Gentlemen two full hours to do it—earth time—(laughter in the audience) although I'm sure they can produce such work in no less than five minutes; five minutes for Saint Augustine and less in the case of Jesus—he is supposed to be one with God; he could produce it instantly.

Please observe how indulgent, how generous I am: I'm not just asking any believer to do this task, although according to Saint Augustine it would be an easy undertaking for a body possessed by the Holy Spirit to overcome it and prove a far more superior advantage. I solicited instead that the Biblical *Son of God* and the famous *Saint,* the Father of the Church, to do it. It's more than fair considering the "no risk," isn't it? It should be extremely easy for them to write those with a whistle and a joy, since they are both possessed by the Holy Ghost (who is omnipresent) and since they both have God on their side. No excuses from them are accepted. For they both have all necessary help in case they find themselves in short supply of talent or inspiration.

If they fail to provide at least an equivalent if not a better production of any of the requested tasks, their sanctity as well as lordship, respectively, should become invalid along with the idea of the Holy Spirit and the intervention of their omnipresent, benevolent god, shall prove null and void, their religions fake just as their faiths and their shot-eyed beliefs.

In case they fail this simple test, they will prove likeness to most mammalian primates sitting in this court, including me, but inferior to the geniuses of Ludwig van Beethoven or Dante Alighieri, by farthest.

And here is the good news as I flip the coin on the other side: if Jesus and the Saint Augustine succeed in surpassing the great composer or the Florentine poet I will instantly and without further ado become a Christian. (Rising his voice) not a Muslim, (pausing) unless, of course, Muhammad accepts the same challenge, which I doubt, because he doesn't know how to write, unless he claims to be illiterate for a wise excuse.

(Laughter and chatter)

Fair enough? Do you Gentlemen agree? Do I have the Court's consent to allow this *revelation*? (Heaven shakes in loud chatter.)

PLATO: Objection Your Honor. This is a trial of God not of the witnesses. Mr. Hitchens' irrelevant tender is strikingly wily. His plan is revolting and extremely provocative and discourteous at the same time.

RUFUS: Your Honor, this objection coming from Plato and not from some obscure lawyer from a lost provinciality, strikes me with much adverse surprise. Jesus is claimed to be the Son of God, many a times *god* himself—therefore part of the trinity. It is believed that the Holy Ghost *is* in him or entails him. Saint Augustine also claims superior influence given him by the Holy Ghost.

Mr. Hitchens was nice enough to ask, not a Jehovah witness or a poor parishioner to do this, which should have been compelling enough if you ask me, but the *crème de la crème*. If Jesus could turn water into wine, he could certainly turn a piece of paper into a musical masterpiece way better than the once deaf, poor Beethoven did; or have a witness stand turn into a tuned up brand new Steinway piano. Saint Augustine may write the verses in Dante's style just to teach us a lesson and to show us the divine presence manifested in him, to also validate the hallows around their heads that they are constantly shown in man made paintings.

If ordinary people could produce immortal wonderful works of art, these two superior, ghostly spirited sanctities are expected to match if not surpass their masterworks; that is if they really are who they say they are, and if the power of God and the Holy Ghost are present. If they should get the writer's block, God could take over in a jiffy while the Spirit gives them the proper inspiration. Did I get explained it right, Mr. Hitchens?

HITCHENS: Why, excellent! By contrast, I think the risk *I'm* taking is catastrophic just to think that I'm willing to give up *freethinking* and to become a Christian. If they succeed it would mean death to me, since I'd better be dead than without rationality. Not to say that I'll probably disappoint many of my friends and fans by taking this risk and that will mean signing my own oblivion.

RUFUS: Your Honor, I respectfully ask for your consent.

PLATO: Objection, you Honor. I ask the witnesses Saint Augustine and Jesus of Nazareth not to respond to this challenge and risk their dignities.

JUDGE: Objection overruled. The Court will grant you two hours earth time, gentleman.

ST.AUGUSTINE: This is a *satanic dream*. I reject this temptation in the name of the Lord our God. (His face crimson with fury.)

JESUS: I am a spiritual teacher not a composer or a poet. I agree with Saint Augustine and I'll take Plato's advice: I refuse to deal with such demonic lure. (His arm flings in Hitchens's direction of arrival, chin inside his chest, uttering theatrically) *Vade retro Satana!*

HITCHENS: Have you lost your faiths, gentleman? Where are your faiths? We didn't ask you to design a new spaceship, or paint another Mona Lisa, or to explain the string theory, or to turn your papers into a complete Encyclopedia Britannica, or rewrite the Bible word by word from your minds since it's claimed to be the word of God. Well! Can you prove us wrong?

(Heavy silence)

HITCHENS: I rest my case.

RUFUS: Ladies and gentlemen of the jury, esteemed court: here is your answer! Thank you.

No more questions, your Honor.

CHAPTER
25
THE "HITCH"

"If you would be a real seeker after truth, it is necessary that at least once in your life you doubt, as far as possible, all things."

René Descartes

PLATO: Mr. Hitchens, babies are born innocent, pure at heart, blameless; you were a child of such rewards once, were you not? A baby is said to be the closest thing to God. In that sense you were, too, close to God, when you were born. Please, speak your heart considering all these.

HITCHENS: Rewards or shortcomings? You know very well that the human baby is the most innocent victim of life, the most vulnerable, the feeblest—the most defenseless creature on earth, unlike God. Let's take a look at the baby scorpion—God's creation, too, and see its ammunition by comparison. The scorpion carries deadly poison from inception; the human baby carries innocence. She or he is totally defenseless. And yet, we are told we are the most gifted, perhaps given our intelligence. Yet, according to Saint Augustine and other saints or prophets whose teachings of the Bible are proverbially stringent, we are born already *stained* with biblical sin and will be so forever and ever. All of us are blemished from the time of birth, says the "bible god" or else god would discriminate. But we are in fact "damaged goods," according to religion. God created us sick and ordered us to be well, that's the absurdity. As for being close to God... unless a child is baptized to receive the Holy Spirit he or she is (said to be) predestined to eternal damnation. Think of the millions of children that are born and grow free of this terrible conviction that religion imposes; think of the billions that perished without knowing of Him; and think of what kind of god would show a heart more brutal than that of a wild beast with a mind more wicked than that of a vilest, to judge them and us. I'm sorry, but the hypothesis that a human is close to God might be true for a God who condemns religion firstly, and himself thereafter for allowing it to take form in the first place.

PLATO: And yet, this God wanted himself in court facing His Conscience, knowing that He is being adversely tried; knowing his fate. Don't you think that He reduces himself from His infinite purpose to the size of our human scopes perhaps to recommend his moral composition to our own? What if his message of confession is meant for us so that we may become humble, not before Him but before our own kind? What if His tiredness and long sleep has been an error, not intended by Him, but an error of... *time*?

HITCHENS: Your words are heartrending. However, I must be pragmatic and act in favor of Conscience and ethics regardless of emotions. I am a witness of extinctions, disasters, despairs, plagues, poverty, death and millions of crimes—most of them done in the name of religion (from the Crusades to the Inquisition, to Northern Ireland, to Kashmir, to Kosovo, to 9/11 to the massacres in present day Palestine, Syria, Egypt, Iran, Iraq, Sudan, etcetera,) the blood still warm in the veins of our earth and on the chapters of our history, all witnessed—or left unattended—by *heaven*; all left without intervention for millions and millions of years.

Based on what I saw, based on what I've read, based on what I've experienced and what I feel, I cannot but revile this mythical "god" for the dreadful fate of humanity and for the catastrophic providence of all beings, not to mention that my inner tears still hurt from my last, painful departure heaving leaved a world ready to explode, with my wife and children and dear friends being part of the billions left as helpless spectators. I could be dismembered or recomposed a million times over, but every time my conscience and consciousness revive it'll remain unchanged before my dignity or before any "god" or "gods" in heaven. As for the possible *error of time*— my dear Plato, whom I admire and have learned from so much—how is it, or why does it always happen that it must always be in our detriment, and not in our favor? This question will constantly leave us freethinkers much in the depth of dilemma, doesn't it?

SAINT AUGUSTINE: We go back to *free will*, don't we, I'm sorry to intrude. Mr. Hitchens has the liberty to freely tell his opinion. That doesn't change the weather and our reading on the factual barometer. God will always be God no matter what Mr. Hitchens cogitates for his thoughts *will* in fact change with circumstances. What Mr. Hitchens says today will not be of weight tomorrow—meaning some space of time from now. Suppose, we'll have Mr. Hitchens back here eons from today, his opinion would contrast his present judgments, incontestably, to relate to circumstances experienced by him. Only God's thoughts are perfect for He is far above our comprehension and he sees the whole picture, not fragments like us.

PLATO: Mr. Hitchens?

HITCHENS: I suppose I'm given no choice when it comes to free will, then. (Laughter in courtroom) If our free will is only a part of an incomplete compendium—as Saint Augustine suggests—then the will itself is incomplete, not free.

PLATO: If that is your opinion on "free will" what about "predestination" in God's relation to us," Mr. Hitchens?

HITCHENS: I suppose you heard of my incident while coming to court today, ladies and gentlemen, brothers and sisters? (Dead silence falling, as Christopher is looking around as for permission) Well... as I was half-walking half-floating on the sky-road on my way to court, I came to a fork where two arrowed signs were largely posted. One read "IF YOU BE-LIEVE IN FREE WILL GO THIS WAY;" the other read "IF YOU BELIEVE IN PREDESTINATION GO THIS WAY." I stood for a moment, thinking that I might be in fact put to a test and took the road to "predestination." At the end of this road there was a gate from where an angel appeared to greet me, tersely asking me: "Why are you here? Well, I said, I came to a fork in the road, read the two signs and since I believe in predestination I chose "predestination." He said, "You *chose*? You must go back." So I went back and went on the other road of "free will" at the end of which there was another gate whence another angel appeared. He asked me, sternly: "Why are you here?" I said, "I had no choice! I was sent by... "

(Hysterical laughter stopping his speech; smiling he continued) I went back at the fork-road to where the signs were and all of a sudden another road opened up for me and I ended up in court, right before your very eyes and I thought I was in hell."

(Fans cheering.)

HITCHENS: But no, no: regarding your prior pronouncement Saint Augustine, I doubt that my thoughts will ever change, Sir. They cannot. My judgment will not alter as long as I will not.

SAINT AUGUSTINE: How can you be so certain of that?

HITCHENS: Simply because you and every theologian and believers are saying that god is "unchangeable." Otherwise he shan't be "god."

SAINT AUGUSTINE: God *is* unchangeable, of course, but you Sir, are not. You are in a constant transformation; you will change, nonetheless. Your thoughts, which are part of you, adjust to upcoming events.

HITCHENS: Constant transformation? That sounds like "evolution..." If god is unchangeable, god's events are also unchangeable, including the past ones that, of course, contain yesterdays and today's incidents and tribulations. So yes, I might change, for the better I hope, but I'm *forced* to obey prior causes and facts that are immovable.

ST AUGUSTINE (Looks at Adam for a moment than back at Hitchens): the irony of your story is amusing but it's only a story. I think "the fall" amply explains free choice.

HITCHENS: And "the fall" is not a story? Should I offer a clearer reasoning?

SAINT AUGUSTINE: You have my challenge.

HITCHENS: We do have a "will" which means that yes, we are in control of our actions and *act* as we wish; but, for this "will" to be "free" the will has to be totally independent of, or unlinked to, any prior causes. Chance occurrences are by reference "casual." To them we assume no responsibility. Those two behaviors, "free" and "will" are just another example of a [26]*non-overlapping magisteria*.

SAINT AUGUSTINE: You are responsible for what you say or what you do Mr. Hitchens, are you not?

HITCHENS: I am "morally" responsible for my ethical actions, yes. But morality is of another kingdom, governing personal, in fact "very personal" and self-persuading principles. Another story altogether.

But let's talk about freedom of choice for a moment: I *willed* that my death, per example, would never occur (or for as long as "never" could be extended.) But death occurred regardless of my willpower. That's also the demise of my free will, isn't it? —The death of my desires. To conclude, we are somewhat string-puppets.

SAINT AUGUSTINE: We are puppets you say, but the strings are attached to God, the master puppeteer, if you don't mind.

---

[26] Coined by Stephen Jay Gould

HITCHENS: I *do* mind... If what you said were true, that would be called "predestination," not freedom of will. And it was my dear friend Sam Harris, not me, that said it in such a complete, metaphorical way [27]*a puppet is free in action as long as he loves his strings.*

SAINT AUGUSTINE: it is God that guides those strings, Mr. Hitchens; He is the one that *also* allows "freedom of will."

HITCHENS: A contrasting statement, once again, Sir. It's either free will or predestination in your lexis. Harris' invisible strings (again, a metaphor, meaning that we are at the mercy of risk or "chance") are nothing but prior causes disturbing our decisions, all *chanced* in time and space. "Chance" or "random occurrences" again, they are by definition fortuitous, casual; they free us of culpability, of responsibility. I am not answerable for my death. I did not "will" for my illness to exist or to create the fantastic pain that assaulted me until the end of my living moment. I did not design or produce my terrible disorder. My *will* could not access my inner body or command my cancer to disappear. The people jumping from the twin towers on September eleven's terrorist attack—I guarantee you—they all had "willed" to survive. What did they do? They took a chance! They died, all of them, horrifically. Their wish to live on didn't come true. Had they not taken that chance, *willed* to live, the result had been the same.

I will wrap this up for you, in a different way: I did not have a choice in selecting my parents. Did you? Have you picked your gender? I did not. Ask anyone living in poverty if it is his or her will to be poor and miserable, and when they are they would like to change that fate according to their will. Can they? No. Why? Because they have NO CHOICE. They have no power over random occurrences that shape and govern their lives. When tragedy strikes they say *'I wish it didn't happen;' 'I wish I was born in a different country;' 'I wish I wasn't sick.'* If you haven't heard it often enough you haven't paid any attention to the unfortunate who cry: *'I wish my child*

[27] Free Will – Sam Harris

didn't die.' 'I wish the war didn't kill millions of innocent peo-ple,' I wish God would have listened to my prayer and let my family live.'

The terminal condition in your body is self-determining, ignorant—unconscious of your will. Every cell in your body, although a part of your entire physique, is dependent on, or at the mercy of other parts of you; just as every action is reduced to erstwhile events. There is no free will since you cannot stop a headache. You can't stop an accident. You can't generate your own fate. You can't *self-control* your whereabouts. You can't command your future. And you can't prolong your youth any more than you could cancel your death. As Sam was saying, you can will all you want but leave freedom out of this business, for there is no relation between the two.

SAINT AUGUSTINE: If people were acting without free will, how would any justice in any court system condemn bad actions? Criminals would plead "non-guilty" claiming that their crimes were all "accidents," as they are "victims of chance," they didn't will any crime to happen; it just did since immovable past causes acted against their will. As you know, to be guilty of a crime there must be a voluntary action "*actus reus*" and a culpable state of mind "*mens rea*." If another cause is culpable and not "their selves," how could they be accused of any crimes? Without any of those two, there is no crime.

HITCHENS: I am not a lawyer, but common culture tells us that there is another agent, a more personal, a non-god-related one, called, "morality." Our justice systems apply rele-vant laws to settle different disputes and distribute justice, resolving acts from misdemeanors to mass murders, in the same manner that they've always done, based on moral, social conduct. Morality is the educated negotiator between your "self" and your actions. She is an educated "alter ego" attached to your conscience. A breach of moral actions happens when there's a leak in one's education, or in good upraising or in common sense, or in all of the above.

SAINT AUGUSTINE: Ivan Karamazov of Dostoyevsky's Brothers Karamazov says that without God everything is permitted.

HITCHENS: Not true. What is true is that Dostoyevsky wrote that, but not true otherwise. In fact, the reverse is much more noticeable.

SAINT AUGUSTINE: What do you mean by that?

HITCHENS: Is Jesus of Nazareth considered God?

SAINT AUGUSTINE: Of course He is.

HITCHENS: By Christians only, but all right here's my direct point. Let's make a U-turn and offer a *hitch*, to prove Dostoyevsky and his concept wrong. I say, that *with* God, everything is permitted.

SAINT AUGUSTINE: Nonsense. Arguments please.

HITCHENS: Coming up! By only looking at the meek and mild Jesus of Nazareth, the inventor of hell, the originator of the eternal damnation, you can see that everything is permitted.

ST. AUGUSTINE: To the contrary...

HITCHENS: Well, you are assured by Jesus (your God) to get away with whatever you want, be that murdering, mass killing, raping, pilfering, torturing, corruption, slavery, on and on and on, but only under one condition—to give yourselves to Jesus. Some denominations of Christianity say you must be born again. As long as at the end of those miserable, immoral, criminal lives, criminals repent and let themselves into the hands of Jesus the Savior, they're safe and protected and granted free tickets to heaven. The moral people are condemned to hell if they do not accept Jesus. "All our righteousnesses *are* as filthy rags" (Isaiah 64:6)

Therefore I say it out loud: with God, everything is permitted. Jesus is the Savior of all the criminals, of the depraved, of the flop minded, of evil and the condemner of good people. Is that right ladies and gentleman, brothers and sisters, comrades in suffering, or is it wrong? What better example of immorality would you like me to give you? That reminds me of no other than the presently father and Bishop of Church

Saint Augustine, who drew upon the bible declaring that the infants who weren't baptized should be punished with the penalty of fire and eternal damnation with the devil. The XVI Council of Carthage in 418 codified the Saint's teaching on the fate of unbaptized infants followed by the Council of Lyons II in 1274; followed by the Council of Florence around 1440. Later the Roman Catholic Church—their uncovered cheeks burning with shame—changed this outrageous, shameful verdict to "limbo," an imaginary conceived place conveniently placed between heaven and hell. Then the Church announced that all infants are finally admitted to heaven. What a decision made by the pious and holy Church. What a moral relief—certainly inspired by God!

I suppose *Mr.* Augustine would not have thought of that appalling, immoral exploitation had religion not rebelled against his ethics, acting upon his judgment with authority. The Saint, or for that measure any religious person, might behave decently outside the rigid hard covers of the Scriptures. It takes religion to make a moral person, immoral, insofar as to condemn to perdition billions of unborn or unfortunate babies, let alone innocent people accused for heresy. And it is they who teach the doctrine of obedience.

To recap, if there's any freedom at all it's not the freedom of will but the "freedom of thought," the principled freedom of taking decent actions as oppose to degenerate, unscrupulous ones. It is our freedom of thought wherein evolves our conscience. Take away the freethinking, take the liberal reasoning away from man, give him religion, sell him on faith and you've just killed his character, you've enslaved his mind and destroyed his rationality.

PLATO: Mr. Hitchens, if you were to ask God one single question what would that question be?

HITCHENS (Long pause; his voice drops he speaks calmly in a low pitch): My question would be this: Heavenly Father, would there still be Evil in the world without Satan? If God's answer were "NO" then, the corollary question comes naturally—would your grace pardon Satan and deliver him from the Earth? A one time amnesty if you want.

(Noise in courtroom)

JUDGE: Order! (Gavel thundering.)

HITCHENS: I'll be fair—If it's too much for Him to give up all at once, he could do it only temporarily; say, only for a year. No! For a month or few hours—which would be enough to convince us but it would be nothing next to eternity—just to show everyone that the reason of evil in the world *is* Satan, (I prefer calling him Lucifer.)

Straightforwardly, I propose this to be done by Him immediately. If god's decision does not solve the problem of evil after Satan has been pardoned, we must conclude that all the evil in the world comes from God, himself. (Long pause) I hope I'm not offending the deity or anyone by offering this proposition; it is not my intention. If I do, I sincerely apologize. My intention is, as explained, purposely moral.

SATAN: It would suit me very well. In fact I'm willing to leave Earth if it's okay with God; few hours will be conclusive. (Laughs.) After all, I wouldn't want this assignment to postpone the trial.

(A long silence descended like thick mist. Lucifer's mouth opened wide with a grin. Adam was furious. Hitchens' proposal seemed to have clearly placed a double-snare plan. If God agreed to pardon Satan, and if by delivering him from Earth all evil disappeared, God would still be accused of sending His Angel down in the first place. If God did not agree to it, God would be accused of wickedness. If God would not respond to Hitchens' offer, He would diminish Himself to void forever.

Plato walked to Adam and after few moments of whispering and looking into the light, returned to the center of the court.)

PLATO: Thank you, Mr. Hitchens.

Your honor, I have no more questions.

CHAPTER
26
SATAN'S CLOSING ARGUMENT

(Lucifer rises and walks to the center of the court.)

SATAN: Ladies and Gentleman of the Jury, [28]you have heard the witnesses; you are about to hear my counsel, the truth that infuriates the religious pleases the rationalists and forces the agnostics to contemplate, a story that everybody knows. I am, therefore, at my ease. You have the truth at last, and I am confident it will do its work."

You see there's no righteousness without integrity. There is no goodness without conscience. And it is conscience and integrity the two honorable virtues that we defend. It is integrity and conscience, in its deepest core, to which I direct my appeal. If I stand here before you it is because I have wished it. I *wished* to face God in His obscure behavior to bring the horrendous facts before your authority, before you who are the noblest, the most direct emanation of supreme universal

---

[28] ÉMILE ZOLA, Delivered in Paris, February 22d, 1898, at the Zola Trial for Libel

justice, in order that Heaven, at last, may honor your decision.

It seems to me that I was treasuring a dream in desiring to offer you all the evidence, considering you to be the exclusive earnest, the sole proficient judge deliberating both, veracity and conscience. They began by depriving you, disdaining and humiliating you in your very moral integrity by pretending to accept your noble authority, your worthy power of judgment, while at all times appealing to your sentiments rather than to your intellect, offering their absurdities and affectations to your heart rather than to your minds. Let's not forget that it is the heart that deceives the mind whereas the mind liberates the heart of heaviest burdens. In their hypocrisy they dared assault your good senses offering you beliefs instead of material proof, presenting to you faith based assumptions instead of evidence based on facts. How dare they insult your intelligence? How dare they speak in that tone of voice and try to corrupt your evaluations? How dare they think that by imposing faith and by blinding you with an abstract image of a ghost that they call "holy" they could incarnate into your very souls of reason? To misjudge your position it is just very naïve of them, verily immature, if not impertinent and foolish.

I apologize for them, wholeheartedly. Yet, beloved ladies and gentlemen, I would not dare offend you by assuming that you have yourselves been swindled by this kindergarten tale. I do trust you since I see who you are. You are the heart and the reason of this entire universe, of our great cosmos where all of us were born, not only the pride of evolution, which I adore with immeasurable tenderness. Soon I shall be in thought with you in the same room where you deliberate, and I am truly convinced that your effort will be to preserve your honor, integrity and conscience, which make, of course, the fundamentals of moral character. I know you will not make an error of judgment, for if you did, it could not be reversed.

This is the only trial in which God faces His Conscience, dear distinguished jury. I know you so well since it is I who live with you on Earth, not God whose oversleeping had caused the fabrication of religion and whose permanent absence had produced blind, nonsensical faith but—and this is the drawback—whose conscience the "universal conscience," rebelled against Him because it is proven to be no other than *your* conscience. That's why the dichotomy: God versus His Conscience; the Supreme versus Morality. It is your very conscience that rebels against God; it is your very conscience that is condemning Him.

Mr. Hitchens' proposal seems to me much more than reasonable and equally unprejudiced; it seems to me far more than fare, far more than *godly*—if you'll excuse my being so indulgent. Yet, I do not need apologies, dear ladies and gentlemen, nor do I need to apologize to anyone. But God does. *He* is in trial. My leaving the Earth will only prove a God responsible for sending me there in the first place, if not for detaining me at last. Not to mention that if I were evil, since God created me, it follows that God created evil—a humble syllogism.

Now, to religious people I'd like to address it like this and offer a betting proposition (Pompously): I'll *bet* on their faith and on all their beliefs that God will not pardon me nor will He ever deliver me from Earth. They'll see how good the Eternal Father is. I'll wager their religion, which to them is everything although to me is not worth more than a pointless sentimental speculation, (chuckling) but I'll do that anyway— I'll wager their religion against my liberation proving that Mr. Hitchens's compromise will be ignored by God, yet giving those religious people an offer they can't refuse. And the offer is: If I'll lose the bet, I'll be leaving Earth immediately as if pardoned by God. But let them not cheer and dance yet, since by leaving Earth I'll prove God wrong.

What will they gain if I win? Everything. Including *all* of their confined liberties, which will be set free. They'll become freethinkers, people of reason, rational beings, humanitarians; in other words they'll take much more concern in human welfare through altruistic, charitable, benevolent meanings. I ask you now, isn't that the most moral bargain they have ever had? Isn't that an offer that would be impossible for any rational person to refuse? I'll go a bit further and extend the surprise: suppose the religious classify this proposal as another out-of-print bible-like tricky temptation, refusing to listen to me because I am Satan and my nametag wears a stigma. So I'll do better than that... I'll be willing to get down on my knees and pray to God before you all. I'll pray for forgiveness, I'll pray that He should free humanity of evil. I'll do the praying myself since no one ever prayed for me and no one will. As Mr. Clemens impartially observed, I'm perhaps the only sinner who needs the most praying and has never been prayed for by anyone. Had anyone ever prayed for me? No. Is *now* anyone praying for Satan?

(Silence. Satan gets down on his knees and grovels before the light.) I'll ask God to forgive me and to set me free. I pray to him, Oh dad, my Lord! Please, forgive me for being born. Please, set me free and prove your innocence by showing the world that once I'm gone, the world is delivered from evil. (Shouting) FREE ME! WIPE OUT EVIL!

(Long pause. Everyone is waiting God's reaction.)

SATAN: Nothing? No answer to my offer? (Looks around everywhere. Moments later he addresses the jury):

See that distinguished jury? See this proof of arrogance and make a note of it, please. And make one of this, too: God does not answer to anyone; He never answered any prayers and He never will. When there seems to be no more solutions it's always one more popping in my brain—thank God for this revelation! And here it is—I'll leave Earth forever. I'll do it for humanity. I know of a similar planet, only it's a hundred times larger billions of years away from all this unnecessary chaos and bloodbath. I'm willing to leave Earth without my Father's permission—dear jury—just to prove my point. Would that be enough evidence for you?

Let God execute me for disobeying His orders, for me breaking free of his prison. I'll prove once and for all that evil will still be there on Earth, with or without me. Because evil is innate in Him. He created it. In fact my absence from Earth would have Him show His angry face at once. My leaving will unmask his real being. I wonder what religion will do without Satan when seeing that evil still dominates the world. What would the believers do in absence of Satan—create another Satan?

People have conceived religion so why not reinvent me? They'll do anything not to blame their God—for fear of death, I suppose. They'll bent over backwards not to attach to Him any form of "dyad disorder" similar to Dr. Jekyll and Mr. Hyde's characters. If the devout think that it's sick to dress God in a Jekyll and Hyde moral suit, how sick would they have to be to conceive the devil, or how maliciously prone would they have to be to create another Satan, or use my name as a synonym for evil?

Creativity is a product of the human brain, but this type of creativity is definitely a product of an septic mind. It has to be. A reform once in awhile must take place.

Perhaps Islam is sick of carrying the heavy burden of the blatantly obvious inferiority complex—more and more manifested by a wild ascendency disorder. It needs a new book. Or perhaps Christianity is sick and tired of explaining the thousands of errors, contradictions and mythical aberrations spilled all over their poorly carved countless Bible translations; and they need an improvement, they need some type of an awakening, most likely brand new scriptures. They cannot live without a God. A deity has to be created, because programmed minds need to be told what to do and how to think all the time. They cannot think freely. They need a governor to rule their souls. Their minds unaware of this burden carry the concealed weapon of mass destruction.

All these people are used to genuflecting, flattering, begging, crawling, bobbling, humming and deceiving themselves by speaking in tongues, falling flat to the ground, fainting in frenzied ways hyperventilating, talking to themselves sticking their bottoms up in the air five times a day at precise hours. And they like suffering; (Raises his voice) they like suffering and they like talking about their despairs. If it were it all possible for only "goodness" to suddenly dominate the world and there be no more anguish, what would these people do? They would miss suffering and misery and would suffer even more for not having any more suffering to complain about. That's how loony most people are. They like to weep and they like to show it. So if I were to vanish, man would most probably write other books with new superheroes ready to fight new evil and rename it. Another authors, another God, another Satan. They cannot live without this drivel. You see? Evil itself it's a necessary good. So if evil were—by absurdity— "inexistent" it would create itself through man's compulsion: and I don't even have to be there.

Nonetheless I see a reform taking place. Why would the apologists try to explain, over and over again the grotesquely embarrassing Biblical contradictions? Ninety-nine and nine percent of them can't tell which end belongs where, while the remaining herd honestly tries to figure it all out, hopelessly. A tenth of those people go to advanced Biblical studies, spend years of their precious lives learning how to interpret the Scriptures, each one decoding it differently, most of them coming out lying with their hands on their Books when they face scriptural errors, some doing it naïvely; some, intentionally. Those that read with an open mind understand the rigid immoral fabric of biblical text and shake themselves loose.

The same with the Qur'an: The psychosis in those books is pathological; it is more dangerous than any inhaled smoke or injected substance. All we have to do is watch carefully the theatrical ridiculousness that some Biblical scholars use so that we might quickly realize that its silliness is abysmal. Some of them become doctors in theology, that is to say doctors in gobbledygook. Some of the titles describe the malady: Church Father, Imam, Father of the Church, Doctor of the Church, Doctor, Revered, Doctor in Philosophical Theology, Pastor—from Latin word "pastorem" meaning shepherd—or a sheep herder—one who protects, supervises and feeds (indoctrinates in this case) the *sheep* of people, (sheeple,) etc.

I have here a long list of most common contradictions found in these so-called "scriptures"—the Abrahamic ones— for the court examination. I'm sure they'll be convincingly conclusive as regards to religion madness. To give you an example, in the New Testament alone there are more combined errors than written words. Consider the scribes' translations that are still available. Even if there weren't any inconsistencies in them it wouldn't make the books true. In other words a *real* God would not have absolutely, definitely and categorically anything to do with any books written by people, nor would He ever claim any mystical authorship by way of revelation outside the new commandments, which were given to Muhammad earlier today. Let us make a crystal clear distinction and not confuse anyone: God is not the same personage with the fictitious god that appears in man made fairy tales because there never were any revelations, because they couldn't have been since our deity was far into the non-existing mode, lost in His dreaming archipelago and speechlessness. Saying that it is the same God with the God of the Scriptures it would immediately dismiss Him but will eternally accuse the people that invented Him, as Christopher had said. The Scriptures are but cheap rags tailored by few speculators to suit the primitive inhabitants of Palestine with the intention to dominate and enslave their conscience as well as their followers'. And surprisingly enough stupidity breeds and multiplies. Credulous people have bowed to the written word of smooth talking charlatans' thinking that God has visited these shysters in total secrecy. Those who are not stupid and believe in this are but naïve. Folly is a fantastic phenomenon vastly expanding beyond imaginary gods. If galaxies have margins foolishness has not. That's how prolific stupidity is. Matter-of-factly stupidity is even greater than God! I wonder who came first, stupidity or God? Who created whom? Nonetheless, religion will have to reform. Al Ma'arri describes it so well:

[29]So, too, the creeds of man: the one prevails
Until the other comes; and this one fails
When that one triumphs; ay, the lonesome world
Will always want the latest fairy tales.

To summarize, "[30]If [God] is infinitely good, what reason should we have to fear him? If he is infinitely wise, what doubts should we have concerning our future? If he knows all, why warn him of our needs and fatigue him with our prayers? If he is everywhere, why erect temples to him? If he is just, why fear that he will punish the creatures that he has filled with weaknesses?"

....

Ladies and Gentlemen of the esteemed Jury: I trust you will find God guilty on all counts of evildoing for trespassing into the realm of nothingness letting the universe in total chaos, a world surviving, developing, and reorganizing by itself according to laws self-determining, independent of His reach. The truth stands before you.

---

[29] Adapted from *Studies in Islamic Poetry* by Reynold A. Nicholson. Cambridge University Press, 1921, Cambridge, England.
[30] Percy Bysshe Shelley

CHAPTER
27
THE VERDICT

(The courtroom is hushed as everyone is gazing at Adam who slowly walks to the middle of the courtroom.)

ADAM: If Satan did not exist, God would not exist.

SATAN (Lucifer jumps from his seat, throwing his arms in the air like a victor after a long fight): That's my boy!

ADAM (resuming calmly): And vice versa . . .

Esteemed Court, I didn't make this remark to condemn God and to absolve Satan from wrongdoing or to help his victory. To the contrary, I intend to show you that goodness and evil are necessary opposites like twins born of the same parent, however distinctively opposed of one another. I will give you an example, which I beg you to consider before returning a verdict of not guilty.

You see, God does not fulfill Mr. Hitchens's request for a very plausible reason. You must understand that when God created the world he had to balance it perfectly. He gave it poles or extremes. Everything has counterparts. Minus has its opposite in "plus," hot has its opposite in cold, wetness has its dryness, light has its darkness just as the good has its counterpart in evil. Those are conflicting, contradictory necessary existents all emanating from God who is the Necessary Being. Thus, there are necessary conflicts, necessary contradictions or paradoxes. Without these contradictions nothing would make sense. In reality without these inconsistencies, nothing works. The being of the external world—or material world, as we know it—is born almost concurrently with its opposite, the immaterial consciousness—the unseen dimension. Both, the inner as well as the outer worlds exist necessarily: the inner surviving from within and the outer comprehensible from without. Without one another the world as you know it cannot exist. God, the Necessary Being, could not survive without His external surrounding, just as the material world cannot live without God's energy that produces its dynamism. Therefore, opposites *must* exist. Without "evil" there would be no concept of "good."

If God is good and Satan is the opposite of God, then Satan is the opposite of goodness.

To the question, "Why did God create something, which necessitates both evil and good?" The answer is explained in the property, in the energy and in the substance of our entire universe.

To the question, "Could there be good without evil?" the answer is not in the existence of both realities but rather in the difference between the two. In other words, the good could exceed by far the effect of evil, although, both exist by necessity. Therefore when God created the world, He created it from within outward for the best purpose; so there is better to be "something" rather than "nothing." "Something" always evolves into more something flourishing from the lowest level to highest ones.

If you do comprehend the emanation of evil from the Necessary Being, then you understand and accept the gradual ascending order of "good" vis-à-vis its "evil" applying your moral choice in an effort to diminishing it or to allowing it. The decision is yours to make. Both good and evil are your properties to accept or repudiate. It is not the absence of Satan from the World, which will remove evildoing, since both, the bad and the good, are in everyone. Removing one will remove both. Accepting one will accept both. You can have your choices by selecting any of the two, the good through educating the feelings and character and associating it with good environment or the bad, through letting yourselves guided by the negative side of matter or letting yourselves influenced by the negative side of others'. You must appreciate the merit of your actual existence by realizing these freedoms of choices; and yes, acquiring virtues by way of your morality ennobles you. Therefore Satan's departure from the world would not make God better or worse, nor would his departure diminish the amount of evil that lives at the extremities of all material or immaterial things.

To understand, please imagine, that the radiance from my Father, which dimmed from brightest to softest as I looked at him awhile ago, were to fade out completely until the deepest darkness prevailed.

(Turns halfway toward God and winks at Eve with a sad smile): Dad, can you show everyone, just for a moment what darkness in contrast to light would be like?

(Satan grasps the edge of his seat as God's light increases gradually until it had become unbearable hot. Jesus threw himself facing down. St. Augustine planks near him reaching for Christ's hand. Mohammad is heard crying out loud *Allah, Allah please be good to us, we'll do anything you'll ask us to do; please, do not burn us.* Everyone is roaring, screaming and hollering when suddenly the light shots off to expose a painful blackness. All the stars in the sky followed suit, at first sparkling with grandness, moments later only to extinguish like billions of candelabras before the greatest show on earth. The audience panics as the sky blackens and space itself disappears. There is no more space; there are no more universes, only the cosmos within every one remains. Everyone feels the immensity of empty space pressing against their inner space, which suddenly seems so diminutive. The lack of the outside creates an immediate sense of claustrophobia. The self falls in within itself. The soul embraces the spirit in a manifest unity and desperation and becomes one. All is blackness. It feels like void. The temperature drops gradually. The pressure is unbearable as space condenses more and more until it feels like dense, heavy matter rushing in gravitational breadth.)

ADAM (shivers and yells): *This* is the opposite of light. *This* is what a black hole starts to feel like, my dear people. This is what the end of all existence feels like. Billions and billions of years of creation and evolution compresses into one single pinpoint that would further diminish to the size of . . . *nothingness.*

And we feel this nothingness if we take a journey back to the matrix from which everything came, into this black hole of eternal death and rebirth, where *everything*—gods and demons, dimensions and matter, billions and billions of things become one single atom, the primeval atom in the middle of empty space; an invisible dot of energy and matter before it explodes again into notice.

Do you *now* distinguish something from nothing? Do you now understand the meaning of the presence and the absence of things? Is there a link between the invisible and the visible? Do you see yourselves as one with the God of the universe or with the universe named God? Do you understand that you are part of the whole and the whole is part of you? Do you understand that Muslim and Jew and Hindu and Christian and Buddhist and Pagan, and all the peoples combined and every living plant and animal and every inanimate object, including the Earth itself, are all but one with the body of the Conception? Do you see your alter ego in the mirror of your souls? Do you see the entity you cannot touch but "know" that is *there*—the existing echo, which itself has a personality that feels and thinks? Can you stop looking at your own self as a distinct and independent being and realize that the Self is one of the billions of bodies of selves resulting from billions of causes born of a single cause, without which you would not even exist? Do you realize that evil and good are contingent upon each other and that your existence is contingent on the environment, the portion of Nature, itself nothing more than a set of symbiotic relationships? The [31]*Visuddhimagga* or *Path of Purification* says:

For here there is no Brahmá God
Creator of the round of births
Phenomena alone flow on—
Cause and component their condition.
[FULL-UNDERSTANDING OF THE KNOWN]

You can't be strong without the weak, you can't be good without the bad, your art would not be art without its beauty; you can't be rich without the poor; there would be no loyalty without infidelity and treachery and the God would not be god without a conscious material world who gives Him that definition.

(The low temperature and pressure seems unbearable. There is no pain, only a senseless realization of rapid oblivion. Everyone is pulled by a fantastic gravity into what they realize is an "event horizon." Fear transforms into pain when suddenly all reappears under a soft light as if nothing had happened. Everybody is astounded as Adam continues in an exhausted voice, his disfigured face revealing his drained eyes, his cheeks washed by tears): See? The God that you are condemning as evil, is a God you do not even know. His brightness could have melted all the suns in the universe and you are sitting here impotently condemning Him. If He were a bad God, if he were an evil deity we all would have scorched and vanished, but He always kept us in mild light although you didn't see it and that the lethal reverse-formation of matter was not felt. He will let us come to Him as we advance, as we progress, for one day we could be looking him in the face and be as brilliant as he intended us to be. Until then, we still learn how to crawl, how to walk, how to think, how to progress, how to fly toward a universe of civilizations.

---

[31] Visuddhimagga or Path of Purification Translated from the Pali by Bhikkhu Ñáóamoli. Fist Ed. 1956. Mr Ananda Semage, Colombo

Ladies and Gentlemen: Our limited perceptions shape our reality. We generally judge things by appearances and through impulses. As you can see, the God that is accused of the evil crimes is not in this court. God's Conscience is sentencing the God of the scriptures, the man-created God not the Father of the Universe. The real God is All-righteous. The real God, who materialized in this court today, is the one who allows you to judge Him when He could in fact judge you for your wrongdoing, for you, yes *YOU* mocking His image and His name. He knows you better than you know Him. He loves you more that you love Him. You have tried to make of Him what He is not. His Conscience is His *alter ego.*

SATAN: Who are you? Aren't you Adam, the first man?

ADAM: Ladies and gentlemen of the jury, esteemed court; you must know the truth and here it is:

I was a grafted cell, floating in a universe unknown. I knew that I had arrived from afar after traveling for millions of years, and I knew that I was reuniting with my own self. I remember being surrounded by a sweet, soft, indefinite, continuous music born of a warm steam and reverberating over cozy, limitless waters. I can't describe the sound, but I knew it well; I had heard it often in my dreams.

The protoplasm that surrounded my nucleus tickled and soothed my senses. I remember laughing, seemingly for feeling so happy; merriment mixed with other feelings made me realize that I had arrived after wandering through nothingness. Because nothingness exists, I assure you, like a rest area for passengers through time.

A pre-embryonic voice had spoken to me—I don't know how—telling me—I don't know what. Whoever he was, he had the warm, comforting voice of a Santa Claus, that old fellow who had set many presents beside my Tree of Life. Later, I would forget that voice, remembering it only when I needed something, just like everyone else. Yet, as I planned and arranged my thoughts in an immense, illusory agenda, I heard voices coming from somewhere, reverberating in a familiar way. I loved them so much that I shouted for joy, but no one heard me because no one was there. I kicked and struggled to escape that space, and I would have done just that had my tiny, pellucid legs not slipped and slid helplessly with every jolt.

Before long, I found myself tranquil and blissful, listening to the symphonies surrounding me, which appeared to arrive from beyond knowledge. Now and then, I contemplated my little hands, giving to each of my fingers important names, imagining that they were my friends. And maybe they were, given that they've remained attached to me ever since.

Everything developed peacefully for many months until one day when I saw a light at the end of a passage. I shrank, trembling with fear that beyond my matrix was a very unfriendly world. I kicked around with an inexplicable passion to live, to stay where I was, safe and unhindered. Something told me to hide within my abyss where no one could ever find me, but I was helpless against the forces that pushed me through the tunnel. I winced as a deep, powerful voice suddenly spoke, making my heart almost stop beating. Unexpectedly, the whole history of the world appeared before my eyes from the beginning until the present, and what I witnessed were the fantastic events that I have revealed. Sometimes, I wish I hadn't been born since I have witnessed great suffering. And yet, if I had not seen it all, who would have lived to tell what happened? On second thought, let me take that back. I am not sorry I was born, and I don't regret any living day. Dear believer or unbeliever, this is my story:

When I first opened my eyes I didn't see God; but I saw planets of all sizes and colors and among them there was a little blue world, so pretty and so lonely that all the stars surrounded it with beauty and light as if they were alive and knew what they were doing. And I thought that *that* was wonderful.

I liked it so much that one day I found myself in that world, living in a garden called Eden. And I remember a certain tree and a girl Eve, and a berry feeding us knowledge since without it we couldn't be complete. Believe it or not, I thought that was wonderful.

I didn't know God, but I saw how rivers flowed; blue oceans, high mountains, and dense rainforests of unbelievable splendor gave the Earth a story of its own, later written in thousands of books and millions of tales by beings that looked like me and Eve. And that was so wonderful, too.

It seemed to me that Nature was blind in her creation since she left everything to chance, but with all that magnificence, she began to see and added flowers by the millions and attending butterflies, bees, and insects of all kinds all buzzing hither and thither, perhaps very happy that they lived. And what a wonderful, wonderful thing.

Wild animals filled the forests and the savannas became abundant with life and motion; fish by the billions swam at liberty, lizards of all types and tempers roamed the land, and the lotus flower made men cry with its heavenly beauty.

I didn't know God, but I knew of a snow-capped peak towering over the African plain that made Hemingway famous; and I knew of a forest, which inspired many a poet's verse, one even falling in love with it offering his entire youth to its beauty. And I thought all those were extremely wonderful things.

Birds of all colors colonized deltas, and I saw Zamfir kissing the lips of superb and vibrant Syrinx as he played the Pan flute with divine grace out of which celestial sounds traveled all over the world—a thing that made the birds jealous and many singers retiring or shy. And that alone was indeed, a very, very wonderful thing.

I didn't know God, but I witnessed how Verdi converted his pain into music, how fantastic was that, I thought; and then I watched Rafael painting an immortal smile, and I've seen how Da Vinci made love to an artwork by caressing it with his brushes. I also heard of a reality show called *The Divine Comedy* who became immortal overnight. How breathtaking was that, I thought.

I have took a knee before a child of five who wrote "Twinkle Twinkle Little Star" a melody that I remember even today, and then I watched him write his first symphony when he was eight. Oh, I thought to myself, *that* was so wonderful, too.

I didn't know God but I listened to a man from Copenhagen named Hans Christian Andersen who told his best stories to children, and his stories are still the finest ever told, for they shall live for as long as children will be around, even when they become old children.

I didn't know God but I heard of a one God who fell asleep between the pages of Scriptures and never woke up. I cried at the thought of that, because my heart is good, and I wished I could revive Him with my breath.

I didn't know God, but one day, while I was fingering the blades of grass contemplating at my strange life—by now I was a homeless beggar with no other possessions than a good heart—I heard of a painter who had fit within a single frame the whole universe containing all these wonders and dreams and many more that live within the expanse of space and time. Sudden tears filled my eyes since this artist sounded a lot like the character in the book, and immediately I though of my father. He exposed his art called *Nature* for everyone who wished to see it. Those who see it can never forget the many wonderful, wonderful things that he made. But those who do not want to see; they don't know what they are missing. Then again, not everyone loves art. This painter dressed in Nature's most beautiful garb simply signed his work—*God*.

(As Adam retreats to his seat the light in the courtroom starts again to faint. Adam's vision seems to liquefy as he sees the court veiled in a haze of timeless conflict. He is dizzy, lightheaded, and seems consumed with emotion awaiting the verdict. In a split second he realizes he will pass out. He hears the voice of the Bailiff calling out: *All rise for the honorable Judge!* Then he hears the Judge asking the foreperson, her voice echoing as if bouncing from a galaxy forgotten: *Has the verdict been reached?* There is a silence. Adam's heart is accelerating. He tries to concentrate but his thoughts are troubled by the sound of his pounding heartbeats against his chest. *Why does it take so long,* he wonders. Cold beads of sweat are now dripping from his forehead; he feels a chill of warmness freezes almost instantly. He panics and would like to escape from there, yet he knows he cannot. The discomfort in his chest becomes unbearable. Finally, the voice of an angel announces the verdict:

Under the laws of the universe and by the Natural Laws of Casualty encompassing time and space, we, the jury, find the defendant, on all counts of evildoing—not guilty.

The ring in Adam's ears supersedes the shouts and cries of the people that expand throughout. He feels a sudden relief despite the pain in his chest. He finds himself saying *we won and... we lost.* An unfamiliar darkness is pressing over him. He cries desperately for help: Father, where are you? Light, please give us light.

There is no answer. From the top of his lungs with one last determination he lets out, his voice skipping: Father! I'm cold.

(A thick silence presses again): God, where are you?

(Everything fades out.)

CHAPTER
28
THE FIRST MAN

There was a rainy day when Martin Hefts died in his hospital bed. The doctors were surprised at his sudden cardiac arrest. On Martin's face there was a faint smile that traced so much serenity. His left hand rested on his chest holding what looked like a scroll. A doctor removed it carefully, everyone eyes gliding in disbelief.

The incident became top news, headlining:
UNEXPLAINED DEATH! MARTIN HEFTS A YOUNG MAN IN HIS THIRTIES DIES OF HEART FAILURE IN HOSPITAL BED AFTER SUCCESSFUL BRAIN SURGERY. SCIENTISTS STUDY NEW COMMANDMENTS WRITTEN UPON UNKNOWN MATERIAL: HOAX OR NEW REVELATION?

The manuscript had been published in all languages—

Mark Thomas Wayne

CHAPTER
29

ONE HUNDRED COMMANDMENTS FOR ISLAM

1.   DO NOT believe everything you are conveyed.

2.   DO NOT disobey God's will; Allah is in Conscience, in all forms and beyond all forms.

3.   DO NOT kill yourself or any other person; Allah gives life and only He can break it.

4.   DO forgive your fellow man and woman; Allah is forgiving.

5.   DO NOT obstruct the freedoms of another. Allah gives you the freedom of thought and action, which you must preserve and exercise with moral character.

6.   DO praise righteousness. Allah is righteous and passes to you the gift of righteousness so that you may pass it to your children in words and fair actions.

8.   DO NOT steal; those who steal will be severely punished in the afterlife.

9.   DO NOT commit rape; the one who rapes will earn Allah's punishment.

10.   DO NOT act in the name of Allah. Allah will punish all pretenders.

11.   DO NOT abuse or mistreat a child. The man or woman who abuses a child will be severely punished by Allah.

12.   DO NOT speak disrespectfully to a woman or harm her in any way. The man who beats, molests, mutilates, or kills a woman will suffer Allah's punishment.

13.   An incompatible couple MUST settle separation civilly without the intervention from any other man or woman.

14.   DO NOT throw stones at anyone; stoning shall be condemned with eternal damnation.

15.   If you want to pray DO pray in solitude and DO NOT make a show of your faith in public places.

16.   DO respect the traditions and customs of your brothers and sisters in other lands; they, too, revere Allah in their different ways.

17.   DO be peaceful and live longer. First be peaceful with yourself and then give your goodwill to others.

18.   DO know that revelation is within you. All Holy Scriptures, including the Quran, are the work of man; the Word of Allah is imprinted in Nature.

19. DO NOT try to understand Allah; He transcends the intelligence of man and woman.

20. DO try to understand yourself. To discover Allah, you must fist discover your own being.

21. To meet Allah, DO study nature; to love Allah, DO love yourself and your neighbor.

22. DO learn Love since love, not violence, is the path to Heaven. Those that use violence ask for the wrath of Allah.

23. DO live and let live.

24. DO NOT impose your ways on your fellow man, woman or child. When you are in other people's lands, you will adapt to their cultures and embrace the laws of the land. Take the good from everything and set aside hatred and violence.

25. DO value discipline and knowledge. Science is the second nature of human beings; you were created to find knowledge, and advance. Allah is man's nature of knowing. Allah is synonym with Knowledge, therefore with Science.

26. DO NOT soil your soul and spirit but honor them. Your soul is Allah's gift to you at your birth. Your spirit is the child of your conscience.

27. Allah is your Father, Mother, and Friend. Friendships are the mating of souls, the spiritual gifts between beings and the universe. DO NOT revile anyone on the basis of their color or origin, looks, or gender preference.

28. DO NOT discount the name of God since He is in all things. Everything is Allah, even calamity, which is part of the universe. Live with it. Be reborn through it.

29. DO have only one religion, the eternal religion, which is the love of the universe; seek enlightenment in your mind, which is part of the mind of God you call Allah.

30. DO know this: that to be free is to cast off the shackles of dogma. Allah is Reason, requires no dogma, and is the logical absolute. Embrace and bow to Reason with veneration. You will conquer the universe if you let life evolve.

31. DO look for Allah in within you, not in man-made Scriptures, which contain impudent doctrines and false prophets.

32. DO unto others, as you would have others do unto you.

33. DO NOT criticize one's defects; they have unseen virtues.

34. DO think for yourself; DO NOT let others think for you. Freethinkers are Allah's preferred children. Without free thought you are but a dummy.

35. DO strive to improve yourselves in all you do and help others that need improvement.

36. Hell is the product of your own mind, which condemns your spirit. Allah's punishment is the only hell. Ask your conscience to vouch for you before every action.

37. DO NOT judge others from your flawed perspective.

38. Anger is the enemy of good judgment. You MUST be peaceful and control your emotions.

39. Your own accomplishment is a confirmation of persuasiveness through spiritual contest. Spiritual contests are positive impulses of the universe. You MUST enter into such contests.

40. You MUST abandon torturing others or you will suffer it. Torture is the ultimate expression of cruelty.

41. You MUST be moral and good to others. Virtue is the mother of goodness and morality; her womb will always give birth to decency and reverence.

42. DO NOT believe in miracles; they are brief unexplained phenomena until discovered and explained. Explained phenomena is part of laws exposed through scientific research.

43. DO KINOW: Faith is belief in that which is not evident. Allah is evident for He is the universal absolute.

44. Allah is knowledge. You MUST seek the truth in knowledge.

45. DO NOT leave by the consent of another's opinion, but by your own inner voice based on your accumulated knowledge.

46. DO NOT use threats or violence in sexual interactions.

47. DO NOT confuse belief in Allah with religion; religion breeds fanaticism. Allah forbids intolerance, extremism, frenzy, and fury.

48. You MUST display your good side. Goodness suspends evil.

49. You MUST be just and sensible to all others.

50. DO NOT engage in warfare. Warfare is man's invention, not God's.

51. The depths of one is the surface of another—both oceans apart. You MUST respect the wonders of the deep.

52. You MUST conceal everything with a robe of courtesy.

53. DO NOT be the slave of vulgar temperaments.

54. You MUST have courage not audacity. The first is a benefit; the last is undignified.

56. Wisdom and patience replaces the wrath of Hercules with the wisdom of Ulysses. You MUST be tolerant.

57. You MUST fight against war with peace.

58. To pretend ignorance is to know. You MUST respect the ignorance of others and benefit from their friendship.

59. DO NOT try to reason with the unreasonable. Think!

60. DO NOT mutilate children by circumcision, unless it is a health requirement.

61. DO NOT induce Minors into marriage. DO NOT marry a child.

62. Pederasts and pedophiles will be punished by eternal damnation. DO NOT become one.

63. DO NOT marry by force.

64. DO NOT espouse a member of your immediate family.

65. DO NOT use people as private property or slaves.

66. DO KNOW: Usury, extortion, and blackmail are forbidden.

67. DO NOT compel a woman or her family to provide a dowry.

68. So-called honor killings are forbidden. DO NOT stain your honor with murder and assassination. This beastly act is punished with eternal damnation.

69. Any child who strikes his parent for a reason other than self-defense when threatened with death will be severely punished by Allah. Allah will also punish any parent who molests or abuses a child.

70. DO NOT perform incest. Incest is punished by eternal damnation.

71. You MUST try to set a good example for yourself, your family, your neighbor, and the world.

72. You MUST acquire good manners. Good behavior and etiquette are essential to educated societies.

73. You MUST rise to the merits of your spirit and keep the name of Allah sacred. He made the law for man and woman without discrimination.

74. You MUST respect others, as you would want them to respect you and love them as you would want them to love you.

75. TO LOVE converted strangers, as you love yourself.

76. DO NOT intend evil toward anyone, for you will doom your soul to perdition.

77. Women MUST dress in comfortable, practical clothing of their own choosing. DO NOT compel a woman to cover her face or hair or to wear burka garments.

78. DO NOT pray to a stone. It will not answer. The *al-Hajr al-Aswad* (the Black Stone) is only a falling, worthless meteorite.

79. DO NOT covet another's property. Get your own.

80. DO NOT covet another's wife, or husband.

81. DO NOT betray your country, your brothers and sisters, your children, or your friends.

82. You MUST help the sick, the weak, and the poor, to the best of your ability, as you would want to be helped if you were sick, weak, or poor.

83. DO NOT swear.

84. DO NOT listen to false prophets. Your only prophet is Allah who is in your conscience.

85. DO Condemn all Jihadists for their crimes; DO reject and denounce their behaviors.

86. DO NOT offer sacrifices of any kind. Allah does not require sacrifices.

87. You MUST respect life around you; DO NOT sell your soul, your children, or your wife.

88. DO NOT hunt game for sport.

89. DO NOT destroy the forests.

90. DO NOT be superstitious.

91. DO NOT have children with someone else's wife, unless she is divorced.

92. DO NOT exterminate in Allah's name; you will be doomed to eternal damnation.

93. Suicide bombers and terrorists will receive eternal damnation.

94. DO NOT idolize any place; city or country.

95. You MUST keep the word of Allah and by it you DO earn peace, prosperity, and spiritual wealth.

96. Heaven is not an afterlife of sexual promiscuity. It is a place of spiritual knowledge. DO NOT make an idol of your imagination. Heaven is within yourself.

97. You MUST educate your children in best schools; DO offer them peace, not war.

98. You MUST be indifferent to other people's religions.

99. You MUST worship Nature and Humanity—the synonym of Allah.

100. You MUST abdicate any religion or any gods that contradict these commandments. These commandments are the only word of Allah. You MUST keep them and you will taste Heaven on Earth before you continue your journey into the Universe.

EPILOGUE

[32]The vast World: A grain of Dust in Space.

All science of mankind: Words.

The Nations, the Beasts and the Flowers of the seven climates: Shadows.

The results of your daily thoughts: Nothing.

— The Beginning —

---

[32] The Rubaiyat of Omar Khayyam & Exantus by Chris Sebastian Douglas, Greenleaf Publishing 2008

The Trial

ABOUT THE AUTHOR

MARK THOMAS WAYNE is an American novelist, historian, poet, philosopher, ex-Christian Orthodox evangelist, essayist, law expert, and international businessman. He is an apostate and an untiring skeptic with great appetite for debating gratuitous religious pretense and affectation.

For more information please visit:
www.MarkThomasWayne.com or
www.EverlyBooksPublishing.com

Mark Thomas Wayne

François-Nicolas Chifflart, The Conscience
(La Conscience - 1877)

Mark Thomas Wayne